# THE LAKE EFFECT

The Milan Jacovich mysteries
by Les Roberts:

Pepper Pike

Full Cleveland

Deep Shaker

The Cleveland Connection

The Lake Effect

The Duke of Cleveland

Collision Bend

The Cleveland Local

A Shoot in Cleveland

The Best-Kept Secret

The Indian Sign

The Dutch

The Irish Sports Pages

# THE LAKE EFFECT

A MILAN JACOVICH MYSTERY

# LES ROBERTS

GRAY & COMPANY, PUBLISHERS
CLEVELAND

Gray & Company, Publishers
1588 E. 40th St.
Cleveland, Ohio 44103
www.grayco.com

Library of Congress Cataloging-in-Publication Data
Roberts, Les.
The lake effect : a Milan Jacovich mystery / Les Roberts.
p. cm.
ISBN 1-59851-005-3 (pbk.)
1. Jacovich, Milan (Fictitious character)—Fiction.
2. Private investigators—Ohio—Cleveland—Fiction.
3. Political campaigns—Fiction. 4. Cleveland (Ohio)—
Fiction. I. Title.
PS3568.O23894L34 2005
813'.54—dc22          2005011233

ISBN 1-59851-005-3

Printed in the United States of America

10 9 8 7 6 5 4 3 2 1

*In loving memory of Kay Williams,*
*who left Cleveland, and this writer,*
*far better than she found them.*

# THE LAKE EFFECT

# CHAPTER ONE

I owed Victor Gaimari a favor.

Favor being a broad, all-purpose word subject to many interpretations, you might think I'd be picking up his dry cleaning or driving him to the airport or taking his homely visiting cousin to dinner and a show. But it wasn't that kind of a favor.

Victor is the favorite nephew and heir apparent of Giancarlo D'Allessandro and number-two man in the D'Allessandro family, which pretty much pulls all the strings in organized crime in northern Ohio, their sphere of influence stretching from Toledo through Cleveland and Youngstown clear across the state line into the Pittsburgh area. And families being what they are, especially that kind of family, when you owe Victor you owe the old man too. It's the sort of debt you don't take lightly.

Some time back I went to them with a request for a name I couldn't have ferreted out anywhere else. They supplied it for me, a name that eventually helped me bail the teenage son of an old friend out of a dilemma that might ultimately have killed him. It's the only thing that would have sent me to the mob with my hat in my hand, but you do what you have to. At the time Victor warned me that someday he would call in the favor.

Of course I'd known that before I asked.

The original deal was that I wouldn't do anything illegal for them. Or anything that stretched my sense of morality or ethics. Or anything that wasn't strictly within the purview of my normal business, a private investigations and industrial security operation which is called Milan Security because I have little hope of anyone who doesn't have a European background saying my last name correctly: Jacovich, with the *J* pronounced like a *Y*. For that matter, most people screw up the first name, too. It's Milan, pronounced *My*-lan. That's the Americanized way, because my folks, both immigrants from Ljubljana in Slovenia, had wanted to be good Americans. Not Mi-*lahn*, like the city in Italy, or *Mee*-lahn. Milan Jacovich.

Victor didn't have to remind me of the duty owed when he asked me to come by his brokerage office one bright autumn Thursday. It was tacit between us. The fact of its being had been burning in my stomach for nearly a year like a pierogi that won't digest, and I'd waited for the marker to be called the way you wait for the winter's first blizzard in Cleveland—with a kind of dread, but also with the certainty that it eventually will come and there's not a damn thing you can do about it.

And since Victor Gaimari and I aren't exactly fond buddies, the summons—for that's what it was, an imperative, and we both knew it—had to be about the return of the favor.

Terminal Tower is Cleveland's most famous landmark, dominating the skyline despite the recent construction of the even taller Society Tower, and is arguably the most beautiful piece of architecture between Chicago and the Chrysler Building, the kind of dignified, rococo building no one wants to erect anymore because beauty isn't cost-efficient. Victor, as one of the city's leading stockbrokers, maintains offices there, along with a lot of lawyers and importers and the Cleveland Convention Bureau, and even manages to transact a good deal of legitimate stock market business and make a lot of money for his clients. As a result he's one of the darlings of the very rich and very social set. That happens in Cleveland when you're an eligible bachelor and good-looking and rich, and you always see Victor's name in the society and gossip columns like "Mary, Mary" or Fran Henry in the *Plain Dealer* or Rick Haase in the *Sun-Press*, attending some benefit or co-chairing some good-works committee.

Victor enjoys his status and visibility, playing them like a violin. He's been linked with every attractive, wealthy single woman on the East Side. And some not so single.

When Victor Gaimari dies, his ashes will be scattered over all the elegant restaurants in Greater Cleveland.

I'm a bachelor too—a divorced one—but I don't get invited to the same parties as Victor. My social outings tend to be Sunday afternoons when the Browns are on TV spent with a Stroh's beer in one hand and a klobasa sausage sandwich in the other, in the den of one of my school buddies from the old Slovenian neighborhood where I grew up just off St. Clair Avenue on the East Side.

I asked Victor's efficient middle-aged secretary to tell him I'd arrived, a request fraught with more peril than it sounds. Once, several years ago, I'd punched her employer right in the beezer in that very office and he'd bled all over the expensive carpeting, and now on the rare occasions when I visit him, she regards me the way a Visigoth might the centurion of an invading Roman legion. This time she actually sniffed when she announced me over the intercom, glasses low on her nose so she could fix me with a baleful stare over them. Her boss and I may have more or less settled our differences, but followers aren't as quick to forgive.

"Milan!" Victor said in his peculiar high-pitched voice as he rose from behind his forty-acre desk to shake my hand. "How delightful to see you again." He's almost as tall as I am, and I'm a pretty big guy. He's also classically handsome, which I'm not, in the way movie stars used to be back in the Tyrone Power–Robert Taylor days, with bright dark eyes, a dashing mustache, and a tan that looks as if he works on it. "Sit down, make yourself at home. God, isn't it a beautiful fall day? Have you seen the leaves turning out in the Chagrin River Valley?"

I took the chair opposite him. "No, I haven't been out there." Victor lives on a huge estate in the far eastern suburb of Orange, where there are about two hundred trees for every house. It's the kind of community where the residents don't mow their lawns, they have them tweezed.

About six miles to the northwest is Cleveland Heights, where I rent an apartment at the top of Cedar Hill, a pretty neighborhood with oaks and elms and quaint old houses overlooking lushly forested parks, but it's light years away from Orange.

"Can I get you something?" he said. What he meant was could his secretary get me something. "I know you're a big coffee drinker."

"Not at four o'clock in the afternoon, thanks."

He sat back down behind the desk, beaming at me as if we'd

been friends since kindergarten and had lost touch for a few months. It always amazes me that he can last until so late in the day without getting a single wrinkle in his suit, but Victor somehow never seems to wrinkle, sweat, rumple, get his hair mussed, or spill marinara sauce on his tie. I guess when you're that rich and powerful you hire someone to do it for you.

"How do you like the Browns this year? Their defense is playing great, especially considering the injuries." The Browns were two and three so far, and I suppose my stint as a defensive lineman during my high school days and at Kent State qualifies me in Victor's eyes as some sort of expert. Whatever I said, he'd be sure to get a bet down on it for the next game.

"Victor, you didn't ask me up here to talk sports."

Some interior dimmer switch lowered the wattage of his smile from high to medium. "No, I didn't," he said. "Just trying to be pleasant, that's all. You're so businesslike, Milan. You ought to loosen up a little. You're very tense. Have you ever tried chanting? I can give you my mantra."

"Victor, for Christ's sake!" I said.

He simply grinned at me. We've been butting heads for several years now. He thinks I'm a low-rent chump and I think he's a high-end scumbag, but for some reason my approval is important to him. In some perverse way he likes me, and he was trying to tease me into liking him back. A big kid, Victor—with twenty leg breakers on his payroll. "Well, it's fall already," he observed at last. "You know what that means besides football and pretty leaves?"

"Seventeen new derivative TV sitcoms."

"Ha ha," he said. It wasn't a laugh. I'd never really heard him laugh. He said, "Ha ha."

I was getting annoyed. "What then? Back to school? The World Series? Yom Kippur? What are we talking about here?"

He pointed a perfectly manicured finger at me. "Politics," he announced, as if it were some Tantric key to the secret of life as we know it. "We're talking about politics. It's election time."

"Are you running for office?"

"You know me better than that. I prefer being behind the scenes. It's more fun, and you don't have to take nearly as much flak. No, a friend of mine is running. For mayor of Lake Erie Shores. You ever been out there?"

Lake Erie Shores is a beachside town of about thirty thousand affluent white people up northeast of the city in Lake County but still part of what they refer to as Greater Cleveland. Not my territory, although lots of city folks manage to steal a weekend every year and go off boating or swimming or fishing on the town's waterfront. "I've been there," I said.

"Then you know what a nice place it is. My friend Barbara Corns wants to keep it that way, keep it out of the hands of the developers and the fast-food joints and the taverns. Keep it a good place to raise a family and live like a decent human being. That's guaranteed in the Constitution, right, Milan? So she's decided to stand for election. It'll be tough; the incumbent, Gayton True, has been in office for sixteen years."

I frowned, trying to recall. "I've heard the name. If he's been in office that long I probably read it in the paper."

"Gayton True is a smooth customer—rich and smart and well-thought-of down in Columbus. But Barbara and her husband Evan think it's time for a change. And so do I."

"Okay, so you're a public-spirited citizen and you're backing Barbara Corns for mayor of a city you don't even live in. Good for you."

He spoke evenly and precisely, the way he always did when he wanted to make sure you were getting his point. "As far as Evan and Barbara Corns are concerned, that's exactly what I am. I'd hate for anyone to tell them different. Evan is an attorney in Lake Erie Shores. I handle his portfolio."

I crossed my left leg over my right knee and looked at my shoe. It was a heavy tan brogan, and the toe was scuffed. I would bet that Victor Gaimari hadn't scuffed his shoes since he was eight; if he ever did, he'd throw them away and buy new ones. "What do you want from me in all this, Victor?"

"A favor."

The word hung heavily in the air as we looked at each other in perfect, if uneasy, understanding. After he was sure I got the message he said, "Barbara's behind in the polls. They don't have a lot of money. It's really a mom-and-pop campaign."

"Why don't you just make a contribution?"

"I have." He rose and went to the window, looking northward as though he could see Lake Erie Shores from the eleventh floor of Terminal Tower. You almost could; it was a clear fall day, and the wind was blowing all the gunk out of the air. "But they're floundering around without a real direction. They need help. I think you're just the man."

I had to laugh. Victor hates it when anyone laughs at him, but the chuckle just bubbled out. I tried to cover it with a cough. "I'm no politician. I'm an industrial security specialist. I help companies with plant security and safety. I investigate insurance claims. I tell them how to keep employees from swiping ballpoint pens. I make sure no one peddles business secrets to the competition. Occasionally I hunt down a missing person."

"You're also an ex-cop," Gaimari said, still staring out the window. "A candidate has to have security."

"A small-town mayoral candidate needs the Secret Service? We're not talking about the presidency here—this is Lake Erie Shores. The last time I looked, communities of white, middle-class Methodists and Episcopalians with two-car garages were a little thin in the political terrorist department."

"That may be, but the campaign's gotten pretty ugly out there, and I'd feel better having someone like you look out for her until the election is over. Besides, security wouldn't be your only job. You took poli sci at Kent, didn't you?"

"I took a class in it, yes."

"Well, then, you could be of inestimable help."

"I took an art history course, too, but the Cleveland Museum of Art hasn't made me a curator. I don't want to sound obtuse, but . . ."

He turned back to me, silhouetted darkly against the bright sun behind him. I couldn't see the expression on his face very well. I didn't like that.

"You'd be an advisor. Check over Barbara's speeches, huddle with her before her public appearances so she'll know what to say. You're a smart man, Milan. You have as much education as I do. And you've lived here all your life, you know the people."

"I've lived in Cleveland," I pointed out, "and Cleveland Heights —both of which are socioeconomically a million miles away from

Lake Erie Shores. I couldn't begin to know what a bunch of nou-veau riche WASPs want to hear from a politician."

"Milan, Milan," he crooned, shaking his head at my lack of so-cial awareness. "You're such a reverse snob! You wear your blue collar like a merit badge. Look, the upper middle class is worried about the same things as everyone else: crime, high taxes, the quality of life. They want the same things for their kids as you do for yours." His tone changed from pedantic to avuncular. "How *are* your boys, by the way?"

"Fine." I said it through my teeth. Victor Gaimari even talking about my family was enough to upset me.

"Good-looking kids, both of them. I enjoyed meeting them that time."

"Uh-huh."

"Your oldest—Milan Junior, is it?"

I let my eyes flicker an affirmation; otherwise I stayed as still as an oil painting.

"He playing football again this year?"

"Wide receiver." I begrudged him even that tiny scrap.

"And the little one—well, I guess he's not so little anymore. He's a charmer. Stephen Louis Jacovich, I think he told me his name was. He just stuck out his chest and introduced himself as Stephen Louis Jacovich."

That just about tore it. "Cut to the chase, Victor."

He came away from the window and stood too close to my chair, his cologne making the lining of my nostrils prickle. It smelled expensive—not like the kind you can pick up in KMart. I got to my feet and shifted so I could see his face better.

"All right, Milan." This was the all-business tone now, the one you'd better listen to if you know what's good for you. "Bottom line. I want you on the Corns campaign for the twelve days un-til the election. The title is chief of security, and the pay is three thousand plus any reasonable expenses, and you can set your own hours. I know you have a business to run, so it's perfectly acceptable if you want to work on other things around Barbara's schedule. And if she wins, there's a twenty-five-hundred-dollar bonus. How's that sound?"

"On paper it sounds terrific. But if the campaign is short on money, how are they going to afford it?"

"Let me worry about that," he said.

"That's good, Victor, because I don't like worrying. It makes people old before their time. Now how about dropping the other shoe?"

He chuckled, going back behind his desk to sit down. The leather of the chair squeaked. It was an expensive sound.

"I'm beginning to think you and I know each other a little too well."

"I've thought so for years."

"Ha ha," he said.

# CHAPTER TWO

H e told me the deal. I was to be a spy.

He didn't put it that way, of course; Victor never uses one word when ten will do. But he said he wanted to keep close tabs on how the Barbara Corns campaign was progressing, and toward that end he expected a report from me at least every other day. He wanted to know what she was doing, what she was saying and to whom, how the voters were responding to her, and how many rubber-chicken banquets and luncheons she'd sat through.

Supremely confident that I'd remember I owed him and say yes, he had already made arrangements with the Corns people to receive me. Hell, why wouldn't they, when he was paying for it? An underfinanced run at a suburban city hall needs all the help it can get, even when that help issues from someone like Victor. I didn't buy it that Barbara Corns and her husband truly believed Gaimari was nothing but a downtown stockbroker, and I had to wonder what his assistance would cost her down the line. But he'd called the favor in, and I had to at least play along until I saw how it would lay out. Starting in the morning.

I didn't like it much. It felt like tattling on the other kids when the teacher left the room. But I owed Victor the favor, and it was as painless a way as any to discharge the debt.

I try to avoid walking into situations blindly. I suppose there had been stories about the developing campaign in the newspaper, but since Lake Erie Shores had nothing to do with me, I'd ignored them. It's hard enough just keeping up with world news and sports without reading stories about every two-bit local election. I'd have to bone up pretty quickly.

So I called Ed Stahl, and invited him to dinner.

Ed is a Pulitzer Prize–winning columnist for the *Plain Dealer*. He's also one of my closest friends. We're poker buddies—I usually lose—we take in ball games on the free tickets he sometimes gets, and we have lunch together every three weeks or so, the way pals do. But the quality of the friendship really shines through when one of us needs help.

I frequently do. My work sometimes takes me into areas I know nothing about, and I always turn to Ed to help me sketch in the background, because what he doesn't know about what goes on in Cleveland isn't worth knowing. And because his column shoots from the hip about corruption and stupidity and bigotry, he gets a lot of people mad at him. And on the rare occasions when that anger is translated into something tangible and potentially dangerous, I've been there for him. Unlike Victor, to whom a favor granted is a favor owed, Ed and I don't keep score. That's not what friends are all about.

The nature of my work makes it necessary to maintain contacts all over town with people who can take shortcuts to get me the information I need. Rudy Dolsak, with whom I went to high school, is one of many vice presidents at Ohio Mercantile Bank and frequently bends rules for me when I need the financial skinny on someone whose affairs I'm poking into. Marko Meglich, my best friend both in high school and at Kent State and my rabbi when I joined the police department after I came back from Vietnam, is the number-two guy in homicide, and I can usually count on him to help out when needed, even though he's never forgiven me for quitting the force and going private.

And then there's Ed.

On the surface of it we're not much alike. I'm an easygoing Slovenian and Ed's a dour second-generation German. He's an intellectual and I got through college on a jock scholarship.

He's Jim Beam whiskey and a contemplative pipe smoker, I'm Stroh's and Winstons. And despite my years as a detective, both public and private, I've managed to maintain a fairly optimistic outlook on life, whereas Ed Stahl is a card-carrying cynic.

Maybe the differences are the glue of the friendship.

We decided to meet at the Great Lakes Brewing Company, which earns its name by their brewing beer on the premises. It proclaims itself the oldest saloon in Cleveland, dating back to the Civil War, and the ornately carved wooden bar makes you shake your head and wonder why they don't build them like that anymore. My only complaint is that it's on the wrong side of the Cuyahoga—East Siders like me go into culture shock when we cross over to the West Side. But the atmosphere is honest nine-teenth-century American, and the servers are all young, eager, and happy to give you a rundown of the building's history while you're wishing they'd just shut up and bring your beer.

Ed arrived at seven thirty, his black horn-rimmed glasses making him look, as always, like Clark Kent after he'd gotten too close to some Kryptonite. His head was wreathed in the blue pipe smoke that precedes him into any room. Whenever he comes to my place my drapes stink for weeks.

We ate in the front room where the bar is, even though there are several other dining rooms. Historically a political hangout because of its proximity to City Hall and the courthouse just across the Cuyahoga, a much cherished myth about the saloon is that the two actual bullet holes in the back bar—slugs still imbed-ded—were put there during a shootout back in the old days when a thug tried to assassinate Eliot Ness, famed "Untouchable" and then Cleveland's safety director.

But the way I heard it, although Ness did indeed hang out at the Great Lakes, he always sat at a booth in the corner facing the door, and the bullet holes were put in the bar by a former owner who, under great stress from unpleasant and rowdy weekend customers some forty years ago, had cracked and rushed into the barroom waving a gun, fired off a couple of random rounds, and then blew out his brains in front of the Saturday night revelers. Eliot Ness hadn't even been there.

I'm not sure which story I like best.

We ate in the barroom because Ed is a barroom kind of guy, always in shirt sleeves or baggy tweed jackets or ancient cardi-gans, or Ohio State sweatshirts when he can get away with it; when he's forced into more businesslike attire, he sports duds from Kilgore Trout and looks as though he's on the tenth day of wearing the same suit, which he augments with one of the ugliest ties on earth, bought ten at a time from T. J. Maxx. He rags on me about my own loud jackets and too-wide ties, accusing me of shopping at a thrift store in a bad neighborhood. But I only own one suit, and I save it for funerals.

After dinner we ordered a Jim Beam for Ed despite his incipient ulcer, and I stuck with the house beer, called Burning River in honor of the conflagration on the Cuyahoga thirty years ago that has helped give Cleveland its unjustified lousy reputation. As a Cleveland booster I dislike perpetuating the legend of one of the city's bleaker moments, but I sure enjoy the way Burning River tastes. Ed and I clinked glasses and then I told him about my upcoming job with the Corns for Mayor campaign.

"Lake Erie Shores," he mused, puffing on his pipe. "One of the last bastions of the white middle class. Are you changing Milan Jacovich to Mark Johnson?"

"No way. They probably think Slovenians are exotic—I'll be a big attraction. Tell me about this election."

He shook his head. "Politics isn't like it used to be in Cleveland. It was fun. You knew all the players and who owned them. In the old days the bulldog edition of the *PD* got delivered early to Tony's Bar on West 117th Street. The judges and councilmen and other pols used to gather there for coffee and to read the obituaries—'the Irish sports pages,' they called them—to see what wakes and funerals to attend that day."

"This isn't Cleveland, it's Lake Erie Shores."

"If my column had to depend on hard news out of Lake Erie Shores, I'd be out of a job in three days. But I know a little about it. Your candidate has her work cut out for her: Gayton True is an institution. And his war chest is bottomless, because his wife is only slightly less wealthy than God."

"You know what they say, Ed—people who marry for money wind up having to earn it."

"Surely. The Trues have a volatile marriage, if I recall. The cops have been summoned more than once because he was smacking her around, or she threw crockery at him. And Princess True has a few skeletons in the closet too."

"Princess?"

"Her maiden name was Barnstable, an old-money Lake County family. Her younger brother Earl got himself indicted for the distribution of hard-core pornography. Little kids, real sicko stuff. His trial is set for January—after the election."

"Earl and Princess. What are the rest of the family's names? Duke and Baron and Queenie?"

He allowed himself an amused smile. "It's sad, Milan. An ordinary crook is one thing, kiddie porn is quite another."

I grimaced. "Wife beating and pornography. Sounds like Gayton True has an uphill fight to get himself reelected."

"Not necessarily," he said. "True's domestic troubles are public knowledge. Have been for years. But they always get swept under the rug somehow, and to their constituents Gay and Princess are the devoted couple, king and consort of Lake Erie Shores. And when election time comes around, the voters conveniently forget they're returning a wife abuser and the brother-in-law of a smut-meister to office."

"Coupled with the real anger that most people seem to direct against incumbents these days, you'd think that would sink him with women voters, and lots of men too."

Ed held up a cautionary finger. "There's one thing people vote more than political correctness, or even morality: their wallets. Lake Erie Shores has one of the lowest tax rates in the county, and a school system that sends more than seventy percent of high school graduates on to college. Property values out there have gone up for the last twelve years or so, and they make a small fortune in summer from Clevelanders who go up for the weekend to boat, swim, fish, and drink beer. When they check around and see themselves so much better off than their neighbors, it's easy to look the other way when a rich lady named Princess wakes up with a black eye every once in a while. Or when a mayor skims a little off the top."

"True is on the pad?"

"Every politician alive takes in one way or another. And a sub-urban midwestern mayor is one of the last absolute monarchs left in the world." He took the pipe out of his mouth and looked into the bowl like he was reading auguries in a teacup. Seemingly content with whatever he saw, he stuck the stem back between his teeth.

"If they're all so happy with Gayton True," I said, "why is this Barbara Corns so anxious to run against him?"

"Over *the* big suburban issue of the nineties—growth. True is gung ho for it. He's ramrodded some tax abatements through on a couple of housing tracts, some new commercial developments, and a gradual buildup of lakefront property, all of which increase the tax base and keep the homeowners happy with the services the town is able to provide.

"Barbara Corns, on the other hand, is antigrowth. She'd like it to be the quieter, more bucolic small-town America our parents came to after the Second World War. Lake Erie Shores is one of the last outposts like that left around here—Andy Hardy, Ozzie and Harriet, like that. And the white middle class who escaped from Cleveland to Lake County, well, that hits them right where they live."

"Nothing wrong with that," I said.

Ed waved away the blue smoke from in front of his face. "I forgot who I was talking to for a minute, there. A guy who still says 'Victrola' and 'ice box.' You're so retro, Milan."

"Maybe," I admitted. "But you can't say that the quality of life is better now than it was forty years ago."

"Hiding your head in the sand is no answer."

"Is that what Barbara Corns is doing?"

"I don't know," Ed told me. "But from all I've heard she doesn't have a program. Just some vague idea of keeping Lake Erie Shores the way it's always been."

He slumped so far down in the corner of the wooden booth it all but swallowed him. "What makes the cheese really binding is that Barbara was Gayton True's administrative assistant for four years. She knows every nickel he's skimmed and every dirty deal he's rubber-stamped. He fired her about a year ago, and that's when she decided to run against him. Or her husband decided."

"What does that mean?"

"Evan Corns is a successful attorney. He's the guy with the political connections and the fire in the belly. He got her into city hall when they got married. Whatever political awareness she possesses has been filtered through Evan. He's the real candidate, but he doesn't want to give up his law practice, so he talked his wife into running instead. It's pretty common knowledge that a vote for Barbara is really a vote for him."

"There are precedents for that," I said. "But you'd think it's the

Trues who'd be in trouble; recently we've had people bounced right out of politics for immorality. Look at Gary Hart, or the buzz saw Bill Clinton ran into just because of a loose zipper."

Ed smiled. "That was national, my friend. O beautiful for spacious skies and all that. You know how pious we Americans get when anyone waves a flag at us. This is as local as a hot stove in a general store. Peeking into your next door neighbor's bedroom just isn't done, even if he's mayor. Gay True is one of Lake Erie Shores' own, his rocky marriage and his brother-in-law notwithstanding. Besides, Mrs. Corns's skirts aren't as clean as they could be in that area, either."

I had no desire to be involved in this election in the first place; finding myself in the middle of a scandal wasn't going to make me like it any better. "Aren't clean in what way?"

He pulled at his Jim Beam, making a face as it hit his stomach. "The Cornses have been married for about four years. They've lived together for six, which is no big deal anymore. But prior to that, Evans Corns was married to another lady, one of those benefit harpies. He left her for Barbara. It caused a minor stink."

He pushed his glasses up onto his forehead, which made him look less like Clark Kent. "But you've got more pressing concerns than who does what to whom behind their bedroom doors."

"I do?"

He sucked hard on his pipe, which had gone out, making a disgusting slurping sound like when you're drinking a milk shake through a straw and you get down to the last few drops. "I don't pay much attention to Lake County politics," he said, "so I don't have any answers. But hasn't it ever occurred to you to wonder why anyone as exalted and connected as Victor Gaimari should care about a little bitty pissant local election?"

I waved to the waiter to bring us another round. "It's occurred to me," I said.

## CHAPTER THREE

To get to Lake Erie Shores you take Interstate 90 north past the pristine communities of Mentor and Kirtland. Seen from the highway, the white Cape Cod colonials and oak and catalpa and maple trees turning color and the soaring steeples of clapboard Protestant churches put one in mind of New England. Indeed the whole area around Cleveland used to *be* Connecticut; it was part of the original land grant from England, called the Western Reserve. It's not a bad drive unless the road is under construction, which it always is during good weather, when the Ohio Department of Transportation is out there every day with their bright orange barrels, patching up the cracks and potholes brought on by the annual ravages of snow and cold. In Lake County, especially, the winters hit hard. You could make a fortune up there if you could figure out some way to get the orange barrel concession.

But there's a payoff for the long gray months of Ohio winter. In spring there's no greener place on earth, and in fall the foliage rivals that of the more heralded New England autumns.

I got off the freeway and consulted the directions Victor Gaimari had jotted down for me. The sun shone without warmth, and a breeze blew off the lake. Football weather; unfortunately the Browns were playing Seattle on the road Sunday.

Not too long ago Lake Erie Shores was strictly a middle-class small town. But along about 1982 some white middle-class Clevelanders who'd begun making bucks from Reaganomics fled to Lake County for the services offered, a more bucolic way of life, and to make sure they didn't have to see anyone over the back fence who wasn't the same color they were. Now many families who live there have a disproportionate amount of discretionary income, which they spend on Saabs, Volvos, and Acura Legends, and lovely homes and elegant attire. The shops and boutiques in the town's main square might best be described as deliberately quaint.

Just off the square, in a storefront whose awning still bore the name of a women's clothing store, was the Corns for Mayor campaign headquarters. I'd be seeing a lot of it, but this morning I'd been instructed to go to the candidate's home.

I drove past woods thick with pine and scrub oak and beech, and over a concrete bridge spanning a lazy river. The rivers of the Midwest have high, wooded banks, and when you cross them on the highway and steal a look downstream you might think you were in the middle of an eighteenth-century painting of rustic serenity. It was hard to believe the muscular and energetic community of Cleveland was within hailing distance.

Barbara Corns's house was a pleasant three-story center-hall colonial painted white with black trim, perched on a slight rise on a north-south side street about two blocks from Lake Erie. On the tree lawn at the curb were two cardboard signs on wooden stakes driven into the ground announcing BARBARA FOR MAYOR. A big oak spread its branches over the front lawn, its vivid yellow and red leaves detaching themselves from their moorings and swirling around in the crisp fall air so that it seemed to be snowing in Technicolor. I parked, climbed the steps, and rang the bell. Inside I heard it go bing-bong.

A pretty black woman in her late thirties wearing a smart green wool executive suit opened the door. Her body language announced that she had the situation well in hand.

"We've been expecting you," she said, smiling. "I'm Cassandra Pride, Barbara's campaign coordinator. Please come in.

I stepped into the vestibule. Inside on the left was a living room with solid Shaker furniture I knew was expensive and a dominating forty-inch TV against one wall. To my right was a dining room, its black walnut table covered with stacks of mailers and campaign literature. A phone on the table was one of the off-brand extensions you buy in a hardware store and put in the basement, and I had the feeling it had only lately come to live in the Corns's dining room.

Cassandra Pride closed the front door behind me and turned to give me a strong handshake. "Welcome," she said.

"Nice to meet you, Mrs. Pride," I said, noticing the thick gold wedding band on her finger.

"Call me Cassandra, please."

"It'll be a pleasure—it's a beautiful name."

"Cassandra I can thank my mother for. And when I met Jim Pride I figured his last name would sound terrific with it, so I married him." She smiled. "There were a few other reasons too. Can I call you Milan? We're pretty informal around here. Barbara likes it that way."

I surrendered my trench coat and she hung it in a hall closet already bulging with outerwear and umbrellas. She pointed through the dining room. "There's always fresh coffee in the kitchen. Come on—I'll give you a crash course."

We went into the living room, at the end of which was an enclosed sun porch, and through the windows I could see a lot of colorful fall foliage in the back yard, reds and oranges and eye-popping yellows. I imagined they had about an acre back there, well-planted with tall oak and catalpa and maple, and the buckeyes that give the state its nickname. The trees must have provided a wall of privacy in the summer; in another few weeks the branches would be bare.

At Cassandra Pride's invitation, I sat at one end of a birch-framed couch with off white cushions. "Victor Gaimari told us all about you," she said. "So let me tell you about us. About Barbara."

She took a chair opposite me and crossed long brown legs encased in sheer white hose. "For the last eight years Barbara's been active in city government, either as a volunteer or on a professional basis. She's no career politician. But she worked in the mayor's office for many years, and the things she saw, she didn't like. So her decision to run stems from a deep-seated desire to effect some positive changes. This isn't a step toward congress or the governorship. She just wants to be the best mayor she can be." She smiled again. "Kind of refreshing in this day and age, isn't it?"

I smiled back and nodded, unready to commit myself until I knew a lot more.

"Barbara surprised everyone by getting only seventy-eight fewer votes than Gayton True in the June primary, which indicates deep voter discontent with a guy who's simply been mayor for too long. So they have to run off in the general election. Frankly, twelve days isn't a lot of time."

"For what?"

"For anything. As yet neither candidate has gotten the endorsement of the Lake County party chairman, for one thing."

"How important is that?"

"Very. That's who gets out the vote. An endorsement by the local paper and the local radio stations would help too."

"Who is the party chairman?"

She grimaced. "Naturally an old buddy of Gayton True's. His name is John Guilfoyle."

The name was familiar. "Didn't he used to be a judge? The one who got canned for drinking on the job?"

She nodded. "That's how they punish miscreants in a political party—they kick them upstairs. He's got twice the political power now than he had on the bench." She swung her foot lazily. "Our main problem, though, is getting the message across. Barbara isn't much of a public speaker. She's very shy, actually. Speaking to large groups can be painful for her."

"Shy people usually don't go into politics," I said.

She nodded wearily. "I know. So you can imagine the depth of her commitment, to put herself through a campaign."

I wanted a cigarette, but there were no ashtrays. What's become of the hallowed political tradition of the smoke-filled room?

"What is her message?" I said.

"'Back to the basics,' if that tells you anything."

"It tells me everything except where I'm going to fit in all this. I can give advice all I want, but this isn't my business or my territory, so I don't know what it'll be worth."

"A lot," she said. "But mainly we want to utilize you for security. You'll be with Barbara whenever she makes public appearances. You'll go in, check the microphone and the lights, and make sure she presents herself in the best possible setting. And with your police background—I told you we know all about you—you'll be right there in case any trouble starts."

"I can't imagine there being that kind of trouble in a place like Lake Erie Shores."

Her eyes narrowed just a millimeter. "Why? Because it's all middle-class whites?"

"No," I said quickly. "Because . . ." I blushed furiously. "I'm sorry. I guess that's exactly what I meant."

She relaxed. "Well, you're right. The crime rate here is only twenty percent of what it is in Cleveland. That's still a lot higher than it was twenty years ago; times change even in a place like this. But there's different kinds of trouble."

"Like what?"

"Voters are angry all over the country—especially when their tax dollars are involved, or the investment they've made in their homes. The growth issue is a pretty volatile one. Barbara's yard signs have been torn down within twenty-four hours of our putting them up, and they cost about a dollar apiece." She sighed. "Not that the damn things do any good anyway."

"Why bother then?"

"We have to have them if our opponent does. Besides, Evan, Barbara's husband, cruised the streets the other evening and had a fit because there were seventeen more True signs on the north side than Corns signs." She fiddled with the hem of her skirt. "But the most disturbing thing has been the phone calls."

"What phone calls?"

"She's been getting harassed on the telephone, usually after midnight. And hate letters—anonymous, of course. Morons like that never have the guts to sign their names."

"What's in the letters?"

"Pretty ugly stuff about Barbara's marriage. I'll show them to you later." She shrugged, somehow making the gesture elegant. "This is a pretty conservative town, and Gayton True will use anything he can. No one expected Barbara to do so well in the primary, and he's running scared."

"You think True is behind these anonymous letters and calls?"

"I wouldn't put it past him," she said. "He's a mean, conniving son of a bitch, and as corrupt as they come. He's been riding roughshod over this community for sixteen years."

"Do you live here?"

She snorted. "Be serious. I live in Cleveland, near University Circle. Not too far from you, actually. I worked on Mayor White's campaign, and for several other local and statewide candidates. I'm a professional political consultant."

"Then you aren't really as passionate about Barbara Corns being elected as you sound."

The edge in her voice was as sharp as a Gillette blade. "Of course I'm passionate. I'm paid to be," she said, pointing one long acrylic fingernail at me. "I'm a hired gun, Milan. Like you." The half smile just barely took the bite out of it.

She uncrossed her legs and got out of the chair in one fluid motion. "Come and meet the candidate," she said.

I followed her up the stairs. Sepia lithographs lined the stairwell, French street scenes. She led me to what was obviously a spare room that had been hastily transformed into an office. It was furnished with battered metal file cabinets, tops of which were stacked with papers. On a desk pushed against the wall beneath a window was an inexpensive copying machine. The carpet was faded yellow shag, and the wallpaper had a sort of bamboo motif.

Barbara Corns sat at a card table. On the wall over her head was a large poster with her picture on it; she smiled stiffly over the legend BARBARA—BACK TO THE BASICS.

Cute.

In person she wasn't smiling at all. She was on the phone, holding the receiver to her ear with her shoulder and drinking muddy-looking coffee from a mug with her name on it. About forty, she wore a pink shirtwaist dress and low heels, and her figure was trim and compact. Her dun-colored hairstyle had gone out of fashion in the Eisenhower era. I didn't know how she usually looked, but there was no mistaking the lines of strain and fatigue around her eyes and mouth. The redness at her nose and the tissues next to the phone told me she was fighting a cold.

"We'd really appreciate your support, Mrs. Styles," she was saying into the phone. "The people of this town deserve a mayor who looks out for their interests, and I think I can be that mayor." Her voice was an unpleasant whine. She held the receiver away from her face and sniffled. In front of her was a reverse telephone directory, and she doodled in the margins with a red pencil. I could see that several names were crossed off, a few were circled, a few others starred.

She chatted a few more minutes, then hung up and slumped down in her metal folding chair with her head back, her eyes closed, and her arms hanging limply at her sides. "I don't see how I'll ever make it through another three weeks," she said.

I didn't either. She opened her eyes, straightened her spine, and looked at me.

"Milan Jacovich," I said.

Barbara Corns stood up and came out from behind the table to take my hand. Her handshake was limp, without energy, but she had bright blue eyes that made her almost pretty. "It's nice to meet you. We're so glad you're going to be with us." She sniffled again, looking around as if seeing the room for the first time. Then she dragged two more folding chairs from against the wall and set them up so Cassandra and I could sit down across the table from her. "We're a cash-poor campaign; we borrowed these chairs and the ones in headquarters downtown from a local funeral home. I hope it's not an omen." She ran her fingers through her hair.

"I told Milan you were the best one to explain what the campaign is about," Cassandra said. "If you have a few minutes."

"I haven't had a few minutes since all this started." She sat down again, folding her hands in front of her. She looked ready to explain the significance of the Protestant Reformation.

"Well, Milan, we're campaigning on a platform of 'back to the basics.' We're sick of so-called progress that cuts down our trees to make room for ugly new homes and strip malls. We're tired of the increased traffic they bring so that it's not safe for our kids to cross the streets anymore. We're against commercial developments that the taxpayers have to foot the bills for. We don't want what happened to Cleveland happening to us—we don't need any new stadiums or museums or shopping centers at the expense of our schools. We want it to be the way it was when life was easier, more pleasant. That's what the American Dream is all about, isn't it?"

It occurred to me that her thinking, while undoubtedly well-meaning, was in a way dangerously simplistic. Life was certainly more idyllic forty years ago, but it was a very different world then, one where people kept the same jobs and the same spouses for fifty years and everyone was white except the hired help. Back then the American character and family values meant Ward and June Cleaver.

I said, "How do you plan on going about this?"

What might have been terror flickered across Barbara's face for a second, and she looked quickly from me to Cassandra Pride and then back again. "By going back to the basics."

I decided I'd be an old man if I waited for her to explain her catchall slogan in detail. I said, "Let's talk security a minute. Tell me about these letters and phone calls."

Barbara colored and looked away. "Show him, Cassie."

Cassandra stood up, went to one of the file cabinets, and rummaged in the bottom drawer, fishing out a folder. "The first one came two weeks ago," she said. "The second one last Monday."

I opened the folder. There were two pieces of lined yellow paper inside. The one on top had been scribbled on with a red felt pen: *Drop out! No whores in city hall!* The second was neater, with underlined block capital letters written in blue ballpoint: GET OUT OF THE MAYOR'S RACE, ADULTERUS SLUT!

"Illiterates!" Cassandra scoffed. "Can't even spell 'adulterous.'"

"Maybe they'd like us to think so," I said. I closed the folder. "Did you keep the envelopes?"

"No."

"From now on, do. And only handle them by the edges. What about the phone calls?"

Barbara Corns pursed her lips again and looked at her campaign coordinator for help. Cassandra said, "There's been, how many Barbara? Three?"

"Four. All between twelve and two A.M."

"Man or woman?"

"It's hard to tell. They whisper."

"What do they whisper?"

She looked away. "They call me . . . those names. Once Evan answered and they hung up without saying anything."

"Well, turn on your answering machine at night, and unplug the phone in your bedroom. They probably won't talk on tape, but at least you'll be able to get some sleep. And if they do say anything, we can go to the police. It's illegal to make threatening phone calls. Otherwise I wouldn't worry; if they really meant to do something they would have done it by now. Obscene callers usually just leave it at that."

Barbara dabbed at her nose with a tissue and gave me a wan smile. "See? You've only been here ten minutes and already you're worth the money."

I hadn't suggested anything that wouldn't occur to a ten-year-old, but I smiled back and modestly ducked my head. Any minute now I'd be tugging at what was left of my forelock. I've inherited the curse of the Slovenes: thinning hair.

Cassandra Pride took the folder from me, exchanging it for a photocopied piece of paper. "Here's the schedule for the week-end. A chamber of commerce mixer this evening at five, lunch tomorrow with the Women's Political League, bingo at Saint Bonaventure's, Sunday morning a walk through the park to meet the voters."

"Pressing flesh and kissing babies?"

Cassandra regarded me narrowly. I think she was starting not to like me very much. "We'll expect you here for all of these. And then Sunday afternoon Barbara and Evan are having an open-house party for some of the people in the neighborhood. The Browns game will be on. You're certainly invited, but you don't have to stay if you don't want to."

"Fine," I said. "I'll be there."

I heard the doorbell and Cassandra excused herself to answer it, leaving me alone with the candidate. She had a habit of pursing her lips, which made her appear prissy, and she didn't seem to know where to look; she wasn't very good at making eye contact. I could see there were a lot of problems with Barbara Corns's election prospects.

"It's so hard," she whined.

"Keep your energy up," I told her. "Convince the voters that you're a real fire-eater."

She smiled faintly. "Keep telling me that. Sometimes I think my face is going to crack from smiling. I wish I'd never started this, that my husband hadn't talked me into it. He's the one that should be running, anyway. I'm just a housewife."

"This is the New Age, Barbara. There's no such thing as 'just a housewife.' Anyone can make a difference."

"Oh, do you really think so? Do you believe in what we're trying to do here?" she said, like Peter Pan exhorting young audiences to please believe in fairies.

"I'm not sure yet. But I'll help you if I can."

Cassandra Pride came back in, followed by two strange-looking people. One of them, the man, was dressed in blue Wrangler jeans that were so new they were still stiff with sizing, a wrinkled blue and white dress shirt with the sleeves rolled up, penny loafers with run-down heels, and a wide-brimmed straw cowboy hat that was several sizes too big for him and as a result rested on the tops of his ears, bowing them out away from his head. His wire-rimmed glasses had been broken at the bridge and were patched together with black engineer's tape, giving him a rather cross-eyed look, and he squinted through them, lifting his upper lip and exposing his crooked teeth. The young woman with him was about five foot two and must have weighed upward of three hundred pounds; clearly the fibers of her black polyester stretch pants were stressed to dangerous limits. One of those brightly colored Mexican serapes was draped over her broad shoulders like a couch cover in a summer house that's been closed up for the season, and a mustache shadowed her upper lip. Both appeared to be about twenty-five years old. Milan junior would probably have characterized them as "dweebs."

"Hi, Barbara," they chorused, descending on her like a well-loved aunt for hugs and kisses, firing questions about how she felt, whether she'd had a good breakfast, whether she slept well.

Cassandra introduced them as Dennis Babb and Laurie Pirkle. When she told them I was Barbara's new security man they looked resentfully at me as though I were an interloper. Dennis even moved closer to Barbara and put a protective arm around her shoulders, and she reached up absently and patted his hand.

"Barbara doesn't need security," Dennis said sulkily. "She's got us." He all but stuck his lip out.

"Well, now you're free to do more important things," Cassandra said. "Come on, guys, there's a million envelopes to stuff. Milan, why don't you wait for me downstairs?" She herded them into the next room, Dennis looking back at me like I was a fox who'd just been invited into the henhouse for a drink.

I wasn't particularly surprised. There is a whole subculture who bask in the reflected glow of celebrities. Rock stars, actors, athletes, TV news anchors, even politicians, all have their hangers-on and their sycophants, mostly people who don't have lives of their own. I could understand Laurie and Dennis not wanting me in the picture; I was taking up Barbara's time and attention, and they wished it would be spent on them.

I turned back to her. "I'll see you later, Barbara," I told her, and went down into the living room to wait. Through the front window I saw a battered Dodge Dart at the curb, one fender the orange of raw primer coat. The car had Dennis Babb written all over it.

Cassandra appeared momentarily, a folder in her hand. "Those kids take their toll on me sometimes. And on Barbara, too.

"Where'd you find them?"

"Laurie is a student at Lakeland Community College. Dennis works over at the salt mines. I don't really know where he came from. He just appeared one day. It's tougher finding volunteers than it used to be. In the old days most of them would be housewives passionately committed to the candidate and the issues; now, with so many women working outside the home, free labor is harder to come by.

"You have to understand about kids like that," she continued. "There aren't many places they fit in, or where they're accepted. Laurie's unfortunate appearance, and Dennis—well, Dennis isn't exactly retarded, but he's very childlike and naive, and completely inept socially. But around a campaign there's always donkey work to do, so it's one of the only places they're welcomed with open arms. On a local level like this there's a good chance they can get close to the candidate and hope some of the stardust will rub off."

"They don't present a very good image."

"We don't dare turn them away. Public relations. They might set up a yell, and we don't want to be perceived by the voters as elitist or exclusionary."

"Political groupies."

"In a way," she said, sitting down at the other end of the sofa. "Most of our volunteers are committed and helpful, but Dennis and Laurie absolutely *adore* Barbara. They'd do anything for her, including stuffing envelopes and licking stamps and even cleaning up. I don't know what we'd do without them."

"I'm not much good at stamp licking," I said, "so you'll have to tell me what it is I'm supposed to do."

"Mr. Gaimari said you used to play football," she said leaning toward me and looking very serious. "So you know about blocking. Well, that's your main job—to keep people away from Barbara at public functions so she doesn't get distracted or upset. When one of Gay True's people says something that makes her feel bad, she goes into a blue funk, screws up her speech, and winds up looking like a fool. We simply can't let that happen."

"Sounds a little ugly."

"It is. The mayor calls her a traitor, and his wife is just beastly to her. But then she's beastly to everyone."

"Princess?"

"More like the Wicked Queen." She handed me the folder. "These are the remarks Barbara's supposed to make at the chamber mixer tonight. We'd like your input, of course. And there's all our literature and throwaways in here, so you'll know the direction we're going in, and some of True's campaign pieces too. Later this afternoon I'll introduce you around headquarters and give you a quick briefing." She stood up. "We'll take Barbara to the mixer a little after five. Do you mind driving?"

I shook my head.

"Make yourself comfortable then," she said. "If you need me I'll be down in the basement. We've put in a phone and desk down there for me—right next to the hot-water heater." She gave me a wry smile. "The glamour of politics."

After she left I sat there with the folder on my knees, pondering my career choices. I've set up security systems for medium-size industrial plants and companies, I've been an armed bodyguard, I've tracked down miscreants who've stolen or embezzled from the people I worked for, and on a few occasions I've gone head to head with hoodlums and murderers. But this was the first time I'd ever been hired to keep anyone from hurting my client's feelings.

## CHAPTER FOUR

The Lake Erie Shores Chamber of Commerce Friday mixer relocates from business to business each month, giving everyone a chance to strut their stuff. October's meeting was at a large real estate company's offices on the square, just down the road from an enormous white shopping mall that covered approximately three city blocks. The office was one of those house-selling factories, sixteen fake-wood metal desks jutting out from both sides of the long room in military precision, walls festooned with licenses and plaques and Jay Cee awards, and sales associates working the phones like a Gypsy boiler room. It was about as warm and personal as the Ohio State Correctional Facility at Mansfield.

We arrived at about twenty past five, me chauffeuring Barbara and Cassandra. Dennis and Laurie didn't actually join the gathering but hung around near the door, not fitting in with the people who typically attend chamber mixers. We all sported BARBARA: BACK TO THE BASICS buttons we'd picked up at campaign headquarters that afternoon. Mine made me feel a little silly.

Men and women between thirty-five and sixty, in proper business uniform, stood around with disposable plastic cups of no doubt wretched red or white wine or carbonated beverage, waving canapés consisting of cream cheese and a slice of black olive on Hi-Ho crackers. Most of the women were in tailored suits or dresses and the men all sported power ties. I was the only guy in the room whose pants didn't match his jacket. We were issued paper badges saying HELLO, MY NAME IS _____. I put mine in my pocket. No one could have pronounced my name anyway.

Some of the revelers came over to give a cool hello to Barbara. They were business types, bottom-liners committed to growth and profits. Barbara's political philosophy must have struck them like *The Communist Manifesto*.

I managed to snag a cracker from a passing tray. Barbara introduced me to several people whose names I didn't catch, and who doubtless didn't catch mine because they'd already decided I was no one with whom they needed to network.

Who was it that first decided *network* was a verb? Networking seems to consist of being in constant motion, handing out business cards the way John D. Rockefeller used to distribute dimes, and talking too loudly so everyone else can hear you. It was a party, but for the attendees it was work every bit as much as sitting at their desks doing mysterious computer stuff or hondeling on the phone. The only festive touch seemed to be the Hi-Ho canapés.

As the head of security, I stuck close to Barbara, but no one tried to call her bad names, and I was feeling a little bit superfluous until the front door swung open and a palpable burst of nervous energy raced through the room like a shock wave.

It was the Gayton True contingent, led by His Honor himself, a pompous man in his fifties with a full head of gray hair, a slight paunch, and fiery blossoms of exploded capillaries on his patrician nose. He was wearing a blue suit, a white shirt, and a patterned blue and gray tie that was thunderingly drab. Just behind him, clutching a clipboard, was an overweight young man, sweat plastering a few strands of his vanishing hair to his forehead. From Cassandra's informative briefing that afternoon I took him to be True's administrative assistant, Tyler Rees. A smattering of applause greeted the mayor, but no more than that; the business community obviously wasn't too crazy about Gayton True either. Like so many political contests of the recent past, this one would garner votes for the lesser of two evils.

After a moment a woman who could only be Princess True swept in; she must have paused a few seconds so her entrance would have more of an effect. She was a few years younger than her husband, and what is often euphemistically referred to as "full-figured." She sported a Nancy Reagan red suit that her figure was a tad *too* full for over a yellow silk blouse revealing more cleavage than necessary, and her blonde hair was swept up and sprayed solid. She looked rather like Tammy Faye Bakker unsuccessfully trying to kick a five-hundred-dollar-a-day makeup habit.

She smiled radiantly at almost everyone she seemed to know, a little less so at those she didn't recognize. But when her blue eyes met Barbara Corns's they turned cold and nasty, and her lip actually curled. Standing next to Barbara, I could feel her shrink. I stepped between her and Princess, shielding her from the venomous glare, and Princess gave me a flicker of annoyed contempt before she moved on through the crowd, following her husband.

But the new arrival who really caught my attention came in just behind Princess. A huge, solid bull of a man with a twenty-inch neck, a military crew cut, hardly any nose at all, and a big, ugly jaw that seemed hacked out of a block of old cement, he looked just off the boat—from across the River Styx. No one had to introduce us. We were already acquainted.

Al Drago, formerly of the Cleveland Police Department's vice squad, where he had been known as the Dragon, both for his netherworld look and for the way he used to beat up and terrorize the hookers and pimps and penny-ante crapshooters and poker players he busted. He was a vicious bastard and an abusive cop, and he'd been kicked off the force in disgrace because I happened to be in what was for him the wrong place at the wrong time, camera in my hand, and had photographed him sexually brutalizing a fifteen-year-old prostitute in an alley off Euclid Avenue. Internal Affairs had taken one look at the picture and asked not very politely that he turn in his shield and his weapon. Of course he didn't feel kindly toward me.

The feeling was mutual.

I don't mind tough cops. I used to be one. Tough is part of the job description. Out on the streets the weeping Willies get themselves—and sometimes their partners—killed. And if the daily rigors of the Job wear away some of a cop's natural human compassion like a river sculpting a rock, we can understand it, if not overlook it. But deliberate brutality for the fun of it cannot be condoned. Let cops get away with torture and rape and assault, they just might take it into their heads that on-the-spot executions are okay, too, and you'd have a true police state, a domestic Tontons Macoutes.

I was glad I'd blown the whistle on Al Drago.

What I wanted to know now was what he was doing in Lake Erie Shores with Gayton True.

"He's your opposite number," Cassandra Pride said when I asked her. "True's head of security."

I shook my head. I knew the real reason I was there, but I couldn't figure out why a longtime suburban mayor needed a guy with Al Drago's peculiar but limited talents.

"Am I missing something here?" I said to Cassandra. "Isn't this a lot of security for local politicians?"

"It's a changing world," she said, "and a dangerous one. I suppose True hired Drago to be on the safe side." She shivered. "He's the scariest-looking man I've ever seen."

"Wait till he gets mad," I warned her.

Drago's mean little pig eyes swept the room, finally resting on me. Most people's eyes widen in surprise, but Drago's got even smaller. Any minute I expected them to glow red like a demon's in a bad horror movie. An ugly flush crept up over his too tight collar, coloring his fish-belly white face. When a man's neck is that thick you're never sure when he's moving his head, but I thought he gave me a small nod, and something happened to the corner of his mouth that might have been a smile. I think he was imagining me dead and figuring how he could make it happen.

Small world. I would have bet that Al Drago hadn't ever been farther north than Lakeside Avenue in his life, and yet here he was out in Lake County, on the opposite side of my fence.

I nodded back, watching as he whispered something into his candidate's ear. True turned and looked at me with interest.

The mayor backslapped his way through the crowd of suits to where Barbara Corns and I were standing. "Well, good evening, my dear," he said loudly to Barbara, taking her hand and smiling. "Always a pleasure to see you."

Barbara gave her lips a prissy purse. "Mr. Mayor."

"Come to give these good folks your message, have you? I'm sure they'll hang on every word."

I glanced around. They were certainly hanging on every word now; True was speaking loudly enough to assure it.

The mayor turned to me and extended a hand. "Mr. Jacovich, is it?" At least he pronounced it correctly, which led me to believe that he'd been briefed. "Welcome to Lake Erie Shores. How do you like our little town?"

"It's very nice," I said.

"We think so too," he said in that ringing voice, turning his body slightly away from me so everyone in the room could see him too. "And we want it to be even nicer. More prosperous. More responsive to the needs of the folks who live here. You know, a place the size of Lake Erie Shores, why, it's just like a shark. It's got to keep moving forward or else it suffocates. We can't afford to play the cards we have—we must draw newer and better ones so our city can grow. So we can be major players in this state."

The bastard was making a campaign speech—paraphrasing Woody Allen to boot—and he still hadn't let go of my hand.

A harried-looking man in gray stepped forward, begging for quiet. His paper badge read JOSH WILDER. I learned later he was the chamber's executive director.

"Ladies and gentlemen," he said, none of whom made any effort to stop talking, so he repeated it. Finally he had to rap loudly with his Cross pen on the side of an empty wine bottle.

"We're very fortunate," he said when he finally had everyone's attention, "to have both our candidates in the upcoming mayoral election here tonight. And they've both kindly agreed to say a few words to us. So if you'll all please move to the sides of the room here and give them a little space . . ."

He made shooing motions with his hands. Muttering, the businesspeople cleared the center aisle, leaning against walls or sitting on the edges of desks, many of them picking up drink refills as they went. I found a place next to Cassandra, directly across the room from the Trues and Al Drago.

"It used to be ladies first," Josh Wilder said, "but this is the nineties and we don't do that anymore—especially not in this crowd." There were a few titters, a few insider-type laughs, but not many. "So we'll just do it alphabetically and it'll work out the same way."

"Shit," Cassandra said quietly. "I hate going first."

"Uh, you all know Barbara Corns," Wilder continued. "She's been a vital part of our community for a long time now, and this year she's decided she'd like to be mayor."

Cassandra stiffened beside me. "Condescending son of a bitch," she said out of the side of her mouth.

"So," Josh Wilder went on, "she's going to talk to you for a few minutes, and then the mayor will say a few words, I'm sure." He stepped back out of the way, then reconsidered and moved forward tentatively. "Uh, Barbara Corns," he announced.

Everyone tapped their patties politely; Cassandra did so vigorously, earning more than dirty looks.

Barbara stepped into the middle of the room, her every move broadcasting her reluctance. She reminded me of a child called on to recite in third grade.

"Our message is simple," she said in her piping little voice. "Back to the basics. Back to the way Lake Erie Shores used to be when it was a nice, quiet, family place to live."

Princess snorted audibly, and a few people glanced over at her, including Dennis and Laurie, who looked as if they wanted to shoot her. Her husband remained calm, rocking forward on the balls of his feet as though he didn't want to miss a word.

"Most of us came out here to get away from all the problems of a big city," Barbara said, nervously looking everywhere in the room except at Princess. "To raise our kids where there was grass and trees and a blue sky free of pollution, with two-lane roads to walk along in the hazy summer evenings. But now it seems everywhere we look there are bulldozers plowing up the fields for new houses, new industry, new commercial developments. And then we have to widen our streets and roads to take care of the new traffic that that brings. We never wanted to be urban; we wanted _sub_urban, that's why we moved here.

"Elect me mayor, and we'll have the band concerts on the square again. We'll grow at our own pace. Because you know what happens when you grow too fast?" She paused, took a deep breath, and delivered her biggie; I'd read the line earlier so I knew what was coming, and I had to admit it was pretty good.

"You get too big for your britches," she said, as convincingly as her little wallflower voice allowed.

Princess laughed out loud, so derisively that even her husband shot her an irritated look.

What little color there was in Barbara Corns's cheeks that

wasn't courtesy of Revlon fled. Mrs. True seemed to have a real evil eye on her. Barbara looked around for a sign of support, finally settling on me. I smiled and gave her a thumbs-up; it must have helped because she straightened her shoulders and continued.

"This can be the town we all want to live in," she went on more confidently, "but only if someone puts the brakes on this helterskelter growth before it gets any worse. As your mayor, I'd be that someone."

She waited for the applause that she expected and didn't get it. Ducking her head, she almost backed out of the center of the room. When they realized she was finished, the crowd clapped politely, because that's what you do at functions like this one, and a few people even reached out to pat her back or take her hand as she worked her way toward where I stood with Cassandra, but it was obvious she hadn't made many converts here.

"Wonderful, Barbara," Cassandra said, giving her a hug. "You were just wonderful."

Barbara looked up at me for further reinforcement. I said, "Way to go, Barbara." What else in hell could I say?

Josh Wilder moved to the middle of the room and raised his hands for silence again. The crowd didn't quiet until they felt like it; Wilder, after all, was only an employee.

"Uh, Gayton True has been mayor here for so long that most of us don't remember what it was like when he wasn't. Well, he wants to be mayor another four years, and he's here to talk to you about that tonight. Mayor True."

The ovation was larger than the one they'd given Barbara, but it was hardly enthusiastic. I gave Cassandra a worried look, but she shook her head almost imperceptibly.

"These people are progrowth, for business reasons," she told me. "The votes we're after, the ones that count, are the commuters who work in Cleveland and return here at night to escape."

"I am so pleased," Gayton True thundered. His voice was strong and mellow, with just a hint of country in it. "I am so pleased and proud of my good friend Barbara Corns. Eight years ago when she came to work in my office, she was earnest and eager and smart as a whip, but she didn't know much about the business of running a city like ours. In the years she worked for me I watched her grow and blossom. And here she is, standing against me for election as mayor of Lake Erie Shores. I'd say that was quite an accomplishment, and I applaud her."

And he did, just like Joan Rivers, arms straight and fingers splayed, slapping his palms together. Everyone in the room joined him except Cassandra and me, and his wife, who had resumed glaring daggers in Barbara's direction.

Brilliant, I thought. In just a few sentences he'd reminded everyone that she was just a few years past filing his letters and emptying his wastebasket, that he'd taught her everything she knew, and that she'd betrayed him by challenging him. True understood political nuances.

"Lord knows I hope she didn't mean me when she was talking about being too big for your britches," he went on, tugging at the belt around his comfortable girth, and everyone chuckled. "Because I love this town. I've lived here for thirty-two years, raised three children here. This is my home. I don't want it turning into a big city, with big-city problems. I remember when this was one of the nicest little towns in America.

"But here Barbara and I disagree—I think it still is! It still is, friends, but it's moved forward. We're poised on the brink of the twenty-first century. I'd like to remind Barbara that thirty-two years ago our property values were probably one third what they are now, dollar for dollar. We didn't have a sewer system. We only had one grocery store. And if we wanted to shop for clothes any fancier than blue jeans and work shirts we had to drive into Cleveland to do it—and there was no freeway to zip us in there in forty-five minutes or less, either.

"All we had then was what Barbara calls 'the basics.' And I must ask you if we're not just a teensy bit better off now.

"I stand for the same good old American values that Barbara and Evan Corns do."

I winced as he reminded the voters that Barbara was really only a figurehead for her husband's political agenda.

"I believe in morality and the sanctity of the family."

Another shot, this one directed at the scandal that had tainted the Corns's marriage. Princess's already ample chest puffed up like a ruffled grouse's, and the vitriolic glare she aimed Barbara's way became slightly diluted by a triumphant smirk. Al Drago loomed behind her like a natural landmark, no expression on his face except a gleam behind his mean pig eyes when he looked at me. An overpainted middle-aged lady and a brutish, almost prehistoric-looking cop—of the two of them, Princess scared me far more.

"I believe in safety in our streets and homes," True rolled on. "I believe in the small towns and cities of this great country of ours, because here is where the real folks live."

"Meaning white," Cassandra hissed in my ear.

"But I also believe in progress, my friends, because progress means prosperity. And progress . . ." He paused here, filling his lungs with air. "Means *not standing still!* Because when you stand still the rest of the world passes you right by and you find yourself eating their dust!"

He shook his head from side to side. "We're not going to eat anybody's dust in my town, friends. Not in *our* town !"

Tyler Rees began a vigorous ovation, which was after all why they paid him, and the lemmings in the business suits got caught up in his enthusiasm. I glanced over at Barbara, who looked ready to cry.

I'd cry too if someone had carved me up so publicly. If this was small-town politics, I thought, give me the rough-and-tumble of the gritty, honest streets of Cleveland, where the gloves were always off and a stab in the back was only what was expected. As a social event, the chamber of commerce mixer was about as exciting as an Amway party. And as a campaign vehicle for Barbara for Mayor, it was pretty much a disaster.

# CHAPTER FIVE

Barbara wanted to leave right away, but Cassandra explained that it was important to stay and talk to the chamber members so it wouldn't look as if she was slinking away in defeat. They set off, working one side of the room while the Trues worked the other, with Laurie and Dennis offering little pigeon cooings of congratulations and love.

I found myself face to face with Al Drago. Literally. True was circling the room clockwise and Barbara counterclockwise, so it was inevitable that Drago and I cross orbits.

We didn't shake hands. The handshake originated as a gesture of good faith among warriors, to show that they were unarmed and not hostile, so for Drago and me to have gone through the motions would have been hypocrisy. As a cop he'd abused the badge and abused citizens, and I hated everything he stood for—and he hated my guts. There was no reason to act civilized.

He bulked in front of me like an abandoned earthmover on a path in the woods. His eyes were working full time, shifting back and forth to see who was listening, who might overhear something he didn't want to become public knowledge.

"I didn't expect to see you out here, Drago."

"Hello, fink," was his reply. He had a voice that sounded like a cave-in at the bottom of a coal mine. His already huge chest expanded like a driver's-side airbag, and I thought for a second he was going to swing on me right there; I tensed for it, watching his hands. But he didn't seem inclined to get physical. Instead, without raising the decibel level much above a soft murmur, he loosed a torrent of obscenities at me that included a few I'd never heard before—and as an ex–army MP and ex–cop, I'd thought I'd heard everything. No one else in the room seemed to notice, and since he barely moved his body during the tirade, a casual observer might have thought we were having a friendly conversation.

He kept up the spew of filth until he ran out of breath, and for someone with a chest the size of his that took a while. Then he inhaled again, leaned his trunk forward, and whispered in my ear, "Paybacks are rough, fink."

He stepped back but not aside, so that if I wished to continue circling the room with Barbara and Cassandra I'd either have to go around him or through him. I thought about it for a long while.

Despite a youthful football career spent on the defensive line, where it always gets pretty physical, and my years in military and civilian law enforcement, I've always believed there are better ways to settle arguments than with fists or guns or bombs or missiles. And since I spent most of my adult life married to a woman of Serbian descent who could escalate even a disagreement over what TV show to watch into open, take-no-prisoners warfare, I'd learned to curb my temper and look for peaceable resolutions to conflicts whenever I could.

Yet everything in me wanted to smash Al Drago.

But there is a right time and a right place, and a chamber of commerce mixer was neither. So I stepped to one side and passed, the negativity like an electrical charge as our shoulders bumped. I wanted to brush off my sleeve where it touched his.

There would be no physical hostilities—not today.

Inevitable, too, was the meeting of Barbara Corns and Gayton and Princess True, which occurred just moments after. The mayor smiled benignly, except I was close enough to see that his eyes were marble cold. "Barbara," he said, taking her hand in both of his, "we're going to be seeing a lot of each other the next week and a half. Take care, now." He dropped her hand and went on by her. He might as well have patted her on the head.

His wife was not so pleasant. Close up, Princess True looked her age. Her orange pancake base was thick enough to write in with a fingernail, and the false eyelashes, which I thought went happily out of fashion twenty years before, were beginning to work loose. Perfume rose from between her breasts like swamp gas. "If you only knew," she rasped in Barbara's ear, "how pathetic you appear. You foolish, dowdy—*drab!*"

The color left my candidate's face again like blood down the drain in an autopsy table, and her knees almost buckled. If I hadn't been there to steady her she probably wouldn't have kept her feet. Dennis Babb moved in, peering past the tape on his glasses, and put a protective arm around her, glaring at Princess.

"Barbara, there's someone over here that wants to meet you," I said, and steered her to the other side of the office, literally taking her away from Dennis.

"There's no one," I whispered when we were out of earshot. "I just wanted to get you away." I looked back over my shoulder at Princess, who continued to glare. "What a witch."

Cassandra came up, tension pulling at the corners of her eyes. "You can talk plainer than that, can't you, Milan?"

Dennis and Laurie came trotting over and patted at Barbara like makeup people around a movie star. Laurie said loudly, "I really hate her."

"I don't know if I can put myself through this again," Barbara said.

"The trick is," Cassandra said, "not to take it personally. When Princess glares at you, just glare right back."

The crowd was thinning out some, since the informal festivities had ended and there were no more Hi-Ho crackers left, so when Evan Corns walked through the front door of the realty company, everyone who was still there noticed. Evan was a bespectacled bantam rooster of fifty, a high-energy little guy as dynamic as his wife was mousy, He came in smiling—beaming—and slapping backs, even kissing the hand of one of the women. My dislike for him was instant and visceral.

"How'd it go?" he said, giving Barbara's cheek a perfunctory peck.

"I blew it," Barbara said before Cassandra could answer for her. "I was dull and boring and he wiped the floor with me."

"Damn it, Barbara!"

"It was Princess," she protested. "She kept giving me dirty looks all the time I was talking, and it threw me."

"When are you going to start standing up for yourself?" The pitch of his voice got higher, and a few of the suits turned to listen. "I can't nursemaid you every minute! You gotta get tough. True's a crooked, conniving bastard, and his wife is more so, and nobody knows that better than you. If they make you look bad, you gotta make them look worse. This is hardball! Don't pussyfoot around like it's a damn church social."

Barbara's face grew even more ashen, and her eyelids flickered as if she were about to pass out. As Evan geared up for another broadside, I stepped between them—after all, my assigned task was to keep people from upsetting her equilibrium.

"I thought she did a pretty good job," I lied. "I can say that because, unlike you, I was here."

Barbara's look of gratitude bordered on worshipful, but her husband caught the dig and stared up at me with surprise, his jaw at a pugnacious angle. Evidently people didn't often talk that way to him. "Who the hell are you?" he snapped.

"Evan, I'd like you to meet Milan Jacovich," Cassandra put in smoothly. "He's going to be working security for the rest of the campaign."

Evan's face changed from pugnacious to sullen and he offered an uninterested handshake. "Oh. Okay, then, Jacovich."

"People who know me call me Milan," I said, "and everyone else calls me Mr. Jacovich. The last time I was called just plain Jacovich was when I was in the army—and then I *had* to take it."

His face reddened, and he puffed himself up for another fusillade. But then pieces began falling into place in his head, and I could almost hear the synapses firing. He squinted up at me, taking my measure. "You're Vic Gaimari's man."

I tried to stifle a smile. Probably not once in Victor Gaimari's entire life had anyone ever called him "Vic."

"Mr. Gaimari arranged for me to work with you," I said. "But I'm nobody's man."

"Well, I kind of run this ball game," he said. "I know politics, I know this town, and I know Barbara. So I call all the shots. We'll get on better if you remember that."

My snappy riposte was stillborn as he turned away from me toward his wife. "Come on, Barbara," he said. "Let's go home and have a nice quiet martini and dinner. It's been a long day."

"You're coming back tomorrow, aren't you Milan?" Barbara said almost fearfully.

I squeezed her hand. "I'll he here, Barbara. I'm on the team now."

Cassandra waited until they were gone before wheeling on me, her eyes like shiny lumps of obsidian. "Was that necessary? Things are tough enough without any internal friction."

"That's why I wanted to get the ground rules straight from the beginning."

"It doesn't help to get Evan pissed off. He's very volatile."

"That's just another word for abrasive," I said. "I don't like the way he treats his wife in public—but that's their business. How he talks to me is mine."

"Fighting with him just makes Barbara more upset."

"Sorry, but if it's a choice between Barbara's being upset or me, Barbara's going over the side every time."

"Don't be such a baby," she snapped. "Evan didn't mean anything by it. It's just his way."

"I have my own way. If there's one thing I've learned it's that in order to survive you *demand* from the people you come in contact with the respect and dignity that is due you as a human being. If someone refuses to give it to you, you have two choices: you can eliminate that person from your life—or, if you can't, you start kicking ass."

Her eyes lost their hard glitter and the starch went out of her spine. "I'm sorry," she said. "This campaign is getting to me. You're right, of course. And Evan is a pain in the butt."

"World class," I agreed.

She rotated her head around on her neck. "God, I'm tired. Sometimes I feel as if I'm teaching nursery school."

"Looks like you need a drink. May I buy you one? There's a few things I need to know."

"Sounds like a plan to me," she said.

We decided that such a crisp fall night was best enjoyed on the water, and in our own cars, we headed to a bar I knew in Grand River.

It's a little blue-collar town that hugs the shoreline, distinguished by a couple of first-rate seafood restaurants, a beach-front recreation area, the Morton Salt factory, with its offshore mines beneath the waves of the lake, and the LTV Steel lime plant. Silky white smoke billowed out of the single high smokestack of the

LTV plant as if a genie were going to suddenly materialize and offer three wishes. Most of the homes were within hailing distance of the plant, older and smaller than the ones in Lake Erie Shores and several rungs down the socioeconomic ladder.

We drove west into the black and blue sky. Along our route from the freeway, we passed a white clapboard church. On its signboard out front was the legend JESUS SAID, "IF YOU LOVE ME, BE TRUE TO MY WORD." Beneath it, big black letters spelled out PIEROGI SALES FRIDAYS.

Cap'n Andy's Saloon by the water was a happening place, its parking lot jammed, mostly with older-model American cars.

It's probably not a good idea to go anywhere for a drink on a Friday evening unless you're under twenty-five and head for one of those noisy, overpriced bars on the banks of the Cuyahoga in the Flats that seem to open and close with monotonous regularity. Fridays I normally stick close to home, because like New Year's Eve and Saint Patrick's Day, that's when the amateur drunks come out. But the strain of my first day in politics made a cold beer seem awfully inviting.

Things weren't yet in full swing at Cap'n Andy's. It was only seven thirty, sort of the lull between the after-work parolees going home and the end-of-week party-hearty crowd coming in. Nevertheless there were no seats at the long wooden bar, and Cassandra and I took a table near the window, where, if we craned our necks, we could see the dark outline of the lake in the dregs of the twilight. High above us a blue marlin was mounted on a large wooden plaque. It must have once lived at least a thousand miles from Lake Erie, and its eyes were wide open as if it were startled to be hanging on a wall in Ohio.

At this early hour Cap'n Andy's was a neighborhood kind of bar. Everyone seemed to know everyone else, and the decibel level was higher than I liked. But a beer was a beer, I figured.

There were two bartenders on duty, both watching Alex Trebek on *Jeopardy* on the TV set behind the bar. At one point the younger bartender, who wore an earring and a Eurotrash ponytail, shouted out, "Who was Edward the Confessor?" and beamed at his compatriot when he turned out to be right.

We sat for about five minutes without anyone coming to take our order, although several of the customers, including three hard cases at the bar, were paying open attention to us. Not many blacks find their way to Grand River; still fewer black women walk into a local pub with a white man.

The waitress who finally approached our table was young, probably just past the age at which she could legally serve alcohol in the state of Ohio. Her dirty-blonde hair was permed and teased and dull with hair spray, and a flaky layer of pale orange makeup covered a pitted complexion.

She didn't ask us what we wanted; she just stood there and waited, hip cocked, sneering at me with undisguised nastiness. I figured her disapproval was something I could live with. Cassandra ordered a vodka tonic. I stuck with my usual Stroh's, and our server moved off without a word.

"Watch to see she doesn't spit in the drinks," Cassie said, and I didn't think she was joking.

I figured the best way to survive the stares and mutterings of our fellow drinkers was to ignore them. Besides, I had business to transact. "Tell me about Evan Corns, Cassie."

She put her purse on the table. "Before I came aboard a few weeks ago, I checked with some of my friends in Cleveland, just so I could keep all the players straight. What I found out is that Evan would like to be the one running for mayor, and he makes no bones about it."

"Then why put his wife through this kind of torture?"

"He's smart enough to know that he's not electable."

"Why not?"

"You've met him—do you really have to ask?" She let one corner of her mouth smile. "Actually he was in one of his more charming modes this evening. Most of the time he makes everyone want to choke the shit out of him. I haven't found three people who would vote for him for rat catcher."

"Barbara doesn't seem like the best surrogate," I said. "She's not exactly a dynamic campaigner."

Cassandra rolled her eyes. "Tell me about it."

"Does she really *want* to be mayor?"

"Oh, she wants it," Cassandra said. "*Now* she wants it. There's something about running for office that gets the blood moving a little faster. But originally she wanted it because Evan wanted her to want it."

Our drinks arrived, and the waitress told me without smiling that the bill was eight dollars and sixty cents, which seemed a little high for one mixed well drink and a domestic beer. I wasn't going to argue with her—I was just glad to know she had a voice. I gave her a ten and waved away the change because it seemed too much trouble not to. She turned and headed for the bar, probably rolling her eyes, because one of three guys in sweatshirts and Browns caps sitting by the serving station snickered as he looked from her to us.

Or maybe I was just being paranoid. They were all in their early to mid thirties, solidly built workingmen who'd stopped off for a few beers after a day of hard labor. One of them had a blond Fu Manchu mustache and kept licking the ends of it as if he'd just finished eating an ice cream cone.

"How did you happen to get involved with this campaign, Cassie?" I asked, ignoring the men at the bar. "Lake Erie Shores is as out of your way as it is mine."

She raised her glass to me before taking a sip. "I'm a political professional, and Evan Corns hired me because I'm damn good at what I do. But if you're asking how they found me, I was recruited by Victor Gaimari, the same as you."

"Do you have any idea what Victor's interest is?"

"Maybe he wants to get back to basics," she said, her eyes twinkling.

The guy at the bar who had snickered levered himself heavily off his stool and came walking across the room, heading for the men's room at the far side of the restaurant. He walked on the balls of his feet the way John Wayne used to, rolling his beer gut in front of him; that he was only about five nine to Duke Wayne's six four made him look a little ludicrous.

"Changing your luck, fella?" he mumbled as he passed our table.

I started out of my chair but Cassandra put a firm hand on my arm and shook her head no.

"Forget it," she said, but her eyes were drawn up at the corners. "You think it's the first time I've heard shit like that? Some people just never get the word."

I looked over my shoulder to where the rest rooms were. "Maybe it's time they did."

"Don't be a damn fool," she said. "His buddies over there are just waiting for you to get out of that chair. You want to take on all three of them?"

The two other guys at the bar were looking my way, swung around on their stools so they could get up quickly. They were both big men—not as big as I am, but big. Cassandra was right; if I went three-on-one with them I was going to get my clock cleaned.

"Relax, Milan. In politics it never pays to get mad."

"I'm not in politics—at least, I wasn't until this morning. And I feel a certain obligation, since your husband isn't here."

"If my husband were here they wouldn't have opened their mouths. They would have resented our being in their precious lily-white bar but they would have shut up about it."

"Why?"

"Because he's a six footer and black, and they think all black men carry a razor."

"Does he?"

She laughed. "He's a CPA. He'd poke them in the eye with his automatic pencil." She tapped a fingernail on my beer bottle. "Come on, drink up. We're here to talk about the campaign."

I swallowed my anger because she asked me to and shifted mental gears. "Okay. We have problems, as far as I can see, but the biggest one is, how can we neutralize Princess True? She really seems to have put the double whammy on Barbara."

"Isn't she a trip? Every once in a while you get opposing candidates who really don't like each other, like Bush and Perot, but most of the time it's understood that it's just politics."

"Then what's Mrs. True's problem?"

She shrugged. "For some reason Princess really hates Barbara on a personal level, and she knows how badly she upsets her. She always seems to show up wherever Barbara's speaking, just to rattle her."

"I've heard that Princess and Gayton have domestic difficulties. Isn't there some way we could use that to keep her out of the way?"

Cassandra shook her head and took another sip of her vodka tonic. "Evan won't hear of it. He says he doesn't want the campaign to get sleazy."

"In light of those letters and phone calls, I'd say it was too late to worry about that."

"Maybe so. But Evan is adamant, and he's running things. We have even better stuff that he won't use either."

"Like what?"

She shifted in her seat as if trying to find a more comfortable position. "For the primary there was a big push to get out the elderly vote. College kids were dispatched to take elderly or disabled voters to the polls. Lake Erie Shores has a home for the blind—quite a well-known one—and guess who showed up on the morning of the primary to help the sightless mark their ballots?"

"I'm afraid to ask."

"Darryl True, Gay and Princess's son. He's in his second year at Lakeland."

"You're kidding."

"When I found out, I wanted to take it straight to the papers. But Evan said it would make us look bad, like we were against helping the disabled. He won't use it, and he won't mention True's brother-in-law being under indictment for distributing child pornography; he goes berserk if I even talk about it."

"Is the brother-in-law here in town?"

"He has a house here, but he's holed up somewhere so no one can find him until his trial."

I shook my head. "Don't they want to win? You're the pro here. What do you think?"

"I think if the election commission had investigated, they would have invalidated those ballots, and that might have made Barbara a clear winner. But without a complaint . . ." She shrugged. "People don't go out looking for extra work."

"They pay you for advice. Why don't they take it?"

"You tell me," she said.

The John Wayne walk-alike came back from the men's room, fingers fluttering at his fly. The swagger became more exaggerated the closer he got.

"Some guys like their women the same way I like my coffee," he said loudly, ostensibly to his buddies at the bar, who guffawed merrily as if they hadn't heard the punchline a hundred times before. When he sat back down on his stool he turned and gloated at us, his watery blue eyes glittering.

I started to rise, but Cassie leaned forward again and pulled me back down. "Don't do that. Please. That's just what they want—an excuse to gang up on us, or to run us out of here."

"I don't run so easily."

"Pick your own battlefield, Milan. I've dealt with morons like that since before I went to kindergarten. And I've been beaten up enough to know that if you fight them in the courts, you fight them in the schools, you fight them at the ballot boxes you can win. But in a redneck bar like this . . ." She shrugged. "Actually they're not so bad. They haven't gotten physical yet, and they haven't even said the N-word."

"They will. They've taken two shots at us, Cassandra. And fatheads like that like the number three."

"Then let's get out of here."

"I'm not letting them run me out."

"Remember when Dick Gregory spent six months sitting in, trying to integrate Woolworth's lunch counter in the sixties?"

"Sure."

"He said when they finally agreed to serve him, there wasn't anything on the menu he wanted. This place is like that. They water their vodka. So why don't you just finish your beer?"

"I don't want it anymore," I said.

"Then let's hit it."

We got up to leave. Our three tormentors cackled and hooted as we left. Fortunately we didn't have to pass the bar on our way to the exit; whether fortunate for us or for them I haven't yet decided.

I walked her to her car. She unlocked it and turned to me. "One question."

"Shoot."

"Were you ready to fight those guys in there because of their racist attitudes, or was it your wounded machismo?"

The question took me by surprise, more so because I had to think about it. "Both," I admitted finally. "I played ball with black guys, and kicked ass in Nam with them. Some were among the finest men I ever knew, and some of them didn't come back.

Slobs like those three bastards crap on their memory." I ducked my head a little. "But your being a beautiful woman probably had something to do with it, too. So . . . both."

She smiled. "Thanks for being honest." She shook my hand. "It's going to be very interesting working with you."

I waited until she was safely in her car with the door locked and watched her drive out of the parking lot. Then I went back to my own car and sat with the window halfway down, puffing on a Winston. Smoke curled out into the night air, which was beginning to turn foggy. Cap'n Andy's was only about a hundred yards from the edge of the lake, and a stiff breeze cleaned the tobacco smoke away almost immediately.

It was boring just sitting, doing nothing. But I'd spent plenty of watchful nights on Cam Ranh Bay, staring into the darkness, waiting for a movement, a sound. And I'd done plenty of stake-outs before. I'd learned patience.

Seventy minutes later the Three Musketeers weaved down the rickety steps of Cap'n Andy's and into the parking lot with lots of high fives and backslaps, real male bonding stuff, as if they'd just made it into the NBA playoffs. They were loud the way teenagers are, not giving a damn who heard them.

Finally one of them climbed into an Isuzu and roared off, his rear wheels spinning and kicking up gravel. The other two stood and talked for about as long as it takes to smoke a Camel. Then the one with the Fu Manchu found a red Dodge Daytona that had seen better days, unlocked it, and squeezed himself in. Before he shut the door he gave the third guy one more high five, almost like a lover stealing a final kiss before parting for the night.

The last of the three, the bigmouth with the John Wayne strut, wandered around, disoriented, until he located a rusting Chevrolet pickup. He swung himself up into the seat, kicked over the motor, and lit a cigarette, the flare from the match making his pasty features seem demonic. Then he pulled out of the parking lot. I counted to ten and followed him.

He didn't lead me out toward the highway but deeper into the residential section of town, through streets lined with small houses built close to the sidewalks. He finally pulled up in front of an old crackerbox with a ratty patch of front lawn and a sagging porch. Farther up the driveway near the back door, an ancient

Corvair was up on blocks. Inside the house a light burned yellow behind faded curtains, and I could hear the insistent drone of a TV. Some cop show, it sounded like, with gunshots and squealing brakes.

He was heading up the path to the house when I glided to a stop. "Hey!" I got out of my car, walking around the front of it. He stopped and peered at me through the darkness. He couldn't tell who it was until I got near enough for the semicircle of light from inside the house to illuminate my face.

His cheeks sagged, and a little white saliva bubble appeared on his lower lip. I'd been sitting down back in Cap'n Andy's, and I don't think he'd realized how big I am. He mumbled something unintelligible, head down and chin on his chest—a classic posture of submission, the young male baboon giving way to the dominant elder.

"We never got to finish our conversation," I said.

He shifted nervously from one foot to the other. I was about six inches taller than he was, and outweighed him by a good forty pounds. Standing there in the yellowish light, I must have seemed like his worst nightmare.

"I got nothin' to say to you," he said.

"You had plenty to say back at Cap'n Andy's. I thought you might want to finish, face to face." I moved toward him. "Well, come on, let's hear it."

"Come on, man, I don't want no trouble."

"Tough shit, sailor. You've got some."

His knees were actually shaking, and I think if I'd taken another step he would have fallen over from fright. I wanted to take that next step.

The screen door screeched open and a towheaded kid came out on the porch, letting the door slam behind him. He wore a long-sleeved T-shirt and jeans, and hugged his own arms to protect himself from the wind.

"Dad?" he said. He was about as old as my younger boy, Stephen, and had the same shock of unruly blond hair and the same pug-nosed, pig-face as his father. He looked anxiously from one to the other of us. He probably hadn't heard anything that was said, but he could read the body language.

"Go inside, B.D.," the man said in a quaking voice.

But all at once I was out of gas. "That's okay, B.D.," I said. "Your dad and I just finished up our talk."

The father moved back a few steps so he could lean against the front of the porch without collapsing.

"How old are you, B.D.?"

"Ten," the boy said, and relaxed a little.

"Nice-looking kid," I said to the father, whose face was clammed with sweat despite the fall chill. "I hope you're teaching him right. Teaching him to respect people—no matter who they are. Be lousy if he grew up to be the kind of guy who judges people by the color of their skin or the church they go to. The kind of guy that says mean things that make other people feel bad. But he looks like a good kid. You're a good kid, aren't you, B.D.?"

He shrugged. "I dunno."

"Sure. I can tell." I looked back at his father, turning slightly so the kid couldn't see my face. "Your dad's lucky to have a good kid like you. *Real* lucky." I leaned hard on the word. "Well, nice talking to you, B.D." The father shifted his feet, and his arms flapped at his sides.

I got back into my car, drove up to the end of the street, and turned the corner; then I pulled over and sat gripping the steering wheel to keep my hands from shaking.

I'd wanted to scare the redneck bastard into peeing in his pants, and I was ripping because I didn't get to.

But not in front of his kid. There are some things you just don't do.

# CHAPTER SIX

Early Saturday morning I made my first telephone report to Victor Gaimari. I saw no necessity to regale him with Cap'n Andy stories, but I did tell him all about the chamber mixer, and the hex that Princess True seemed to have on our candidate.

"Princess is formidable, all right," he said in that fluty high-pitched voice of his. "But Barbara can't win this election if she falls apart every time that bitch looks at her."

"The trouble is, Princess knows it," I said. "She floats around like Banquo's ghost, glaring at Barbara, and Barbara just folds up and dies. I wish I could think of a way to level the playing field a little."

"Italians make the sign of the horns and spit to ward off the *malocchio*, the evil eye."

"That would be my second choice."

"You have any suggestions then, Milan?"

I didn't like the way he said it. But then, I didn't much like the way Victor said anything. Victor being who he was, a simple good-morning held portents of doom and disaster. "How about a crash course for Barbara in assertiveness training?"

He chose to take me seriously. "That'll be your job then. Pump her up with confidence and enthusiasm. Give her an old football pep talk, if you have to."

"'Win one for the Gipper' won't make it with Barbara, Victor. She's a Democrat."

"I'll leave that up to you. But do what you can about her energy level. Don't let her be lackadaisical. Voters should see her as energetic, competent, someone who gets things done."

"A word in her husband's ear might not be amiss either," I said. "He's very critical of her—in public too—and that intimidates the hell out of her."

"Evan does have a personality problem. But there's not much anyone can do about that, I'm afraid, except work around it." He sighed wearily. "What's on the schedule for today?"

"Lunch with the Women's Political League."

Victor chuckled. "You're earning your money, Milan."

"I just have to remember to hold my pinkie out when I drink my tea."

"I'd like to see that. What else? I can't believe that's all on such a nice Saturday."

"Bingo tonight," I told him, "at a Catholic church."

"Saint Bonaventure's, sure. Say hello to Father Tarantino for me when you see him."

"I have a question about the bingo game."

"What's that?"

"If I should happen to win tonight, Victor, what's your skim?"

There was silence on the line for a moment, and I could hear him breathing. "Ha ha," he said finally.

The Women's Political League luncheon was in the home of Mrs. Arlen James. I had no idea what her own first name was, because that's how she introduced herself: Mrs. Arlen James. Mr. Arlen James just nodded briefly at us on his way out the door with his golf clubs.

I felt out of place and awkward in this elegant, country-style living room, one of only two men among forty-some women. The second was an aggressive little piece of work named Donald Straum, who said he was the political columnist for the *Bulletin*, a weekly newspaper addressing itself to the concerns of the various eastern suburbs and publishing several different editions in different communities. He seemed surprised that I'd never heard of him.

He was a burly little guy, all wild curly blond hair you could see his scalp through, unkempt beard, and perfectly round granny glasses, the kind I thought went out when John Lennon died in front of the Dakota. He had the annoying habit of standing too close to you when he talked, crossing that invisible boundary of your personal space so you could smell what he'd had for breakfast. He spent about ninety seconds off to the side with Barbara, doing all the talking, earnestly whispering in her face; he seemed to make her almost as nervous as Princess True did.

A buffet was set out in the dining room, and everyone filed through, piling their plates with quivering orange Jell-O with julienned carrots suspended inside, German potato salad, and slices of not very rare roast beef in glutinous gravy. After lunch they went back through the line for coffee, which had the unmistakable medicinal taste of decaf. So fortified, they arranged themselves in a circle beneath the cathedral ceiling of the James's sprawling living room and fired not always friendly questions at Barbara Corns between sips. Cassandra hovered outside the circle, the only dark face in the crowd. The women had greeted her politely and then pretty much ignored her, but that was to be expected. Barbara, after all, was the main event.

I hate decaf, but it was something to do with my hands, so I drew myself a cup, which I balanced on a saucer before Straum cut me out of the herd. The two of us stood off to one side, him with his shoulders hunched up nervously beneath his wide-wale corduroy jacket and me drinking coffee while I tried to keep one ear cocked toward my candidate. He kept his head thrust forward, looking a little as though he didn't want anyone to notice the double chin beneath his beard. I put him in his early forties, but he could have been ten years older or younger; it's hard to tell with those aging hippie types.

"You can cut the tension around here with a knife," he observed. His intensity made me back away from him.

"Why?"

"The excitement of an upcoming election. It's do or die the next week and a half. The *Bulletin* is watching this campaign pretty closely. And Columbus is watching it too."

"I wouldn't think the guys in the capitol give much of a damn about a suburban mayoral election," I said. "Neither candidate seems to harbor any statewide ambitions."

"There's more to it than that." The light through the windows flashed off his glasses, making it hard to see his eyes. He pulled out a Spiral notebook and a mechanical pencil. "What's your place in Barbara Corns's campaign?"

"I'm nobody," I said. "Write about the candidate. That's who we're trying to get people to vote for."

"You might make an interesting sidebar."

I shook my head. I wasn't about to stand still for an interview; I'd only wind up shooting myself in the foot.

He moved in still closer. "You have something to hide?"

Only my annoyance, but I didn't say that. "I'm just not the story here," I told him.

He leaned close enough that I felt his breath on my face. "How well do you know Barbara? What's your relationship with her?"

He was making me uneasy, which I supposed was the object of the game. "Am I talking for publication now?" I asked.

His bushy eyebrows climbed ceilingward. "You have a problem with that?"

"I don't like publicity much."

A muscle in his cheek twitched. "Off the record, then."

"Off the record it doesn't make any difference," I said.

"I find it interesting that a man such as yourself is so spooked by the press," he said, the hairs of his beard quivering. "What are you trying to cover up here?"

I was tired of being crowded. "Beat it," I said. I pushed myself off the wall he'd backed me up against and strolled over to Cassandra Pride. Through the windows behind her the James's back yard stretched off into seeming infinity, the oaks and sugar maples interspersed with an occasional pine.

"You've met our little local newsie," Cassandra said.

"Kind of intense, isn't he?"

"He thinks he's Woodward and Bernstein sometimes," she said, shaking her head. "I don't know what Barbara ever saw in him."

I almost spilled my coffee. It's tough enough trying to juggle a cup and saucer without someone throwing a high hard one at you. "Excuse me?"

She looked amused. "Didn't you know? They went around together for a while before she moved in with Evan." She lowered her voice, even though no one in the room was paying attention to her; they were too busy asking Barbara Corns questions she wasn't having an easy time answering. "He was pretty bitter about the breakup. He called her up and begged her to come back to him, left crazy messages on her answering machine, knowing Evan was sure to hear them, and hung around outside their house until Evan threatened to get a restraining order. I guess he's still bitter, even though he fancies himself a stud."

"That little hairy caterpillar?"

She laughed out loud, causing a few of the Women's Political Leaguers to look our way in annoyance. "I think of him more as Lassie, because of the hair. But he's actually sort of a vulture. On the rare occasions when there's a divorce, Donald is right there to feast on the carcass. Barbara says he's very possessive and jealous about his women, even his exes."

"No wonder she looks so nervous," I said. "What's he doing here?"

Cassandra waved a hand at me. "He says he's covering the campaign, but I'll let you decide the real reason."

Donald Straum might have been looking daggers at me—his head was turned my way—but the light from the windows was reflecting off his glasses again, making him look like a Nazi in an old movie, so I couldn't be sure.

Barbara sat in the center of the circle of Women's Political Leaguers. She was obviously on the defensive, and I'd noticed that at times like that she developed an irritating whine. Barbara Corns in the role of femme fatale seemed an unlikely bit of casting, but Evan had divorced his first wife to marry her, and Donald Straum still lusted after her years after their affair ended, so maybe there were facets to her I hadn't seen yet.

Barbara was saying, "A small town used to be a wonderful place to live, to bring up a family. There was no traffic, there was no pollution, there was no street crime—"

"There was nothing to do, either," Mrs. Arlen James said. She had a voice like a crinkling paper grocery sack. "If you wanted to eat anything fancier than meat loaf or a burger you had to drive clear into Cleveland. You couldn't even see a movie without burning up half a tank of gas. None of us want to live like that again. This isn't a sleepy little lakeside town anymore, Barbara. Times have changed."

"Change for change's sake isn't necessarily good," Barbara

answered, but there wasn't much punch in it. "What about the school dropout rate? What about teenage pregnancy."

Mrs. Arlen James drew herself up to her full height, her monolithic bosom inflating as she inhaled deeply enough to deplete the oxygen supply in the room. "We certainly don't need to talk about that in Lake County," she said, making it an edict handed down from on high.

The other members of the group murmured and nodded agreement, and Barbara accepted the rebuke meekly.

Cassandra Pride did not, however. "I think that the statistics show that we do, Mrs. James."

The woman looked at her almost pityingly. "You only say that because you don't live here, Mrs. Pride."

Cassandra turned away, her mouth a thin scarlet slash of anger. Across the room Donald Straum folded his stubby arms and crossed one foot over the other like Sean Connery in those old James Bond movie ads, although the effect was hardly the same. Barbara looked at him nervously, then away.

The kaffeeklatsch broke up in about ten more minutes. Barbara shook everyone's hand and told them she hoped she could count on their support, but I thought she'd made few converts.

"Why don't you get some rest this afternoon?" I said to her when the three of us were outside by the car. "You've got to be sharp for bingo tonight."

She sighed, shaking her head. "I'll be glad when this is all over."

"If you win," I said, "it's just the beginning."

She rolled her eyes skyward.

"You're going to win," I assured her.

She smiled wistfully. "You're a nice man, Milan," she said, and laid a hand on my cheek for a brief moment, then got into the front seat of my car. Cassandra folded herself into the back, and as I walked around to the driver's side I noticed Donald Straum standing just outside Mrs. Arlen James's front door, chewing on the end of his pencil. His face was clouded by suspicion.

I glowered right hack.

My afternoon was spent in the Corns's living room reading from a scrapbook what little press coverage had been garnered by the Lake Erie Shores campaign. In the *Plain Dealer* there had only been a brief announcement of the results of the primary several weeks before, buried in coverage of more glamorous statewide races and ballot initiatives. Most of what had been written appeared in the *Bulletin,* and much of that bore Donald Straum's byline. It was ostensibly reportage and not editorial, but an interview he'd done with Barbara one-on-one right after the primary was pretty rough, and she came off sounding like an airhead.

I wondered if his editors were aware of their past relationship, and if so, how they squared his coverage of the Corns campaign with responsible journalism.

I thought about what could possibly be done before Election Day to make Barbara appear a more interesting choice for the voters. My political experience was limited to handing out buttons for Bobby Kennedy when I was too young to vote in 1968, but as an adult I'd never shirked my duty at the ballot box and tried to keep myself relatively well informed.

Looking at the image problem Barbara Corns was facing, I came up with a few ideas, but I decided I'd hold off until I had both the candidate's and her husband's attention the next day at the football party.

Cassandra made sandwiches for everyone, corned beef, which wasn't bad but hardly the equal of the corned beef at Jack's delicatessen in South Euclid. There probably weren't many Jewish delicatessens in Lake Erie Shores. Then we wiped the mustard off our mouths and headed off to Saint Bonaventure's for bingo.

Tables had been set up in the basement, where the fluorescent lights cast a bright, ghastly glow over everyone. All the people there except Cassandra were white, most were over sixty, and all of them played bingo with the concentration of a heart surgeon doing a triple-bypass operation. Barbara made virtually the same speech I'd already heard twice before, although the crowd of bingo players seemed a lot more supportive than the chamber of commerce or the Women's Political League.

I bought a card just for the hell of it. And that's how it turned out. Four times I got three numbers across, plus the free space, only to be aced out by several little blue-haired ladies shouting "Bingo!" with ear-shattering enthusiasm.

None of the True people showed up, for which we were all grateful. But Dennis and Laurie did, and when they could manage to tear themselves more than two feet away from their be-loved Barbara, they walked along the lines of players, kibitzing and occasionally pointing out to one or another the fact that a number had been missed. Neither one had said hello to me when they came in, like second-graders freezing out the new kid in class. Maybe they were just ticked off that I was getting paid and they weren't.

Just before Barbara's speech Donald Straum walked into the church basement and stood by the door, taking in the whole scene. He didn't seem to undo Barbara as much as he had that afternoon, but I don't think he helped matters any. She glanced up at him, colored, and turned her face away, chatting with the bingo players in a voice that was a little too loud and shrill.

For that matter, Straum made me nervous. He had that angry glower down to a science.

"I wish he'd stare at somebody else," I said to Cassandra. "What's his problem, anyway?"

"He's jealous."

"He should get over it. Barbara's married to Evan now."

She looked amused. "Milan—I think he's jealous of you."

According to the divorce agreement between my ex-wife Lila and me, I get the pleasure of my children's company every other Sun-day. This particular Sunday was one of the off days, and I missed the boys a lot. Of course now that Milan junior is so grown-up, a high school football star and shockingly handsome, with his Ser-bian mother's dark hair and eyes, he doesn't find a lot of time for his old man, even on the appointed Sundays. The pack instinct runs high in teenagers. I have to accept that, to try to sneak some time with him on a weekday evening for a movie or a ballgame or just pizza. Stephen, my little one—now not so little at eleven—is still his dad's son, especially when there are no other kids around, but I figure I've got only a few years left with him before he gets interests of his own and wants to spend his weekends with his peers too.

In the meantime, every other Sunday is lonely.

I took the Sunday *Plain Dealer* up Euclid Heights Boulevard to

Arabica, the sixties-style coffeehouse near Coventry, got a coffee and a bear claw with almonds, and sat near the window reading the sports section. The Browns were three-point favorites over Seattle. I stayed about half an hour, sipping, nibbling, and looking across at the Coventry Library, one of the prettiest old Tudor-style buildings in Greater Cleveland. Arabica's clientele was mostly couples, a few pairs of men, several more pairs of women, and one mother with three school-age kids. I was the only one that was alone. I was also among the oldest people in the room.

At ten fifteen I headed out across the street for my car. I wasn't out the door before someone pounced on the newspaper I'd left on the table.

The morning was crisp and sunny, with the temperature hovering around sixty, one of those fall days that put the jewels in Ohio's crown. A walk through the park so the candidate could meet and greet the people was a pretty good idea; even if it didn't garner a single vote it was going to be a great way to spend a Sunday morning.

Out at the Corns house, Cassie was looking terrific in an ivory-colored pants suit, and Barbara was in another of her seemingly endless supply of sensible dresses, this one topped with a drab blue cardigan sweater to ward off the chill. Evan was off breakfasting in Painesville with some of the party bigwigs, including Judge Guilfoyle, the county chairman.

We stood in the entryway of Barbara's house while Cassandra went and got stacks of brochures with Barbara's picture on them to be handed out in the park. I don't do that sort of thing very well, but I supposed it would beat hell out of walking around with my hands in my pockets looking for terrorists in the trees. Ugly phone calls or no, it just didn't seem as though Barbara was in much need of bodyguarding.

The civic park in Lake Erie Shores is just behind the square, a six-acre greensward with sandy playground areas at either end and a wading pool in the middle surrounded by cement and benches. We walked around it counter-clockwise, Barbara stopping to talk to everyone who would listen, shaking hands and asking for support on Election Day, while Cassandra and I passed out campaign literature and reminded people to please vote. Finally I realized that someone as big as I am approaching a stranger in a park was intimidating, so I stopped pamphleteering and just kept my eyes open for trouble.

There wasn't much trouble on this idyllic Sunday.

Although many of the citizens to whom Barbara spoke seemed fairly receptive, several others had never heard of her, hadn't even known there was a mayoral race and didn't much care now they'd found out. Barbara seemed to diminish after each encounter, like Alice after she'd drunk the contents of the bottle. Although they weren't around that morning, I began to understand why she tolerated Dennis and Laurie. Besides doing the scut work, they offered her unconditional acceptance and approval, something she didn't seem to get from anyone else.

Just about the time we finished the circuit of the park a cold wind kicked up off the lake, and the temperature dropped about ten degrees. Not a moment too soon, I thought; Barbara's energy level was fading fast.

When we got back to the Corns's at about three o'clock, Evan had returned from his breakfast, several campaign volunteers had set out a buffet, and Dennis Babb and Laurie Pirkle were manning the cooler full of Bud, Bud Light, and various soft drinks, Dennis's attitude that of a guardian in a seraglio. The giant TV was on and several retired football luminaries were analyzing the matchups in the National Football League that afternoon. A couple of other guests had wandered in already and so managed to snag good seats right in front of the set, beer and sandwiches firmly in hand.

I grabbed a Cheez Whiz–covered Triscuit and went into the kitchen to talk to Evan, who was removing giant plastic bowls of macaroni salad from the refrigerator. A small black-and-white portable TV buzzed irritatingly on the breakfast table, tuned to NBC like the big set in the living room.

He barely looked at me when I came in. "Good walk this morning?" he said as though a smile might cost him money.

"Not bad. I've got a few ideas to run by you."

He gestured at me with a bowl. "I don't have time now, buddy, I've got fifty people coming to see the game."

"It's kind of important," I said. "The election's getting closer every day."

"Talk fast, then." He moved from the refrigerator to the kitchen counter, deposited the salads, and went to the oven to remove two warm loaves of Cleveland's famous Orlando's chiabatta bread.

"I think we ought to release to the press that business about True's son helping the blind punch out their ballots during the primary."

It stopped him in his tracks. He shook his head. "I've already said no to that."

"It could help us win."

He stuck his chin out. There was more than a little of Jimmy Cagney's brashness in him, with none of the charm and insouciance. "I don't happen to think so—and I'm the one that makes those decisions."

"It's dirty," I said, "as well as being illegal. I think the voters ought to hear about it and make up their own minds, and that could translate into a lot of votes."

Barbara came into the kitchen as though she'd never been inside it before. She stood there miserably, picking at the skin beside her thumbnail.

"I don't want to play that way, *Mr.* Jacovich," Evan said. "We smear him on a personal level, he smears us, both of us get spattered with the mud, and the voters forget about the real issues. Besides," he added, reaching into one of the cupboards above the counter, "we make an issue out of True's kid helping the blind to vote, every group yelling about rights for the elderly and the disabled comes down on us with both feet, and the last thing we need is to lose the senior citizen vote."

He slammed two bottles of mustard onto the counter and turned back to me, his face red all the way up into his hairline. "If it won't offend your sense of dignity, let me observe that you don't know squat about Lake County or about this community. You don't even live here. So I think I know what's best for Barbara just a little bit better than you do."

Barbara said, "Evan, Milan's only trying—"

"To take over," he finished for her, still glaring at me. "I don't appreciate it, either. I told Cassandra and I'm telling you—that primary business is a dead issue. Let's not talk about it again.

"All right," I said. "Then I have another idea that might be helpful."

"Look, this is not the time or place. We're in the middle of a big party here." He looked smug. "Today what's important is the Browns winning."

"Why don't we ask Barbara if the Browns are more important?"

He pushed his glasses up on his nose, picked up the two bowls of macaroni salad, and took them out into the dining room. I turned around and looked at Barbara, but she dropped her gaze to her shoes and wouldn't meet my eyes.

Screw it. I wasn't getting paid enough to take Evan Corns's crap. I grabbed a beer—a Bud Light, which was all they had, but beggars can't be choosers—and went into the living room to join the growing crowd and watch what seemed to be the day's biggest priority, the Browns versus the Seattle Seahawks.

It was late in the first quarter, and Touchdown Tommy Vardell had just plunged six yards through the middle for a first down when the phone rang. There was so much noise in the living room that most of the guests didn't hear it.

Barbara went into the kitchen to answer it. The Seahawks called a time-out, and I turned away from the TV and saw her standing in the entryway to the living room, her hand to her mouth and her face the color of a white marble tombstone.

I tried not to attract attention as I snaked my way through the throng to reach her. "What's wrong, Barbara?"

She took her hand away from her mouth and put it on my arm. "That was Tyler Rees on the phone, True's campaign manager," she said in a pinched voice.

I nodded.

"Princess True was killed this morning by a hit-and-run driver."

## CHAPTER SEVEN

I found out later that the Browns had won, but even Evan
Corns wasn't quite callous enough to leave the game on after
the news of Princess True's death had been announced. The
guests, deprived of their weekly football fix, went home in a snit,
and those of us who remained—Cassandra, Dennis, Laurie, and
myself—wore worried faces. Barbara was so upset that she retired to her bed for the rest of the day, only emerging for pills to
take the edge off what she called a blinding headache.

After calling the local florist to arrange for a wreath to be delivered to the True home, Evan got on the phone with his political
cronies, trying to get the details, but all he could learn was that the
accident occurred just after noon in downtown Cleveland. Princess had gone to meet some friends for brunch at Piccolo Mondo
in the warehouse district and was on her way to the Avenue, the
dining, entertainment, and shopping complex beneath Terminal
Tower, to shop. As she crossed Prospect Avenue a pickup truck
creamed her and then roared off. She was dead by the time the
police got there.

When I got home later that afternoon I called Victor Gaimari
to tell him. I wasn't surprised to learn that he already knew; Victor has eyes and ears in the woodwork.

"I'm very dismayed by this," he said. "I didn't particularly like
Mrs. True and I'd be a hypocrite if I said I did, but no one deserves to die like a dog in the street. This is a terrible thing." I
heard him take a sip of something; Victor, I knew, favored bloody

Marys at home on Sundays. "Milan, find out what you can about what happened to her, will you?"

"She got hit by a pickup," I said. "What's to find out?"

"It doesn't smell right to me, that's all."

"This wasn't part of the deal," I said. "I was hired to help out on a political campaign, not to get involved with police business."

"I don't mean to sound crass," he went on, "but this may have great bearing on this election. It's going to throw it right into a cocked hat, as a matter of fact."

"How do you figure?"

"Well," he said. I knew Victor enough to realize that a "well" followed by a pause was a harbinger of something pontifical and significant. "It's hard to tell which way the wind will blow now. Is Gayton True going to get the sympathy vote? Is it going to shake him up so badly that he'll make a mistake and Barbara will breeze through the election?"

"I somehow doubt that."

"Well then, we don't want to tie Barbara's hands. She can hardly attack him on political grounds now without seeming like an insensitive and opportunistic bitch."

"I wouldn't worry about that last part," I said. "The Corns campaign doesn't do much attacking, on any grounds you might want to mention."

He paused for a moment. "I don't understand."

I told him about Evan's refusal to use the incident with Darryl True and the blind voters in the primary.

He thought it over for a while. Then he said, "Nothing wrong with a clean campaign. People proved in 'ninety-two that they were sick to death of mudslinging and negativism in politics."

I shook my head even though he couldn't see me. I'd never in a million years understand the arcane workings of the political mind. And for Victor Gaimari to speak so reverently of cleanliness was a particularly biting irony.

"There's another possibility you haven't thought of," I told him. "Gayton True might be too grief-stricken to continue with the campaign and drop out altogether."

He gave a dry laugh. "I've known him fifteen years," he said. "Put that little scenario right out of your mind."

• • •

The Cleveland Third District Police Headquarters at Twenty-first and Payne is a big ugly rock pile of a building, one I worked out of several years when I wore a blue uniform. It was the nerve center of everything until about ten years ago, when a lot of the brass moved downtown to the then new Justice Center, taking Cleveland's principal lockup with them. Now they're doing some remodeling, and lately there's been talk of refurbishing the old jail cells to accommodate the overflow. Anyone who's been behind a badge ten years or more still refers to the Payne Avenue facility as "the old Central."

When I walked in I got a volley of hellos as well as some suspicious looks, but I knew my way around here. Many of the men and women who still work at the old Central are friends of mine, or as close to friends as a cop ever gets with a civilian.

The one exception, the true friend, is Marko Meglich, lieutenant, homicide. We went through St. Clair High School and Kent State together, football buddies at both places, and it was Marko who talked me into joining the force after I got back from Southeast Asia, so as not to waste my experience as an MP at Cam Ranh Bay.

He took it as a personal affront when I turned in my badge four years later; he also takes it hard that I always call him Marko, which he'd anglicized to Mark because he thought his more ethnic, real name would be a hindrance to him in the rough-and-tumble of station house politics. But a twenty-five-year friendship dies hard, and even though our jobs put us at odds once in a while, I knew I was always welcome on Payne Avenue.

Marko is a big bear of a guy given to three-piece suits and solid-color silk ties, and he's affected a dashing mustache for the last couple of years that looks like he should give it back to his grandfather, but every time I see him I remember the burly, fresh-faced kid in football pads with lampblack under his eyes. In high school we'd been inseparable, and at Kent State our teammates had jokingly dubbed us "the Slovenian tag team."

I found his office and told him what I wanted. He shuffled through some file folders on his desk and came up with one marked TRUE.

"Where do you figure in this, Milan?" he said, thumbing through the papers in it.

"Probably not at all," I said. I sat down across the desk from him and wondered, as I so often had, why the police department couldn't find a few bucks for comfortable chairs. "I'm doing some work on the Lake Erie Shores mayoral campaign. Princess True was the wife of my candidate's opponent."

"How did you get involved in Lake County politics?"

I shuffled my feet under my chair. "I work for a living and they hired me."

He wasn't buying it. "Why you? Why not somebody local?"

I didn't want to tell him, but I had to. "Victor Gaimari recommended me."

"Victor Gaimari?" He slumped back in his chair, scowling at me from under his eyebrows. They're bushy ones, and as he grows older they tend to fly off in all directions. "You never learn, do you?"

"What?"

He slapped the flat of his hand onto the pile of folders. A cloud of cigarette ashes rose from the ashtray and settled on the surface of the desk. "Victor Gaimari is pond scum! You know that, Milan, you know it better than I do. And yet every time I turn around you're cuddling up to him."

"I'm not cuddling up!" I said with some heat. "I'm a businessman, Marko, and this is legitimate."

"Gaimari and D'Allessandro don't know the meaning of the word."

"Maybe not, but I do. They might not be the Vienna Boys Choir, but they've always been straight with me, and that's more than I can say for a lot of people."

Marko fingered his mustache. He's never gotten really accustomed to it and continually treats it like something alien has taken up residence beneath his nose. "I don't like the way they make a living."

"Neither do I. But this seems fairly on the up-and-up."

He sighed. "On the surface, anyway. Did you bother to wonder why Victor Gaimari gives a damn about Lake Erie Shores?"

"Evan Corns is a customer of Victor's brokerage, and his wife Barbara's running for mayor. It's a favor, as far as I can see."

"Okay, fine. Let's pretend Gaimari is a candidate for sainthood,

Mother Teresa in a Palm Beach suit. That still doesn't explain your interest in Mrs. True."

I shrugged. "Call it healthy curiosity, Marko. Instances of hit-and-run are more rare than other kinds."

He opened the folder and scanned it. "That's exactly what it looks like, though. A pickup truck, older model, white, probably a Ford, heading west on Prospect, according to one eyewitness. It hit her, knocked her about thirty feet, then ran over her and went on its way. No one saw the driver, no one got the license number. Probably some drunken cowboy."

"A drunken cowboy downtown at noon on a Sunday?"

"It happens all the time."

"Maybe. But I think you ought to look at this pretty carefully. It's going to be a very close election out there, and plenty of people might have wanted Princess True out of the way."

He folded his hands across his stomach. Sometimes Marko acts like he's ninety years old. "Name a couple."

"There's her husband, for one. They didn't have what you'd call an idyllic marriage. There've been reports of physical abuse on both sides."

"There's no such thing as a perfect marriage. That's why you and I aren't married anymore, remember?"

"Lila and I never hit each other, and I never considered murdering her. As far as I know she didn't want to kill me, either."

He conceded the point. "If it turns out to be foul play, the spouse is always Suspect One."

"But even if he wanted her dead," I went on, "a week before an election is a peculiar time for a politician to kill his wife."

He looked up at the discolored acoustical ceiling. I figured I was boring him.

"On the other hand, you might be right," I said, mostly to re-claim his attention. "It could get him the sympathy vote."

"Who else?"

"Evan Corns."

He took a slug of coffee. "Now you're being dumb."

"Princess True had a real whammy on Barbara Corns. Every time she walked into a room Barbara would fall apart. Evan is nothing if not driven to get his wife elected. It might make things a lot easier with Princess out of the picture. And he wasn't any-where in sight on Sunday morning."

He stretched out his arm. "You're reaching."

"Okay, try this one: Barbara Corns has been getting hate mail, and obscene phone calls late at night. I only met Princess once, but I wouldn't put that kind of thing past her."

"Oh Christ, Milan, get some perspective, will you?"

"I just give the news," I said.

"Then stop editorializing." He stood up and moved over to the Mr. Coffee atop his bookcase. "Want some?"

I shook my head and watched while he poured the jet black coffee into his own personalized ceramic mug. Marko convinced himself a few years ago that plastic and polystyrene cups cause cancer and had charged the department for an oversized mug bearing his name and gold shield. He sat back down and took a sip, patting his mustache.

"Any way you can get hold of the telephone records of those calls and trace them back?" I asked him.

"Sure—if the caller was stupid enough to call from his own phone."

I picked up a pencil and began doodling empty gallows on a scratch pad on his desk, an old habit of mine dating back to high school. My parents had always thought it was morbid. "You're probably right. Nobody'd be that dumb."

"Knowing you," he said, "you've got more."

"Did you know Al Drago was working on True's campaign?"

He winced. "The Dragon, huh? I heard he'd gone into body-guarding, but I haven't seen him since you showed up at that In-ternal Affairs hearing with his formal portrait. He must be happy as a pig in shit to see you again."

"I'm trying to keep out of his way as much as possible," I said.

"I know Al Drago. He's got a long memory. He'll carry it to you if he can."

I tried to pass it off. "Maybe."

"What happens then?"

"I guess we'll dance."

"Watch yourself, Milan. He fights dirty." Deep in thought, he played the piano on the edge of his desk. It sounded like "The

March of the Wooden Soldiers," but I couldn't be certain. "Drago's a beast, but he's no killer. I don't like him for Mrs. True."

"Anything he's involved in has to be kinky—and there's lots of things about this election that are. Evan Corns used to be married to someone else, but he dumped her and moved in with Barbara. And before that, Barbara was running around with some small-change suburban reporter named Donald Straum. It was pretty heavy, and when *she* dumped *him* for Evan he took it badly."

"Okay, so she's not a virgin."

"Yeah, but Straum hangs around the campaign a lot making calf eyes at her, even after all this time."

"None of which has anything to do with Princess True—what the hell kind of a name is that, Princess?"

"Her family's kind of Lake County royalty."

He sipped his coffee, rolling it around on his tongue as if it were a fine cabernet. "What about the candidate herself?"

"Barbara?"

"If this True woman was such a pimple on her ass, squeezing her would be a lot simpler than dealing with her."

"You don't know Barbara Corns. She redefines timid."

"Doesn't mean she couldn't order it done. There's a million guys walking the streets that are more than happy to snuff a perfect stranger for the price of a gram of nose candy."

I shook my head. "I don't think so, Marko. Do you know about Earl Barnstable?" I said.

"Who's that?"

"Princess True's brother. He's under indictment for child pornography."

"Kiddie porn? That's mob stuff."

"Yeah, but not the D'Allessandro mob, and you know it. Anybody in his outfit who peddled dirty pictures of children, the old man would have him skinned alive. Literally."

Marko took a deep breath and blew it out through his lips in a sort of tired razzberry. "This gets better and better. Okay, I'll check with the sex crimes unit and see what they have. Barnstable?"

I nodded as he wrote the name down. "When do you need it?" he said.

"This afternoon would be terrific."

He gave me a weary look. "I'm so glad I know you, Milan. You really enrich my life."

I went downstairs and sat in my car for a while and thought about it. Barbara was scheduled for a "coffee" this morning, a little gathering in the home of one of her volunteers. Cassandra Pride had told me that sometimes fewer than ten people showed up at these things, but in a small-town race even five or six votes is well worth an hour of the candidate's time.

It costs approximately forty thousand dollars to run a local campaign, more if it gets messy. There's no limit to the amount any one person can contribute, but if you don't want your participation made public, there are all sorts of ways to hide it, like giving ten different people a thousand dollars each to throw in the pot, or by paying a campaign worker's salary through your own company—the way Victor Gaimari was doing with me.

All campaign contributions had to be reported by October 17, and I thought about obtaining that list, but Marko was probably right, I was reaching. Even so . . .

One thing I could take to the bank, though: Gaimari and his uncle had nothing to do with Princess True's accident. It wasn't their style—and it was well known around town that even though the old man was ruthless, and crooked as the Cuyahoga River, his rigid moral code wouldn't allow him to even entertain the thought of killing a woman. I didn't like him, but over the years I'd developed a kind of grudging respect for him.

I still hadn't put together the pieces to figure out the mob's interest in Lake Erie Shores. It was out of their territory, both geographically and professionally. Even Corns's custom at Gaimari's brokerage house didn't seem like a compelling enough reason to fork over several thousand dollars toward his wife's cause. It wasn't going to bother me very much, though, until Princess True's death got explained. Compared to life and death, especially violent death, who gets to be mayor in a small suburban community seems kind of unimportant.

I took the five-minute drive downtown and parked on Huron Street in a metered space, which are pretty rare in the downtown area. Most parking lots and garages cost upward of four dollars for an hour or two, and it can get pretty dear if you aren't on an expense account. Where I parked was not much more than a seven-iron from Gateway, the new sports complex Cleveland built for the Indians and the Cavaliers. When they first broke ground for it, cynical Clevelanders called it "the Gateway Hole," but now it's a beauty of a complex, and our teams are beginning to play up to it.

It's nice having pro basketball downtown instead of clear out in Richfield, and the new ballpark is great for bringing people to the city, but I'll miss watching baseball in the cavernous old stadium on the lake, especially in April, when it's still winter on the North Coast. Just one more piece of my youth, like the closing of the May Company on Public Square, that progress has changed forever.

It was only a few blocks' walk to where Princess True had been run down the day before. I stood there and stared at the place where it had happened. The police had drawn a yellow chalk outline around the body, but Monday morning traffic had all but obliterated the marks. I peered down the street, noticing that at regular intervals there were some dirty brown discolorations on the pavement, and my stomach lurched when I thought they might be Princess True's blood. I visualized her stepping off the curb to cross over to the elegant shops and boutiques in Tower City, and the pickup hurtling toward her. I took a deep breath as if trying to inhale some sort of mystic vibrations that would give me a clue, but all I got for my pains was a lungful of exhaust fumes and the creepy awareness of sudden and violent death.

I crossed the street and chatted briefly with the security guard outside the entrance to Tower City, a big brown-skinned man with an open smile and the plodding gait of an offensive line-man. There's a bus stop right in front, and of late there had been problems with homeward-bound school kids getting rowdy and scaring away some of the upscale shoppers, but otherwise there wasn't a lot for him to do, despite the fact that the shopping mall was only a few blocks away from some of Cleveland's toughest and most dangerous streets. He'd been off the day before, however, and had only heard about the hit-and-run when he arrived at work that morning.

"People just don't care no more," he rumbled sadly. "Run down a woman and then keep on going, that's not right." He shook his head. "If that was me, I wouldn't be able to sleep another hour for the rest of my life. How can people do that?"

"Who was on duty yesterday?"

"I can't remember his name," he said. "He's a swing guy, works all different shifts. But they said downstairs he was inside when it happened."

Another dead end. I thanked him for his time and went inside to grab a bite of lunch. The Avenue at Tower City is an enormous shopping arcade constructed in the late eighties from the guts of the old railroad terminal, with a wide variety of shops that are mostly upscale. Several office buildings are reachable from the Avenue, as well as Stouffer's Tower City Plaza Hotel, often called "Cleveland's Front Doorstep."

The complex features one of those food courts down on the lower level, a whole enclave of fast-food joints clustered together to give diners a wide range of varying cuisines from which to select their heartburn of choice. It's one of the best people-watching sites in Greater Cleveland. I picked a table by the window so I could see the river traffic while I ate my burger and fries and downed a Diet Pepsi from a waxed paper cup.

The Cuyahoga, an Indian word for "Crooked River," raggedly bisects Cleveland, separating the East Side from the West geographically and socially. It not only gives the county its name but for me it defines our city; the smoke-belching steel mills on its banks give way to the glitter and grandeur of downtown, the beautiful buildings encompassing several eras of architecture, which house the movers and shakers of the community. The river is part of Cleveland's elegance and sophistication as well as its good, honest grit.

I've always loved the Cuyahoga, although not quite enough to go splashing around in it the way I had the winter before. But then I hadn't exactly decided to go for a swim—I was pushed.

I watched a flat oreboat glide inland from the lake toward the two steel mills, LTV and Deming. My life would have been less complicated if I'd gone to work in the mills like my father. But Louis Jacovich hadn't had my options when he emigrated to Cleveland from Ljubljana more than fifty years ago, and so he'd spent his life sweating at the firebox at LTV, and his labor had enabled me to get two degrees from Kent State.

I studied business for my B.A. without having a clue as to which business might interest me. When I decided to stay in the safe cocoon of academia for a while, I took my master's in psychology. How I parlayed my education into a career as a cop, an industrial security specialist and private investigator, I'm not sure. Watching my father wither and die working like a dray horse imbued in me a fierce desire to be my own boss—or maybe I'm just too ornery to take orders. But I like my work, and sometimes I do something that makes a difference.

And once in a while I end up in the Cuyahoga River.

But this political job had seemed fairly benign at the start, even though it had come from Victor Gaimari. A nice suburban woman was running for mayor of a nice suburban town, and all I had to do was herd away hecklers. Now all of a sudden someone was dead, and Al Drago was staring out from the Stygian pit of his existence, no doubt wishing it was me.

Life do get complicated.

I finished my lunch, dutifully dumping my trash into the receptacle and stacking my dirty tray atop several others, and walked back down Huron to my car. The parking meter ran out just as I got to it, and I hustled away before one of the beat cops came over and decided to earn his money.

It only took me five minutes to get back to Marko's office on Payne, and another ten to find a parking spot.

"The vice guys wouldn't let me take the Earl Barnstable file out of their area," Marko informed me. "Just as well—you wouldn't want to look at it." He shuddered. "Jesus, the filth! I almost lost my lunch. Little kids, nine, ten years old."

"Was the stuff locally produced?"

"Why? You think some irate parent decided to take revenge on Barnstable by mowing down his sister? Earl Barnstable is looking at some heavy time—just being in possession of this stuff is a felony. But there's nothing in his file about Princess True one way or the other, so I don't see a connection."

"That doesn't mean there isn't one," I said. "When is his trial date?"

Marko flipped open his leather notebook. "Set for January the eleventh."

"Well past Election Day. I wonder if that's a coincidence too."

"You're seeing ghosts in the closet, Milan," Marko said. "There's no reason to think True's death was anything more than an accident that scared the driver enough to make him take off. We'll find him—or her. Don't worry."

"How?"

He rummaged around for the True file again and opened it. "Remember, I told you the truck hit her and knocked her halfway down the block and then ran over her?"

"That's not something I'd forget."

"There were tire tracks—nice clear traceable ones."

"On the street?"

He cleared his throat. "On the body."

"Will you keep me informed?"

He folded his arms across his chest. Like me, Marko is a big guy. Unlike me, he has forearms as thick as most other men's legs, and with them crossed in front of him, he looked fearsome. "Not if you're going to keep Victor informed. Look, Milan, you're my oldest friend, and I've helped you out in the past—"

"I've helped you out, too."

"I appreciate that. But you working for the Gaimari people rubs me the wrong way."

"I'm not breaking any legs for them, Marko."

"The principle remains. The taxpayers don't cough up my salary so I can be on the earie for the mob, even to help a buddy. Go back out to Lake County and do your electioneering, and when you're back to taking clean money, we can do business." His dark brown eyes bored a hole in my forehead. "Because right now it seems like you've developed a very selective sense of morality."

I felt myself flush. "That's a shitty thing to say."

"It galls me. You're the mob's favorite PI." He rubbed his hand across his face, making a few long hairs of his mustache stand straight out from his lip. "God damn it, why didn't you stay on the job where you belong?"

"Thanks for your help," I said, getting to my feet, "but if you think I have such a slippery set of morals, maybe I shouldn't be here."

It was a poor exit, not up to my usual standards. But as bad as I felt, stalking out in a huff was the best I could do.

## CHAPTER EIGHT

lcohol consumption has always been strictly social for me. I often go for days without a drink, and I don't miss it a bit. But that evening I cracked open a can of Stroh's as soon as I got home, even before I took my coat off. I needed one.

Friendship is a funny, fragile thing. I'd maintained mine with Marko Meglich for almost thirty years. It had survived punchouts in sixth grade over things neither of us would care about the next day, squabbles over girls in high school, arguments that came with our playing football together at Kent, a serious disagreement when I'd opted to turn in my police badge and go private, and several differences of opinion when our paths had crossed professionally since.

There were more personal areas of friction as well.

His politicking within the department made me sick, and I had little patience for his womanizing since his divorce, especially with a series of interchangeable twenty-year-olds whom he dropped as soon as they had to get vertical and talk. For Marko, my lone-wolf status, except for eighteen months in a relationship with Mary Soderberg, was a subject of scorn and derision, and the way I sometimes ignored the rules that he, as a badge-carrying officer of the law, had to uphold, frequently bent him out of shape. Maybe, in a peculiar way, we were jealous of one another.

But until now, all of these quarrels had been minor bumps and potholes along the road of a lifetime of respect and trust. When you stop and think about it, what good is a friend who agrees with you all the time?

Now Marko perceived me as a mob errand boy, an opinion that threatened to permanently rip that delicate fabric that binds any friendship together.

And it hurt—more so because there was a kernel of truth in it. Sometimes it can be very traumatic to look in the mirror, to realize that without your knowing it you've gradually been turning into some creature you don't recognize—one you'd step on if you saw it crawling on your kitchen floor.

You have few real friends in your lifetime. Lots of acquaintances with whom you can drink, bowl, play cards, or go to the ball game, but even if you're lucky, there are only a handful of people you know you can count on no matter what, the ones who are there for you on your dark days as well as on your bright ones. The ones you can ask for help and they don't stop to inquire why or how much.

We all maintain emotional bank accounts with each other. You start out even, and each act of kindness or friendship is a deposit. If you've made enough deposits, a withdrawal, doing something the other guy doesn't like or gets angry about, might strain things between you, but unless it's a huge and unforgivable withdrawal, it won't close out the account. That's why old relationships are the strongest, because there have been many years during which to add to the balance.

But I guess I'd been making big withdrawals lately. I'd lost my old friend Matt Baznik when I almost got killed helping his son out of a jam and the resulting awkwardness had driven a wedge between us that didn't seem to be going away. I'd lost Lila, my ex-wife, because my preoccupation with my work had depleted the account until one day she decided that being married to me was no longer what she wanted.

And now I was losing Marko Meglich, not because I gave a damn about how well Victor Gaimari was paying me but because I owed him a favor, and to a cop like Marko, Victor represented everything that was ignoble and corrupt. And even if we were able to patch things up, as I supposed we would, it would always be unspoken between us. Life is a continuum; no thought is ever lost. It just becomes part of the unconscious.

I was running out of friends.

My living room is really my office, with my desk and files and office supplies. I normally see my clients at their workplace, but I do maintain a couple of chairs for the rare occasions when they visit here. So I do most of my living in the little parlor off the main room where the bay window looks down on the triangle formed by the coming together of Cedar Road and Fairmount Boulevard, and on the Mad Greek restaurant and Russo's Stop-N-Shop. It was to the parlor I retreated like a bear crawling into his cave for a long winter. I sank into my easy chair still wearing my coat and gnawed angrily at the beer.

I called Barbara, but Cassie Pride answered.

"It's been a difficult day for Barbara," she said. "I've decided not to let anyone talk to her. Of course, you can, if you really want to."

"I just wanted to find out how she was feeling. She was in pretty bad shape yesterday."

"She's not a hundred percent, so I canceled that coffee she was supposed to go to and she's spending the day resting."

"What about Gayton True?"

She sighed, and it sounded like a hurricane through the receiver. "True is staying in the race—Evan had breakfast with Tyler Rees this morning. But they've asked for a moratorium on campaigning until after the funeral on Wednesday, and under the circumstances that seems reasonable. So until we hit the hustings again Friday you won't have to come out here every day. If we need you, we'll just call you, if that's all right."

I agreed that it was. "Have the Cleveland police contacted Barbara yet?"

There was a long pause. "Why would they do that?"

"There's been a crime committed, Cassandra, a major one. They call it vehicular homicide."

"What's that got to do with Barbara?"

"Nothing, I hope. But she had a good reason for wanting Princess out of the way."

Cassandra gasped. "You can't be serious."

"I'm not, but the cops are."

"I thought it was a simple hit-and-run."

"Nothing's simple when somebody dies."

"They surely don't suspect Barbara?"

"They suspect everybody. It's their job."

She dropped her voice to a nervous whisper. "Don't even breathe anything like that to Barbara. She'd be shattered."

"I won't," I said, "but I can't vouch for the police."

"My God, Milan, it would ruin her. She's been in seclusion for two days as it is. And if word got out that she was suspected of . . ." She couldn't bring herself to pronounce the word. "She wouldn't get ten votes."

I didn't say anything, just sat there and shook my head. A woman was dead, and Cassandra was worried about votes. Politicians have peculiar priorities.

"You've got to get this cleared up, Milan. Before the election. It's Barbara's only chance."

"It's not up to me to clear it up," I said. "By law, I can't interfere with an open police investigation."

She sniffed. "Who said anything about interfering? Just look around a little. Is that so much to ask?"

"If it costs me my career, yes."

"There are a lot of careers on the line here, including my own," she said in the icy tone I'd learned to recognize, one that came on quickly and then went away again. "You were hired to help Barbara get elected mayor. And the best way you can help right now is to remove any suspicion directed at her, anything that will keep people from voting for her."

I fought down a wave of irritation. "How do you suggest I go about that?"

"That's your job, Milan," she said, and hung up.

I got up and took my coat off and then pounded down another beer.

All that business about being independent, about wanting to be my own boss and not be beholden to an employer who might one day take it into his head to retrench or to replace me with a nineteen-year-old who'd work for three bucks an hour, was a wagonload of crap.

I had hired out to Victor Gaimari, and by extension to the Cornses and to Cassandra Pride, and I was obliged to do what they wanted, even though it was going to mean alienating Marko even further. Even though now I just wanted to get out.

But it wasn't going to be that easy. It never is.

Everybody, whether self-employed like me or a wage slave in

the steel mills, whether a corporate lawyer in a paneled office in the Society Tower downtown or a security expert cum private detective, is dependent upon someone else for their income. Unless of course they happen to have been born filthy rich, which brings its own set of problems and treacheries.

No matter how fiercely independent and self-reliant you think you are, you come to that point in life where someone who has the power and the purse strings firmly in their grasp says "Jump!" and survival dictates that your only possible response is "How high?" Independence is illusory—it's all done with mirrors.

But there are some things that even the saddest hooker lurking in the midnight shadows of Prospect Avenue will refuse to do, no matter how much money she's offered. Everybody draws that line somewhere, and the point at which each individual draws it is called integrity.

I had to think long and hard about where my line was drawn. About what Marko Meglich had said to me, and about Victor Gaimari and where the money I was earning had come from.

And about poor Barbara, whose husband's ambition had gotten her in over her head and who was now in danger of being totally swamped.

I stomped around the apartment for about half an hour, wanting to break something. Then I pulled myself together, sat at my desk, and took up my trusty packet of three-by-five cards.

When I'm trying to put a case together I usually inscribe all the elements on cards and then spread them out on my desk and shuffle them around until I can make some sense out of them. Up until Princess True was killed on the street, this hadn't been a case at all, but a simple matter of security, complicated only by the vagaries of the political process. Not so unlike the industrial jobs that make up the bulk of my work.

Now all of a sudden it had darkened and soured, and both Victor Gaimari, who was signing the checks, and Cassandra Pride, who represented the candidate I was supposed to be looking out for, had decreed that I jump.

I made out individual cards for Barbara and Evan and one for Gayton True. Then I wrote Victor's name on a fourth, even though I was sure he had nothing to do with Mrs. True's untimely end. The four cards looked kind of lonely on the surface of my desk, so

I put Earl Barnstable into the shuffle. After staring at them a few minutes I added Al Drago. I couldn't think of a motive for him to kill Princess, but he got a card of his own just for showing up.

Another five minutes and I made a Donald Straum card. There was something about him I didn't like—maybe his habit of standing too close to people. After further consideration I decided there was nothing about him I *did* like, and his past relationship with Barbara Corns got him tossed into the pile.

Then I started thinking about how Evan didn't want to use the information about True's son marking the primary ballots, and I scrawled *ballots* atop another card.

Eight white cards, seven names, and shuffling them around didn't bring me any revelations.

I had another beer, sipping at it slowly this time, because I was unused to drinking so many this early in the day and they were starting to hit me just a little. Earl Barnstable's card seemed to jump out at me. I held it in my hand, even picked my two front teeth with the corner of it. Then I decided I would have to do some of the detective work I hadn't thought would be necessary when I signed on as chief of security for Barbara Corns's campaign.

I went to the window and looked out. The sky was darkening to an intense medium blue, and the fluffy clouds were pink from the rays of the afternoon sun.

I went back to my desk, sat down, lit a Winston, and called Victor Gaimari. "I'm sorry to bother you in the middle of a workday," I said.

"No problem. The market's already closed."

"We have to talk, face to face. And I'd appreciate it if Mr. D'Allessandro could be there too."

He didn't say anything. I suppose he was trying to make me uncomfortable.

It worked. I was the first one to break the silence. "I wouldn't ask if I didn't think it was important."

"You aren't thinking of pulling out on us, are you?" His tone got a little harder, more jagged. "We had a deal."

"The game has changed. Someone's been killed, and I want to make sure we're all in synch."

"Why does my uncle have to be there?"

"I'd rather explain it to both of you at once."

"You'll have to do better than that."

I ran my thumb over my jawline, noting that my five o'clock shadow had arrived a few hours early. "Did you ever play a game called telephone when you were a kid? You whisper a joke to one person, he whispers it to the next, and by the time it gets to the end of the line it's a completely different joke?"

"My game is blackjack," he said.

"Well, I used to play telephone all the time—and I want to make sure that you and I and your uncle are all laughing at the same joke."

He gave me the silent treatment again.

I said, "Come on, Victor, you're always telling me how much Mr. D'Allessandro likes me, wants to have dinner with me. Here's his chance. Only I'd rather make it breakfast than dinner. How's tomorrow morning?"

"Well," he said, one of his famous "wells," this time drawn out as if he was thinking it over. "My uncle always has breakfast at eight o'clock at the Vesuvio on Murray Hill. Is that too early for you?

"Eight o'clock is fine."

"All right then, meet us there in the morning. Unless I call you back and tell you different. You know the Vesuvio?"

"Sure. I didn't realize they were open for breakfast."

"They're not," he said. The sound he made might have been a chuckle, or he could have been clearing his sinuses.

You could never tell with Victor.

## CHAPTER NINE

The next morning was cheerfully clear and sunny, a picture postcard of an October day, and the trees of Cleveland Heights had trotted out their autumn brilliance for me, bright yellows and vivid reds and warm oranges. This was probably the peak week for fall colors in Ohio. In another few days the weather would turn colder, the winds would slash down from Canada and bring the rain with them, and all the glorious leaves would simply be something the householders have to rake.

I missed the house I'd lived in with Lila and the boys. I missed taking care of it, changing the screens for storm windows and doing minor repairs like tightening faucets. But renters have it easier; one of the advantages of apartment living is that I don't have to rake October leaves anymore.

Another advantage in my case is that I'm within ten minutes of practically everything, including University Circle and its museums, jazz clubs, parks, gardens, churches, hospitals, and Severance Hall and Case Western Reserve University. Murray Hill Road really is on a hill; it runs perpendicular to Mayfield Road and is the heart of that quaint section of Cleveland just south and east of the Circle known as Little Italy. Some of our finest art galleries are hidden in the old buildings on Murray Hill, along with several good Italian restaurants. The street itself is cobbled with red bricks, which adds to the old-world feel of the neighborhood, and my tires sang merrily over them as I navigated the hill toward the Ristorante Vesuvio.

It was about five minutes after eight when I pulled into the unpaved parking lot behind the building. Besides the older models parked out of the way down at the far end, which probably belonged to the restaurant's employees, there were only two other cars. One was a sleek black Acura Legend looking like it had rolled off the showroom floor fifteen minutes ago. The car pretty much conformed to what I thought to be Victor Gaimari's style. The other was a gray Lincoln Town Car as big as a battleship, with dark tinted windows and an extra antenna on the trunk that probably served a TV set in the back seat. The Lincoln was undoubtedly the old man's. Leave it to a naturalized citizen like Don Giancarlo to buy American.

The heavy wooden door to the restaurant was locked, so I rapped on it, hard enough to make my knuckles ache. After a few moments it was opened by one of D'Allessandro's ever present punks, who was wearing a shiny gold down-filled jacket with a collar of fake fur. I think his name was John. We'd had a run-in several years back—more than a run-in actually. He and two other punks had shown up at my apartment one night on Victor Gaimari's orders and thumped me pretty good. But I realized I hadn't seen him around for quite a while. Maybe he'd been an unwilling guest of the state at the Graybar Hotel. It wouldn't have surprised me.

He looked me over, nodding as he recognized me. "You carrying?"

"You think I'm stupid?"

He shrugged, not wanting to commit himself one way or the other. "Let's have a look."

I held my arms away from my body while he ran expert hands up and down the length of me, paying particular attention to my ankles. Off-duty policemen often favor unobtrusive ankle holsters, and even though I hadn't been a Cleveland cop for years, John wasn't going to take any chances. Something in my gut tightened up; I dislike being pawed. But that's what he got paid for and it wouldn't do my cause any good to make a fuss about it.

When he was satisfied I was clean, he turned on his heel and stalked into the interior of the restaurant. I supposed I was to follow him.

Victor Gaimari and Giancarlo D'Allessandro were at a booth over in the corner. The old man had a bright red napkin tucked under his chin, which made it look as though someone had cut his throat, and he was gumming at a steaming bowl of oatmeal that had been sweetened by Sugar Twin, to judge from the three torn-open yellow envelopes on the table. On a plate to one side were two half slices of unbuttered toast and a fragile-looking poached egg. A tumbler of orange juice stood nearby.

Victor seemed to be sticking to coffee. He waved me over.

"Good morning, Milan," he piped. It always amazes me that a man his size had a voice like a castrato.

"Victor," I said, nodding. "Good morning, Don Giancarlo. I appreciate your seeing me."

The old man smacked his lips and dabbed at them with the napkin. "I had to eat anyway," he said. He was nothing if not practical. He looked up at John and waved him away to a small table all the way across the room.

Giancarlo D'Allessandro was well into his seventies, as far as I could figure out, though he could have been older than that. Each time I saw him he seemed to have grown more frail, a bag of brittle bones wrapped in yellowing parchment that a strong lake breeze might pick up and carry across the street. He was one of the last of his breed, an old-line *capo di tutti capi* born in Sicily and come to the United States to pursue his own slightly skewed version of the American Dream.

It gave me a start to realize he was a slice of American history walking around. He'd run with the best of them, sat down and shared wine and food and espresso with Frank Costello and Charlie Lucky and Joe Bonnano and Cleveland's own Jake "Greasy Thumb" Guzik and Shondor Birns. They were all gone now, but D'Allessandro survived, a dinosaur who had stopped evolving several epochs ago but who still hung on and whose footsteps still made the earth tremble.

Victor Gaimari had a degree from Ohio State, which he put to use laundering dirty money and running the operation from a computer terminal, but the don had done all his learning on the street, and even though he functioned under a feudal system that was becoming as antiquated as a Victrola or a Model A, there was respect for his accomplishments and honor for his white hairs throughout the organized crime families of America, especially from the older and wiser heads.

The young Turks, impatient and hotheaded punks who hadn't yet been made, who had seen too many Martin Scorcese movies and who neither remembered nor cared about the glory days when the outfit left its fingerprints on almost every surface of big-city life, might snicker at him and scornfully refer to him as a "Mustache Pete."

Except never to his face. Nobody laughed at Giancarlo D'Allessandro to his face.

I shrugged off my coat and slid in next to Victor.

"Have some breakfast, Milan," he said, and snuggled into the corner of the booth to make room for me.

"No, just coffee, thanks."

"Eat!" D'Allessandro commanded. "The doctor says I gotta eat this slop, but you're a young man. You need meat on your bones."

"Thanks for the 'young' part, Don Giancarlo."

He gave Victor's coffee cup a look of unutterable scorn. "Victor here, he's afraid to eat, afraid he'll get fat and the women won't like him no more."

Victor accepted the rebuke with a fond smile at his uncle. It was apparent that his affection for the old man was real. "My uncle would eat pasta puttanesca for breakfast if the doctors would let him," he said, smiling.

"Pah! Doctors! Look at me, Victor. I eat like a pig all my life, I never weigh more than a hundred sixty-three on my fattest day." The old man regarded his low-calorie breakfast glumly. "Don't look like I ever will, either."

He had been sick for a long time now, old age and decades of good living finally catching up with him. The last time I'd seen him he had been drinking espresso like it was Gatorade and chainsmoking heavily, and every few minutes his skinny old body would be nearly torn apart by a cigarette cough. Now his doctors must have cracked down on him hard, don or no don. And perhaps he had lived long enough or was simply tired enough to finally do what they told him.

He beckoned the waiter over, a young man who looked as though he'd fought bantamweight—not very successfully, judging by the sharp bend in his nose.

"Bacon and eggs and Italian potatoes and toast for this man,"

D'Allessandro said. Apparently Victor could get away with skipping breakfast, but since I wasn't family I was going to eat whether I liked it or not.

He looked at me. "How you like your eggs? Scrambled?"

"Over easy."

"Over easy," he told the waiter. "And bring coffee right away."

"Yes, Don Giancarlo," the waiter said, almost bowing, and backed away. It was all pretty formal for eight o'clock in the morning, but that was D'Allessandro's style. The old organization from which he'd sprung maintains a code of conduct as rigid as that of the U.S. Marines, and he knew how to be a gentleman, polite to a fault, even while he was thinking about having you put in cement galoshes and dumped in Lake Erie.

The don bided his time until the waiter brought my coffee. "I envy you," he said as I took my first sip. "One cup a day they got me down to. One lousy cup a day, and it's that decaf shit. Like drinking the water you wash your socks in."

They must have had him on a pretty severe regimen. I'd never seen him without an espresso and a cigarette, and neither were in evidence this morning. I lifted my cup in a sort of toast, and he nodded his acceptance.

"So, Milan Jacovich." The don always had trouble fitting his Mediterranean tongue to my Slavic name and had to twist his mouth out of shape to do it. But he'd never mispronounced it in all the time I'd known him; he'd lived enough years to understand the value a man puts on his own name. "How do you like politics?"

"It's not what I thought it would be," I said.

"Nothing ever is." He had some more oatmeal, making a face. The trouble with hot cereal is that it doesn't stay hot very long, and there's nothing worse than cold oatmeal. "You get along okay with the woman? Corns?"

"She seems nice. But she has problems talking to people. And her husband is a real . . ." I searched for the right word, then selected one D'Allessandro would relate to. "A real *strunz*." I know very little Italian, and most of it is rude.

His eyes twinkled at my use of the word, and he nodded. "I don't like him either." He looked at Victor. "I don't like the husband, Victor. He's skeevy."

Victor translated for me. "Diseased, unclean. A wrong guy "

"Is that an Italian word?"

"That's a Collinwood word, skeevy," the old man said, naming an area of the East Side, now integrated by blacks, in which many of the Italian immigrants settled before the middle of the century. After the war there had also been a lot of Slovenians in Collinwood, and quite a bit of intermarriage had gone on between the two cultures.

"Well," I said, "we have our work cut out for us. Getting Barbara Corns elected is going to be tough."

"That's why we got *la chocolata*," he said, biting into a piece of toast.

I must have looked puzzled, because Victor explained, "Mrs. Pride."

Cassandra Pride. *La chocolata*, the chocolate-colored woman. I heartily disapproved of who he was, how he thought, and what he did, but Don Giancarlo D'Allessandro was never less than interesting to talk to.

"Nothing worth anything is easy," the don said, chewing noisily. "You want what you want, you gotta break some eggs." By way of illustration, he poked at the poached egg with a fork, rupturing the yolk. He watched with distaste as it spread across his plate.

My breakfast arrived. As I took a bite of the Italian fried potatoes, D'Allessandro said, "But you didn't come here just for breakfast, eh?"

"No, sir."

"And you didn't come to talk politics, am I right?"

"You usually are."

He liked that. He smiled a little, as much as I'd ever seen him smile, and began sopping up egg yolk with his toast. "So then, what?"

I took some perfectly cooked, crisp bacon. "You've heard about what happened to Barbara Corns's opponent's wife, Mrs. True?"

He bobbed his head before taking a bite of the dripping toast. "It's too bad. I was sorry to hear that. Goddamn people shouldn't be allowed to drive!"

"Both Victor and Mrs. Pride seem to think that it would be better for Barbara if we found out who was responsible."

"All right," he said, wiping his fingertips on the edge of the napkin. There was a splash of yellow at the corner of his mouth and he licked at it. "So?"

"Are you aware that Mrs. True's brother, Earl Barnstable, is currently under indictment for child pornography?"

The old man's nose wrinkled so that it matched the deep creases in his cheeks and around his eyes and mouth. He wiped some more egg yolk from his bottom lip. "Makes you sick, don't it? Little kids! There's no punishment bad enough for a man who'd do a thing like that." He glanced at Victor for affirmation and got it. Surprise, surprise.

"You suppose there might be a connection between that and Princess True's death?"

His eyebrows climbed toward his hairline. "It was an accident. We heard it was an accident."

"A pretty convenient accident, isn't it?"

He pushed his plate away from the edge of the table. "What are you saying?" There was no mistaking the saw teeth in his tone, or the way the corners of his eyes kind of flattened out, giving him an almost oriental look. All of a sudden it became difficult for me to get my food down.

Victor jumped in. "I don't think Milan's implying we had any knowledge of this."

"No, sir, I'm not."

The don relaxed—not much, but some, and when he did, I did, too, and was able to swallow a mouthful of egg and toast.

"What it comes down to," I said, "is that I need some help from you."

"Why?"

"If I'm going to put Barbara in the clear on this killing—and Victor thinks it's important—I have to check out the angles."

"Angles? I don't understand what you mean, angles."

"The brother angle."

The don broke off another piece of toast and dabbed absently at the egg. "I—we—don't know this brother, this guy who deals in filth. Why do you come here?"

"Don Giancarlo," I said, "I know that your organization has nothing to do with distributing pornography."

"You damn right!"

"But I also know that most of the porno trade in this country is controlled by . . ." I flailed around like a goldfish on the living room carpet. I didn't know how to put this to Giancarlo D'Allessandro, what expression to use that wouldn't offend him. The mob? The outfit? The family? Organized crime? Certainly not the M-word, which was more of a media expression than a reality anyway.

I glanced at Victor beside me. He was grinning, obviously enjoying my discomfort and not about to help out. That's the kind of guy he is, Victor.

"Controlled by people that you might know," I finished up lamely.

The old man sat back in the red leather booth, one hand touching a fold of papery yellow skin that sagged beneath his jaw. "People that I might know," he repeated woodenly.

"Earl Barnstable—Mrs. True's brother—is under indictment and goes to trial in January. Could it be possible that his sister was killed as a warning? For him to keep his mouth shut in court?"

"Milan," Victor said, "where did you develop this melodramatic flair of yours? Did you take drama in school?"

I turned slightly in the booth to look at him. "You hired me to work on Barbara Corns's campaign because you thought I was smart enough to handle it. Smart enough to consider every possibility, and that's what I'm trying to do here."

"You know we don't touch porno. Why even bring it up?"

I locked eyes with D'Allessandro, who was still playing with his jowl. "Because I have nowhere else to turn."

Nobody said anything for a long while, and I used the time to finish my breakfast. It was a lot more than I'm used to eating in the morning, but it was very well prepared, good enough to eat and then skip lunch.

"I wish I didn't have to ask you," I said.

"Don't waste wishes," D'Allessandro told me, flapping his napkin under his chin as if he were shooing away a mosquito. "You only get a few in your lifetime—you shouldn't waste them. There's only one thing worth wishing for in this world anyway."

"What's that, sir?"

"An easy death," he said.

The waiter bustled over to refill both my coffee cup and Victor's. As soon as he went away, the don sighed and leaned forward, his elbows on the table, his hard old eyes shiny bright and the napkin dragging in the remnants of the poached egg.

"You're asking me for a lot. We don't talk about our own, ever. You know that."

I nodded. And waited.

"Even if I gave you a name, you think you could just walk in and ask your questions?"

"I hoped you could arrange for me to do that."

He jerked his head back, and his derisive laugh was like a single shot from a cap pistol. It sent him into a paroxysm of coughing that shook his body from within; he clawed the napkin from under his chin and held it over his mouth, his other hand clutching the edge of the table.

Victor shifted in his seat and leaned across the table to put one hand on his uncle's arm. "Relax," he said. "Just relax."

D'Allessandro kept coughing, his usually parchment-colored face turning as red as the napkin, and Victor and I could only observe impotently. The waiter came back and hovered, as uncertain as to what to do as we were, but Victor motioned him away. Across the room John swung his legs out from the booth where he sat, concerned, but he didn't get to his feet.

After what seemed like several years the coughing fit subsided, and the don slumped back against the seat, using the napkin to wipe the mucus from his nose and the tears from his eyes. His whole body was limp, as though someone had carefully removed all his bones.

"Are you all right, Uncle?" Victor asked.

The old man didn't have the breath to answer at once and struggled painfully for it. Then he gasped, "I look all right to you?" He signaled the waiter. "Bring espresso."

"Now you know you're not supposed to—"

A fierce wave of D'Allessandro's hand silenced his nephew. "Don't say what I supposed to. You want I should keep alive so I can do *that* every ten minutes?"

Victor had no answer, so he just squeezed his uncle's hand. The don slumped back again, his head lolling on the skinny stem of his neck. Then he raised his eyes to mine. "Don't never get old, Milan Jacovich. It's a piece of shit, being old."

From the back of the restaurant came a hiss of steam from

the espresso machine. After a moment the waiter bustled over with a tiny cup and saucer, four sugar cubes, and a twist of lemon peel and set it before his patron, then cleared away the old man's breakfast.

D'Allessandro carefully ran the lemon peel around the rim of the cup, then took a sugar cube from the bowl in front of him, put it between his teeth, and drew the thick black coffee through it with his lips. He held it in his mouth for several moments before he swallowed, sighing deeply.

"Good," he said. "I forget how good it is anymore."

I sipped at my own coffee. I'd had enough dealings with Giancarlo D'Allessandro to know that he took his own sweet time about things. Maybe it was his age, but more likely it was his style. This was no hothead, no firebrand; this was a man who had survived the violent, often deadly power struggles at the highest levels of organized crime by being judicious and careful.

"You got a pair of brass balls on you," he said at last. "Coming in here and asking me . . . What if I say no?" His eyes crinkled. "What then?"

"I'll have to back off. Off the campaign."

"You've already been paid," Victor said.

"I'll refund your money in full."

"You always have to have it your own way, Milan. Why are you like that?"

I shrugged. That's the way I am, and Victor knew it when he hired me. I may have owed him a favor, but I was going to repay it on my own terms or not at all.

The most powerful organized crime figure in northeastern Ohio just stared at me, his eyes black and steady on my face. "I can't make such a decision on my own," he said at last. "I have to talk to people, to get permission."

"With all respect, sir, I always thought you *were* the permission."

"In my family that's true. This—this *porno* . . ." he said, his lips curling back over his long front teeth. He pronounced it as though it were almost unspeakable, which I guess it is. "That's not my family. We don't do that shit with little children. Disgusting." He looked sad. "I gotta talk to people."

"When can you let me know?"

"When I let you know!" he snapped.

"In the meantime, Milan," Victor said, "we expect you to stay on the job. Barbara Corns needs you, and it would be really cruel to desert her now, so close to the election." His big brown eyes were so wide and innocent I almost wanted to laugh.

Instead I said to D'Allessandro, "Then I'll wait to hear from you?"

"You'll wait," the don assured me.

I stood up and took my leave of them, shaking the don's skinny hand. The bones just beneath the skin felt like a small bird's. John saw me to the door and unlocked it for me.

"See ya," he said. Nice and casual, almost friendly, as if he hadn't once beaten me until I couldn't stand up. He had nice manners, John.

It wasn't until I was back in my car, rumbling over the red brick cobblestones of Murray Hill, that I remembered I hadn't thanked them for breakfast, an unconscionable breach of etiquette.

Only the fear of looking like a complete fool kept me from driving back to the Ristorante Vesuvio to correct the oversight.

## CHAPTER TEN

I t was about two o'clock when I got out to Lake Erie Shores. The temperature had dropped several degrees since morning, courtesy of a cold front slicing down across the water out of Canada, and there were more colorful leaves lying forlornly on the front lawns of houses than there had been a few days earlier. In anticipation of the inclement weather to come, many homeowners had taken down their screens over the weekend and replaced them with storm windows. Winter doesn't take you by surprise in Ohio; it gives you plenty of warning it's on its way.

As per Cassandra Pride's instructions, I went directly to the campaign headquarters in the little storefront off the square. Election placards covered the door and windows, but the green awning, flapping in the wind, gave mute testimony that Randa's Casual Boutique had been one of the victims of the Bush recession that had decimated the lower and middle classes of America's heartland. Randa, whoever she was, probably had little interest in maintaining the sort of status quo that Barbara Corns espoused, so there was a particularly cruel sort of irony to the big BACK TO THE BASICS sign that took up most of the right-hand window.

There was a sprawling public parking lot for the convenience of the shoppers just off the square, with meters that could be fed for up to six hours, and I left my car there and walked back out onto the sidewalk a buck and a half poorer. One of the reasons the huge mall down the road had taken such a fearsome gouge out of the business on the square was that mall parking was free. But the city couldn't afford not to charge for parking on such valuable real estate right downtown, and as a result everyone was suffering.

It wasn't a long walk, but I was grateful to get in out of the wind. Inside the headquarters a space heater was churning out warm air. The light fixtures overhead and in wall sconces had been designed for a women's wear boutique; the stingy illumination must have made working and reading a bit difficult. A series of folding metal picnic tables crowded the one large room, interspersed with scarred wooden desks, and there was a wealth of gray metal folding chairs, only a fraction of which were occupied by volunteers. BARBARA FOR MAYOR signs were everywhere.

At one table three young women were busily folding pamphlets and making up packets to be delivered all over town. At another table along the wall four well-dressed matrons were working a bank of phones with all the fervor of a well-schooled boiler room crew. One of them held her left hand out as she spoke, fingers splayed so her nail polish would dry.

A tall, rather pretty woman about five years younger than I with dark golden hair in a Dutch boy cut came over to greet me, smiling broadly and brandishing a blue and white BARBARA button. She was dressed down, compared to the other volunteers, in gray slacks and a maroon turtleneck sweater that made her look even taller than she was, which was about five foot nine. She was also without a wedding ring, I noticed.

"What every well-dressed man should wear," she said, smiling, and pinned the button onto my lapel. The smile made me catch my breath. Her hair smelled of citrus shampoo. "Especially in here. There, now you're in the height of fashion. Besides, it matches your eyes. Hi, what can I do for you?"

"Is Mrs. Pride here?"

"She just ducked out to grab herself a sandwich. Would you believe it's been so crazy in here this was her first chance? Can I help you with something?"

"I sort of work here," I said. "On the campaign."

"Hi," she said again, extending her hand. "I'm Kellen Charles—Kellen with a *K*."

"My name is Milan Jacovich. Jacovich with a *J*."

"Nice to meet you. Cassie should be back in a little while. Why don't you come keep me company?"

The prospect of keeping her company certainly was a pleasing one. Her face reminded me of sunlight when it hits the water, constant and yet everchanging, and even though I kept staring at her eyes, it was hard to decide if they were brown or green. It depended on how the light struck them. There was something in them that made me want to smile.

I followed her over to one of the tables stacked high with election brochures, where I took off my coat and draped it over a folding chair. We sat down opposite each other. The view was terrific, but the metal seat was cold and very uncomfortable.

"Who designed these chairs?" I asked. "Torquemada?"

"They were loaned to us through the good offices of the Winslow-Edison Funeral Home just off the square. You take any donations you can get in a small-town campaign like this one. Let's just hope nobody dies until after Election Day." She caught herself and put a hand over her mouth for a moment. Her blush was rather pretty.

"Sorry," she said. "I guess that was insensitive . . . under the circumstances." She pushed a pile of pamphlets at me. "Here, make yourself useful while you wait. Fold them in thirds, like this." She demonstrated.

I began folding. "You're a volunteer?"

She nodded. "I can't give as much time as I'd like—I have to make a living. But it's very important to me that Barbara gets elected."

"Why?"

"Self-interest, I guess, like everybody else. I'm the director of the Lake Erie Shores Homeless Project. Barbara cares about the homeless and Gayton True doesn't. It's that simple."

"I don't live in Lake Erie Shores," I told her, "but I wouldn't think they'd have much of a homeless population."

Her pretty eyes got smaller and the bright smile died aborning. "Don't kid yourself. Homelessness isn't just a big-city problem any more." She shook her head resolutely, her shiny hair swinging back and forth like a model's in a shampoo commercial. "I just refuse to believe that people are going to be allowed to starve or freeze to death in the United States of America in the twentieth century. And so does Barbara." She waved a pamphlet at me before she folded it.

"Barbara hasn't said anything about the homeless."

"She wouldn't. That kind of advocacy isn't exactly popular in Lake Erie Shores, so she doesn't mention it much in public. But I've talked to her at great length, and she believes in it, so I believe in her. As for Mayor True . . ."

She looked up as Cassandra Pride walked in through the front door carrying a paper sack from Wendy's with a large grease spot on its side. Dennis Babb and Laurie Pirkle tagged along behind her like the Pied Piper's rats. She spotted us and came over to our table.

"Milan, I'm glad you're here," she said, and then looked from Kellen to me. "I see you two have met." She set the bag down on the table, a safe distance from the pamphlets, and gave Dennis her coat to hang up. Then she went to the coffeepot on a small table in the corner and poured herself a cup. It smelled strong enough to stand a pencil in upright.

"Fill me in, Cassie," I said as she sat down. "What's happening around here?"

Cassie took a few moments to arrange her thoughts; it must have been a busy and trying day for her. "Let's see. We had our expected visit from the Cleveland police. It seemed pretty routine, but then what do I know? They asked a lot of questions—where was Barbara Sunday morning, things like that. I was proud of her; she didn't fall apart until after they left. She's pulling herself together, though. She has to make an appearance at a cocktail party and dinner tonight. It's a private party, a regular thing they hold in the banquet room of a restaurant the last Tuesday of every month. Not so much the business leaders who go to the chamber functions, but more the super-rich types that hang out on the benefit circuit. The town's movers and shakers who like to get together to see who's wearing what and trade gossip. Gayton True was invited as well as Barbara, but of course with what's happened, he won't attend. He'll probably send Tyler Rees in his place."

She began unwrapping her burger and french fries. "I hate fast food," she said, making a face, "but it does live up to its name, and I've been swamped all morning."

"Isn't True going to campaign at all anymore?" I said.

Cassie regarded her burger with some mistrust. "He hasn't let us know, and we haven't asked. I don't like him much, but I can't help pitying him. Princess was a real partner to him."

"Sparring partner," Dennis put in, and grinned delightedly at Laurie. I was getting the idea that Dennis's elevator didn't go all the way to the top floor. He was wearing another variation of his urban cowboy drag, this time with a purple knit sports shirt, and with the straw cowboy hat and the patched glasses, he looked like the funny sidekick in an old Hopalong Cassidy movie.

"One thing, though," Cassandra said, and then she stopped and glanced up at the two of them hovering over her shoulder, living cartoons of a haloed angel and a pitchfork-wielding devil. She changed her tone to that of a nursery school teacher. "Come on, guys, there's lots of fliers to be folded. Why don't you go on over there and grab a pile?"

Dennis glared at me, his lower lip extended in a pouty sneer that was half three-year-old and half Jerry Lee Lewis. "Why doesn't *he* fold some?"

Being talked about as though I weren't present is one of my pet peeves, but I smiled gamely and took a pamphlet from the stack between me and Kellen. "I'm going as fast as I can, Dennis," I said.

Dennis slouched away like a stray dog who's been kicked, Laurie following after him, her wide body banging against the metal chairs on either side.

Cassandra leaned across the table toward me. "There was another letter," she said softly.

I shot a quick look at Kellen, but Cassandra said, "It's all right, she knows."

"Do you have it?"

She shook her head. "It's back at the house. I put it in a big manila envelope for you. But I did what you said and only handled it by the edges."

"What did this one say?"

She looked around to make sure no one could hear except Kellen and me. " 'First adultery—now murder. Where will you stop, cunt?' "

"Jesus," Kellen breathed.

"Did Barbara freak out?" I asked Cassandra.

"I picked up the mail this morning. I didn't let her see it. There didn't seem to be much point."

"That's good," I said. "She doesn't need any more worries right now. Let's see, Princess was killed on Sunday; that means the letter was probably mailed just yesterday. I'm impressed with the mail service out here."

Kellen said, "Isn't sending threats through the U.S. mails a federal offense?"

"Nobody's threatened anybody," I said. "Hate mail is also a crime, but the Lake Erie Shores Police Department basically works for Gayton True, and I don't think they'll get too exercised about someone sending Barbara a nasty letter."

"Can't we go to the FBI?"

"We could. The question is, do we want to? The publicity wouldn't do Barbara any good, unless we could pin the letters on True. And that seems pretty unlikely."

"But if Barbara needs protection," Kellen began.

"It's a possibility," I told her, "but there've been no threats so far, just nasty comments. It's been my experience that phone freaks are just that, and more of a nuisance than a danger. But I don't think this is an ordinary pervert."

"Why?" asked Kellen.

"Someone's obviously trying to shake Barbara up so badly that she either drops out of the campaign or makes a serious error," Cassandra said. She tore open a paper packet of salt and sprinkled it over her fries.

"And we know who'd want to do that," Kellen said.

"Who?" I said.

She glanced at the inexpensive sports watch around her wrist. "Oh, nuts, I have to go. I've got a meeting at three."

Smiling apologetically, she stood up and got her coat from the rack and shrugged into it. "It was nice to meet you, Milan. I hope I'll see you again."

"I'll be around," I said. For a well-educated guy it sometimes amazes me how banal I can be.

I watched her as she went out the door, hunching her shoulders against the wind. It was typical of me to allow the most attractive woman I'd seen in a long time to just walk away. But I'd never learned the art of making a positive move toward someone I'm attracted to when there is a third party present. I guess I was just married too long, during the era in our history when things like that were fairly commonplace. I'm out of touch, I suppose.

Cassandra put a Wendy's french fry between her teeth with long, delicate fingers. "I thought you'd like Kellen."

I blushed in spite of myself. Damn my fair Slovenian skin for betraying me!

"I've been talking around town all morning," she said, switching into her get-down-to-business mode, "and the wind seems to be blowing in our direction—or at least, not away from us. Everyone feels sorry for the mayor, but not enough to vote for him out of sympathy alone."

"Who were you talking to? Barbara supporters?"

She nodded, almost embarrassed that I'd caught her out. "At least what happened to Princess isn't going to cause them to switch." She took a bite of hamburger. I've never understood why Wendy's makes their hamburgers square, but I guess Dave knows what he's doing.

"Have you talked to the police?" she said after she'd chewed and swallowed.

"They're treating it pretty much as an accidental hit-and-run." Now it was my turn to be embarrassed. "I'm afraid we can't count on much help from the Cleveland police on this one."

"Why not?"

I gestured impotently, then decided not to even try explaining about my conversation with Marko. "Let's just say it has a lot to do with Victor Gaimari."

She took some coffee and sighed. "I was afraid that was eventually going to get in the way."

"Cassie, why is Gaimari so interested in this election? I didn't think he'd ever even been in Lake County."

"I have no idea, unless it's his friendship with Evan. He asked around to find out who was good, and available, and I guess my name came up. He contacted me six weeks ago and told me he'd pay me well to run Barbara's campaign."

"You never worked for him before?"

"I never laid eyes on him until he called and asked me to come to his office and then offered me the job."

"But you know who he is? Who his . . . connections are?"

"You hear rumors," she said. "Believe me, if I hadn't liked Barbara and believed in her, even Victor Gaimari wouldn't have been able to pay me enough to get me here. But when I heard what she had to say I signed on."

"You want to go back to the basics too?"

She laughed. "I know—it sounds like George Bush's 'family values' pitch, which was pretty lame at best. And when Republicans say family values, they mean white middle-class families. The Nelsons and the Beaver and *Father Knows Best*."

"So what is it that appeals to you?"

She stared into her cup for a moment. "I'm not against progress, God knows. Without it I couldn't have gone to college and I'd probably be cleaning white women's houses. But lately the word has come to mean making it easier for rich people to build housing tracts and malls to service other rich people. The prevailing theory is that the money trickles down, but in reality there's damn little trickling. And it doesn't matter that there aren't any blacks in Lake Erie Shores; there are poor people, homeless people even, as Kellen must have told you. The money needs to be invested where it's needed—in schools and jobs and community centers, in *people*. It shouldn't go to line the pockets of developers and large-scale entrepreneurs, most of whom probably live somewhere else."

She was quiet for a few moments. "I guess," she finished, "that's what Barbara's about. And why I'm here." She gave me a piercing look, and said, "What about you?"

"Me?" I said. "I owed Victor Gaimari a favor."

# CHAPTER ELEVEN

When we got back to Barbara's house to pick her up for the evening's ordeal, I was appalled to discover that Dennis and Laurie were going with us to the restaurant. If Barbara was trying to convince the voters of her maturity and judgment, dragging those two to a fancy cocktail and dinner party given by some of the most influential people in town was a funny way of going about it. I expressed my doubts to the campaign manager.

"We can't say no, Milan," Cassandra explained.

"Why in hell not?"

"You know how sensitive they are."

"Who? Dennis and Laurie? We'll take them out for ice cream tomorrow."

"That's not going to cut it." She lifted her hands to indicate futility. "Our hands are tied, I'm afraid."

"Why?"

"Let's suppose we tell them they couldn't come," she explained like a fifth-grade history teacher. "What if they got mad and went to the newspaper and complained that they were good enough to do the hard work for Barbara, the running errands and licking stamps and dragging chairs around, but she was ashamed to be seen with them in public? How would that look?"

"A hell of a lot better than showing up at this elegant private party with them, I'd imagine."

"We might even get the mental health people all over us because of Dennis."

"What's wrong with him, anyway?"

"I'm not sure. But whatever it is, we can't keep him locked in the attic like an eccentric uncle. Dennis and Laurie are part of the campaign, and this is a small town. We do what we have to do. It's politics, Milan, and you know what kind of bedfellows that makes."

I knew when I was licked. "Do one thing for me," I said.

"What?"

"Just for tonight, try and convince Dennis to lose the cowboy hat."

"Why don't *you* tell him?"

I had to laugh at that one. "Because he doesn't like me. He'll just stick his tongue out at me and go sulk in the corner."

Her eyes raked the ceiling. "All my trials, Lord," she mumbled as she went upstairs to help the candidate get ready.

The late October sky had dimmed from pewter gray to inky black before we left for the restaurant. We formed a four-vehicle caravan—Evan and Barbara Corns in their Buick Park Avenue, Dennis and Laurie in his old beater, and Cassandra and I each driving our own cars. I'd been hoping Kellen Charles would show up too, but I supposed that was too much to ask.

Laird's Olde English Steak and Chop House was the fanciest eatery in Lake Erie Shores, I was told, and seemed to be just what its name implied, complete with discreet green wallpaper, wall sconces that looked like torches in a British country home, and hunting prints and copper tankards hanging on the walls. The cocktail lounge didn't look too lively, but then it was only seven thirty in the evening. An electronic keyboard arrangement and an elaborate system of microphones and speakers crowded a tiny stage in the corner.

The party, if one could call it that, was being held in one of the chop house's banquet rooms, in which the decor wasn't quite as fussy as in the public part of the restaurant; there were no hunting prints on the green walls. Six round tables were set with ten settings apiece, place cards at each setting. Of course there was the ubiquitous wooden lectern with its inevitable microphone on a skinny flexible stalk like the neck of a praying mantis, set up beneath a large black and gold and green coat of arms with a dragon sejant-erect hanging on the wall, probably bought at a garage sale.

Over in one corner a portable bar had been set up, over which a young man in a white tuxedo shirt and a green vest presided in a rather bored fashion, perhaps because everyone there was old enough to be his parent. Against another wall was a long buffet table, and on it were platters of Melba toast and cheese, celery and carrot sticks and cauliflower in beds of shaved ice, mushrooms stuffed with something I didn't care to think about, and a bilious-looking gray dip.

I immediately noticed Mr. and Mrs. Arlen James in the center of a knot of well-dressed peers; all were holding glasses in that peculiar way people have at cocktail parties, elbows tucked tightly into their sides. The women were all drinking white wine as though it was required, while their husbands were fortifying themselves with what appeared to be stronger stuff. They moved with the easy and brittle familiarity of the rich, who only patronize restaurants that are frequented by other people whom they know and are comfortable with.

Mr. Arlen James looked even more glum than most of the other men. He smoked a cigarette, which he held between the second and third knuckles of his right hand.

I recognized two of the women as having attended Mrs. James's "coffee," and I amused myself trying to figure which men belonged to them. I stopped when it hit me that I didn't care whether I was right.

Mrs. Arlen James came over to Barbara and gave her an air kiss and nodded to the rest of us, looking somewhat askance at Dennis, who had left his cowboy hat at home but was wearing a sports jacket of blue corduroy with tan elbow patches over a western shirt tucked into his ratty low-slung jeans and a ridiculous bolo tie, as out of place as a bustier and garter belt at a meeting of the Epworth League. Laurie's outfit was her customary black polyester and a red fringed shawl and was hopelessly gauche, but at least she didn't look as though she was in costume for an old Randolph Scott movie.

Mrs. James took it upon herself to guide Barbara and Evan around the room and make sure everyone met them; she was the kind of woman who was born to organize parties and brunches and benefits. She elevated hostessing to an art form.

She wasn't quite so gracious with the hired help, so she left Cassandra and me to our own devices. We wandered over to the bar, where Cassandra conformed, asking for white wine. The bartender's stores seemed to be somewhat deficient in the beer department, and for a moment I considered going out into the cocktail lounge to get one, but I decided that would be rude, so I opted instead for a Perrier with lime, just to have something to hold in my hand. I didn't enjoy it very much.

"They do this every month?" I said.

Cassie nodded. "Yes, and I can't imagine why. This crowd looks about as much fun as a coronary bypass."

"Maybe they like to rub their money against everyone else's to see if it'll breed."

Mrs. James left Barbara and Evan in what I assumed were good hands and floated over to the door to greet two new arrivals. Gayton True's campaign manager, Tyler Rees, was probably wearing the same jacket, shirt, and tie that he'd had on all day, which had the appearance so common to the wardrobes of overweight men of having been worn hard. Rees looked harried and uncomfortable, but not nearly so much as Al Drago, who lumbered in behind him like a freight car. His idea of dressing for the party was a phlegm-colored suit with a windowpane check right off the rack from the Big and Tall Men's Shop, and a startling yellow tie which reached just below his sternum, leaving a white expanse of shirt, buttons straining over his wide, hard belly.

His watchful little eyes scanned the room, seeking out bomb-throwing Hezbollah terrorists and finally settling on me as though I fit the category. His pasty face turned a ruddy color and his almost invisible lips tightened into a downturned scowl. His itch to get his hands on me and rend me apart was as palpable as lust. Al Drago frightened me as few men ever had.

In the meantime Mrs. James was guiding Rees around the room, taking the same route she'd used to introduce Barbara and Evan, and the assembled revelers all clucked their tongues over Princess's death and expressed their sympathies. If Tyler Rees was Gayton True's surrogate speechmaker this evening, he was going to have to accept the condolences as well.

Cassie regarded Drago with something akin to awe. "God, he's creepy," she whispered. "What's he doing here?"

"Since Princess isn't around to intimidate Barbara any more, they're sending in a sub, I imagine."

"Keep him away from her, whatever you have to do."

"Whatever I have to do?" I said. "That means shoot him." She laughed lightly, and then her expression changed to one of horror. "You haven't got a gun, have you, Milan? Jesus, what if someone were to see it?"

"No, I don't—I didn't know Drago was invited."

She looked at me closely. "You two know each other from somewhere?"

I nodded. "I got him kicked out of the police department about a year ago."

"And from the way he glares at you he still remembers."

"An elephant never forgets," I said.

Mrs. Arlen James tinked a spoon against the side of her wineglass. "People, people. Excuse me, but shall we all take our places? They're about to serve dinner now."

Everyone milled around like cattle that had been separated from the herd until they found their names on the place cards. Evan and Barbara were seated at one table up near the front and Tyler Rees and Al Drago at another. Cassandra and I had been assigned seats at a table near the door, and Dennis and Laurie were banished to one in the corner, where I couldn't help notice that no one else spoke to them. Probably just as well.

Our tablemates introduced themselves. I didn't catch their Anglo-Saxon names and I'm pretty sure they didn't catch our names, but it was one of those polite rituals one goes through to make life a little more bearable.

One woman in particular, a forty-something matron with teased, frosted hair and acrylic nails like Masai spears, seemed very interested in how the campaign was progressing. At least she talked a lot about it, which may have stemmed less from a burning interest in politics than from an inability to remain silent for more than forty-five seconds at a clip. I'd wager she was being groomed to take over leadership of the group when Mrs. Arlen James retired to her condo in Naples, Florida.

"Have they taken any polls?" the woman asked me between bites of salad. "Do you know who's ahead?"

"This is a local election," I told her. "I don't think either candidate can afford pollsters."

"Well, everyone in this town who cares about good local government is keeping an eye on things. And they're talking to one another. You know what a lot of us are concerned about?"

"What's that?"

"Potholes," she said, thus identifying the problem of the nineties that was going to push peace, race, poverty, and a cure for AIDS right out of the public consciousness. Both she and her husband, who wasn't listening to anything she said, had terrific tans, the kind of bronze you don't get living in Cleveland. I imagined they spent a lot of time in Florida during the winter, and someplace exotic in the summertime like Tahiti, with trips to the local tanning salon in between. They both looked like skin cancer waiting to happen.

"Potholes are a menace and a safety hazard," she continued. "If Barbara gets elected, is she going to do anything about the potholes on Lost Nation Road? It's a real problem, you know. Last winter they were absolutely terrible. I totally ruined a tire."

I indicated Cassandra. "That's not my department. You'll have to ask the campaign manager."

She just looked at Cassandra for a moment. "Oh," was all she said, her bright smile fixed on her face, and then she got very interested in her Caesar salad. For all I knew she picked out the anchovies the way I did. In any case, it was preferable to having to ask a political favor from a black woman.

Cassandra didn't meet my eyes or indicate visibly that she considered the woman's quick change of attitude racially motivated but went on calmly eating her own salad. I wondered how long the professional politician was going to hold sway over the human being. Probably one more week—until Election Day. The civil rights advances of the past thirty years may have changed the laws, but they haven't always changed attitudes.

It's a good thing I harbor no ambitions toward holding public office, or even toward behind-the-scenes power, because I'm not cut out to smile politely at people who piss me off. One of the reasons I work for myself is so I don't have to. But it didn't seem to matter much to Cassandra Pride that the overbearing woman didn't think she was worth talking to because she was black. Politics, I think, requires a much thicker skin than I'll ever possess.

When my entrée was served by a waiter even younger than the

bartender, it proved to be a small sirloin steak with green pep-percorn sauce, a baked potato the size of a baby's fist, and green beans with slivered almonds. The portions were niggardly, but I had to admit that what was there was several notches above most banquet food.

Dessert came in the form of some sort of chocolate mousse, which I noticed almost no one was eating except me, and I won-dered whatever happened to the notion of ice cream or apple pie. Maybe Barbara was right about going back to the basics.

Donald Straum's unexpected arrival coincided with that of the dessert. He just appeared at the door to the banquet room in his scruffy sports jacket and open-necked dress shirt, his notebook at the ready, looking balefully at Barbara and Evan Corns through his granny glasses. When Barbara looked up and met his pene-trating gaze, her face lost what little color it had, so that the rouge on her cheeks stood out like clown makeup. She didn't acknowl-edge him, in fact turned her whole body away from him, but she couldn't help shooting covert looks over her shoulder, alternated with worried glances at her husband, who was so busy election-eering with Mrs. Arlen James that he didn't even notice.

But Mrs. Arlen James soon spotted Straum, and she left her untouched mousse to come over to our table and lean over me anxiously. The skin at her neck beneath the lavish gold necklace was crepey, and her Chanel no. 5 made me giddy at close range.

"Mr. Straum wasn't invited this evening, Mr. Javitz."

I thought about correcting her, but I didn't really care if she knew my name or not. "If you don't want him here, ask him to leave."

"I certainly don't want him here." Her mouth was white with anger. "This is a private party, and the press is definitely not wel-come. I was hoping you'd explain that to him. Nicely, of course."

"Why me?"

To Mrs. Arlen James the answer was obvious. "You're in charge of Barbara's security, aren't you?"

I inclined my head toward Al Drago's broad checkered back. "Why don't you ask Mayor True's security man?"

She looked at Drago and shuddered. "I couldn't possibly bring myself to talk to that person," she said.

I had to sympathize with her.

I put down my spoon in mid mousse. I hated it anyway, it had the texture of library paste. I got up from the table and went over to where Straum held up the wall. He watched my approach the way he might that of a charging Cape buffalo, hunching his shoulders, balling up his fist, waiting.

"Can I talk to you outside?" I said.

"What for?"

"Just for a minute." I held open the door until he moved reluctantly through it.

The noise from the adjacent cocktail lounge was loud when we got outside the banquet room, with revelers yelling over the band, which was performing a radical tunectomy on a Beach Boys medley. Apparently business picked up later in the evening at Laird's Olde English. "What's this about?" Straum said, sticking out his chin like Mussolini. He was a truculent little bastard. Barbara's taste in men seemed to follow a pattern—she liked them short and nasty.

"Our hostess has just reminded me that this is a private party."

"So?"

"So you're crashing."

"Didn't you ever hear of freedom of the press, pal?"

I like being called pal somewhat less than being dragged naked over cobblestones by a team of Clydesdales. "I'm not your pal, Mr. Straum, and you can write whatever you like, but you have no business at a private function."

"It's a political function."

"Nevertheless, it's private. You can go sit at the bar, have a drink, and wait for people to come out, and if they want to answer your questions, that's fine with me. But you aren't invited into the banquet room."

"Bull shit!" he said, making it two words with the accent on the second, and started back inside.

I took his arm rather firmly and halted his forward progress. "I don't think so."

His eyes widened behind the thick pebble lenses. "Are you touching me?" he demanded. "How dare you touch me?"

"Mrs. James doesn't want you in there, and Barbara doesn't

either. As far as that goes, neither do I. So that just about settles it, doesn't it?"

He looked down at where I grasped his arm as though it was his first experience ever with human contact. "I can't believe you're touching me." One would think I'd just felt him up in the movies.

"Look, Mr. Straum, you're just making trouble for yourself. Now, I'm asking you nicely, as per instructions. I can just about guarantee that if Mayor True's security chief asks you he'll not only touch you but there's a good chance that afterward you'll walk funny for the rest of your life. So be a good fellow and take a hike, okay?"

He slapped at my hand and wrenched his arm away almost violently, and in doing so popped a jacket button, which had evidently been hanging by a single thread. We both watched it hit the tile floor, sounding like the ball in a roulette wheel.

He was outraged. "You'll pay for this, Jacovich," he sputtered.

"How much could a lousy button cost?"

It was a pretty good riposte, I thought, and I left him standing there hyperventilating and went back inside, feeling righteous that I'd earned my money for the evening.

Mrs. Arlen James had resumed her seat, but she arched her eyebrows at me and I nodded back, letting her know that the problem had been dealt with—at least for now.

I did wonder, though, why she'd been so anxious to get him out of there when she'd welcomed him into her home for the informal coffee just a few days before.

After the dessert plates had been cleared, Mrs. James rose once more from her place and went up to the podium. She had a little trouble getting the microphone turned on and needed help from the bartender, and after an ear-shattering screech of feedback, she finally said, "As you know we have some special guests here this evening, and we're very appreciative that they took time out from their busy schedules to talk to us."

She looked around the room, clearly expecting to be given credit for enticing the candidates to speechify at their little dinner party. She obviously loved attention and did whatever she could to get it.

"Election Day is only a week away." She announced it with

all the solemnity of a network anchor reporting the news of a presidential assassination. "And all of us, naturally, are concerned about who is going to be mayor of our city for the next four years. I know we're all going to vote, but some of us haven't yet made up our minds who we're going to vote for. So we invited the two candidates to come and speak to us this evening."

She paused for a moment, scanning the audience as though she expected applause. When she didn't get it she went right on. She was a gamer, Mrs. Arlen James.

"Unfortunately, Mayor True couldn't be with us, due to the tragedy we're all aware of. But he sent along a worthy substitute. And of course Barbara Corns is here, too."

On my left, I could sense Cassandra wince as Barbara was mentioned as an afterthought, but I doubt if anyone else caught her at it. That's how the game is played: never let them see you sweat, no matter what.

"So if you all have enough coffee to get through the next fifteen minutes," Mrs. James continued, "we'll start our program now."

It would be nice to report that an anticipatory murmur rose from the assemblage. It would also be untrue. Most of them figured rightly that sitting through a couple of political speeches at a party was going to be a pain in the ass, something to be borne with fortitude.

"To begin with, we'll hear from one of the candidates herself. You all know Barbara, so no long introductions will be necessary. Barbara?"

Barbara Corns stood up at her place, a few limp three-by-five cards in her hand, and marched to the podium as though mounting a gibbet. The tepid applause garnered by the nonintroduction wasn't quite sustained enough to get her all the way there, and by the time she reached the lectern the room was silent except for the wild clapping of Dennis Babb and Laurie Pirkle. The folks at their table looked at them as though they were little green people who'd just stepped off an alien spaceship.

Barbara fiddled with the microphone, then cleared a frog from her throat. It was the wrong order in which to do things—magnified by the speakers, the little cough sounded like a fender crumpling.

"First of all," she began, "I want to express my deepest sympathies to the True family in their bereavement. Everyone in our campaign feels terrible about what happened, and we want the Trues to know that our thoughts and prayers are with them."

Cassandra nodded her approval at me. Barbara probably meant it sincerely, but Cassie the election pro chose to think of it as a canny political move.

"But even in times of personal tragedy, the business of government must go on," Barbara said.

Al Drago stood up slightly and shifted his chair around so he was facing her directly, his mean eyes scorching her. It was clearly calculated on his part, and I could tell it shook her up pretty badly. She stared at him for a moment, faltering, forgetting her lines. Then she took a deep breath, glanced for too long a moment at her index cards, and proceeded to repeat what I had come to think of as The Speech.

It might as well have been on a cassette. I'd heard it before—so had several other people in the room, and I could sense their attention wandering. Mine, too, as Barbara went on in her thin little monotone. I took the opportunity to check out the guests. One silver-haired gentleman's chin sank quietly onto his chest; his wife didn't even bother giving him an angry nudge the way she might have during a Mahler concert at Severance Hall. I hoped he wouldn't snore aloud.

Next to me Cassandra Pride was chewing on the inside of her cheek, and I looked over and saw Evan Corns twisting his napkin as if he were wringing the neck of a chicken.

We heard again about why everyone had moved to Lake Erie Shores in the first place, and then finally, mercifully, it was over. There was some more applause, unenthusiastic except for Dennis and Laurie, and Barbara literally staggered back to her seat like a conventioneer on a three-day binge. Her husband glared at her fiercely.

Mrs. Arlen James took the podium again.

"Thank you, Barbara," she said. "That was very nice. And now, speaking for Mayor True, Mr. Tyler Rees."

As Rees sprang to the microphone I had to give it to Mrs. Arlen James for subtlety. Praise didn't get much more faint than "very nice." She might as well have patted Barbara on the head. And she was careful to call her by her first name while always referring to True by his full title.

Rees's blue jacket was shiny, and so was his pink scalp, but at least he didn't sweat as heavily as at the chamber mixer. He held no notes in his hand. He kept murmuring, "Thank you, thank you very much," until the applause had dwindled.

"Mayor True wants to convey his gratitude to each and every one of you for your good wishes and your expressions of sympathy," he said, leaning too close to the microphone and making the speakers resonate. His voice was a surprisingly deep baritone. "He wishes he could be here tonight, but of course it isn't possible. But he wants you to know that after the election he's going to be right back at City Hall, looking out for the interests of this town that he's served so well for so long."

Some people applauded, and Dennis Babb took it as a personal affront, skewering each of them with an angry scowl through his taped glasses with quick, erratic jerks of his head like an angry owl.

"The mayor has suffered a deep personal loss, and the fact that his wife's death is shrouded in mystery makes it all the more difficult for him."

A few of the listeners at the tables squirmed in their seats. They didn't want to hear about death shrouded in mystery. They wanted to hear about taxes and potholes. And more than that they wanted to go home.

"But Gayton True's love for his family has given him the strength to carry on." Rees's voice got louder, and he leaned in closer to the microphone, gripping the sides of the podium with both hands. "Lake Erie Shores is what they refer to as a bedroom community—and that means families. Families like yours, families that stay together through the bad times as well as the good. There's been a lot of talk lately in the political arena about family values—and a lot of laughs, too. But those are the values that made this country and this state and this town what they are. And I think the True family represents those values much better than the Corns family."

I turned to Cassie; her eyes were wide and unbelieving. In an era where fighting dirty has become a constant in political life, this was going to be the ultimate cheap shot, and from the expressions of shock around the room, completely unexpected.

But Rees wasn't through. His face was shiny with perspiration as he stared directly at Barbara and Evan. "I'm sure you all know what I'm talking about, and if you don't I'd be glad to tell you privately. It has to do with Evan and Barbara Corns's marriage."

The crowd gasped collectively, and Barbara jerked in her chair as though it had just been electrified. The circumstances of the Cornses' marriage—Evan having divorced his first wife to marry her—was, I supposed, an open secret in Lake Erie Shores, and in any event old news. But it wasn't the sort of thing one brought up publicly. Until now.

Rees had drawn blood and was hitting his stride. "Maybe the issue of character isn't so important to voters on the national level when it comes to dealing with the economy or with foreign powers or with health care. But in a city like Lake Erie Shores, I think it's doggone important, and I think you do too.

"So I came here tonight to ask for your prayers for Mayor True in his hour of bereavement, and I ask for you to say a loud and emphatic no to immorality and adultery, and I humbly beg your support in allowing him to continue keeping this community what it was meant to be—a textbook example of what Middle America is supposed to be about. A place where innocent people aren't run down in the street. A lovely, peaceful town where your families can flourish and grow in a climate of decency." He took a deep breath. "Will you help me?"

He paused then, staring from one face to the other, almost demanding applause. It was late in coming, and was engendered more by shock than any real enthusiasm.

Cassandra Pride's pretty brown face had turned gray. She shook her head and leaned close to me so I could hear her over the clapping. Her breath was warm in my ear. "True didn't have the stones to say that himself, at least not in public, but he let his pit bull say it instead, and he comes off clean."

"How much damage did it do?"

"You really want to know?" She smiled ruefully. "We're dead in the water."

Tyler Rees returned to his table like a victorious tribune reentering Rome, looking smug and self-satisfied. Crimson-faced,

Evan Corns jumped to his feet and started over to him purpose-fully, hands balled into fists, but Al Drago rose up in his path, wide as a shopping mall. I stood up quickly, ready to move, but it wasn't necessary. Evan stopped in mid step, a groundhog re-thinking his frontal assault on a rhinoceros. Drago just glared down at him, and all the air seemed to go out of him. He went stumbling backward, his hand groping behind him for his seat. When Drago was sure he'd made his point, he and Rees smirked at each other.

Dennis and Laurie rushed over to where a stunned Barbara sat, flapping around her like magpies, hugging and patting her, but she didn't even notice them; she had wished herself into an-other place, perhaps even another dimension.

"Where is the first Mrs. Corns these days?" I asked Cassie, thinking that perhaps she was a factor in this strange equation.

"They had a condo in Naples," Cassie said. "Naples, Florida. She moved there after the divorce. In a town this size she'd be running into Barbara and Evan every few minutes, so she figured she'd better get out of here."

I touched her hand. "I think we all better get out of here—the sooner the better."

She nodded and pushed herself away from the table.

Quite a few of the guests were standing now, in tight little cliques, muttering *sotto voce* about Rees's attack on the Corns's marriage. Nobody dared look at Barbara and Evan. Seeing their next-door neighbors naked was nearly as embarrassing for the inadvertent peepers as for the victims.

Cassandra and I moved toward the front of the room, and I squatted down beside Barbara's chair. "I think it's time to go," I said.

Evan Corns glowered at me, his mouth twisted into a snarl and the veins in his neck throbbing and bulging like an interactive exhibit at the Cleveland Health Museum. "We're damn well not going anywhere. If that fat son of a bitch thinks he can get away with—"

"Not here," I said sternly.

He blinked. "What?"

"I said not here. Let's go home and talk about it in private."

"Milan's right, Evan," Cassandra put in. "Let's just get out of here now."

His anger, barely contained behind his popping eyes, threatened to explode all over us, but then he took a good look at his wife and reconsidered. There were white lines of shock around her mouth.

Evan's chest heaved a couple of times and he finally managed to stand up, using the table for support. "All right then," he said in a choked voice, and took Barbara's elbow and almost lifted her out of her chair.

We made our way toward the door, and the crowd parted for us like we were ringing a leper's bell.

## CHAPTER TWELVE

The wind was tearing off the lake and across the headlands when we got out of Laird's Olde English Steak and Chop House. All the way out to the car Evan Corns was hissing obscenities through his teeth, and his neck was puffed out like a bullfrog's.

Cassandra put a hand on my arm and spoke softly so Dennis and Laurie couldn't hear her. "Let's meet back at the house, Milan."

She went off to her car and I joined the others at Evan's Buick. "We'll see you guys tomorrow, all right?" I said to the two volunteers.

"We want to go back with Barbara," Laurie whined.

And Dennis chimed in, "She needs us now."

"Barbara's very tired and needs her rest," I explained gently. "But I know she wants you at the office first thing in the morning, if you're free."

Dennis pouted but I ignored him. "Are you okay?" I asked Evan.

He shook his head angrily. "How in the name of Christ am I supposed to be okay?"

"Drive carefully then." I turned and started for my car, parked at the other end of the lot. I was nearly there when I saw Al Drago walking toward Evan and Barbara, and I felt the muscles in my neck and shoulders bunch up. I headed back for the Corns's car, trying to make it look casual.

Drago marched right up to Barbara, looming before her like a small mountain, and she shrunk away from him, holding her husband's arm for support. He stared her down for a very long moment and then shook his head, his lip curling with contempt.

"Why don't you fuckin' hang it up?" he said in his grating voice.

Barbara cried out and fell back against the front fender of the car, which was the only thing that kept her from hitting the ground. If Princess True had intimidated her with only a look, Drago could scare her half to death.

I quickened my pace, but before I could get there, little Dennis came tearing up, planting himself between Drago and Barbara, chest heaving and hands in front of him, ready to fight.

"Get out of here," he piped shrilly. Drago outweighed him by a hundred pounds and outclassed him by twenty years' street experience. But it didn't faze Dennis, whose adrenaline must have been coursing through him like the Colorado River.

"You keep away from Barbara, you big shit!" he yelled in Drago's face.

For just a second the huge man looked absolutely nonplussed. Then one corner of his mouth twitched a little—bad news. The only thing that made Al Drago smile was inflicting pain on another human being. He took a fistful of Dennis's corduroy jacket in his huge hand, lifting him up on tiptoes.

"You leave him alone!" Laurie screamed.

Drago looked at her as he might have a squirrel that had run across his path. "Mind your own business, you fat, ugly sow. Go take a bath—I can smell you from here."

She staggered backward as though he'd slapped her. In fact, from her point of view it might have been preferable.

I got there just in time to prevent a punch to the face that might have killed Dennis. "That's enough," I said.

Drago swiveled his neck around to me, his pig eyes like two lumps of black coal in his pasty white face. His right fist was drawn back ready to strike, and Dennis still dangled helplessly from his left one.

"Let him go," I said.

"Mind your business," he rumbled.

"He's a kid and he's littler than you. Take your hands off him."

He spat out an epithet, and I made a show of unbuttoning my coat so I could shrug it off in a hurry.

Evan Corns opened his mouth to say something but then wisely reconsidered.

Drago took his time thinking about it, but he finally released his grip on Dennis's jacket, dropping him the way he might drop a sack of garbage into a Dumpster. The kid shuddered and staggered away.

That left me. Drago turned and faced me directly, and it was as though a Sherman tank had just swiveled its cannon in my direction. He lowered his chin onto his chest and stared, his tongue flickering out to lick his nearly invisible lips. He looked like a huge lizard.

My past knowledge of him as a brawler was that he liked to eye-gouge and knee, and especially to butt with his head at close quarters; apparently he'd yet to find anyone with a skull harder than his own. Even as big as I am, my only chance was to not let him get close.

"Go home, Dennis," I said, but I didn't take my eyes off Drago.

For a long while nobody moved. Evan and Barbara were frozen to the spot next to their car, and Laurie and Dennis were watching from about thirty feet away. Drago was absolutely motionless, as if he'd been built there, and I wasn't going to be the first one to flinch. It was absurdly like the final facedown on a frontier street, black hat versus white.

He took a deep breath, expanding his already enormous chest to the size of a parade float. I bent my knees slightly, shifting my weight forward on the balls of my feet to make myself as mobile as possible.

And then something took the fight out of him, or seemed to. He expelled most of the air from his lungs, rocked back on his heels like a house settling onto its foundation, and relaxed—at least as much as Aloysius Drago ever relaxed. He lifted his head slightly, and his black eyes glittered.

"Some other time, asshole," he said. I remembered where I'd heard a voice that sounded that way before: Mercedes McCambridge in *The Exorcist*.

He did a one-eighty like a battleship changing course and walked back across the parking lot toward the restaurant, his gait rolling and his shoulders hunched.

It was my turn to be stunned. I'd been ready for a fight and never more surprised when it failed to materialize.

I waited until Drago climbed into his own car, a black Ford LTD that probably had once belonged to the Cleveland Police Department. As he rumbled out of the parking lot I went back to Evan and Barbara.

"Go on home," I said to Barbara, and opened the door of their car for her. "I'll meet you there."

Barbara puddled onto the passenger seat, almost falling over backwards.

"Get hold of yourself, Barbara," Evan commanded, but he seemed almost as rocky as she.

"Not tonight!" It was as firm a declaration as I'd ever heard her make. "I just want to crawl into bed and forget tonight ever happened." She smiled an apology up at me. "I'm sorry, Milan. Come by in the morning and we'll talk."

She squeezed my hand and then drew the tail of her coat around her legs and shut the door.

Evan jangled his keys in his hand, and his voice was subdued. "I had no idea they'd ever play this dirty."

"Rees is the mayor's hatchet boy," I said. "He can say things True can't. Get some sleep, Evan. We'll talk about this tomorrow."

He put a gloved hand on my arm. "I've been shitty to you, Milan. I want to apologize. It's just my way sometimes. I've been under an awful lot of pressure."

"Take it easy, all right?" I shook his hand. As I crossed the lot to my car I noticed Donald Straum near the chop house entrance talking feverishly to the pothole lady whom I'd sat next to at dinner. Her husband, who I realized hadn't spoken a single word all evening, stood off to one side not paying any attention to them. His hands were in the pockets of his cashmere overcoat, and he was gazing off toward the far horizon. Maybe he was thinking about Tahiti.

A fine drizzle misted the windshield as I drove back home, and my car heater was keeping me toasty as jazz music from WCPN public radio kept my toe tapping. I'd kicked in for a membership during their fall pledge drive, so listening to their station gave me a proprietary feeling.

It had been a difficult evening for everyone, and I was glad it was over. But it had given me a lot to think about.

First of all, after welcoming Donald Straum into her home for the kaffeeklatsch a few days before, Mrs. James had seemed rather agitated when he showed up at the restaurant. I wanted to know why. I made a mental note to make an index card for Mrs. Arlen James as soon as I got home.

And then there was Al Drago.

There are very few certainties in this world, but one of them was that Al Drago hated my guts. I knew he wanted to mess with me, needed to, the way he needed food and water—in fact, I'd been rather expecting him to pop up in some dark alley for the last year. I couldn't imagine why he had let the opportunity to tear my head off go by.

But he'd just walked away, his snarled obscenity a hanging echo on the cold wind, and there I was with my coat half off my shoulders, ready for a battle that wasn't going to happen. At least not then.

It wasn't like him at all, and it troubled me.

Something else was bothering me, too, buzzing behind my ear, but I couldn't seem to call it up and bring it into focus. Too much had gone on in the last few hours, and I was approaching sensory overload.

I shivered despite the efforts of my heater. There was no question about it, winter was coming, and along with the cold and the snow, it meant Cleveland wouldn't be seeing much of the sun again for several months. The advent of the cold weather didn't really bother me; I rather enjoy the winter, except on the few days a year when we get battered by real blizzards, and those are the days I'm even more glad I'm self-employed and can work out of my apartment. My office is twenty feet from my bed, and when Dick Goddard, Channel Eight's weather maven, warns people about whiteout conditions on the Shoreway, I simply turn up the thermostat and live off whatever food happens to be in my freezer. Unless it's absolutely necessary, I never go outside.

But I do miss the warming touch of the sun now and then.

When I got to my apartment door I heard the chirrup of the

phone inside. There's nothing more frustrating than being on the wrong side of a locked door when your telephone is ringing. Fumbling with my keys, I managed to get both locks open and grab the call before the answering machine did.

"Mr. Jacovich, this is John Terranova." The voice was vaguely familiar. I couldn't place the name, though, until he added, "From Mr. D'Allessandro."

John. The guy from the Ristorante Vesuvio. The guy who, six years ago, came to my door with two other goons and beat the crap out of me with gloved fists and a sock full of sand. That John.

"What's up, John?"

"Mr. D'Allessandro asked me to deliver something to you." I checked my watch; it was a few minutes after ten. "Now?"

"I'm right down the hill at the Vesuvio," he said. "Having a couple of pops. I can be there in five minutes."

"The last time you delivered something to me, I didn't like it very much. I don't forget things like that, John."

"That was a long time ago. Besides, it isn't like that." He waited for a few seconds. "If you wanta do something about that I guess I'll oblige you, but to tell you the truth I forgot about it a week after it happened."

"That's because you were pitching and I was catching."

"Look, this is my night off, but the old man asked me to deliver this to you, and if I don't I'm gonna get yelled at in the morning, okay? Gimme a break—it won't take but a second."

I sighed. "Come alone, then."

"Hey!" he said, dropping the *h*. "So who'm I gonna bring?"

Five minutes was more like fifteen, enough time for me to take off my coat, suit, and tie and throw on a sweatshirt and jeans. The shirt was from the University of Maryland, white with red letters, and I don't even remember where I got it.

Pretty soon John Terranova was standing in my hallway, wearing the same jacket with the fake fur collar, and a shiny brown sports shirt buttoned to the neck. The jacket was too bulky for me to make out whether he had anything hard and metallic under his arm.

"Come on in," I said.

He kicked at the worn carpet outside my door. "I don't wanta bother you."

"It's all right, I just got home. I'm going to unwind a few minutes."

Hesitantly he crossed the threshold, looking around at the front room I use for an office.

"You work here and live here too, huh?"

"Saves a fortune on office rent."

"Pretty nice."

"You've been here before," I reminded him, and he looked down at the floor. "Make yourself at home. You want a beer or something?"

He seemed pleasantly surprised. "I wouldn't say no."

I went into the kitchen and got two cans of Stroh's. When I got back he was sitting in my most uncomfortable chair with his ankle crossed over his knee. He hadn't taken off his jacket, but he'd unzipped it all the way, and I still couldn't see any hardware.

He wasn't a bad-looking guy, with close-cropped black hair and thick, sensual lips. His sideburns were a little too long to be fashionable and curled in toward his mouth like those of the older, fatter Elvis, but he sported a five o'clock shadow that I supposed women like these days. A curved pink scar about three inches long ran from the side of his mouth up toward his ear. His natural complexion was swarthy, but his face had an unhealthy gray undercast, and the whites of his brown eyes were yellowish.

After facing down Al Drago earlier in the evening I'd had my fill of hard guys, but there was something about John Terranova that gave you the feeling he came close to the state of evolution most of the rest of us have reached, and I found myself strangely comfortable with him.

I handed him a beer and sat down on the other client chair. I figured that going behind my desk and looking businesslike was a little too much for that time of night. "So, John. I haven't seen you around for a long while."

"I been outta town." He pulled the tab on the can and a spume of foam shot out through the hole. "Not too far outta town, though."

"Lorain?" There's a correctional facility in Lorain, one county west of Cuyahoga.

He nodded. "Good guess."

"Shot in the dark," I said.

"It wasn't too bad. I got to work in the liberry. I kind of enjoyed that part."

Not enough to pronounce it properly, I thought. "How long you been out?"

"Three months. I'm still on parole, which is why I'm not packing heat." He grinned. "I saw you checking that out."

"A girl can't be too careful," I said.

He toasted me silently with the beer can, took a deep swallow, and exhaled noisily. His expression could best be described as beatific. "Three months back on the outside now and I still can't get over how good a cold beer tastes."

"I've got more."

He shook his head. "I don't wanta take up no more of your time."

"John, you had a guy you worked with back when I first met you. Mean little punk, wore sunglasses with mirrors all the time. Joey."

"Joey, yeah."

"He's usually hanging around Mr. D'Allessandro, but I didn't notice him this morning. Where's he?"

"He's outta town too."

"That figures. I never liked him, Joey. With him I took it personally."

"Yeah, well Joey could be a real *strunz*, you know? Bad temper. Like that guy Sonny in . . ." He smiled, thinking about what must have been his favorite movie and his favorite character, Sonny Corleone, but clearly thought better of making the analogy. He cocked his head at me. "Hey, do me a favor?"

"What's that?"

"Fill me in."

"On what?"

"On where you fit."

I took a gulp of my own beer. "Where I fit?"

"Last time I saw you Mr. Gaimari was pissed off enough at you to have you punched out. Now all of a sudden you're having breakfast with him and the old man and I'm delivering secret messages to you in the middle of the night. And you ain't even Italian."

"So?"

"So where do you fit?"

The question made me uncomfortable, because it was one Marko Meglich had asked me, one I'd been asking myself a lot in the last few days. I cleared my throat. "Life takes funny turns, John. It just happened that I got involved with a few things that your people were into, and from what I heard, Don Giancarlo likes my style. So every once in a while when he's got a need for someone like me, he throws the business my way. No muscle stuff, and nothing illegal. I'm not in the family yet—and I won't ever be."

"That's it?"

"That's it. And he pays well." I couldn't believe how hollow that sounded, and I nearly emptied the beer can in one long guzzle as if that might wash away what I'd just said. It didn't, but it made my eyes tear.

"Hey, lemme give you what I came to give you and then I'll get outta your hair." He set his drink down on the desk and reached into his back pocket for a slightly worse for wear number-ten envelope and handed it to me. It had my name typed on it. "Mr. D'Allessandro says everything's in here. I guess you're supposed to know what that means, huh?"

"I guess," I said.

"Hey, about that business a few years ago. You know."

"Yeah, I know."

"I just want you t'know I never had nothing against you. I work for a guy, I take his money, I gotta do what he says to. Right?"

"Right."

"Yeah. Well, I just wanted you t'know."

He unwound from the chair and I got up too and walked him to the door.

"John?" I said when he was out in the hallway.

"Yo?"

"What were you—out of town for?" It's the kind of question one isn't supposed to ask, but my curiosity got the better of me.

He didn't seem to take offense, though, and his gaze was level. "Manslaughter," he said. Then he headed off down the corridor and disappeared into the stairwell.

I closed and locked the door and leaned against it while I thumbed open the envelope he'd given me. Then I went and sat down behind my desk, switched on the little desk lamp with the green shade, and extracted the single sheet of paper inside. Elegant paper with scalloped edges and a high rag content, too small for the envelope in which it came, and wrinkled from several hours in John Terranova's hip pocket.

On it was typed an address on Old Furnace Road in Youngstown. Beneath that, *3 p.m. Thursday. Mr. C.*, was written in longhand. It looked to have been done with a fountain pen, and I recognized the handwriting as Victor Gaimari's.

## CHAPTER THIRTEEN

When I arrived at the Corns household at ten the next morning, the candidate was still in her bathrobe, with no makeup to disguise her natural pallor and her bangs in two large pink curlers bobbing over her forehead. She paced the living room like it was a zoo cage, her fuzzy slippers slapping on the rug and her coffee mug clutched in both hands, and when she stopped moving to sip from it she reminded me of a little girl drinking juice from a plastic cup. Her eyes were red-rimmed and puffy.

Cassandra Pride had answered the door, and now we were seated at either end of the sofa with nothing to look at except Barbara moving back and forth across the room. Cassandra had a clipboard to which a yellow legal pad had been affixed, and she clicked the button on her ballpoint pen in and out. She seemed anxious to get started, but so far the yellow pad was virginal.

"Evan'll be down in a minute," she said, more to calm her own impatience than mine. "He's been on the phone half an hour."

Barbara glanced up at the ceiling, as though she might see through it to discover what was keeping her husband. The house was warm, but she shivered nonetheless.

After a few more minutes the silence got to me. "How are you doing this morning, Barbara?"

She just looked at me.

"You're not going to let a little nerd like Tyler Rees upset you, are you?"

"It wasn't you on the receiving end," she said quietly. "How could he have said something like that in public—with Evan and me sitting right in front of him?"

"Modern politics," Cassie said. "I think we're getting off easy. Look at the Mary Rose Oakar and Margaret Mueller congressional races, and Mike DeWine's campaign against John Glenn for the Senate in 1992 right here in Ohio. Politics doesn't get much uglier than that."

"And don't forget Bush calling Clinton and Gore bozos," I reminded her. "We've come a long way from when politicians used to refer to one another as 'my distinguished opponent.'"

"If it makes you feel any better," Cassie said, "the ones who slung the most mud that year all lost."

"Small comfort," Barbara said.

Evan came clattering down the stairs, making enough noise for a man twice his size. He was in his shirt sleeves and a flowered tie, and he didn't bother saying good morning to any of us. He looked almost as pale as his wife, and the muscles in his face had tightened and solidified into an instant facelift.

He parked himself in the middle of the room, fists on hips. "Okay. Let's identify our problems and then solve them."

*Identify* is one of those new business buzzwords that go along with *network* and *impact*.

"Let's talk damage assessment. Cassie?"

"It's not good, Evan. How could it be?"

"It could be worse," I said. "There were no more than fifty people there."

Evan wheeled on me. "By lunchtime half the town will have heard about it, and the rest by dinner. I'll bet Alice James was on the phone ten minutes after the party broke up."

Alice. Now I knew Mrs. Arlen James had a first name.

"Even if she wasn't," Cassandra said, "fifty votes in a town this size is a lot."

"I don't imagine anyone there hadn't already heard about your marriage, Evan," I said. "And Tyler's having the bad taste to mention it right in front of you and Barbara just might backfire on him."

Cassandra spat air from between pursed lips. "It might, but I'd hate like hell to count on that."

"The question is," Evan grated, "what do we do about it? How do we get those fifty votes back? Suggestions?"

Nobody said anything for a while, and Barbara, who had been standing perfectly still against the windows at the far end of the room since Evan's arrival, began her pacing again.

"How about fighting fire with fire?" I ventured.

"Talk English, for Christ's sake!" The olive branch Evan had extended to me at the end of the previous evening seemed to have withered and died overnight.

"Take off the gloves, like they did. Let the voters know about True's son helping elderly blind people mark their ballots in the primary. That's unethical, and probably illegal."

Evan Corns gnawed on his lower lip. "I don't like it," he said. "I never did like it. Besides, it's old news. The primary was four months ago."

"So what?"

"People will ask why we didn't bring it up sooner."

I shrugged. "Tell them it just came to our attention."

"That won't fly. I don't like it. And I'm tired of talking about it. At this late date it's a nonissue."

"All right then, how about this? Tyler Rees talks about the kind of family voters want representing them when the mayor's brother-in-law is under indictment for peddling dirty pictures of small children? Is kiddie porn a nonissue, too?"

Evan swatted his hand in my direction as if giving me a slap on the side of the head, even though I was halfway across the room. "He can't help who his brother-in-law is."

"You asked for suggestions, Evan. I gave you two. It's admirable that you don't want to start slinging mud. But they threw the first shovelful."

"Two wrongs don't make a right."

"Evan, we've got to start fighting!" Barbara said suddenly. "We've got plenty of ammunition."

I said, "They had a hell of a nerve bringing up the circumstances of your marriage when the whole town knows Gay and Princess used to go ten rounds every Saturday night."

Evan shoved his hands into his pockets. "Well, they didn't come right out and accuse us of adultery."

Barbara gasped.

"Screw it, Barbara! Let's call a spade a spade."

Cassandra drew her legs up under her, "The woman is dead. We start attacking her now, we're going to look like the monsters of the midway."

"Yeah, how about that?" Evan came and stood over me with his fists on his hips, glad to have a new rat to shake. "You were supposed to be checking up on the hit-and-run, Milan. What's happening with that?"

"I have a lead to follow up tomorrow," I said uneasily.

"What lead?"

"I can't tell you."

He crossed his arms across his chest. "What kind of shit is that? The election is less than a week away, you've got a lead, and you can't tell me?"

"It may be nothing, and until I get something concrete there's no point in talking about it. Besides, it was given to me in confidence."

"Who the hell's paying you, anyway?"

"Victor Gaimari."

He must have forgotten that for a moment, because it set him back on his heels. He dropped his hands to his sides, his eyes flickering around the room. Then he got his composure back. "Well, I just talked to Victor," he announced pompously, making it sound like he had been on the phone to the White House. "And he thinks the Princess True accident needs to be cleared up ASAP. So you better get your ass in gear and be a detective, because you really stink at being a politician."

I stood up, my sheer bulk backing him off a few steps. "Evan," I said, "when this election is over, you and I are going to have a long talk about employee-employer relations. Look forward to it."

Hollow threat number 453.


The Lake Erie Shores Homeless Project was housed in a two-room office in a red brick Georgian office building about three blocks off the square, one of those buildings designed expressly to look quaint. The project announced its presence with an inexpensive cardboard placard taped beside the door at the rear of the second-floor hallway.

The reception area looked a lot like the Corns campaign head-quarters, with makeshift furniture, two used-looking filing cabinets, and several cardboard cartons stuffed with papers and folders placed out of the way against the wall. A middle-aged woman at the desk cradled a phone between chin and shoulder. She raised a hand to me, indicating she'd be through in a minute.

"Is there any way you can have those delivered directly to the shelter?" she was saying. "We're on a small budget here, I'm afraid, and we don't have any extra manpower available to come and pick them up."

She listened for a while, and I could hear a metallic voice filtering through the earpiece. She made a sour face at me. "All right, then, if you can't, I suppose I'll have to come by and get them myself on my way home. About five thirty?"

Her eyebrows climbed almost into her hairline as she listened some more. "Not until seven?" Her shoulders slumped and she had to catch the phone before it fell onto the desk. "Okay, I'll be there around seven. Thank you so much."

She put the phone down grimly. "If I don't start getting home in time for dinner once in a while, I'm going to be homeless my-self—my husband's going to toss me out on the street." I wasn't sure if she was talking to me or to herself.

"Hi," I said. "I'm looking for Kellen Charles."

Kellen appeared in the doorway to the inner office, looking even better than I'd remembered. "You found her, and not a moment too soon." Her hand went up to touch her golden bangs. "This has been one of those mornings. What a pleasant surprise."

"I was in the neighborhood," I said lamely.

I followed her into her office, and she shut the door behind me. The office was furnished even more spartanly than the outer room. A huge corkboard had been mounted on the wall behind the desk, and it was nearly obliterated by all sorts of papers and notices affixed with yellow-headed push pins to its surface. Against the wall was a swaybacked couch with orange plaid upholstery that must have come from someone's rumpus room, probably donated after the kids grew up and went off to college. The one wide window looked out on a stand of trees behind the building, which, in autumn anyway, was a decided improvement over a view of the nondescript street in front.

"How did the political shindig go last night?" Kellen asked, sitting down at one end of the couch and patting the cushion next to her in invitation.

"It ranks right up there with the *Titanic* and the *Hindenburg*," I said. I encapsulated the evening for her, including Tyler Rees's remarks. A vertical line of worry appeared between her pretty eyes.

"They're not going to quit," she said sadly. "There's too much at stake."

"*What's* at stake, Kellen? You started to tell me at campaign headquarters the other day, and then you ran off."

"I did?"

"You said that everybody knew who wanted Barbara to lose the campaign, but you didn't stick around long enough to elaborate."

She stared at me. "You're kidding. You're one of the honchos on Barbara's team and you don't know?"

"I haven't even been around a week."

She leaned toward me, obviously warming to the subject. "Why do you suppose I'm so committed to getting Gayton True out of City Hall? He doesn't give a damn about the homeless because they don't vote, and that makes me angry. But the big thing—and this will tie up so much public money that we'll be lucky to get a trickle coming into this office for people that have nothing to look forward to this winter except maybe freezing to death—is that if True gets in again, he's going to push through a progambling ordinance in this town, and a tax abatement for a big casino out on the lake to go with it.

I sat back against the thin cushion. "I never heard anything about that," I said weakly.

"True hasn't gone public with it, for a lot of good reasons. But when it happens, he can justify it because the construction will provide a lot of jobs—except you and I both know damn few of those jobs will get any homeless people off the street. It'll be business as usual. And he'll claim—rightly—that a casino will expand the tax base and bring a lot of money into town. And the fat cats will like it because it'll put Lake Erie Shores on the map. So there's a lot of people around here, and elsewhere, that would like to see Barbara crash and burn."

I tried not to notice how attractive she was when she was angry. "Even so," I said. "This is a family community, as True has taken pains to point out. People like the Arlen Jameses are going to be damn upset about a casino down on the corner."

"Milan, do you have any idea the type of people legalized gambling will attract?"

"Bookmakers and hookers and pickpockets, I'd imagine."

"That's only the beginning. One casino opens the door to another, and pretty soon Lake Erie Shores is another Central City, Colorado, with charter buses coming in from Cleveland and Erie and Pittsburgh every hour. They'll turn some public land over for parking lots—some of the little pocket parks we have all over town—and that means cutting down trees and pulling up grass and flowers. Or else they'll tear down some of our old, beautiful buildings. Traffic will be a nightmare, the air will get polluted and so will the lake, and they'll have to double the police force. The town won't be fit to live in anymore."

"If True did that," I said, "he'd never win another election."

"Do you really think he'll care, Milan? He's been in somebody or other's pocket since before he got elected the first time. Right now it's the heavy money behind the casino. He'll be rich enough not to care about getting reelected."

"He's already rich."

"What's too rich? And if he pulls this off there's always the county party chairmanship, and that means power. To a man like Gay True, power is a lot more important than money."

"I thought Judge Guilfoyle had that all sewed up."

"Guilfoyle is an embarrassment and a drunk. If True builds the casino he can ease Guilfoyle out with a nudge."

I pulled a pack of cigarettes out of my pocket; I suddenly had to do something with my hands. "Mind if I smoke?"

"Go ahead," she told me. "I'd like one, too, and I don't smoke. What I'd really like is a drink, and it's not even lunchtime yet." She ran both hands through her hair, and I thought how pretty it looked as it slipped between her fingers.

I lit one up and tried to blow the smoke away from her. "Why hasn't Barbara made an issue out of this, or at least brought it to anyone's attention?"

Kellen Charles shrugged her shoulders fetchingly. "Don't even talk to me about how the Cornses have run this race," she said. "The word that comes to mind is inept."

"But you're still working for them, still going in and folding campaign literature. What makes you think Barbara won't be just as inept in the mayor's office?"

"She will be," Kellen said. "But that's better than letting True sell this town out to line his pockets, isn't it? I'd rather have a wimp in City Hall than an out-and-out crook!"

"Sometimes an ineffective public official can do more damage than a crooked one."

She wrinkled her nose. "Whose side are you on, Milan?" I sucked a lungful of smoke deep, feeling the bite. "I'm beginning to wonder."

# CHAPTER FOURTEEN

I didn't leave before inviting Kellen Charles to dinner on Friday night. I'm slow, but I'm not stupid.

But my mind wasn't on romance as I headed down I-90. I was thinking about what she'd said, about Gayton True and the possibility of a casino, which would turn Lake Erie Shores into a glitzy lakeside mecca for all sorts of people the solid citizens wouldn't particularly welcome.

And I was wondering why in hell nobody connected with the Barbara Corns campaign had told me about it.

I wheeled my car into the old neighborhood, St. Clair Avenue in the east Sixties. Before World War II the area just north of here, built on landfill, was a kind of Slovenian shantytown often referred to as Chicken Village, because almost every house had an occupied chicken coop behind it until the terrifying East Ohio Gas explosion in 1944 that practically obliterated it.

Parking in a one-hour zone with the hope that if I overstayed my welcome no sharp-eyed traffic cop would notice, I dropped into Azman & Sons on St. Clair and bought some freshly made klobasa sausage. The store has been there since 1919, and the sons in question are three cheerful men in their seventies and eighties who work behind the meat counter six days a week. Cleveland is a city of immigrants' children.

The Slovenian Country House is a mile further west in a store-front, mere steps from where I was born. Its wood-paneled walls and cheerful prints and artifacts from Slovenia add to the ambience, as does the pretty blue-eyed lady who runs it. Slovenian women tend to have lots of dimples.

Marko was at a table near the window, surrounded by hanging plants, a diorama of Slovenia on the wall behind him. I sat down across from him without being invited.

"The desk sergeant told me you were here," I said. "I should have figured."

He wasn't happy to see me. "I'm not buying you lunch."

"I can buy my own lunch. You still mad at me?"

"Mad at you? Jesus, Milan, you're like a little kid, I swear to God! Mad at you." He forked roast pork with gravy into his mouth as if someone were timing him.

The waitress came over and I asked for a Goldhorn Club, a tangy beer brewed in Slovenia that's sometimes hard to find in the stores. When it arrived I ordered the same thing Marko was having, since it looked so good.

"We have to talk about D'Allessandro and Gaimari," I said when the waitress had returned to the kitchen.

He wiped his mouth angrily. "I don't discuss disgusting things while I'm eating. Go sit at another table."

"Can you just listen to me?"

"What, God damn it? You want to tell me why you're taking dirty money and I don't want to hear it."

"Dirty money is redundant," I said. "Everybody has a hustle, everybody cuts corners."

"You never did," he said accusingly. "That was the one thing about you—you never cut a corner in your life. You've been beaten up and shot at because you wouldn't cut corners, you lost your girlfriend over it. You were the one constant, the guy Diogenes was looking for. One stand-up guy I could always count on like the sun coming up in the east. Milan Jacovich always played it straight."

"I still do."

He pointed his knife at me, and a blob of gravy dripped off onto the table. "Not if you're taking from the mob. If you're taking from the mob, you're twisted."

I sat back in the wooden chair, frustrated. "Will you try looking at this with some kind of perspective? It's election time. There's a little woman up in Lake Erie Shores who's trying to become mayor, and she's been getting threatening phone calls. Her husband does legit business with Gaimari—they're friends—and Gaimari asked me to go and make sure she doesn't get hurt."

"Over a small-town election? Cut me a break."

"It's more than that now. A woman has been killed—and in your ballpark, too, Marko."

"Accidental hit-and-run, until I hear otherwise."

"Maybe it was an accident, maybe not. I don't want it to happen to Barbara too. What I'm doing is not only legitimate, but it falls right into line with how I make my living. What's the difference who's paying for it?"

"Time was, it would've made a difference to you. Jesus, if you need the money that bad I'll loan you some."

"It's not the money."

"Then what?"

The waitress brought my lunch, but I didn't start eating right away. I just pushed the chunks of pork around in the gravy with my fork, trying to frame my answer carefully. "Last year Gaimari and D'Allessandro did me a favor."

His eyes flashed. "I know about their favors."

"Well, this was a biggie."

"They break somebody's legs for you, Milan? Or was it even worse?"

"You know better than that."

"I don't know jackshit."

"They helped me keep a kid out of jail—maybe out of the morgue. A kid we know."

He stopped eating. "You talking about Paulie Baznik?" I nodded.

"How?"

"That's not important. They did it. Or at least they tried."

He frowned, trying to remember. "That's why you wouldn't talk to the feds, isn't it? You wouldn't roll over on whoever told you."

"Something like that."

He took a sip of water. Marko is as big a beer drinker as I am, but he was on duty. "I still don't see what that's got to do with Lake Erie Shores."

"Nothing. It has to do with paying back. I told them I wouldn't do anything kinky for them, but when they asked me to get in on this election it sounded legit, so I signed on. But I just learned a new wrinkle this morning, if it's true, and I thought you might be interested."

"Try me."

"Rumor is that if Gay True gets reelected he's going to legalize gambling in Lake Erie Shores and build a casino."

"So?"

That stopped me for a minute. "What do you mean, so?"

"I don't care if Jeffrey Dahmer opens up a meat-packing plant in Lake Erie Shores," Marko said. "In case you forgot, I work for the city of Cleveland, and believe me, I've got enough problems right here."

I shook my head sadly. "And you accuse me of selective morality!"

"I'm doing a job."

"I'm talking about your job. About finding out who ran down a woman in broad daylight, on your street, in your territory. Maybe I can help you and maybe you can help me."

"I don't need your help!"

"So if I find out what the deal was about Mrs. True I should just keep it to myself?"

"That's withholding evidence."

"Christ, Marko, are you that desperate to make a collar?" His shoulders slumped. "Shit," he said quietly. "What do you want from me? Blood?"

"Just some help. On the Princess True hit-and-run."

He didn't say anything for a while. Then he took another sip of water. "I guess it wouldn't hurt anything." He settled back in his chair, weary, I supposed, of fighting with me, crumpling up his napkin and tossing it onto the table. "Hurry up and eat your lunch," he said, "and then come on back to the office."

"I'm so thrilled I have your blessing." I couldn't disguise the sarcasm.

"I got your blessing right here," he said.


Marko picked up his messages from the sergeant at the desk and I followed him upstairs to his office. He hung his overcoat and his suit jacket on plastic hangers on a hook behind his door. Marko Meglich is probably the only cop in the world who uses hangers.

He ruffled through the message slips. "You'll have to wait," he said, pointing a manicured finger at the chair across from his desk. Then he sat down and proceeded to return four phone calls, making notes about each of them. Fifteen minutes of my life ticked by, each one lasting a week.

Finally he opened his desk drawer and pulled out a file I'd seen before, except that it was a lot fatter than it had been two days earlier. He perused its contents for a few minutes, being careful to hold it so I couldn't see them. His brow wrinkled in concentration; he might have been studying the Koran.

"We called in a forensic tire specialist," he said. "More often than not an unsophisticated police department will screw up tire evidence, or ignore it. But we were right on top of it, got the forensic guys from downtown in on this. It's amazing what they can do. They took some pictures and—here, you want to see them?"

"Sure."

"Not pretty," he warned.

I took several eight-by-ten glossies from his outstretched hand. They were photographs of Princess True, nude, laid out on a steel table in the morgue. One side of her body looked almost caved-in, with lacerations and deep black bruises. A jagged end of her hip bone poked out through the torn skin.

The roast pork I'd eaten for lunch was reminding the back of my throat how good it had been. I pushed the pictures back at him.

"It was kind of fascinating, really," Marko said. "The guy took these with a tripod at an absolutely perpendicular angle. See, if you take the shot at an oblique angle, everything gets distorted—like a circle will appear as an ellipse." The way he recited this made me believe he'd only recently memorized it.

"What's this ruler doing next to the body?" I said.

"That's so they can get the scale right when he's figuring out the tire treads."

"What tire treads?"

He pushed the photos back toward me and pointed to places on the first one with the tip of his pen. "Look here, Milan. See those bruises?"

"How could I not?"

"Tires can leave tracks on the skin, you know."

He put on his glasses—those half-glasses people use for reading, and I'm sure Marko never wears them where anyone can see him. I guess he's just known me too long to be vain. I've seen him in the shower room.

He came around to my side of the desk and shuffled the pictures to an extreme close-up of the bruises. "Now every tire has what they call sipes. You know what a sipe is?"

"I know what a *Brian Sipe* is. Quarterback for the Browns before Bernie Kosar."

"Cute, Milan. Sipes are small, random cutouts put in tires to give them their wet pavement traction. The sipes wear down, the patterns change the longer you drive on them. Sometimes there'll be a small stone or a pebble in one of the sipes and it'll stay there for thousands of miles. See there, that little irregular mark? That's from a little rock in the sipe."

"I don't see how any of this—"

"Shut up and you will. Now. This is a retread, the guy could tell. You know what a retread is, don't you?"

"It's a reconditioned tire, right?"

"Well, yeah. But what they do is, they take the carcass of the tire and they butt-splice the retread around it with a bonding agent before it's vulcanized." He said this with great authority, as if he'd written his master's thesis on the subject. Marko can be a pompous ass sometimes.

"Did you know that most tires on commercial airplanes are retreads? They have to replace them fairly often, what with all the friction of landing and braking and all that stuff, so retreads are much more economically feasible than new tires." He laughed. "The airlines don't talk about that very much."

"You mean Mrs. True was run over by an airplane?"

"Don't be funny," he said severely. "This isn't funny. Okay, so the forensics guy comes in, takes the pictures, checks out the noise treatment—"

"The what?"

"There are varying pitch lengths of tread pattern on every tire, mostly random. That's called the noise treatment, they make tires like that because otherwise we wouldn't be able to hear ourselves think on the highway. Now you find the tire, and there's only one section on it where the pattern would be similar."

"That's the trick, Marko. Find the tire."

"It's not as much of a trick as it was two days ago. The guy said that this is a retread of a one nine five seven five fifteen."

"What does that mean?"

"That's a tire size, and it means that it probably came from a Ford pickup, somewhere around 1983."

"We already knew it was a Ford pickup."

"Yeah, but not 1983. So I'm having the Motor Vehicles Bureau run all the eighty-three Ford pickups in Cuyahoga County."

"You're forgetting something," I said.

"What?"

"Mrs. True lived in Lake Erie Shores. If the hit-and-run was deliberate, like I think it was, chances are the vehicle is from Lake County, not Cuyahoga."

His face fell. "Shit," he said. Marko had a limited vocabulary these days.

"I want to know why I wasn't told!" I barked. I had my desk phone to my ear and was walking the perimeter of my office–living room as far as the cord would reach, puffing furiously on a cigarette. The can from my first beer of the afternoon was on my desk, squeezed in the middle, and the second was in my hand.

"I don't see what you're getting so excited about," Victor Gaimari was saying on the other end of the line, and his voice was soothing, placating, syrupy.

"I'm getting excited, Victor, because I don't like walking into situations blind."

"Would it have made any difference in the way you did your job, knowing about True's plans for bringing in gambling?"

"That isn't the point!"

"It's exactly the point," he said. "If I hire a man to paint the outside of my house, I don't give him a schematic of the electrical wiring, hand him my Dun & Bradstreet report, or tell him what I had for breakfast, or share with him who I was with on Saturday night. You were told what you needed to know, and I thought that was sufficient. I still do."

I stubbed my cigarette in an ashtray like I was mad at it.

"You were told all you had to know about Barbara's campaign,"

Victor continued. "That's where you were going to work. But the election's less than a week away, and neither you nor the police have come up with any answers about what really happened to poor Mrs. True, and that's very disappointing."

"I'm working on that. That's why I'm going to Youngstown tomorrow."

He sighed rather pettishly. "That's going to be a waste of time, if you ask me. Barbara needs you there with her."

"Victor, you've known me long enough to realize that I do things my own way."

"Well, frankly, it's a pain in the ass."

"You want your money back?"

"Don't use that tone with me, Milan, I don't like it. Now, it's been a long hard day and I'm not going to argue with you any further. You aren't the guardian of the world's morals, you're a security specialist, and for the next few days, a campaign advisor. Wearing the first hat you're going to find out what happened to Princess True, and wearing the second you're going to do whatever you can to help Barbara Corns get elected, and to keep her shielded from any unpleasantness." He cleared his throat discreetly. "You haven't forgotten about our bonus arrangement if she wins, have you?"

"No, but I'm not running out and pricing Cadillacs."

"Oh?"

"It doesn't look good, Victor. Barbara's a terrible campaigner, for one thing. She doesn't know how to talk to people. For another, True's crowd has gone after Barbara and Evan about his divorcing his first wife to marry her. And worst of all, nobody in the Corns camp seems even slightly interested in fighting back."

There was no sound on the other end of the line for a while, and I was afraid he'd hung up, but then he said, "No one ever promised you it was going to be easy."

## CHAPTER FIFTEEN

Before 1992, driving from Cleveland to Youngstown was a major production, getting on freeways, getting off freeways, getting on surface roads, then onto turnpikes. But after thirty years of sitting on their hands, the state finally approved and completed a connector link of U.S. 422 that provides a practically straight shot from Cuyahoga County east into the Mahoning Valley.

Although it only takes ninety minutes or so and is a pretty drive through one of the most heavily wooded sections of the state, most Clevelanders have never been to Youngstown. This visit was only the second in my lifetime.

Youngstown used to be a steel town; it isn't any more. Back in the forties there was an exceptionally classy welterweight boxer named Tony Janiro who claimed Youngstown as his home, but other than that it's never gotten a lot of press.

Youngstown is one of those small cities in the midwest that practically define the ugly but accurate term "Rust Belt." The decline of the steel industry was Youngstown's decline as well, and now the downtown area resembles sections of bombed-out Beirut, with large buildings on main streets boarded up, and a pedestrian population of down-and-outers. Even men wearing suits and ties and carrying briefcases seem to be painted in muted grays and browns, as if industry sucked the vitality out of them when it left. Along once bustling Market Street, prostitutes on the stroll shout and wave at passing motorists.

But Mr. C's address was in a much more elegant part of the city, a hilly, wooded area of six- and seven-figure homes that managed to appear as though they had turned their back on Youngstown's troubles, which were none of their own. The superrich know no recession; their idea of belt tightening is going to Europe only twice a year instead of three times.

The house itself was a fortress. Surrounded by a high stone wall with a locked and barred iron gate, it was built of solid gray stone and heavy timbers, turreted and gabled and patrolled by a security guard walking a brace of rottweilers on a leather leash as thick as my wrist. Close by Mill Creek Park, near the western boundary of Youngstown, the property backed onto a stand of trees from which it separated itself by another high wall, brick topped with a roll of concertina wire gleaming dully. It looked like a federal penitentiary, with virtually no front lawn, the house itself built very close to the wall and the street.

It was funny, I thought, about mob guys. They spend millions of dollars on slick lawyers to keep them out of jail, and then turn their own homes into virtual prisons.

I parked out on the quiet road and checked my watch. It was a minute past three; I hate being late to anything. I went to one of the two columns of quarry stone that served as gateposts and pushed a discreet white button. The dog walker looked at me curiously, waiting to see what would happen. He didn't seem very concerned, whoever I might be, because the rottweilers stopped too, regarding me the way they would a chew toy, their bright alert eyes never leaving my face.

There was a whirring noise above my head as a remote control–operated TV camera swiveled toward me, its red eye glowing warm against the gray sky. A speaker in a steel plate set into the gatepost crackled with ambient sound, and a metallic male voice said, "Yes?"

"My name is Milan Jacovich," I said. "I'm here to talk to Mr. C." I felt silly speaking into the metal plate, even sillier calling someone by just an initial.

"Wait there," the voice said, and the speaker squawked and went silent. After a few minutes a tall slim man wearing an unlikely tweed suit and gray-tinted glasses came out of the house and down the driveway. The dog handler, satisfied everything was under control, resumed his patrol of the perimeter.

"Mr. Jacovich?" the man in the tweed suit said through the bars of the gate.

"Yes. Mr. D'Allessandro said—"

"That's all right." He unlocked the gate with a big iron key that must have been cut during the Spanish Inquisition and swung it open for me to walk through, stopping me when I'd gotten onto the grounds and locking us both in. The medieval-style keep was at odds with the high-tech video cameras.

He made a little upward gesture with both hands. I raised my arms from my sides for a thorough, professional patdown. When he was sure I carried nothing more threatening than a telephone beeper, he led me across the wide driveway to the house. The carpet of fall leaves crunched under our feet.

The front door must have been six inches thick. It led us into a two-story entryway with a broad staircase sweeping up to the second floor. Everything was done in dark woods and warm rich earth colors, and I was struck by the unmistakable odor of Lemon Pledge. To my left was a high-ceilinged, beamed living room with heavy furniture that looked very expensive but was not upholstered in the best taste. The bright blues and reds of the velveteen fabrics warred with the stately elegance of the walls and ceilings, and the painting on the hearth, a fanciful depiction of the Bay of Naples on a sunny day, was as out of place as a portrait of Elvis on black velvet. Mr. C was desperately in need of an interior decorator.

The tweed man led me away from the living room to the right, through sliding double doors into a large room that had been conceived as a library. There weren't many books on the shelves, though, but a lot of black plastic videotape storage boxes. Over against one wall was a projection-style giant TV set in front of a grouping of black leather sofas. The stone fireplace, big enough to roast a wild boar in, was dark and cold; in fact the whole house had an unpleasant chill to it, the kind that made old bones ache. It must have cost a fortune to heat.

"Make yourself comfortable," the tweed man said. "Can I bring you anything?"

"No, thanks."

He wiggled his eyebrows as though I must be crazy to turn down a free drink, shrugged, and left me alone in the room. I walked around the big room looking at the videotape boxes, but it wasn't as much fun as checking out someone's bookshelves because none of the cases were titled; they all had numbers on them, as though they were coded. Was #1742-E *Debbie Does Dayton*? Finally I got bored, took off my coat, threw it over a chair, and sat down on one of the leather couches to wait.

After about ten minutes a large, blocky-looking man wearing a bright blue ski sweater and black ski pants came in. There was nowhere nearby to go skiing, but I imagined he dressed that way to stay warm in the big drafty house.

"I don't have much time," he said without introducing himself. Physically he was the antithesis of Giancarlo D'Allessandro. About fifty, he looked in robust health, with wide shoulders, a thick neck, a fairly flat stomach, and a ruddy olive glow to his skin. There were deep pouches under his eyes, and his full mouth was like the torn pocket of an old raincoat beneath a fleshy nose. A few errant strands of silver highlighted otherwise jet black hair. He looked neither friendly nor hostile; he didn't look like much of anything and was obviously working hard to keep his expression noncommittal.

"Are you Mr. C?" I asked, knowing that he was; I recognized him from some newspaper photos taken at the time of one of his indictments several years before, and I knew his full name too. But I figured I'd better play along.

He sat down on one of the other sofas and cocked an ankle over his knee. His socks were fuzzy and yellow. "What can I do for you?"

"I'm a private investigator," I said.

"I know who you are. What do you want?"

I was put off by his abrupt manner, but I pressed on. "I'm trying to get a line on a man named Earl Barnstable."

"Why ask me?"

"Barnstable is a small-time peddler of kiddie porn."

He waved a hand around the room. "One, does it look to you like I'd know a small-time anything? And number two, I'm not in the pornography business. I'm in the erotica business."

"What's the difference?"

He looked at me scornfully as if everyone in the world but me knew the difference. "Erotica's legal."

That brought up the question of the indictments, but I didn't think it was a good idea to ask it.

"The trouble is," he volunteered, "these damn new amateur videos that are around now. Real people make a tape of themselves fucking and sell it for five hundred bucks to a distributor, and the next thing you know it's copied and it's all over the country." He clucked his tongue. "Can you imagine such a thing, letting God and everybody see you doin' it with your own wife? Jesus Christ!"

Now that I'd gotten him talking I realized he spoke with a slight accent, New Jersey overlaying long-ago Italy. I tried to get him back on my track. "So Earl Barnstable never worked for you?"

He shook his head. I waited for him to say something else, but he didn't seem so disposed.

"Look, Mr. C, I'm representing Mr. D'Allessandro on a matter that might or might not involve this Barnstable. Mr. D'Allessandro wouldn't have sent me here to see you if you didn't at least know the guy."

"I didn't say I didn't know him."

"So how about giving me a break?"

I waited again while he thought it over; this time I waited long enough.

"Earl Barnstable is a goddamn chicken hawk," he said at last. "You know what that is?"

I nodded.

"There's a big difference between what I do and what he does. I supply erotic fantasies for people; Earl Barnstable likes to have sex with little kids! That's disgusting!"

"So how do you know him?"

"He come to me, maybe a year ago, maybe eight months, wants to do some business." He snorted. "I wouldn't have nothing to do with him."

"What kind of business?"

"What the hell kind you think? You think I sell machine tools here?" He waved a hand at all the tapes on the shelves. "You think I sell eggs and cheese?"

"You sell dirty movies," I said.

He uncrossed his legs and put both feet on the floor. "Don't get all moral on me, okay? It just makes me tired. You people who get all moral are the worst sickos of all, 'cause they get their kicks in the closet."

"So everybody's a sicko?"

"More or less," he said. "And I got a fortune in beaver movies here to prove it. You gonna tell me you don't like pictures of beautiful women naked? What are you, a fag?"

"Why? Do you sell male erotica too?"

He drew himself up in his seat and looked down his nose at me. "I wouldn't touch that shit," he said, and shuddered. "Whaddayou think I am?"

I knew what he was, but I figured it was politic to keep quiet about it. "I'm trying to find out about Earl Barnstable. I don't give a damn what you do for a living."

Scratching his head vigorously, which caused a minor snowstorm to fall on the shoulders of his sweater, he gave me a weary look. "First of all, you gotta understand that most legitimate dealers don't go near the kid stuff. Most of us think it's sick to begin with, and it's also the quickest way to get the feds climbing all over you.

"See, the kiddie collectors, the chicken hawks, they're different from the ordinary whack-off freaks who buy porno. They get personally involved, they hang on to the stuff they got, or they trade it with other collectors. They gotta be discreet. Every once in a while the dumb ones, they advertise in one of those underground fuck magazines, *Screw* or the *Fetish Times*, trying to connect with other sickos like them. That's how the feds nail them, with sting operations."

"Then how do they come by the material in the first place?"

The corners of his mouth turned down in disgust. "Mostly they take the pictures themselves."

"So what did Earl Barnstable want here?"

"A distribution deal. He wanted to expand, y'know? Not bad enough he's a sick fuck, now he wants to make a buck off it too." He shook his head sadly like Geraldo Rivera, unable or unwilling to comprehend the injustices of the world.

"But you weren't interested?"

His laugh was as dry as the Sahara. "Interested? I had him thrown out on his ass. I mean really on his ass, in the middle of the road. He's lucky I didn't turn the dogs loose on him, a god-damn sickoid like that." He pondered that for a while, regretting his sin of omission.

"Was that because what he does disgusts you, Mr. C, or because you knew there was no profit in it?"

"Jeez, you don't let loose, do you? I already told you, we don't touch that shit." His tone grew pompous. "We got standards, for crissake."

"Is that the last you heard of him?"

He scowled. "Last I saw him, but I hear lots of things. I hear the feds nailed him a couple months back, caught him in one of their stings." He smiled with a kind of satisfaction. "I hope they give him the fuckin' hot seat."

"Where is he now?"

He shrugged. "Word I get, he's hidin' out someplace outta state until the trial."

"Mr. C, his sister was killed Sunday. Hit-and-run."

"My sympathies," he said, and didn't make the slightest effort to sound sincere.

"What I'm wondering is, could her death possibly have anything to do with him?"

"You mean, did he kill her? Get real, okay?"

"She might have been killed as a warning to him, to keep his mouth shut when he goes to trial."

He got up from the couch and wandered over to stand by the stone fireplace, crossing his arms across his chest. When he was satisfied with his pose, he frowned down at me. I stood up, too. I don't like being looked down at.

"You work for Don Giancarlo in Cleveland," he said, "you oughta know better'n that. If anyone in the organization wanted Barnstable's mouth shut, they'd shut it for him, direct. We don't mess with people's families, especially women, you hear what I'm saying to you?"

I heard.

"There's probably a lots of people wouldn't want him talking, but it'd be a personal thing. Guys into that kiddie stuff you wouldn't believe—straight types, executives and lawyers. A lot of 'em married, too. If it ever came out, even a rumor, they'd be ruined." He uncrossed his arms and rubbed his hands together;

maybe the chill in the room was finally getting to him, ski sweater or no. "But these aren't the class of guys who kill people."

"Anybody who's backed into a corner is the class of guy who kills people," I said.

He regarded me with sudden interest. "You know all about that, huh?"

"I know enough. I used to be a cop."

He obviously didn't like cops, even ex-ones. "Not no more?"

"Not no more," I said.

"Then go someplace else and look for a desperate sicko in a corner," he said. "I got nothing for you here."

"No names?" I said. "Not even a hint as to where to look?"

"A hint? What the hell you think this is, a game?"

"It's no game, Mr. C."

He put his hands in his pockets and walked around for a few seconds. I could hear his loose change jingling. "When Barnstable come to see me, all he wanted was my connections. He told me he had the financing for a distribution operation."

"He has plenty of his own money."

He wrinkled his brow as though I'd suddenly started speaking Farsi. "You don't put your own money into something like that! What're you, nuts?"

"Okay," I said, properly chastened. "Where was the financing coming from?"

"He didn't give me no names," Mr. C. said. "Even Barnstable's not that dumb. But he mentioned it was a guy owns some electronics firm out in Lake County, someone with—how'd he say it? The same interests."

I nodded at him. "That's more like it."

Putting up a traffic cop hand, he said, "You didn't hear it from me." He walked over to a Queen Anne table, opened a silver humidor, and took out a cigar, raising his eyebrows to see if I wanted one. I shook my head.

After neatly clipping off the end with a little silver nipper on the table and putting it in a big crystal ashtray, he licked the cigar up and down its entire length; it was almost too embarrassing to look at. Then he took out a Dunhill lighter, snapped it, and began warming the leaves carefully, taking obvious pleasure in the ritual. When he was satisfied, he passed the cigar under his nose, inhaling noisily. The rich aroma filled the room. "As a matter of fact," he said, "we never even talked at all. And be real clear on this point—whatever it is you're doing, if my name even gets as much as mentioned, you better make sure your life insurance is paid up, D'Allessandro or no D'Allessandro." He stuck the cigar between his teeth and flicked the lighter again. "You hear what I'm saying to you?"

Once again, I heard—and the skin on the back of my neck crawled, and for a moment my chest felt constricted. I don't like being threatened, but he had said it as a statement of fact, without any apparent rancor. He touched the lighter flame to the end of the cigar and smacked his thick lips around it noisily. When it had caught he took another puff and blew the smoke toward the ceiling.

"I don't even know your name, Mr. C," I said.

He twiddled his fingers along the length of the cigar the way Groucho Marx used to before firing off a bon mot and shook his head almost sadly. "Don't jerk me off, Mr. Jacovich."

The field of industrial security, which is where I earn the greater part of my living, has become a complicated one. The uniformed Pinkerton dozing at the door is long gone, replaced by sophisticated audio and video hardware, cameras that see in the dark, scanning devices, international trade treaties, federal guidelines, and complex computers that used to be found only at IBM. The dazzling array of technology requires constant study just to keep abreast.

I, however, am a low-tech guy. I have a calculator that I've practically mastered, an electronic typewriter on which I can bang out about forty words per minute, a telephone beeper, and a digital clock. I also have an electronic security system at home that is as easy to use as a push-button phone, but half the time I forget to arm it.

I don't have a cordless telephone because anyone with the right frequency can eavesdrop on a private conversation—and I have those sometimes. I haven't yet given in to a VCR because I've never met anyone over the age of fourteen who knows how to program one. Besides, I rarely turn on the TV unless it's the news or someone is doing something with a ball, and I can't imagine watching a sporting event on tape three days later.

I also don't own a personal computer. If I wanted to learn another language I'd probably choose French and not computerese. To me a RAM is a male sheep, "booting up" means putting on your shoes, a window is what you open when the weather is nice, a laptop is where you invite someone to sit that you like a lot, a byte is something you do to their neck while they're sitting there, a megabyte is one that leaves a gigantic hickey, and interfacing goes on strictly between two consenting adults, preferably behind closed doors.

One of the aids I keep on hand to help me in my business, hidden away in a messy cupboard, is as low-tech as you can get—a complete set of telephone directories for everywhere in Ohio, as well as directories for Pittsburgh, Detroit, Chicago and, for some strange reason I can't seem to remember, Tulsa, Oklahoma. I also have a reverse directory for Greater Cleveland, the kind in which you can look up a given number to discover in whose name the phone is listed.

I got home from Youngstown hungry as a bear, but before I even thought about dinner I pulled out the directory for Lake County and made a list of all the entries under "Electronics, Research and Development" and "Electronic Equipment and Supplies, Wholesale & Manufacturers."

It took two whole pages of yellow legal paper.

I sighed, placing the telephone console on top of the yellow pad, not that there was any reason to—the list wasn't going anywhere. Unfortunately. Tomorrow was going to be a busy day.

It was six thirty at night and there was nothing in the house to eat except mild cheddar cheese and crackers and the butt end of an Italian salami, plus a few spoonfuls of praline pecan ice cream left over from when my sons had spent the weekend. I thought about walking down a couple of blocks to Nighttown, but I hate eating dinner in nice restaurants alone. Call it single paranoia, but I'm convinced everyone in the place is staring at me and feeling sad that such a loser can't even find someone to join him for the evening.

Fast-food joints aren't nearly as intimidating, but I wasn't in the mood to decide whether or not I wanted "fries with that." My hand hovered over the phone to order a pizza, but neither sausage nor pepperoni nor mushrooms sounded particularly appetizing. I'm not a big pizza fan anyway, especially since the yuppies started making them designer. Finally I gave up and ate the cheese and crackers and salami, washing it down with my last two remaining beers. Then I looked up a number in my notebook.

The voice on the other end of the line was an impossibly deep basso.

"Mr. Pride, my name is Milan Jacovich. I work with your wife."

"Sure," he rumbled, "she's told me about you. Nice to finally get a chance to talk to you. Hang on, I'll get her."

When Cassie finally got on the phone she sounded out of breath.

"I hope I'm not interrupting your dinner," I said.

"I just got home about twenty minutes ago. We were getting ready to run over to Club Isabella in University Circle for some pasta, as a matter of fact. Want to join us?"

I gritted my teeth over the lost opportunity. It would have been nice to eat dinner with Cassie and her husband, to simply relate as people and not talk about politics or porno. "Thanks," I said, "but I just ate."

"What's happening?"

"I need a favor, Cassie. I need a list of Barbara's campaign contributors."

She hesitated. "I don't think that'll be a problem."

"And True's contributors also, if you can."

"Well, I can get them all right. That's public record. But I can't imagine why you need them."

"I'm not sure why myself, yet."

"What does that mean?" She sounded a little tense. "You don't think there's some sort of irregularity, do you? We don't need a smoking gun at this point."

"It might have something to do with Princess True."

"The campaign contributions?"

"Maybe," I said. "I won't know until I look. Can you have them tomorrow by lunchtime, do you think?"

"Tomorrow noon?" she said with a little indignation. "I'm not a magician."

"I'm sorry about the rush, Cassie, but tomorrow is Friday. That means if I don't get them by tomorrow I can't move until Monday—and that's the day before the election, which is too damn late."

"Any other miracles you'd like me to perform?"

"None that I can think of, thanks. Enjoy your dinner."

"Fat chance," she said. "But if I can get those lists by noon tomorrow I can probably save some money at dinner tonight."

"How's that?" I said.

"By changing water into wine."

## CHAPTER SIXTEEN

I had a little trouble getting started in the morning. Maybe it was because I'd been awakened from a sound sleep at one A.M. by a phantom phone call, the same kind that Barbara Corns had been getting, but mine contained a specific threat.

*"Stay out of Lake Erie Shores or you're dead, fucker!"*

Snake venom dripped from the whisper.

Other than disturbing my sleep, it didn't bother me very much. It sure didn't scare me. Anonymous phone callers usually stop there; if whoever it was had really meant business they wouldn't have bothered calling. But it gave me something to think about for the rest of the night, and I was up early and trying hard to make a pot of coffee disappear before the sun came up. The days were shortening, and daylight was beginning to come late in northern Ohio.

I'd learned two things, however, at the cost of a good night's sleep. If the caller who had disturbed my wee hours was the same person as who was harassing Barbara, it certainly wasn't Princess True. Not only couldn't she get to the phone these days, but the caller was definitely a male. Something in the timbre of the whisper. And the choice of words, as well.

I started my day by calling Marko. He sounded cranky; maybe I wasn't the only one with a case of morning disposition.

"I told you I'd let you know when I had a computer printout for the Ford pickups," he snapped. "We have other priorities down here, you know. And calling me up every ten minutes isn't going to make it go any faster."

"I haven't talked to you for two days," I said.

"Why do you always push me, Milan?"

"Because I'm getting close. But I need your cooperation."

I heard him lighting a cigarette, heard the snap of the lighter and then his satisfied exhalation. "I can only move as fast as the motor vehicle people. Call me tomorrow, all right?"

"Tomorrow's Saturday."

"Yeah, well, explain that to the bad guys. I'm a lieutenant now, I've got to stay on top of things whether it's the weekend or not."

"And you wonder why I left the force."

He suggested I try an interesting anatomical impossibility and hung up.

That morning's *Plain Dealer* was full of last-minute election news and political endorsements, but most of it concerned statewide and national races and issues vital to the residents of Cuyahoga County. Poor little Lake Erie Shores was presumed to be of interest only to its residents and was ignored. The sports page was its usual Friday self, analyzing to death the weekend's football matchups with grammatical errors that would put a sixth-grader in a remedial reading class, and the regular weekend entertainment insert held little interest for me. I turned to Ed Stahl's column; today it centered on a love-starved spider monkey in the Cleveland Metroparks Zoo's Rain Forest exhibit, which had opened in late 1992 and was supposed to be pretty spectacular. I'd like to see it, but I could imagine the look my boys would give me if I suggested going to the zoo some Sunday.

I decided to put a bug in Ed's ear.

The newsroom at the *Plain Dealer* has the annoying habit of playing commercials for itself when it puts callers on hold, but they finally tracked Ed down before I became too aggravated. "Did you know," I asked, "that Gayton True's going to build a gambling casino in Lake Erie Shores if he gets reelected?"

"That rumor has been around since Christ was a corporal, Milan. Sometimes it's about Lake Erie Shores or Painesville, sometimes about Youngstown or Elyria. Nobody on the paper pays attention anymore." He chuckled. "Is one of your campaign duties to plant items with the media?"

"I don't care if you use it or not," I told him, trying to hide my disappointment. "Just thought you'd be interested."

"It might explain D'Allessandro and Gaimari's interest in the election. Gambling would be right in their wheelhouse."

I listened while he lit his pipe. This seemed to be the morning where everyone I spoke to was smoking in my ear. It made me want a cigarette, but it was still too early; I was trying to hold it to a pack a day. "That doesn't fly, Ed. They're backing Barbara Corns, not Gayton True. And if I know Barbara, gambling is the last thing she'd let happen in her little town."

"The outfit, like the Lord, works in mysterious ways."

"Don't blaspheme."

The chuckle turned into a full-out laugh. "I haven't heard that word in twenty years, but coming from you it's par for the course. How did you get so damn quaint?"

"It's those reruns of Donna Reed on cable," I said.

After we finished chatting about the Browns' seeming inability to put points on the scoreboard, I hung up, folded the paper, and took it out to the kitchen, where I keep bags of recycling, news-papers, cans, and glass. I noticed the bottles from the Stroh's I'd polished off the night before, wondered if I might be drinking too much, and reminded myself to lay in a new supply.

After shaving extra-close, I took more time than usual with my hair, making sure it was combed to show the least possible amount of scalp, and dressed carefully in a brown sports jacket and tan slacks with a brownish-greenish tie that was narrower than most in my collection. I took an extra dress shirt with me so I could change before picking Kellen Charles up for our date and at the last moment grabbed my electric shaver too, just in case my five o'clock shadow got out of hand before dinner.

I was really looking forward to seeing her, enough so that it bothered me a little. I hadn't felt that kind of nervous anticipa-tion about anyone since Mary Soderberg had dumped me for her boss, Steve Cirini—I hadn't let myself feel it. You can only hit yourself on the head with a hammer so much before deciding that it feels good when you stop.

Today was Halloween, and I was sad to miss staying home that evening to hand out candy bars to the local kids, but the electoral process wasn't going to stop for ghosts and goblins with a sweet tooth. I wondered what costume Stephen would don for his trick-or-treat sortie through the neighborhood and felt a momentary pang that I wouldn't see him. I hoped Lila would take pictures of him before he set out on his candy-scavenging mission, but I didn't hold out too much hope. Lila can be remarkably unsentimental.

I headed up Cedar toward the freeway, stopping on the corner of Taylor Road at a convenience store to pick up a six-pack while I was thinking about it. Taylor Road is one of the centers of Hasidic Jewry on the East Side, and I had to wait a few minutes while a youth of about fourteen, wearing a black suit with no tie, a blue and black brocade yarmulke, and long *peyeses*, the unshorn earlock curls of his sect, hassled in vain with the African American clerk behind the counter, who was refusing to sell him a plastic-wrapped copy of *Hustler* magazine.

It was one of those moments that make me thankful I live in Cleveland, with all its bustle and its color and its ethnic diversity, and not in a white-bread-and-mayonnaise community like Lake Erie Shores.

But that's where I had to go to earn a buck. I tossed the beer into the back seat and headed up Cedar for I-271.

Cassandra Pride was on the phone, frowning, when I got to Barbara's house. When she hung up, she sat down at the dining room table and put her head in her hands.

"What's wrong?" I said.

"Judge Guilfoyle wants to meet with Barbara this afternoon," she said.

"The county party chairman?"

She nodded. "He's going to come out with an endorsement in time for Monday's paper and he says he hasn't made up his mind yet."

"Is she up to it?"

Cassie just wiggled her eyebrows at me. "Grab some coffee. I'll call Evan and get him back here for the meeting."

"Will he be any help?"

"I'm not sure anyone can help us now," she said, and picked up the phone again.

I took off my coat and hung it in the hall closet, got my coffee, and went into the living room to wait for Cassie. Out the back window the sky and everything beneath it was dull gray.

Barbara drifted down the stairs like a wraith and wandered

into the living room, her beige negligee thrown on over a matching nightgown. She looked drawn and puffy-eyed, as if she hadn't slept, but then that seemed to be her usual appearance.

"Milan," she murmured when she saw me. "You came back? I thought that what happened last night would scare you away and we'd never see you again."

"I work here," I said.

She gave me a wan, brave smile and sat down next to me on the sofa. "You're a trooper."

"How are you, Barbara?"

She stared at her knees. "I feel like I'm mainlining Valium. Everything is kind of hazy and unreal."

"It's the weather."

"I wish." She chewed on her lower lip for a while. "There was another call last night."

I thought about telling her I'd gotten one too, but she was in bad enough shape. "What time?"

"About one o'clock."

I nodded. The caller had probably made himself comfortable with a drink in front of a warm fire before setting about his night's work. "What did they say?"

"The usual." She held up a trembling hand. "I know you told me not to answer the phone at night, but after what happened at the restaurant I was so jumpy I picked it up without thinking." She watched her own hand shaking almost as if it belonged to someone else and then quickly put it in her lap. "I'm wearing down, Milan. Like an old car with too many miles on it."

Cassie came briskly in from the dining room. "Barbara, we have a meeting with Judge Guilfoyle at three o'clock, so think about what you're going to wear. Something businesslike, okay?"

Barbara's hand flew to her throat. "No!"

"You don't say no to the county chairman," Cassie said sternly, and then compassion flickered across her face. "It can't be helped, sweetie. Evan's in court this morning; I'm trying to track him down to see if he can cut loose."

She turned and started back for the dining room. The muted tones of the doorbell stopped her in mid stride, and she veered off to answer it.

Barbara looked at me for clemency I was unable to grant, and all of a sudden tears welled up in her eyes and spilled out to run down her cheeks. "I can't. I can't do it anymore. I don't have the strength and I don't have the guts."

"Sure you do, Barbara. It took guts to start this campaign, and you've still got plenty. Just fake it." I smiled encouragement and took her hand in both of mine. "Pretend it's a Tupperware party. From what I hear, Guilfoyle'll probably be too tanked to notice."

She squeezed my hand and slithered closer to me. "It's funny," she said, "two weeks ago I didn't even know you, and you've turned out to be my sturdy oak. Thank you."

"For doing my job?"

"For being so solid," she said. "For being here for me." She leaned forward and kissed me on the cheek.

Dennis and Laurie walked through the front door just in time to see it. Laurie came running over to Barbara to hug and kiss her, poncho flapping; Dennis just stood there in the doorway for a second, his cowboy hat low over his ears, looking at me as if he were the sheriff just walking into the Last Chance Saloon and I were Black Bart. Then he scrambled over for his kiss, too. He didn't quite get there in time.

"Kids, please!" Barbara's eyes were suddenly frightened, and she put up a protective forearm to fend them off. "My God, I'm still in my nightgown," she said, and clutched her peignoir around her chest.

She jumped up and, snaking through Laurie, Dennis, and Cassie like Eric Metcalf heading for the sidelines and daylight, rushed upstairs. Laurie reached out after her, empty arms pitifully outstretched, a ballerina signifying loss. As we heard Barbara pounding up the stairs, she dropped her hands to her sides and hung her head.

Dennis Babb's eyes turned to slits behind his thick glasses. "God damn you, anyway," he said to me before Cassie hustled both of them upstairs to the makeshift office.

I was getting pretty tired of being cursed at, but I considered the source.

Going into the kitchen, I poured myself the last of the coffee and made another batch, and then I went back out to my post on the sofa to wait for Cassandra Pride.

She came downstairs with two computer printouts in her

hand and tossed them onto the cushion next to me. "I hope you find something in here," she said. "I had to promise my firstborn child to get them so quickly."

"I didn't think you had any children."

"Sometimes with Laurie and Dennis I feel as if I do."

I stood up. "You have a few minutes, Cassie?"

She snorted—I think it was supposed to be a laugh.

"Sit down with me and let's go over these."

We went into the dining room and I pulled a chair around so that we could sit at the table side by side. I unfolded the first printout to its full length, three pages' worth, doublespaced. It was the list of those who'd made contributions to Barbara's campaign.

"Who are these people?" I said.

"I don't know all of them, of course. But let's see . . ." She ran a red-nailed finger down the list. "Victor Gaimari you know," she said. "A thousand dollars. And Giancarlo D'Allessandro, too."

"They each gave a thousand?"

"On paper, yes. But Victor's actually given a lot more. Like he's paying your salary—and mine—through his brokerage. He's also renting the headquarters. And he sent several of his people out here to put up yard signs."

"When you put up a sign on somebody's lawn, you have to ask their permission first, don't you?"

"Sure," she said, and I had to smile at the thought of some of the bent-noses who worked for Victor wandering around buttoned-up Lake Erie Shores, knocking on doors and intimidating the hell out of the homeowners.

I started with the name at the top of the list, Albert Blossom. He'd kicked in five hundred dollars. "Who's he?"

"He's one of the two dentists here in town," Cassie said, and then pointed to an Irving Glassfeld, who'd contributed four hundred. "He's the other one."

I moved to the next name, and the next. Some of them were familiar to Cassie, some she didn't know. The ones whose contributions were under a hundred bucks I didn't even ask about. I did recognize Laurie Pirkle's name; she'd given fifty dollars.

"Dudley Klane, six hundred dollars. Who's that?"

"Retired insurance broker, a widower. Lives about half a block from the lake. Nice old guy."

"Nathan Lerner, one thousand."

"Search me."

"Henry Ludlow, a thousand. And Virginia Ludlow, also a thousand."

"He's a local businessman," she said.

"What kind of business?"

"Electronics of some sort. Capacitors, I think, whatever they are. He has a small plant just outside the city limits, but he lives in town and votes here."

The adrenaline rush was almost as good as an orgasm. I leaned forward. "You know him personally?"

She shook her head. "He's just a name on a list."

I went down the rest of the list with her, making notes here and there, and then turned to the other printout, the list of Gayton True's contributors.

The end of the list caught my eye first. Josh Wilder, the executive director of the Lake Erie Shores Chamber of Commerce, was a four-hundred-dollar contributor. From the way Wilder had introduced the two candidates at the mixer, that didn't surprise me. And obviously he'd worked with the current mayor and felt his job would be secure if True's tenure in City Hall continued.

I scanned up the list, stopping at the seventh name from the bottom. It had a familiar ring, and I searched my memory to figure out why.

"Cassie, who is this thousand-dollar contributor here?"

She followed my finger. "John Terranova? I never heard of him. Why?"

Then it hit me. Of course, it might have been another John Terranova. Sure—just like there was another Richard Milhous Nixon, only this one ran a Hallmark card shop in Knoxville, Tennessee.

John Terranova had been at my house three nights before, carrying an envelope from Giancarlo D'Allessandro. But I didn't tell Cassandra that. "Just wondering," I said.

So, I asked myself, where does a guy only a few months out of the joint get a thousand dollars to donate to a campaign? And why was he contributing to the opponent of the candidate his boss was supposedly backing?

I came up with an answer, but it wasn't one that I liked. Not even a little bit. I felt as though I'd been sucker-punched. Or gut-shot.

Cassie went upstairs to get Barbara ready for Judge Guilfoyle's impending visit, and I tried to get a rope around my own emotions. Victor Gaimari, I discovered when I called him, wasn't at his office. I finally wormed out of his secretary that he'd gone to New York for a long weekend of Broadway shows. I hoped he had lousy seats way off to the side, or that the chandelier in *Phantom of the Opera* fell on his head.

I thought about phoning Mr. D'Allessandro, or even going to see him, but I discarded it as one of my less felicitous ideas. At least with Victor I could lose my temper, something I didn't dare do with the old man. I felt frustrated, impotent, blocked at every turn; also stupid, used, and ripping mad.

I studied the rest of the list without any names jumping out at me, but then I'm sure that most of the people in Lake Erie Shores who had enough money to give some away to a politician weren't in my social circle anyway. I did note that True's campaign had raised about eleven thousand dollars more than Barbara's. I wondered where he was spending it.

Cassie was up in the converted office on the second floor with Laurie and Dennis, and as I climbed the stairs there was an unpleasant burning in my stomach that had nothing to do with drinking too much coffee. "I have an errand," I told her, "but I'll be back at three o'clock in time for Judge Guilfoyle."

"Oh, fuck you. Who cares?" Dennis almost spat at me.

It was the wrong morning to screw around with me. I took another step into the room. "Dennis," I said, "I'm getting awfully damn tired of your mouth."

"Milan!" Cassie rose, took my arm with a firm grasp, and steered me out into the hallway. "What's the point of that?" she said.

"None," I said. "But it's the first thing in the morning and already it's turning into a hard day, and that's the second shot he's taken at me in the last half hour."

"You have to learn to rise above things, Milan. Poor Dennis

doesn't play with all fifty-two cards; you can't hold him responsible for what he says."

"He's bright enough to drive a car, he's there enough to have formed a political opinion. He'd better learn to watch his mouth. If I hadn't been there last night, Al Drago would have turned him into Cream of Wheat."

Cassie's spine straightened perceptibly. "I'd hope you had a little more compassion than Al Drago."

I really was sorry once I thought it over. Dennis was indeed one of the world's Poor Things, and even though I was pretty upset at what I'd learned from the lists of contributors, it was no excuse to turn into Al Drago.

Cassie walked back downstairs with me and watched as I got my coat from the hall closet.

"Did you find anything?" she said, indicating the computer printouts I'd left on the dining room table.

"I'll let you know later," I said. "Go up and wipe Dennis's nose. I'll see you at three."

I let myself out, hunching my shoulders against the wind. The end of October and it was already getting cold enough for a scarf. I sat in my car with the motor running, smoking a cigarette and wanting very badly to punch someone.

# CHAPTER SEVENTEEN

Not all of Lake Erie Shores is a Connecticut clone. Just northeast of the town, vast forest lands had been cleared of trees and grass, converted into flat plains for the construction of long, low brick and concrete buildings for industrial and small manufacturing use set well back from the highway and surrounded by blacktop parking lots. For several years now some of the plants had been standing vacant, their unoccupied lots mute testimony to George Bush's recession of 1990, their former employees struggling to make their house payments as they grasped at day work and tried to stretch their unemployment checks. Many jobs had gone south to foreign countries where workers earned one fifth the money for the same work. The empty factories had a sullen, angry air about them, or maybe it was just the half-light of the tarnished sky that made them look that way.

The electronics industry hadn't taken quite as hard a hit as some others, and Ludlow Electronics was one of the survivors; its parking lot was more than half full, mostly with low-end domestic cars several years old, all looking in need of a good wax job. The plant itself was about eighteen thousand square feet of cinder block, broken up by windows of glass brick. I squeezed my car into a visitor's space near the main entrance and went through a glass door into a waiting room with three chairs, some backdated magazines on a low table, and a glassed-in cubicle behind which the guardian of the gate crouched. She had a ponytail on the side of her head like Pebbles Flintstone, scrunched down by a Madonna-type headset. She looked as if she'd rather be almost anywhere else.

"May I see Mr. Ludlow?" I said, and told her my name.

"Huh?"

From the puzzlement in her dull brown eyes, a jumble of foreign-sounding syllables was all she heard. I repeated it for her, slowly, and when she still didn't get it I spelled it for her, only I used a *Y* instead of a *J* to head off any mispronunciation, figuring that it wouldn't matter because we weren't going to be pen pals anyway. She couldn't have been much more than eighteen and had on a straight black skirt and one of those Value City white blouses; you could see through to the white bra beneath. "You have an appointment?"

"You can tell him I'm with the Barbara Corns campaign."

"The what?"

I repeated it. It was looking like a long afternoon.

I waited for about ten minutes, and then the inner door swung open and Henry Ludlow came out. He was remarkably unremarkable-looking, dressed in the trousers of a nondescript gray suit and a black and gray tie with the knot pulled down about an inch below the unbuttoned neckline of his blue and white striped shirt. A plain gold wedding band was on his left hand and some sort of class ring on his right. In his early forties, with a ruddy face and glasses with ice blue plastic frames, he was starting to develop jowls and a small paunch, starting to lose his hair, and, I imagined, becoming uneasily aware that time was drifting by more rapidly than it used to. He probably drove a three-year-old Olds, and had a wife who folded his clean socks instead of rolling them. The kind of man you spend two hours talking to and then a week later don't recognize.

"So you're with Barbara's people. I hope you aren't here to ask me for more money," he said pleasantly, shaking hands and chuckling softly. "What did you guys do with the money I already gave you?"

"We appreciate your generosity, Mr. Ludlow. I'm not here for a contribution. I don't want to disturb you if you're going to lunch."

"I can't eat lunch," he said. "Doctor says I have to lose twenty pounds." He patted his round belly. "No problem. Piece of cake." I saw he was unaware of the irony.

"Good, then. I'd just like a few minutes of your time to talk to you."

"Okay, if you don't mind talking on the run. I can show off the store to you at the same time."

He looked pointedly through the glass at the receptionist, and when the idea finally permeated she pushed a button somewhere, acting put-upon, as if he'd asked her to shovel a ton of coal. A buzzer sounded and he was able to open the door he'd come in through, and I followed him into a long cinder block corridor with offices all along one side. We headed down toward the end and then turned into a huge fluorescent-lit room with long work tables at which about two dozen people sat. Most were women, and about half were either black or Hispanic. They were bent over complicated-looking little mechanisms on which they screwed or welded things. The room was bare of decoration except for a brave, drooping aloe plant at one of the work stations.

"I guess it must be getting pretty hectic over at campaign head-quarters, huh?" he said as he walked briskly. "Just a few more days. How does it look?"

"Too close to call," I said. "So we need your support more than ever."

He slowed down a little. "You got it. I'm telling everybody I know to vote for Barbara Corns."

We turned off into another large room, this one obviously the shipping department. A steel door in a recessed bay was open onto a loading dock, and the workers, all male and mostly black, had on outerwear to protect themselves from the wind that was blowing in.

"You're a big supporter of 'Back to the Basics,' then, Mr. Ludlow?"

"I'm a big *non*-supporter of Gayton True," he said. "I'll bust my butt to try to keep that son of a bitch out of public office." He looked around and then called out, "Luther!"

A tall, well-proportioned black man wearing a wool cap looked up from some shipping orders on a stand-up desk. He came and met Ludlow in the middle of the room, moving with an easy, self-assured strength. Ludlow spoke urgently to him, a hand on his shoulder, and Luther nodded, checking the watch on his thick wrist.

"Okay?" Ludlow said, backing away from him. "Can do, Luther? Don't let me down now."

He turned and came back to me, rubbing his stomach, a pained look on his face. "Damn rabbit food I've been eating lately gives me heartburn. All so I can keep my girlish figure. It's not worth it. So, Mr. Jacovich, what can I do to help Barbara? Give a speech, talk at a pep rally or something?"

"Mr. Ludlow, do you know a man named Earl Barnstable?"

The ruddy glow drained from his cheeks, leaving them a chalky white. I'd come to see him on the flimsiest of hunches, made a wild stab and hit pay dirt. I would count coup with Henry Ludlow.

"Barnstable. Ah, that's an unusual name. I don't—ah, Barnstable . . . no," he said. His hand fluttered to his mouth, and he pulled at his bottom lip.

"Earl Barnstable is Princess True's brother."

His laugh was nervous and high-pitched. "I don't exactly socialize with the True family," he said. "No disrespect for the dead intended."

"You might not socialize," I said, "but I thought perhaps you might have done some business with Barnstable."

Despite the cold of the shipping room, a mustache of perspiration popped out on Ludlow's upper lip in round beads, and he blinked rapidly. "We deal with lots of different people. I can't remember all of them. Thank God, business has been pretty good. This Barnstable, ah, he's in electronics?"

"I think you know what business he's in, Mr. Ludlow."

His sweat glands were working overtime; dark half moons appeared beneath the armpits of his shirt, and a drop trickled from his forehead and beneath his glasses and made its way down his cheek like a single tear. His eyes darted here and there, like a rabbit's before it ventures across the highway. Over at his desk, Luther looked up curiously.

"I, ah, as I said, I can't remember . . ." He swallowed, his Adam's apple bobbing. "Come on out here a minute," Ludlow said suddenly and in a different voice. He led me out through the shipping bay onto the loading dock. The wind off the lake hit full force, and I was glad I'd kept my coat on. Ludlow must have been freezing; beneath his white shirt and undershirt his nipples stood up stiffly.

"All right," he said, his former affability now only a memory.

"What is this? What do you want? Is this a shakedown or some-thing? I don't even know you, and you come in here and—where the hell do you get off . . ." His words trailed away, his anger ban-ished by fear.

"First, I'd like to know where you were Sunday morning."

He flushed. "None of your business!" The wind was disturb-ing what little hair he had left, mercilessly exposing his balding scalp.

"No it isn't," I said, "but the police might think it's theirs."

"Police?" He shivered. "What are you talking about?"

"Somebody ran Princess True down in the street in Cleveland on Sunday morning. The police might want to know where you were."

He wet his lips. "Why would they want to know that?"

I just looked at him. It made him a lot more nervous than if I'd said anything.

"All right," he said, crossing his arms across his chest, his body language louder than his voice. "It so happens about a hun-dred people saw me Sunday morning. I was in church. With my family."

"You have kids?"

"Yes, a daughter who's eleven—" He stopped cold. Maybe it was the expression of disgust on my face, or maybe it was some-thing else, something inside him that was dead and putrefying he'd just gotten a whiff of. His chin was quivering, whether from fear or anger I couldn't tell. "Who the hell are you to come here and make accusations?"

"I haven't made any accusations, Mr. Ludlow. And you don't have to talk to me, I'm just a private investigator working on the Corns campaign." I gave him my card, but he didn't look at it, just crumpled it in his sweaty hand.

"You and your wife contributed two thousand dollars to Bar-bara Corns. I wonder why."

"I've told you," he said, speaking into the wind but not neces-sarily to me. "I don't like Gayton True."

"Maybe it's important for you that he not get reelected," I said, "because if he does, his family connection with Earl Barnstable might come out, and then your name might come up. Because you were ready to bankroll Barnstable in a business that would not only make you some money, but would—how can I say this politely, Mr. Ludlow? Feed your habit."

He turned away from me. There was a raised brown mole on the back of his neck, just right of center, and it somehow diminished him, made him smaller and more vulnerable. Rather like a child, I thought, and there was something satisfying in that.

Dark rage was bunched up below my sternum, but I kept my voice low and intense. "I think you contributed to the Corns campaign with the stipulation that Evan Corns not bring up Earl Barnstable as an issue, because once that cat was out of the bag, others might be let out—including your connection to Barnstable. How'm I doing so far?"

He stared out across the parking area and beyond it to the rolling fields of grass and the stand of oak and maple trees that cut off the horizon, their branches skeletal and black against the sky.

"Maybe you thought if Mrs. True died her husband would pull out of the campaign and you'd be safe."

That seemed to galvanize him, where he had almost meekly accepted the rest. "You're crazy!" he said, raising his voice. "That's murder. I'm no murderer."

"That's no worse than what you are, Mr. Ludlow."

He took a deep, shuddering breath, and the starch seemed to go out of him. I didn't say anything. I just waited.

"Look, Mr. Jacovich, I don't know exactly why it is you've come here, but I'd be happy to make another contribution to Barbara's war chest, if that will put an end to this business."

"It's a little late for that."

He started to talk, but there seemed to be something in his throat that prevented it. He coughed, licked his lips again, and said, "Then how about if I give *you* a—contribution, and you can do with it what you like? Ten thousand, let's say?"

I just shook my head.

"You want more? Look, I can't put my hands on that kind of money right away. Maybe we could work out a payment schedule."

"Mr. Ludlow," I said, "I wouldn't use your kind of money to wipe myself with."

His face reddened, and the veins in his neck bulged. His mouth was a thin slash across his face, his breath was ragged. "You moralizing son of a bitch! What the hell do you know?"

"I know you're a pedophile."

He recoiled from the word as though it were a blow. He seemed to have aged ten years in ten minutes. He didn't fit the stereotype we all have of child molesters—the wild eyes, the dirty fingernails, the crazed expression. He just looked like a sick, pathetic man. "You think I chose to be? That I selected it like you'd order a cheeseburger off a menu?" His voice had risen and he made a conscious effort to lower it, although even as close to him as I stood, I could barely hear him over the wind. "It's a sickness, Mr. Jacovich." He shuddered again. "And there's no known cure."

His shoulders sagged, and he closed his eyes. For a moment I thought he'd fallen asleep on his feet. "I can't help the way I feel," he said at last, "any more than you can help being attracted to blondes or redheads or whatever your thing is."

"But we can help what we do."

"Goody for you being a wonderful human being," he said with a kind of tired scorn. I figured he'd had this same conversation with himself more times than he could count.

"Yours is not exactly a victimless crime."

His chin dropped low onto his chest. The scalp at the crown of his head looked gray through his thinning hair. At least he had enough of a shred of decency in him to feel ashamed of himself.

"So," he mumbled, "what are you going to do?"

"I'm going to talk to the sex crimes unit and let them take it from here."

"You don't have to do that, y'know."

"I'm afraid I do."

He raised his head, a frisson of defiance running through him, and for just a moment I caught a glimpse of the person he might have been if he hadn't been deeply sick. "I could stop you from leaving if I wanted. Luther and these other men are very loyal to me."

I looked over my shoulder at Luther inside. He was watching us closely while trying not to seem like it, and not doing a very good job. If he was indeed loyal to his employer, I wondered whether that loyalty would survive if he knew what Ludlow did with his spare time.

"And what would you do then?" I said. "Kill me and bury me out in the field over there? That wouldn't be smart, Mr. Ludlow. You think I came here without letting anyone know where I was headed?" I cursed myself silently—that's exactly what I'd done. But Henry Ludlow didn't know that.

He chewed at his lower lip hard enough to make it bleed, but he didn't say anything, nor did he meet my eyes. If I had been he, I wouldn't have been able to look me in the eye either.

"And if you had nothing to do with what happened to Mrs. True," I said, "I sure hope that you don't own a white 1983 Ford pickup."

"I don't," he said quickly. He put two fingers beneath his glasses and rubbed his eyelids, poking at them as if his eyes pained him. "Have pity, all right? Don't you have enough dirt on me already without trying to add murder to it?"

"You're the one that has dirt on you," I said, and started down the concrete steps to the blacktop. I believed that he wasn't responsible for Princess True's death, but I was going to blow him out of the water like an enemy battleship anyway. I had to.

"Mr. Jacovich?"

I turned and looked up at him. His head had sunk onto his shoulders so that he appeared to have no neck at all.

"I don't suppose I could appeal to your compassion to give me a break here?"

"Mr. Ludlow," I said evenly, "I'm going to do better than that. I'm going to cut a break for your little girl."


There was no doubt about it, judge John Guilfoyle was a formidable presence in his three-piece gray pinstriped suit and his heavy tortoiseshell glasses, worn low on his nose, on which capillaries destroyed by alcohol abuse blossomed rosily. Twenty minutes late, he walked into Barbara Corns's campaign headquarters with the special confidence of a man who is accustomed to power and knows how to use it. A hush instantly fell over the volunteers, some of whom didn't even know who he was, like when the high school principal unexpectedly walks in on an unruly shop class. Even Dennis and Laurie seemed a little awed. He had that kind of charismatic aura.

Guilfoyle was tall, and handsome in a kind of dissolute middle-aged Irish way, sonorous of voice and broad of shoulder.

He was also drunk. Drunk in the manner of habitual drinkers, with a grave, almost comic dignity.

I don't know how he'd managed to drive to Lake Erie Shores from wherever he came, but he was having a bit of trouble standing. He swayed dangerously in the doorway until Cassandra Pride rushed to his rescue and, like a tugboat piloting a listing liner, got him to a seat near the back of the store, where I waited for him with a nervous, near catatonic Barbara.

"Well now, Miz Barbara!" the judge said, slumping in his chair and hanging on to the edge of the table. He had a voice like someone shaking a tin can full of tenpenny nails.

Barbara just nodded, tight-lipped. I winked at her, and she managed to squeeze out a smile.

Cassandra said, "We really appreciate your coming to see us, Your Honor."

He swiveled his entire head around to stare at her, squinting as though trying to figure out who she was. Then he turned back to Barbara. "So we got ourselves a little election here, don't we?"

She nodded again.

"Now there's a few things I want to speak to you about," Guilfoyle slurred. His tone was confidential, learned in a thousand back rooms, where the political process really takes place. "You know, there's a lot of good people working here for the city. Good loyal party workers, been around a long time making things run smoothly. And I'd certainly hope that if you become mayor, those people would be taken into consideration."

"I'll look at each one of them individually, Judge," Barbara ventured meekly.

He frowned, and all pretense of friendliness fell away from him like a discarded garment. "What the hell is that supposed to mean?"

The color rose in her cheeks. "Just that—that I want the best people available."

He shifted around in his chair. "Public works, for instance?

Marty Holbrook has been running that department for seven years now. Doing a pretty good job, wouldn't you say?"

I thought about the pothole lady.

"I-I really haven't thought about any sp-specific jobs," Barbara stammered.

I jumped in. "Mrs. Corns has concentrated all her energy on getting elected, Judge."

He looked over at me. "And you are . . . ?"

"Milan Jacovich. I'm with Barbara's campaign."

"You speak for Barbara, do you?"

"No, sir, I—"

"Then kindly keep out of this," he ordered peremptorily, as though he were still sitting on the Common Pleas bench in black robes banging a gavel. I kept quiet.

"So how about Marty?" the judge asked Barbara again. "I'd like to know what your plans are in that area."

Barbara's fists were clenched so tight that her knuckles looked bloodless. "I don't feel that I can make any commitments right now, Judge Guilfoyle, one way or the other."

Good for you, I thought, even as I knew she was sinking her own ship.

"The director of public safety? Jack Boyle?"

"I haven't decided." She seemed to be gaining a little strength.

"Administrative assistant? You used to have that job, Miz Barbara, you know how important it is. We going to have Abby Osborne stay on?"

"I think I'd prefer someone who wasn't quite so closely associated with Mayor True," she said.

The judge cleared his throat, and his voice became louder, enough so that a few of the campaign workers at the front of the store glanced nervously back at us. "You're not giving me the answers I was hoping to hear."

She wavered for a moment, and then she filled her lungs with air and herself it seemed with confidence. "I'm sorry to hear that, Judge, but I can't make promises until I've thought it out carefully."

"There's such a thing as party loyalty," he said. "Reciprocation. Reaping reward for services rendered."

"I'd be doing the people of this city a disservice if I ran city hall like a private boy's club," she said, and her eyes widened as she said it, as though she couldn't believe the words that were coming out of her mouth.

The judge sat there staring at her for a moment, a great ruined statue of a man, his hands flat on the table in front of him all that kept him upright. Barbara was probably the first party politician to tell him no within his memory. He must have cut a dashing figure as a fire-breathing young lawyer thirty years ago, before sour-mash whiskey had tarnished some of the glitter and Lake County's political machine had ground his idealism into bone meal. If I'd been in a better frame of mind that day, if I hadn't found that morning that my employer had betrayed me, if I hadn't just spoken to a man whose sickness translated into evil, I might have felt some pity for Guilfoyle instead of only contempt.

But he wasn't much interested in what I thought. "Mrs. Corns," he said slowly, finally according her that much respect, "you're turning into quite an interesting woman."

"I take that as a compliment, Your Honor."

He nodded, still studying her as if she were a lab specimen. "I think probably that you should," he said finally, and hauled himself out of his chair to stand, weaving a little but upright and tall. "You'll be hearing from me."

Cassandra and I stood up, too, and Cassie helped him make it up to the front door, one hand firmly on his elbow.

Barbara sat where she was, her eyes scrunched up like she was about to cry, her lips practically disappearing. "I screwed up," she said.

I reached out and took both her hands in one of mine and squeezed reassuringly. "I'm proud of you, Barbara."

"Really?"

"Really. You were terrific."

She dropped her eyes, and I think she might even have blushed. Then she got up and went to the coatrack and began struggling into her coat. Dennis ran to help but I got there first, which brought on his now familiar sulk. As I eased the coat over her shoulders she leaned back against me for a moment. I could smell her herbal shampoo; the moment was almost touchingly intimate. "So are you, Milan. I can't express what having you around here has meant to me."

I was going to say something else, but Cassie came back from seeing to it that Judge Guilfoyle didn't keel over before he left. Her pretty face looked drawn and stressed. I didn't even want to think about him behind the wheel of a two-thousand-pound automobile.

"You're lucky you have a date tonight," she said. "You can get your head away from this campaign for one evening, anyway. I've got to go home and chew on it."

Annoyed, she glanced at Dennis, who was standing there with his thumbs hooked into the belt loops of his jeans. "Dennis, go find something to do, all right?"

He slouched away, sending one more dirty look my way over his shoulder. I seemed to have become his bête noire.

"So," Cassie said, "now you've met the judge. Isn't *he* a piece of work?"

I leaned in close to her ear so Barbara couldn't hear me. "Do you think he'll give us his endorsement?"

Her smile was bitter. "When elephants fly," she said.

# CHAPTER EIGHTEEN

I don't have any connections at the Lake Erie Shores Police Department, and I didn't feel like going through twenty-six different people and twenty-six lengthy explanations, so I simply took the easy way out and called Marko in Cleveland, told him what I'd learned about Henry Ludlow, and asked him to take it from there. Even though the spirit of cooperation between law enforcement agencies of different jurisdictions sometimes hangs by a thread of the finest gossamer, I figured the complaint would be taken more seriously coming from the number-two guy in Cleveland homicide than from a carpetbagging private eye. And maybe the cop who answered the phone in Lake County would feel the same way about the victimization of children that I do and would get the ball rolling.

Simple possession of child porno is a crime in Ohio; whatever else Mr. Ludlow might have been doing, I didn't even want to think about. Marko assured me he'd alert the proper people in Lake County but couldn't make any promises beyond that.

It's funny. People get hysterical about such silly things sometimes, like those who expend enormous amounts of energy trying to convince the world that the Procter & Gamble logo is a sign of devil worship or that *Snow White and the Seven Dwarfs* is obscene, and yet so often they ignore the very real evil that just might be living next door.

Pedophilia is, as Ludlow had said, an affliction rather than a life-style choice, but we all have to control our urges when other people are involved. And when those other people are children that we're supposed to be protecting, the whole subject becomes nonnegotiable.

So I made myself a quiet promise. If Marko's efforts didn't pan out, if someone in authority in Lake County couldn't get to Henry Ludlow, I'd take it further. I had to, for the sake of Ludlow's kid, and a lot of other kids I didn't even know.

There wasn't much I could do about anything that evening, though. I wasn't any closer to finding out what had really happened to Princess True, and Barbara, by showing some backbone for the first time since I'd started working for her campaign, had probably cost herself the valuable endorsement of the county chairman. Victor Gaimari had suckered me and then left town so I couldn't even tell him what a shit I thought he was until Monday morning. It had been a stressful and frustrating day, and I was wound pretty tight.

But I hoped the evening would change all that, because I was looking forward to having dinner with Kellen Charles.

I went into the small washroom at the rear of the Barbara for Mayor headquarters, ran my electric shaver over my jaw, and changed into the fresh shirt. Then I put my tie back on. The mirror in there was about the size of a dinner plate, and the ghastly fluorescent light mounted over the sink could have transformed Tom Cruise into a clone of *The Night of the Living Dead*, but the reflection of the finished product was at least presentable. I don't consider myself anything more than okay-looking, but I clean up pretty good.

Kellen lived in a rented red-painted cottage with white trim about three blocks away from her office, not too far from the square. A big white globe of light on the porch was bright enough to illuminate a movie set, but it made the house number easy to spot from the road. There wasn't much lawn, and what there was slumbered under a carpet of fallen leaves, and the house had only a tiny driveway big enough for her Honda CRX, red to match the house, so I parked at the curb and went up the walk.

She came to the door with a glass of red wine in her hand, wearing a long wool plaid skirt and an ivory-colored blouse with a dark green sweater thrown over her shoulders. "My rescuer," she said, her pretty brown eyes lighting up when she saw me. "All that got me through the afternoon was knowing that you were coming tonight and I could relax and forget about the cares of the day. And there were plenty, believe me."

"You had a rough one too?" I said, coming into her living room. A fire crackled merrily on the hearth, the popping of the burning logs like music. The place had a rustic feel to it; the floor was uncarpeted hardwood, polished to a gloss—pretty, but it wouldn't hold much heat. The furniture was well-worn and old-fashioned but of high quality, and on nearly every flat surface Kellen had placed old black-and-white family photographs of another vintage, all in rather ornate gold and silver frames. A fat orange cat with one fang jutting out from its lower jaw skulked in from the living room, gave me a resentful stare for having invaded her private fiefdom, and disappeared. A CD player was cranking out a symphony I wasn't familiar with, which is any symphony at all besides Beethoven's Fifth.

"I'm so tired of writing grant proposals," Kellen groaned, "especially when I want to be out there doing something. I think the world would be an easier place to deal with if the Egyptians hadn't invented paper."

"I hope you're not too tired to eat," I said.

She grinned. "Not until they nail down the lid of the box." She took my coat and hung it up on a coat tree by the door. "It just seems like I'm hollering down a well sometimes. There are so many causes. They all want money and they're all worthwhile. Health charities, educational charities, arts charities—it makes me dizzy."

"Well sit down, then, before you fall down."

"I won't fall down," she said. "I'm a survivor." She put her hands on her hips. "Are you in the mood for seafood? There's a great oyster bar at Cap'n Andy's in Grand River."

I hesitated just a beat. "I don't think so."

"Meat and potatoes guy, right?"

It didn't bear explaining. "Something like that."

"Well, let me pour you a glass of wine, then, and we can talk about it."

I'm not much of a wine drinker. For the year and a half I was seeing Mary I drank a lot of wine because she enjoyed it and would always comment on the "nose" or the "finish," and I'd mumble politely without the foggiest notion of what she was talking about. I didn't want to start things out with Kellen on the wrong foot, so I decided to play it safe. "You wouldn't happen to have a beer, would you?"

"Sure," she said. She went into the kitchen and came out with a Budweiser. Close enough.

She flopped down on the sofa beside me, and I clinked my beer bottle against her wineglass. We each took a swallow, and then stared at the flickering fireplace for a while, the music soothing and almost sensual. When I inquired, Kellen told me it was Mozart.

"What's happening over at Barbara's?" she finally said.

"A nightmare. I don't even want to talk about it."

"Boy, we're a jolly pair, aren't we?"

"I'm sorry," I said. "Come on, let's go get something to eat.

She held up a hand. "I've got a better idea. I don't think either of us is in the mood to frolic around in a crowded restaurant tonight. I've got some salad fixings in the fridge, enough beer for a party, and we can send out for something. Pizza, Chinese, whatever."

"That's the best idea I've heard in a month. If you're sure you won't mind?"

"I'd prefer it—under one condition."

"What's that?"

"You take that damn tie off and at least look comfortable."

I was going to like Kellen Charles, I thought, as I yanked off my tie and stuffed it in my pocket and unbuttoned the collar of my shirt. My neck felt delightfully liberated. I'm not a suit-and-tie kind of guy. I normally wear a lot of sweaters, and sweatshirts bearing the logo of my alma mater, Kent State, or of the Browns, or of several colleges I never attended and teams I don't root for. Every once in a while I break down and wear a sports jacket with an open shirt. But my political foray had kept me in starched shirts and ties for the past week.

After some more discussion, largely about calories and cholesterol, we decided to phone the Chinese restaurant just off the freeway exit, about ten minutes away, Kellen having assured me that they didn't use MSG. We chose hot-and-sour soup, spring rolls—which are a very different proposition from egg rolls, I

learned from Kellen—kung pao chicken (very spicy), and something with the horrifying name of ants-on-a-tree, which turned
out to be a form of Chinese hamburger.

The food was eventually delivered by a young man with dirty-
blond hair who didn't look at all Chinese, and Kellen spread it
out on the coffee table along with two sets of chopsticks that she
found in a drawer in the kitchen. I was on the sofa, while she
settled down on the floor; I'm too big and awkward to be much of
a floor sitter. We ate from several of those ubiquitous cardboard
cartons that seem to define Chinese takeout, while the crooked-
fanged cat stalked hopefully around the coffee table muttering
softly, like a lion on the perimeter of a safari campsite.

"Barbara's going to lose, isn't she?" Kellen said. "Anything's
possible, but right now it doesn't look terrific."

"What happened?"

I shrugged, munching on a spring roll. "Don't ask me, I'm no
expert. And maybe that's the trouble. There's no such thing as
grass roots anymore. Politics is a game for professionals, and the
Cornses have frankly run this campaign like amateur night in
Dixie."

"It's rotten," she said. "Gayton True hasn't done a damn thing
for the little people in all the years he's been in office, and it's
going to be four more years of the same." She expertly plucked
a single peanut from the kung pao chicken concoction with her
chopsticks and popped it into her mouth. "The perception of the
homeless is that they're the same winos and bums that used to
hang out on Skid Row and beg for handouts, and it's not like that
anymore. Half of them are decent people who ran into some hard
luck and lost their jobs and their homes, and uneducated mothers whose general assistance ran out. Most of the rest of them
are the mentally ill who got dumped out of hospitals and shelters
and into the mainstream of society when the budget cutbacks
hit. They're harmless but they're helpless—all of them." She put
down her chopsticks, warming to the subject. "When people say
they should pull themselves up by their bootstraps I just want to
scream. And when I see money being plowed into shopping malls
and housing tracts while Americans are living on the streets, I
have to wonder about our system."

"And you think Barbara can change all that?"

She shook her head. "Not really, no. But she won't spend our tax money to help the rich get richer, and that means there's at least a chance we can get our hands on some of it to use it where it'll do the most good."

"We?"

She laughed. "Not *me*, certainly."

I tried a piece of the chicken; the fiery Hunan spices opened up my sinuses in a hurry, and I slugged down a mouthful of beer. It didn't help.

She noticed my discomfort and said, "Take some rice. It'll cool down the fire better than beer."

I did, and she was right. From then on I alternated bites of entrée and rice. "It sounds like you spend a lot of your time banging your head against the wall," I said.

"That comes along with a master's degree in social service. If I'd wanted to get rich I would've become a lawyer."

"Why do you do it?" I said. "You could make a lot more money in the private sector."

"It's not about money, it's about making an impact. A difference. You must understand that. You do the same thing."

"I'm a businessman," I said.

"Sure. But you could make more money doing something else too. You're doing what you believe in."

"Don't assign me too many noble motives," I protested. I was uncomfortable with the undeserved praise, all too aware that I was working for Victor Gaimari.

"Strong, silent, and modest," she said, brown eyes twinkling. "If they ever make a movie about your life, Gary Cooper should play you."

"Gary Cooper? Kellen, I don't want you to be upset, but I'm afraid I have some sad news for you."

She clutched her throat in mock horror. "You mean . . . ?"

"I'm afraid so," I said. "But let's remember him as Lou Gehrig or the Virginian. He would have wanted it that way."

She laughed. She had a nice laugh, like wind chimes in a garden on an evening in spring.

After we finished eating, Kellen cleared away the cartons

and crumpled napkins, put a Cleveland Orchestra recording of Schumann on the CD player, and sat on the sofa next to me. The cat plunked herself strategically between us and gazed at me through narrowed eyes, waiting for me to make a false move.

We talked then about all the things people talk about when they're just getting acquainted: family—she was a native Clevelander whose folks still had a house in Lyndhurst, an East Side suburb not too far from where I live in Cleveland Heights—schooling—she attended Cleveland State University and got her master's at Michigan—and past loves—she'd been engaged once four years earlier but got cold feet at the last minute.

I found out she was a Tribe fan like me but didn't care for football; she said she couldn't accept it until "you guys admit all those pats on the ass are sexual." She rarely watched television, preferred live theater to movies, classical music to rock, and red wine to white. And to my delight, she admitted she loved spicy sausage—only she called it "kielbasi," the way the Serbs do, instead of the Slovenian "klobasa."

It was as pleasant an evening as I could remember. I was almost able to forget my anger at Victor and at Henry Ludlow. But the rough day we'd both had finally caught up to us at about eleven o'clock, and I figured it was time to go home.

"This was fun," she said as I got into my coat. "You're easy to talk to. I'd like to do it again sometime." She sighed then, almost sadly. "But I guess I'm GU."

"GU?"

"Geographically undesirable, living all the way out here in Lake County. After the election Tuesday you won't have any reason to be out here again."

"I can probably find a reason," I said. We looked at each other for a minute and then she came into my arms as if she'd been doing it forever. Her mouth was warm and her tongue tasted of red wine.

"First kisses are always so scary," she said a little breathlessly when we finally broke apart.

"The second one is easier," I said, and proved it. For quite a while, as a matter of fact.

Finally she pulled back a little and said, "You'd better go."

She moved out of the circle of my arms and backed a few steps into the living room. It was safer that way. "If this were the seventies we'd be in bed."

"Bad timing's my middle name," I said, and came and kissed her again, a quick one that was easily ended. Then I went outside.

The temperature had dropped along with the sun, and the icy wind made me wish I'd left my tie on to keep my neck warm. I went down the walk to the curb and around to the driver's side of my car and unlocked it, looking over the roof at Kellen standing in the doorway with the soft light behind her forming a nimbus around her shiny blonde hair. She waved, and I waved back. I was still savoring the taste of her kiss, which is probably why I didn't hear the cough of a motor down at the end of the street, why I didn't notice the white Ford pickup bearing down on me with its headlights off, gathering momentum as it came. A wide wooden push bar was on the front, looking as big as the side of a New England barn.

By the time I saw it, the truck was practically on top of me, a monstrous juggernaut growing larger as it got closer, like everybody's worst nightmare. I remained frozen for a moment, but then instinct took over and I was able to fling myself across the front seat of my Sunbird face first, doubling my long legs in after me. The gear lever dug hard into my ribs, and the entire car shuddered and rocked as the truck slammed into the open door and sheared it off.

I didn't even hear the door skitter about thirty feet down the street. I was too busy thanking God I was still alive.

I lay without moving for a few seconds, taking inventory of body parts. When I finally crawled backward out of the gaping hole where the driver's door used to be, the pickup had roared out of sight around the corner on two wheels, and Kellen was running down the walk toward me, calling my name.

I waved to let her know I was okay, but my heart had taken residence just under my chin and was pounding like a kettle drum, and I was having trouble catching my breath. I leaned against the side of the car for support—that little mechanism behind my knees that locks them and keeps them from buckling seemed not to be working very well.

Kellen ran around the car and came and put her arms around me. "My God," she said. "Are you all right?" She was shaking.

"Call the police," I said.

# CHAPTER NINETEEN

I spent the night, what was left of it after my visit to the Lake Erie Shores Police Department, beneath a cozy down quilt in Kellen Charles's guest room. My seriously wounded car was towed to a police impound lot.

The desk sergeant who took my statement was very sympathetic, especially when I told him I'd been a cop once myself, until he heard I was working for the Barbara Corns campaign, and then his attitude changed. He was a veteran and probably knew the mayor well enough to drink with. So he got very businesslike and assured me they'd put out an APB on the Ford pickup but he was going to treat it as a drunken Friday night hit-and-run, and he only got interested again when I reminded him it might well be the same vehicle that had killed Princess True.

That made him sit up straight. Visions of a gold lieutenant's badge, a reward for busting a big case, danced in his head. At least I left knowing I'd gotten his attention.

Needless to say, I slept fitfully. Attempts on my life tend to have that effect on me. Besides, I was very aware of Kellen on the other side of the wall.

In the gray autumn light of morning, with *Appalachian Spring* playing in the background, she made some coffee and raisin toast, and I didn't have the heart to tell her I hate raisins. She bustled around the kitchen looking very huggable in a University of Michigan sweatshirt, the wearing of which is a hanging offense in Ohio. I arranged for a car rental company in nearby Mentor to deliver a Mercury Sable to her house, and then while she got dressed for work—she explained that the homeless don't automatically get Saturdays off, so she didn't either—I called Marko and told him what had happened.

"Jesus, Milan," he said, and I was pleased to hear his genuine concern, which seemed to supersede how mad at me he was. "You sure you're all right?"

I rubbed the sore place where the gear lever had stabbed into my ribs, but nothing felt broken. "I'm all right now," I assured him, "but until we get this guy off the streets, it's only a matter of time." I decided to use whatever small advantage my misadventure had bought me. "Now will you quit dragging your feet and get me that list of Ford pickup owners?"

He promised he'd light a fire under the motor vehicle people as soon as he hung up the phone. Then he said, "How did you get home last night?"

"I didn't. I slept the night at my date's."

"*Yesss!*" he chortled, and I was too distracted to set him straight. If I spent as much time on my sex life as Marko does on his, I wouldn't have time to do anything else.

Victor was still in New York, as far as I knew, but I thought that the attempt on my life should be on record with the organization. It took me five phone calls to get through to Giancarlo D'Allessandro, all of which were answered by guys who sounded as if they'd been kicked in the larynx.

"Somebody tried to run me down last night," I told him. "In a white Ford pickup. Probably the same one that killed Mrs. True."

There was a long silence while he processed the information. "I don't like that."

"I'm not too crazy about it either."

"Tell you what I do," he said after I listened to him breathe a while. "I'll send some of my people out there to look after you, see that it don't happen again."

"No!" I bit my lip. One doesn't say "No!" to the don in that tone, but the idea of a bunch of slick-haired punks with bulges under their jackets hanging around Barbara's election campaign was one I didn't want to deal with. "I appreciate the offer, sir, but I'd rather you wouldn't."

"Maybe I want to."

"With all due respect, Don Giancarlo, I'm the guy people hire to look after them. I can take care of myself."

"It don't sound like it." His sigh was cut off by a harsh cough. When he could talk again he said, "I don't want nothing bad to happen to you. When we hire somebody, we're responsible he stays healthy." He gave a dry laugh. "Besides, I like you—for some funny reason."

I'm just a lovable guy. "I'll be okay, I promise."

"Uh-huh." He didn't sound convinced. "You carrying?"

"I didn't think it was necessary."

"So," he said with as much of a trace of merriment in his voice as I'd ever heard, "maybe you ain't so goddamn smart as you think you are."

Maybe I ain't, I thought while I waited for the rental car. It was nearly six days since Princess True had been killed, and whoever did it had tried for me, and I still didn't have a clue. I didn't have my three-by-five cards to play with, but I ran through all the possibilities in my mind.

Out of hand, I eliminated anyone in the D'Allessandro organization. The outfit had changed over the years and weren't nearly as disposed toward that kind of violence as they used to be. And they'd hardly pull anything as crude as a hit-and-run in an old pickup truck; they'd be slick—a small-calibre pistol at close range, my body left someplace where it would send a message to anyone else thinking about getting cute with them. And as far as I could figure, I hadn't done anything to piss them off. Besides, I'd given them plenty of reason to be angry with me the several previous times I'd had dealings with them, and they'd allowed me to keep walking around.

Gayton True might want to kill his wife to inherit her money, but he'd hardly pick the week before an important election to do it. And he had no reason to want me out of the way, either; he hardly knew who I was.

Al Drago was another story. He had the motive, but he'd had it for a long time now, and it's not as though he hadn't known where to find me if he'd wanted to. Venal, sadistic, and corrupt as he was when he carried a badge, Al Drago was no hit-and-run artist. Any damage he'd inflict would be on a more personal level, so he could enjoy it to the fullest. And as far as I knew he'd borne no grudge against Princess True.

Nobody in the Corns campaign would want me dead—at least,

I didn't think so. Even Corns hadn't been around on the Sunday morning Princess died, and he didn't like me much more than he'd liked her. He was a possibility, but my gut feeling was that he probably wouldn't resort to murder.

Henry Ludlow, on the other hand, was looking pretty good. It was entirely possible that Gayton True didn't know about his dealings with Earl Barnstable, but Barnstable's sister might have, and after our meeting the previous afternoon he knew that I was on to him as well. Ludlow was at the top of my list of people that might want me out of the way, and I'd already planted the bug about his pedophilia in Marko Meglich's ear.

Casting Ludlow in the role of desperate killer, however, didn't explain the anonymous midnight phone calls to Barbara's home. He'd want to help Barbara, not hurt her, and when I got my threatening call on Thursday at midnight, Ludlow hadn't been aware of my existence.

Maybe the killer and the caller were two different entities. After all, the calls were aimed at Barbara, and it was Princess True who died under the wheels of the pickup, which was certain to shake up Gayton True. Two different targets. I'd have to chew on that for a while.

They delivered the Sable, a dark maroon sedan, at about a quarter past nine. I signed for it, kissed Kellen goodbye like a husband going off to work, and drove over to Barbara's place. The car was much bigger than the Sunbird I was used to, and it felt as if I were driving an aircraft carrier.

Barbara answered the door herself, wearing black polyester stirrup pants and black pumps with medium heels, and an orange and black zebra-striped knit shirt. It seemed to be somewhat out of character for her, but then Barbara had surprised me before.

"You're early this morning," she said.

If I explained I'd only had a five-minute drive to get there I'd have to tell her what happened and where I'd spent the night, and I didn't think she was up to it. I wasn't either. So I just said, "I didn't sleep very well," which was not a lie.

She took my coat. If she noticed that I was wearing the same outfit I'd worn the day before, she was gracious enough not to mention it. "Let me bring you some coffee, then."

"I'll get it."

"That's all right," she said. "Let me wait on you. It's the least I can do."

I went and sat in my usual spot on the sofa. The heat was full up against the morning's chill and the room was stuffy.

"Cassie called; she's fighting off a cold and she'll be a little late," Barbara explained as she came back in with a steaming mug. "And Evan has his regular racquetball game every Saturday morning, so he won't be around until noon."

His wife is three days away from an election and Evan goes off to play jock. Another black mark in my book.

"I guess it's just the two of us for a while," she said, curling up in the opposite corner of the sofa.

"What's on the schedule for today?"

"I think I'm visiting a senior citizen's center later, and then we're going to pass out leaflets in the mall. I'm not really sure. Cassie takes care of all of that for me—or Evan. I can't keep track of it. Evan says I'd forget my own address if it wasn't printed on my driver's license." Her smile was vague. "I'm not very good at taking care of myself, I'm afraid."

"Then why on earth would you want to be mayor?"

"Right now," she said with a kind of wonder, "I can't even re-member. I guess it seemed like a good idea at the time."

I sipped my coffee; it wasn't as good as Kellen's.

"It was something Evan wanted," she continued. "And I sup-pose I'm kind of a throwback: I belong to the last generation of women who want to please their man, no matter what. The last of the dedicated housewives." She pursed her lips in that way she had. "Back to the basics."

"You're putting yourself through this just for Evan?"

"That's how it started. I wish he hadn't talked me into it, but he did, and here we are, and I'm going to fight hard as I can to win because I really believe in what we're doing."

"That's good," I said.

"But I never dreamed it would get so . . . rough. So personal." She put her chin in her hand. "I should have known they'd drag up the business about Evan's first marriage."

"Tell me about that," I said. "Since it's become a campaign is-sue. Obviously I've heard all sorts of things around, but I'd like to get it from you."

A tentative hand fluttered up to her chest. "Why?"

"Barbara, lots of things are going on here besides the election," I said. "Those phone calls you've been getting, what happened to Princess True, and some other things you don't even know about. Maybe if I knew the background I might be able to fit some pieces together."

She sucked on a fingernail. "If you think it's important," she finally said.

"Right now I don't know what is and isn't important."

"It's not something I'm particularly proud of."

"All of us have done things we're not proud of."

"Well, there isn't that much to tell," she said. "I was married before. I married my high school sweetheart. Corny, huh?"

"No. I married mine, too. It didn't last either."

"He was a go-getter, very aggressive and ambitious, and really way too concerned with what other people thought, or might think. He spent so much time on his career—middle management at a textile firm—that there wasn't much left over for me."

Except for the part about the textile firm, that could have been a newspaper profile of Evan Corns. I suppose we all fall into patterns, and apparently her first marriage had been the beginning of Barbara's. I didn't share that particular observation with her.

"After a while we kind of drifted off in opposite directions," she went on. "He began making me feel as though I was holding him back, that he could travel faster alone. So . . ." She gave a sad little shrug.

"Does he still live here in town?"

"No," she said. "His company relocated to South Carolina five years ago, and he went with it. Two years ago he married someone else."

I was beginning to regret having asked, but she was rolling now, the words coming out of her almost as if she couldn't stop them. "I was all right alone—sort of, anyway. I'd always envisioned myself being somebody's wife, so I didn't know how to do anything else. But I went back to school and took some business and secretarial courses and got myself a job. And I dated a little. Quite a lot, actually." She said it as though making a shameful confession. "This was the early eighties, when 'dating' wasn't such a bad word, remember. Well, after a while I met Donald—it was at Laird's Chop House, actually, during a Friday evening happy hour—and we started going around together."

She looked away as though the memories weren't pleasant ones. "He was a lot like David, my first husband. Very driven. I think he always wanted to write a novel and knew in his heart he didn't have the talent."

"They say inside every newspaperman there's a novel—and that's where it ought to stay."

She laughed. "It's made him bitter. He was very demanding, and the most possessive man I've ever met. The relationship was very hard on me, but I guess I just didn't have the guts to get out.

"I started working in the mayor's office—I met Gay True through Donald, as a matter of fact—first as a secretary, and then as an administrative assistant. That's where I first met Evan, and after a while we . . . started seeing each other. I knew he was married, and at first it bothered me, but people are able to rationalize almost anything. Eventually his wife found out about it and gave him an ultimatum: her or me." She preened a little. "He chose me."

I didn't say anything.

"It was a small scandal in this little town, I can tell you. Elizabeth Corns was very active in a lot of civic things and knew everyone, and a lot of people took sides." Her smile was full of rue. "Not many took mine. That's why people like Alice James are so bitchy to me."

"And what about Donald Straum?"

"He and I dated fairly steadily before I met Evan. He's an extremely jealous man. He was always quizzing me about old boyfriends. When we broke up, he'd call in the middle of the night and scream into my answering machine, accusing me of being in bed with somebody else."

"He's even more of a head case than I thought," I said.

She nodded. "He even—what do they call it now?—stalked me. When I moved in with Evan, Donald hung around outside my office, and he was always driving by the house at night. He took it pretty hard—he still does. That's another reason Alice is so bitchy."

I must have looked a little bit at sea, because she added, "She and Donald are having a thing now. Didn't you know?"

"No," I said. "I didn't. Does Mr. James know?"

She shrugged. "I doubt he'd even care, as long as word didn't get around."

"It seems like it already has."

"That's why she was so anxious to get Donald out of Laird's Chop House the other night."

"But she seemed content to have him in her home."

"Probably because Arlen wasn't there."

I gulped down the dregs of my coffee, which had cooled. "Well," I said, "whatever works, I guess."

She bristled. "Why? Is it so inconceivable that Donald Straum would be attracted to someone like me?"

"I didn't mean that at all."

She did that simpering thing with her lips. It was beginning to get on my nerves. "Do you think I'm attractive, Milan?" she asked me.

If on occasion I have questioned the existence of a merciful God, all doubts were assuaged as the telephone rang and saved me from the necessity of a reply.

"You're not off the hook," she warned, and jumped up to answer it, while I wished that I was Lamont Cranston, the old radio Shadow, who years ago in the Orient learned the strange and mysterious power to cloud men's minds so they cannot see him.

"Hello?" I heard Barbara say from the dining room. "Oh, yes— Judge Guilfoyle. Good morning."

I stood up and went in to join her. She was standing with one hand pressed flat on the table to support herself. Her face was very pale.

"Yes . . . Yes. Uh-huh . . . You have?" Her voice cracked and she cleared her throat loudly. "Well, that's—that's very . . ."

Her gaze met mine for an instant and then flicked away.

"I know that, Judge . . . yes . . . yes . . ." Then she took a sudden sharp breath, and her tone of voice changed markedly. "Yes, well thank you. I really appreciate . . . Yes. Yes, I will, Judge. Thank you so much. I appreciate your taking the time. . . . Yes, thank you. Bye-bye."

She put down the phone and turned to lean against the edge of the table. Her eyes were bright.

"Judge Guilfoyle," she said. "The county chairman. He's made up his mind." She put her hand on her chest. "He's giving me his endorsement," she said as though she couldn't believe it. "It'll hit the newspapers on Monday."

"All *right!*"

"He's going to endorse me!" Tears welled from her eyes but they were happy tears, and she threw herself at me, wrapping her arms around me and burrowing her head against my chest.

"Congratulations, Barbara, that's terrific!" I had to squeeze back hard to counteract her bear hug. She was half laughing and half sobbing, her body bouncing in my arms.

I towered over her by nearly a foot, so when she finally got control over her breathing she had to tilt her head back to look up at me. "Oh, Milan, do we have a chance now? Do we really have a chance?"

And then she was hugging me again and kissing my face. Before I knew it her arms were around my neck, pulling my head down, her mouth was glued to mine, and she was giving me her tongue.

I pulled away, more than a little surprised. "Hey!" I said gently, and I sounded to myself like a fourteen-year-old girl who'd been taken advantage of on the front porch after her first date with the stud of the sophomore class.

Her face burned red and she turned away from me and went into the kitchen to stand by the sink. I didn't know quite what to do so I just stood there feeling embarrassed, my hands shoved into my pockets.

Finally I heard her say, "I'm sorry."

"It's okay." I didn't move from my spot. "That was pretty exciting news."

There was silence from the kitchen except for the hum of the refrigerator. Then she turned and came out into the dining room again, walking briskly past me toward the stairs. "I'd better get dressed for the mall," she said.

"Barbara, I couldn't be happier for you about Guilfoyle's support."

She was halfway up to the landing, and she stopped, looking over her shoulder. "It might not even be important," she said.

I meandered into the living room again. There was nothing in there to read, and it being a Saturday morning the TV fare was mostly witless and badly animated cartoon shows for the moppet set, so I just looked out the window for a while and watched the few remaining leaves swirl down from the branches onto the back lawn. Winter was in the air.

I heard the water pipes in the walls of the old house gurgle as Barbara turned on the shower upstairs.

She was something else.

I didn't know the reason for what had just happened, and it troubled me. Judging from Evan Corns and Donald Straum I was hardly Barbara's type. Maybe because she was a little brown wren of a woman who sought out domineering relationships like they were the Holy Grail, vamping every man she met was a kind of affirmation for her. Maybe it had been the excitement of the moment that Evan simply hadn't been around to share with her.

Or maybe it was just devastating, irresistible old me.

Cassandra Pride arrived at about ten thirty, her eyes puffy and her sinuses clogged to the point where she couldn't pronounce her *n*'s and *l*'s very well. Her normally melodious voice was roughened by a sore throat.

She wasn't too sick to notice I was wearing the same clothes I'd had on the day before, though, and raised her eyebrows at me. "I see by your outfit that the date went pretty well," she rasped as she hung up her coat.

"Not exactly." I lowered my voice so Barbara couldn't hear and told her about the attack of the Ford pickup.

She looked genuinely worried. "You told the police?"

"Sure. They're on it."

"I think we need more security."

"A bodyguard for the bodyguard? I don't think so. I'll be okay. I'll watch my own ass now as well as Barbara's."

"You didn't mention this . . . ?" She looked upward.

"No."

"Well, for God's sake, be a little more careful." She studied me for a moment and then took a little pocket pack of tissues from her purse. She pulled one out, and swabbed none too gently at my mouth. When the tissue came away there was red lipstick on it. "In fact, be a lot more careful."

I felt the blood rushing to my ears. "I didn't . . ."

"It's all right," she said. "I've been across the street a few times."

"It's not what you think."

"I know just what it is, Milan." Her disdainful sniff probably didn't have much to do with her cold. "I've been around Barbara for eight weeks now." She shrugged, and stuffed the crumpled tissue into her jacket pocket. "So what else is new?"

"Funny you should ask. Guilfoyle just called—he's giving us his endorsement."

"He is, huh?" She smiled, and it transformed itself into a Cheshire cat grin. And then she laughed out loud. "That sly old bastard," she said. "Talk about watching your own ass!"

She went into the living room and sat down, whipping out another tissue to dab at her nose. "Guilfoyle doesn't want Barbara for mayor any more than he does me."

I followed her in. "Then why didn't he endorse True? Or at least keep his mouth shut altogether?"

"Politics again," she said. "Guilfoyle is the power in this county. He's the puppet master, and everyone dances when he pulls the strings. But he's getting old, everyone knows he's a lush, and they're a little tired of his megalomania. If True wins this election decisively, he's a serious threat to try and take over the party chairmanship from Guilfoyle, and the judge knows it. So he's publicly backing Barbara, even though he hates everything she stands for."

"It's going to be a big push for Barbara; does it matter why he did it?"

"Not now," she said, frowning. "But if by some quirk of fate Barbara gets in, she's going to find it pretty tough sledding if she doesn't fall into line."

"How so?"

"When Lake County has one of their famous lake-effect snows and nobody can get out of their driveway, the new mayor will find that she can't seem to get the salt trucks out to de-ice the roads. County maintenance crews will do their repairs at their own sweet pace, if at all, and there'll be a general slowdown in services. The citizens will scream—rightly—and it's Barbara who's going to take the hits. After a while I think she'll begin seeing things the chairman's way. And he knows it."

I was appalled. "That's blackmail!"

"Milan," she laughed, "you're such a political virgin."

"And I think I'd like to keep it that way," I said.

## CHAPTER TWENTY

**C**assandra and I were drilling Barbara on all the things she was supposed to say at the senior citizen's center. We were fairly certain the Back to the Basics message was going to be welcome in that particular venue, but we wanted to make sure Barbara mentioned some of the social programs she had in mind, a Meals-on-Wheels project, minor improvements for the center, and a part-time police security presence there.

It was all handled in a businesslike, professional, and very intense fashion, befitting the last moments of a political campaign. What had happened between Barbara and me earlier wasn't mentioned or even hinted at. She didn't look at me as often as she normally did, and there was a tightness around the corners of her mouth, but otherwise no one would have noticed anything amiss unless they were looking for it. Cassie had, of course, wiped the lipstick off my face, but she was one of those very focused people who could concentrate on the business at hand—getting Barbara elected mayor—and not allow outside distractions to sway her.

In the middle of the briefing the phone rang, and Cassie left us alone to answer it. It was an uncomfortable time during which Barbara never looked at me. I could hear that Cassie was talking to Laurie Pirkle. Dennis had been scheduled to pick her up at eleven and bring her over to the house, but he had failed either to call or show up, and Laurie wanted to know if someone could stop by and get her.

Cassie hung up and looked pointedly at me. There didn't seem to be anyone else to do it. And as much of a drag as it would be squiring Laurie Pirkle around, I was happy to get away from Barbara and from the house until things cooled off.

My bruised rib bitched at me when I slid behind the steering wheel, but it wasn't the worst pain I've ever suffered. It wasn't even in the top ten.

Laurie lived in student housing about a mile from the Lakeland Community College campus with its landmark bell tower, beyond the corporate limits of Lake Erie Shores; she wouldn't even be able to vote for the candidate whose election she was working so hard to bring about.

She waited just inside the vestibule of her apartment building. When I pulled up, she started out, then noticed who was behind the wheel. I think she actually considered turning around and going back inside for a moment but finally put her head down and traversed the cement sidewalk to the car as though she were walking the last mile.

"Hi, Laurie," I said as brightly as I could.

For a reply she slammed the car door and scrunched herself against it, as far away from me as she could get, folding her arms. The shadow of an incipient mustache darkened her upper lip. "How come they sent *you*?"

"The chauffeur with the limo was busy just now."

She slumped down on the base of her spine, glumly resigned. "Whatever."

I put the Sable in gear. "Where's Dennis today?"

"I don't know," she grumped.

"Kind of surprising that he didn't even call."

"No it's not."

"It's not?"

"Sometimes he bugs out for a couple of days and nobody hears from him." She stared out the side window, her face turned away from me. "He's a dork."

I couldn't have agreed more, but I wasn't going to tell her so. "That must be difficult to deal with."

She spoke in a bored monotone, trying to offer me as few strokes as possible. "You must have me confused with somebody who gives a damn."

"I thought he was your boyfriend."

Her head swiveled around. "Be real, okay?" she said with withering contempt.

"Sorry."

She looked away again. "Just because I'm fat doesn't mean I'm desperate, you know."

I suppose that was my cue to assure her she wasn't fat, but it would have been such a transparent lie I didn't even attempt it. "I've always seen you two together," I said, "so I jumped to a conclusion. I didn't mean to offend you."

"You didn't. Don't flatter yourself."

I pulled onto the freeway. "Why don't you like me?"

She shrugged. "I don't know you."

"You don't know me so you don't like me?"

She picked at the cuticle around her thumbnail. It looked red and angry, as though she worried it a lot. "Why'd they have to hire you? We were doing just fine by ourselves."

I hadn't really talked to Laurie before. Now that I'd heard her speak more than three words at a time, I detected a rural twang, possibly from the southwestern, largely agricultural part of the state. I wondered what kind of rural loneliness had sent a girl like her, overweight and unattractive and introverted because of it, to the outskirts of a big impersonal city where another and possibly sharper brand of loneliness awaited her, the kind that had propelled her into the middle of a political campaign in which she had no stake at all.

"I'm doing the same thing you are. Trying to get Barbara elected."

Her bottom lip stuck out in a pout. "Ever since you came, nobody pays any attention to us anymore."

"That's not true."

"Yes it is," she said.

It was about a ten-minute drive to the Lake Erie Shores exit, and and we undertook it in silence. I finally snapped on the radio and fiddled with the controls until I found WMJI, the golden oldies station. Dion, an inductee into the Rock and Roll Hall of Fame they're building in Cleveland, was singing that he was a wanderer. I guess Laurie and Dennis were, too—there wasn't anyplace they really belonged. Dion sounded a lot happier about it, though, than Laurie looked.

Cassie had decided that she, Evan, and Barbara would go to the senior center by themselves and meet us at the mall, so that's where I headed. The parking lot was fairly crowded with Saturday souls doing their Christmas shopping early, some sort of sign that the economy was struggling to recover.

The sprawling shopping center was set at the top of a modest little hill, and as we walked from our parking space, which was the length of two football fields from the nearest door, the wind slapped us with its icy palms.

The Lake Erie Shores Mall needs no description, because everyone in America has been in it—or one just like it. Shopping centers like this one proliferate all over the country as a greatly expanded and completely depersonalized replacement for the old general store, where the folks could meet their neighbors, talk, and catch up on the local news, except most of the people that use the mall for social purposes are teenagers. Unfortunately, they don't vote.

There were a lot of mothers with babies, pushing the strollers ahead of them like battering rams to get through the crowds. A month from now, in the teeth of the Christmas rush, the mall would resemble the running of the bulls at Pamplona. There were a few families, the husbands dragooned into a reluctant Saturday shopping trip when they'd rather be home watching the Ohio State–Illinois game, and most of the kids younger than two were crying or fussing, their tears stopping only as they passed the toy emporium and were temporarily mesmerized by some little fuzzy battery-operated dogs that barked and rolled over on the carpet outside the store.

There were a very few black faces, many of whom had probably driven over from nearby Painesville to shop, but mostly the Lake Erie Shores Mall was solid white middle-class suburbia.

A few of the volunteers I'd seen at headquarters during the week had set up a little card table in the middle of the mall with a big BARBARA FOR MAYOR sign hanging over the end of it. They were wearing straw boaters with the same message printed on the band and were passing out leaflets to a group of busy shoppers who couldn't have been less interested.

One of the volunteers, a woman in a ski sweater, recognized me. "Oh, hi, uh . . ." I watched her fight for the correct pronunciation of my name and lose. Her name tag told me she was Norma Bish. "Barbara's not due until two. Want to hand out flyers?"

"Let me grab a bite to eat first," I said. I turned to Laurie. "Can I buy you lunch?"

She reacted almost as though I'd made an unexpected and obscene proposition, but then her stomach went to war with her attitude and lost. She gave me the kind of offhand nod designed to make me think she didn't really care one way or the other, and together we walked toward the food court near the center of the mall. She lagged about two steps behind me.

A large arena of food-sticky white metal tables were encircled by about twelve different fast-food franchises. None of them looked enticing. The restaurants pay heavy rent in the malls but make little effort to please—they don't depend on word-of-mouth business.

Laurie decided she wanted Chinese food, and even though I'd had some the night before with Kellen, it still sounded better than the grayish meat patty dripping grease onto a stale bun on sale at the next counter. We waited in line for about five minutes until we finally got served; we'd both selected the egg foo young, Laurie because she liked it and me because I figured it was the one thing on the joint's menu board that they couldn't louse up.

I was wrong. When we finally found a vacant table, I discovered that my meal tasted like soggy, pulped cardboard. I tore open three little plastic envelopes of soy sauce and nearly drowned it. Now the egg foo young tasted like soy sauce–flavored pulped cardboard. It was a culinary nadir in my life.

"You shouldn't have done what you did to Dennis the other night," Laurie said, mouth stuffed. She seemed to relish her food; for all I knew, in her world this was *cordon bleu.*

"What other night?" I gulped from a huge waxed cup of Coke to banish the taste of the egg foo young, but the generous helping of chipped ice in it had diluted its flavor.

"At Laird's Chop House. With that big ugly guy. You humiliated him in front of Barbara. You didn't have to do that. He wasn't going to hit him."

"You don't think so?"

"People don't do things like that, hit other people. The guy was only trying to scare Dennis because he got in his face like that."

Maybe in the small farming towns near Dayton people didn't hit other people, and not at a small, laid-back college like Lakeland, but Laurie was proving herself incredibly naive about life in the big city.

"No wonder he didn't come around this morning," she went on. "You treated him like he was a baby or something, while Barbara was watching. And that just about killed him." She took another bite of her egg foo young and chewed it with her mouth slightly open. "He was ready to cry—or to die. He worships Barbara, you know. I mean he really loves her. She's the only person probably who's ever been nice to him."

She swallowed what was in her mouth and looked down at her broad lap. Unspoken was that nobody else had ever been nice to Laurie either.

"I'm sorry," I said. I seemed to be saying that to Laurie a lot for things that didn't require an apology, and I was annoyed with myself about it. "I'll talk to him when I see him, try to square things with him."

"No!" she almost shouted, throwing down her fork. "Just stay away from him!"

She became aware that we were in a very public place and that several people had glanced over at her loud "No!" She reddened and stood up.

"Thanks for lunch, all right?"

It was all right with me.

She toddled away, a ludicrous and pathetic figure, leaving me alone at the table. And that was all right with me too.


I browsed through the shops in the mall for a while, the egg foo young sitting in my stomach like the iceberg that did in the *Titanic*. I saw a sweater I liked, but its cost could have fed a Third World family for a year. Besides, one didn't buy oneself presents that close to Christmas.

I arrived back at the Barbara for Mayor table just about at the same time as the candidate herself made a quiet entrance through the main double doors of the mall, Cassandra Pride and Evan flanking her like a cut-rate Secret Service team. As they walked down toward the table, Evan and Cassie stopped likely looking

passers-by and introduced them to Barbara. I couldn't help noticing that many of the potential voters they accosted were over
forty. Their campaign message with its back-to-the-basics philosophy was aimed at those old enough to be a little bit wistful for
the good old days.

Someone had placed a boom box on the floor beneath the
card table, and a tape of "God Bless America" blasted out sound
waves that were floating up to the high ceiling and getting lost
there. Norma Bish and Laurie stood at either end of the mall,
right in the path of anyone trying to walk, and they were hawking
Barbara to the busy shoppers like hot-dog vendors at an Indians
game at Gateway. Two other volunteers stood in front of seats
near the table and were busily handing out flyers to whoever was
foolish enough to slow down long enough for them to thrust one
into their hands. And still others were standing nearby with yard
signs mounted on sticks, waving them around like they were
planting the flag on Iwo Jima. I expected a barrage of red-white-
and-blue balloons to be released at any moment from the ceiling
of the mall.

"Have a good racquetball game?" I asked Evan, trying to keep
from sounding sarcastic.

He seemed pleased that I was inquiring, the dumb shit. "Yeah,
matter of fact I did. When this is all over"—and here he waved
his hand at the colorful signs and the straw-hatted volunteers—
"you'll have to come out some Saturday and play with us. Nice
group of guys."

Some people simply don't have a clue.

I walked over to Cassie, who'd armed herself with a stack of
leaflets. A few feet away Barbara was entreating a leather-jack-
eted middle-aged couple who I'm sure had come to the mall on
their Harleys.

"How did it go at the senior citizen center?" I asked Cassie.

Cassie arched those eyebrows at me. "You wouldn't have
believed it. I've never seen Barbara with so much energy." She
leaned close to my ear. "Whatever went on between the two of
you this morning, do it again, will you?"

"Nothing went on. And did you ever stop to think that maybe
Judge Guilfoyle's support gave her a big lift?"

"No," she said, "I never stopped to think that." Then, turning to a mother with a balky kid of about four in tow, she said, "Hi, come and meet the candidate."

I didn't have any leaflets, which was just as well; I'm too big to loom up in front of some stranger and drag him or her over to do anything—I might bring on a seizure in the faint of heart. So I just wandered around the area trying to look like the chief of security that I was, ever watchful that no harried mother tried to blindside Barbara with a stroller. Bored to tears, I let my mind ramble.

I thought about Laurie and Dennis, two charter members of the No Chance Club who had used physical and mental challenges as an excuse to quit trying. I thought about Henry Ludlow, who could so easily rationalize the sexual exploitation of children because it was, as he'd put it, a sickness.

And I thought about what had transpired between Barbara Corns and me in her dining room that morning. And why.

After a time I amused myself watching the earnest, smiling volunteers put the arm on Saturday shoppers. Some of them just shook their heads and walked on with determination. A couple of people declined even to take the flyers. One or two others told Cassie or Barbara, "I don't even live in Lake Erie Shores." Occasionally a refusenik would smile, but most simply looked irritated, and I found myself wondering if we weren't doing Barbara's candidacy more harm than good. I didn't understand politics any better than when I started.

And then I saw a familiar face skulking around the edges of the campaign activity. Like many self-styled investigative journalists, Donald Straum was good at skulking. It's what he did for a living.

He didn't see me until I'd walked right up behind him. His blond curls lay over the collar of his corduroy jacket as he scribbled furiously in his notebook. "Getting a jump on the Christmas crowds, Mr. Straum?"

And jump is just what he did, about three inches off the ground. "God damn it, don't sneak up behind me like that!"

"Maybe you wouldn't be so nervous if you weren't where you're not supposed to be."

He stuck his jaw out at me, presenting a tempting target. "I suppose you're going to throw me out of the mall now, huh?" I tried to dodge the flying spittle but to no avail. "There's five thousand people walking around, and you're going to tell me I can't be here."

"No, I'm telling you to stay away from Barbara Corns until this campaign is over."

He put his fists on his hips and threw back his head like Errol Flynn as Robin Hood. "What are you going to do to me if I don't?"

I got very close to him, for a change invading his personal space instead of the other way round. "How bad do you want to find out?"

"You don't scare me, Jacovich," he sneered, his words at odds with how fast he was backing away from me. He'd switched from an Errol Flynn mode to a Bogart one, although it was coming out more like Walter Denton in *Our Miss Brooks*. "I have the power of the press behind me, and I'll take care of you good. You're dead, fucker. Just remember that!"

He scurried off toward Radio Shack, and I considered going after him until my beeper chirred gently at my waist.

I took it off my belt and looked at the readout. The number was familiar to me—Third District Police Headquarters, Marko Meglich's private line.

I started for the food court, remembering I'd seen a bank of telephones there, but Barbara grabbed me by the arm.

"Milan," she said, "I'd like you to meet Evelyn Culbertson, she's one of our strongest supporters."

Evelyn Culbertson was somewhere around sixty and had draped her tall, angular frame with some very expensive clothes. She had a voice like Beulah Witch on the old *Kukla, Fran and Ollie* show, and she emphasized too many words.

"Well, it's so *nice* to meet you!" she said, pumping my hand. "We're all so excited about *Tuesday! Especially* now that the county chairman has *endorsed* us!"

I started to tell her I was pleased to meet her, but she wasn't the least bit interested in my pleasure or lack thereof.

"You *know*, if Barbara *wins*—and she *will!*—it'll be so marvelous to live in a decent, honest *town* again! I've been here thirty-two *years!* My husband was *born* in our house! And *Barbara* here is going to make it like it *used* to be!"

She went on like that for another ten minutes or so. Every time I started to drift away Barbara would grab hold of my arm and squeeze it. I didn't blame her. It took at least two people to absorb all those exclamation points.

When I was finally able to extricate myself and get to the telephone, the Third District phone operator left me on hold through two choruses of "When a Man Loves a Woman" with strings, then came back on and told me Lieutenant Meglich had left for the day.

I hung up and stood there for a few minutes, thinking it over, until a woman waiting to use the phone demanded to know whether I was going to make another call or just stand there. I moved away slowly; something was bothering me, but I couldn't put a name to it.

I had to go outside in the cold crisp air and have a cigarette after that. The smell from the nearby Chinese fast-food stand was making me queasy.

Finally the never-ending day wound down.

"Thanks, everybody," Evan Corns was saying as the volunteers scooped up what was left of the campaign circulars and started tearing down the little Barbara for Mayor enclave in the middle of the mall. "You did a great job. Barbara and I are going to go home, have a quiet dinner, and get to bed early."

Everyone was kind of milling around, not paying any attention to him, but when Barbara stepped forward everybody listened. They were so unaccustomed to having her say anything at all that the sheer novelty of it captured their interest. Even Laurie and Cassandra were caught unawares.

"I want all you guys to know," she said, her piping little voice surprisingly strong, "that without all your hard work and dedication and commitment there wouldn't have *been* a campaign. I'm very touched that you expended all your time and effort for us because you believe in the same things we do, and whether we win or lose on Tuesday, I love you all!"

Everyone broke into a round of cheering, which attracted more attention from the late afternoon shopping crowd than an entire day of pamphlet distribution and banner waving, and Barbara accepted the accolades by blushing and dropping her head in a kind of offhand bow. Evan was a little stunned by her declaration but nonetheless stood by with his chest puffed out like a proud father.

I found Laurie in the crowd. "I'll drive you home as soon as you're ready, Laurie."

"No!" she said, stamping her foot. I'd never actually seen anyone stamp their foot before. "I want Barbara to drive me home!"

Cassandra Pride, as usual, saved the day; that seemed to be what she did for a living. "Aw, honey, Barbara's just exhausted, and it's way out of their way. I'll drive you home if you don't want Milan to."

Laurie shrugged, put-upon, and walked away to sulk.

"Jesus, I'll be glad when this is all over," Cassie said, rubbing one eye. "This campaign has been . . . strange."

"To say the least," I agreed.

"Well, tomorrow we've got more of the same. We'll be right back here at the mall from noon to three."

I didn't say anything but she caught my expression.

"Problem?"

"Tomorrow is the day I usually spend with my sons. I only get to see them every second Sunday."

"Go ahead and take the day off," she said. "It's probably just as well."

I frowned. "Meaning?"

"Barbara's lipstick is too red for your coloring."

"Let's understand about that—"

"I understand about it, and my guess is it wasn't your fault. Barbara is the most insecure woman I've ever met, and she needs constant reinforcement, mostly from men. I don't really care where she gets it, but I don't want anything screwing up this election more than it already is, so it's probably better if you take a day off and let her get her act together."

"That doesn't sit right," I said. "I've got a professional reputation—"

"So do I." Her eyes got narrow in a way I'd learned to know. "And there's enough scandal flying around already without letting it get complicated."

"You mean I'm fired?"

"I didn't hire you so I can't fire you. Let's just say I have no objection to your spending tomorrow with your kids and let it go at that."

I wanted a cigarette badly, but smoking was a no-no in the mall. "You're tough, Cassie."

"I'm paid to be," she said. "Call me at Barbara's first thing Monday, all right?" She patted my shoulder and went back to the card table to supervise the packing up.

I stood there feeling stupid and almost got run over by a lady with a platinum blond toddler in a stroller. The kid looked like he'd grow up to be an offensive lineman nicknamed Bubba. His mother looked like that now.

I drove home listening to the end of the Ohio State game, which they won by a touchdown, thus keeping the dogs of criticism from nipping at Coach Cooper's heels for at least another week.

I called Kellen when I got back to my apartment, but she wasn't in. I tried Marko at home to no avail, although I left a message on his machine saying I'd be home all evening.

Then I made myself a pot of Earl Grey tea, opened a new mystery I'd bought a week earlier but hadn't gotten around to, and settled down to read.

Another big Saturday night for one of Cleveland's most eligible bachelors.

# CHAPTER TWENTY-ONE

'm usually a little cranky when the telephone wakes me up in the morning, especially on a Sunday at eight o'clock. But this call was from Kellen Charles and as such was more than welcome. At least it got my heart started.

"I just wanted to see if you were all right," she said. "I was hoping I'd hear from you yesterday."

"I called last night but you weren't in. Don't you have an answering machine?"

"God, no! I'm not even listed. I get enough calls at my office. When I'm home I just want peace and quiet. So? How are you? Recovered?"

I felt for my bruised rib and was pleased to find it was still there. "Recovered but watchful."

She laughed nervously. "I've never been through anything quite so horrendous. Any ideas about who might have been driving that truck?"

"Lots of them, but nothing I can put my finger on."

"If you'd like to come over and hang out tonight, I could even be prevailed upon to cook."

"I can't," I said. "Sundays I spend with my kids. Every other Sunday, anyway. Can we make it some other time?"

"I guess so. I know how crazy you are about those boys." She sounded a little wistful. "I'd like to prove we can spend the evening together without somebody trying to kill you."

"Maybe when the election's over," I said. I sounded to myself as if I were copping out and hoped it didn't sound that way to her too. But my sons come first—they always have and always will. I think many divorced and noncustodial parents often have a keener sense of responsibility about spending quality time with their children, and during the years since Lila and I split up, I'd never allowed any relationship, not even Mary, to take precedence over fatherhood.

After Kellen and I said our goodbyes I called Marko at home but got his recorded voice again. He'd probably spent the night with his latest romantic conquest and hadn't come home yet. She was a twenty-two-year-old computer whiz from one of the big law firms downtown who, if memory served, was called Tiff. I assumed that was short for Tiffany, and even more annoying.

I wondered what they talked about. They probably didn't.

I showered, dressed snugly in a turtleneck and jeans, and read the sports page while I drank my morning coffee. The Browns were five-point underdogs. What else was new?

By ten o'clock I was pulling up to the curb in front of what used to be my house and was now occupied by my ex-wife, Lila, my two sons, and Lila's live-in boyfriend, one Joe Bradac. I'd almost stopped being morose every time I saw it; it was the only home my kids had ever known, and I'd done a lot of remodeling and repairing and painting during my tenure. There was a lot of me in that house. Now it had been so long since I'd lived there, it felt like I was visiting, which indeed I was, and that was another kind of sadness.

The door flew open and my younger son, Stephen, blasted out, blond head down, a football tucked under one arm.

"He's at the fifty!" he shouted. "The forty, the thirty, he's heading for the end zone!" In Stephen's twelve-year-old world it was perfectly reasonable to be both tailback and play-by-play announcer simultaneously.

I made a grab for him without any intention of stopping him, and he cut by me—"He dodges a tackler!"—and raced to the sidewalk. "Six points, Jacovich!" he trumpeted, and did a little victory dance that was every bit as grotesque as those you see in the NFL on any given Sunday. Then, forgetting that a moment before I'd been an opposing cornerback, he strutted up to me and gave me a high five, or as high as he could get, anyway.

Stephen had been a remarkably beautiful baby, and was still

a great-looking kid, but his cheeks were beginning to lose their baby roundness, the angel-fine blond hair was starting to darken, and there was a firmness around his jawline that hadn't been there a year ago. The realization of the passing of time knifed through me. My kids were growing up; did that mean I was getting old? The answer seemed irrefutable.

"What's new, kiddo?" I said. Everything in me wanted to hug him, but from a boy of twelve a high five is the absolute maximum expression of physical affection a father can hope for. "Did you get a good haul trick-or-treating?"

"I hid my candy so you and Milan couldn't get to it," he said. I'm afraid that when I was a resident parent I had sneaked candy bars out of my kids' Halloween bags. I wondered if Joe did it now.

"Where we going today?" Stephen asked.

"I don't know. Let's get Milan and talk about it."

Lila was standing in the doorway as we mounted the steps, wearing her usual jeans, which were becoming a tad tight across the hips, and a black and blue checkered flannel shirt over a white T-shirt. "Hi," she said, and then looked over my shoulder at the Sable. "Where's your car?"

"In the shop."

"I thought you had it tuned last month."

"A little accident."

She stood aside so Stephen and I could enter the house, then closed the door behind us and followed me into the living room. "What kind of accident?"

"No big deal—it was parked at the time." Not a lie but several light years from the truth.

"What happened?"

I heard my firstborn, Milan Jr., thundering down the stairs from his room. At seventeen, boys thunder.

"Hey, Dad," he said. He was about six one now, broad of shoulder and enviably narrow at the hips, and with his dark shiny hair and dark Serbian eyes was growing to resemble his mother more every day. There was a fresh bruise on his cheekbone that I assumed he'd earned during football practice.

"Hey." The same urge to hug had to be vanquished. How long had it been since I'd held that face between my two hands and kissed it? I couldn't remember. "What do you guys feel like doing today?"

"Milan, I want to know what happened to your car," Lila said, and planted herself in that wide-stance way she had that told me I wasn't going to be able to put her off.

"You bang up your car?" Milan Jr. asked, seemingly anxious to hear about it.

I tried to shrug it off. "A guy drove by and sheared off the door while I was getting in. It's fixable."

"My God," Lila said. "Was he insured?"

I sighed. "He didn't stop." I turned to the boys. "I thought we could do a little hiking in the Metroparks, maybe out by Squire's Castle. We can go for lunch first, or we can get some takeout and eat it out there. It's probably our last chance before winter hits."

I wasn't getting off that easy. "What do you mean, he didn't stop?"

"What part don't you understand?" I snapped, and immediately regretted it. Lila and I made a strict rule about always being civil to one another when the children were around. In fact, we were almost always civil, because I usually refused to plug into her confrontational mode, just as I had when we'd been married. But this time I'd slipped. I blunted the sharp edge a little. "It was just a hit-and-run."

She grew very pale. "Boys, go on into the den and watch TV for a few minutes. Dad and I have to talk."

"Jeez!" Stephen said, stomping off. I knew how he felt.

Milan Jr. gave me a one of those looks over his shoulder as he ambled out of the room. "Oh, yippee," he said. "I was afraid I was gonna miss *Face the Nation.*"

Lila just stared at me for a long moment, her eyes like twin lumps of shining coal. "Come into the kitchen," she said.

When Lila wanted to talk in the kitchen, it usually meant she was red-assed about something or other. The kitchen was her natural habitat, her own special turf, and she gained a certain strength from its familiar surroundings. During arguments she regarded being in her kitchen as having the home court advantage.

I followed her in, wondering where her consort Joe was. When I came over to see the boys he usually hid upstairs in the bedroom until I was gone; perhaps Lila's wanting me to talk for a bit meant that he'd gone somewhere outside the house to hide. He'd been terrified of me since he started seeing Lila right after our divorce, but especially so since I'd found out things about him that, were I to tell Lila, would wind up with him sitting on his belongings at curbside waiting for the moving van.

The kitchen was warm and cozy, full of extremely healthy house plants, and smelled of recent pancakes. There were no dirty breakfast dishes in sight, but then there wouldn't be; Lila is one of those compulsive neat freaks who make the bed in the middle of the night when you get up to go to the bathroom.

She leaned her bottom against the stove and put her hands on her hips. She might have been tapping her foot, but I wouldn't swear to it.

"Now what about this hit-and-run?"

"I told you," I said.

"Wasn't somebody involved with this political thing you're doing killed by a hit-and-run driver?"

I nodded.

She doubled up both fists, and the color flooded back into her cheeks as though someone had opened a sluice gate. "Milan Jacovich, somebody deliberately tried to run you over!"

It didn't seem to call for a reply.

"Didn't they?"

That *was* a question.

"I don't know that for sure, Lila."

"Well I know one thing for sure—you're not taking those children out of this house today."

"Lila . . ."

"It's non-negotiable. I don't want you anywhere near the boys until this is over. And you know damn well I'm right."

That was the trouble—I did know she was right, and I could have kicked myself all the way down the block for not thinking of it myself. My hunger for my sons' company had clouded my common sense, and I'd almost put them in jeopardy.

I negotiated an extra day with the boys the following weekend and then made my apologies to them. Milan Jr. took it stoically, the way teenage boys take everything, and although Stephen put a brave face on it I could tell he wasn't happy.

"Tell you what," I said, his disappointment magnified in me a thousandfold, "I'll see what I can do about some tickets for the Browns game next Sunday. How's that sound?"

"The Browns! Yea!" Stephen crowed, and even my older son couldn't suppress a grin. As a high school footballer himself, he was a devout Browns fan and had suffered through several bad seasons in a row along with the rest of sporting Cleveland. I respected the fact that he hadn't transferred his allegiance to a more successful NFL franchise.

"No promises," I warned, "but I'll give it my best shot." Like asking Ed Stahl to use his considerable influence to wangle some tickets. My approval rate as a father was often dependent on Ed's good offices, and I offered up a little prayer that he'd come through for me once more.

I went home feeling lousier and more alone than I had in a long time.

I tried Marko again to no avail. At least one of us was having a nice Sunday. Or it pleased me to think so.

I moped around my apartment for a while. Not only was it too early in the day for a beer, but I had left my new six-pack in the back seat of my Sunbird when it had been towed to the impound lot and thence to a body shop in Lake Erie Shores, and since it was a Sunday, Ohio law made it impossible for me to go and buy some more until one o'clock in the afternoon.

I reheated what was left of my coffee, but it always tastes like roofing tar that way, and I dumped it into the sink.

Sundays stink.

Finally an idea hit me. It took some guts, but I called Kellen Charles back.

"I feel like an idiot," I said, "but it turns out I won't be spending the day with the kids."

"Oh, I'm sorry," she said. "Nothing's wrong, I hope."

"Too complicated to explain over the phone. Any chance I could tell you in person tonight?"

"I think that'd be just a fine idea." She really sounded pleased, which did a lot to improve my own mood.

We decided, after some more conversation, that she'd drive in to Cleveland Heights late in the afternoon instead of my going out there—for the same reason that I wasn't seeing the boys. I'd nearly been run over in front of her house, and even though I was listed in the phone book, there was a chance that the driver of the white Ford pickup didn't know where I lived.

That pretty much gave me something to do to pass the long Sunday afternoon: I cleaned my apartment.

The front room, my office, was always fairly tidy. The rest of the place wasn't really all that dirty, but it wasn't neat, either. When you live alone like I do, you tend to leave things around. I could exist very nicely in a house with no closets, as long as there were plenty of doorknobs.

I switched on the football game while I cleaned, but I didn't really watch it. Kansas City was creaming the Raiders like they always do, and I didn't care much, but the sound of the play-by-play made the solitude a little easier to bear.

I called Marko almost every hour on the hour all afternoon but had no luck; finally I stopped leaving messages.

Not being able to get hold of him bothered me. He wouldn't have called Saturday if it wasn't important.

Kellen arrived promptly at seven o'clock. One of the nice things about living at the juncture of two major thoroughfares is that even people who don't know the neighborhood can find me without too much trouble.

Arm in arm, we walked down to Nighttown about two blocks away, and over predinner cocktails I explained what had happened at Lila's and why I happened to be free that evening.

"You did the right thing, Milan," she said soothingly. "But I know how much it must hurt not being able to see your kids. At least you'll make up for it next weekend."

"That's the trouble," I said. "With kids that age there is no real making up. They change so quickly, develop their own interests and their own friends, and pretty soon it'll be a drag for them to have to spend time with their old man. Every day I don't get to see them is a day lost."

She sipped her Pinot Noir. "I guess so. Of course I don't have any children, but I think I understand how you feel."

A jazz combo began playing quietly in the next room, one of my favorite old songs called "Shining Hour."

"Didn't you ever want kids?"

"Oh, sure. When I was a little girl I had all those old-fashioned little-girl dreams about a family of my own, but when I finished school I got on a career track right away, and after a while I realized it was just as well. I wouldn't make a very good mother, I'm afraid."

"Are you kidding? You're a real nurturer. You even have a nurturing job."

"I suppose that fulfills my needs okay. And the nice thing is, when I go home at night I leave all of that at the office. But you can't take time off from children. Some people are born to be parents—like you."

"Me?"

She reached across the table and squeezed my hand. "I see the way your eyes get when you talk about the boys. You're a very kind man. Look at the work you do."

"I don't see that as nurturing."

"The way you are with Barbara."

"I get paid for that, Kellen."

She shook her head. "Kindness comes with the package."

After dinner—we both ordered pasta and tasted each other's choices—we went back up to my apartment, where I boiled a little water, heated up two brandy snifters, and poured some Rémy Martin, a holdover from when I used to keep it on hand for Mary.

I put on an Artie Shaw tape. Maybe, as Ed Stahl had said, I am retro. I'm probably the only guy in Cleveland my age who doesn't know the words to "Louie, Louie." But the silky clarinet gliding through "Begin the Beguine" seemed more appropriate to the mood.

We cuddled up together on the sofa and talked quietly. When we finished the cognac I poured us some more, and when we finished that we moved into the bedroom as though it were the most natural thing in the world.

I was glad that I'd included putting clean sheets on the bed in my housekeeping ritual.

I heard the telephone ringing at about ten thirty, but I didn't bother getting up to answer it.

Would you?

# CHAPTER TWENTY-TWO

**K**ellen left shortly after midnight. She almost didn't, because after making love a few times we were both drowsy and relaxed and were just on the edge of falling asleep. It would have been all right with me if she'd stayed; when you've lived alone for a long time, waking up in the morning with someone is an event. But we both had to get up early Monday morning, so she decided to head out to Lake County before dawn. There would be other times, other mornings—I hoped there would be other times.

Since Mary, there hadn't really been anyone in my life. I'd had a brief romance with an attorney named Shushano Bauch, but we really came from different galaxies, and as an Orthodox Jew she didn't see much future in keeping company with a Slovenian lapsed Catholic. We were still friends—but that didn't keep my feet warm at night.

I suppose I'm at the age where every woman I meet is a potential significant other. Playing the field is fun for a while, but it eventually wears me down. So I'm always looking for that special spark, that moment when you begin to think that this particular relationship has staying power. Most Slovenians get married and stay that way, and the failure of my union with Lila was forever marked on my own scorecard as a strikeout.

The same with Mary Soderberg. When we busted up it had taken the guts right out of me. Now I was finding myself gun-shy, and very reluctant to trust any more—myself or anyone else. Maybe with Kellen things would work out.

Whatever that meant. Whatever I wanted it to mean.

I wrapped up in a blanket and sat in the dark and finished the rest of the cognac. Making love with Kellen had been energetic and full of shared laughter, and I was feeling good in more ways than one. I was so busy remembering that I almost forgot the phone had rung in the middle of everything.

The message on my answering machine was from Marko, concise and to the point: "Where the hell are you? Call." It was too late to do that, so I got into bed and closed my eyes, but my mind was racing. There's nothing like a phone message from a homicide lieutenant to lull you to sleep.

The clock radio blasted me awake at seven o'clock. In between golden oldies from the sixties, WMJI's John Lanigan and Jimmy Malone were doing their daily liberal-versus-conservative shtick and taking no prisoners, and mellow-voiced John Webster was trying his best to mediate without getting caught in the crossfire. I listened and chuckled while I got dressed, drank my coffee, and idly checked the NFL scores in the *Plain Dealer*.

I waited until eight fifteen, when I was pretty sure Marko would be in his office, and gave him a call.

"Where the hell were *you* at ten o'clock on a Sunday night?" he demanded.

"This isn't a school morning and you're not my mother."

"No, but I worry about you like I was. Somebody tried to kill you Friday night, in case you've forgotten."

"I wrote it down in my diary just so I'd remember."

"Any more trouble over the weekend?"

"No," I said. "But I stayed pretty close to home. I tried to call you about twenty times since Saturday afternoon."

"I was with Lindsey," he said.

"Lindsey?"

"I met her Thursday night at Swingo's Silver Quill. "She's the PR gal at one of the big hotels. A real doll."

Ah well. Welcome, Lindsey. Farewell, Tiff, and thanks for the two swell weeks. *Sic transit* Marko's sex life.

"So," I said, "what did you want Saturday?"

"To tell you I've got those motor vehicle printouts for you. The 1983 Ford pickups."

"White ones?"

"We don't separate them by colors, Milan. This isn't an art gallery. Besides, you can get a vehicle painted for under a hundred bucks, so there's no point. Bring a pillow for your ass; you're going to be all day going through them."

My shoulders sagged just thinking about it. "I'll be there directly—if there's coffee."

"There's always coffee. It's a police station."

I fished through the desk drawer for my reading glasses. I don't wear them very often unless I'm going to be doing a lot of close work, but I was already anticipating the headache I'd have by the end of the day. I wasn't quite ready to leave yet, however. I took a chance and called Victor Gaimari at home and caught him before he left his ultramodern house in the far eastern suburbs for his office downtown.

"Good morning, Milan," he said heartily. Of course he said everything heartily; it was his personal style. "I took a few days off and went to New York to hit some of the Broadway shows, if you were trying to reach me."

"I was trying to reach you, all right."

"How's the campaign going?"

"You tell me."

"What's the matter?" he said. "Is something wrong?"

"You know damn good and well there is."

"You're not getting confrontational again, are you, Milan?" he said. I really think he felt bad about it. "I hate it when you do that. We've been getting along so well, too."

"When can we sit down, Victor?"

"I have a pretty full plate today. Shall we have a drink after work tonight?"

He wanted to be my friend so badly it was pathetic, and I couldn't understand it. I loathed everything he was and stood for, and he knew it. "I don't want a drink."

"By six o'clock tonight you might," he said playfully.

After poring over Mark's computer printouts I probably would, but not with him. "Why don't I just come up to the office?"

He sounded stiff and hurt. "Strictly business, is that the idea?"

"That's the idea. Six o'clock," I said, and banged down the receiver before he whined some more. Then I sat at my kitchen table until my hands stopped shaking. I didn't want to get behind the wheel of a car when I was that angry.

Traffic was fairly heavy. We don't have a rush hour in Cleveland—it's more like a rush ten minutes—so I descended Cedar Hill briskly and then headed down Chester Avenue to East Thirtieth and cut over to Payne. It wasn't even nine o'clock when I pulled into a parking space two blocks down from the big rock pile that is Third District Police Headquarters.

Marko's three-piece suit du jour was chocolate brown with a discreet pinstripe, one I hadn't seen before. He owns more than twenty different custom-made suits. He probably spends a quarter of his salary on wardrobe. Personally I wouldn't dress so elegantly to talk to murderers, but then that's me.

There were two dauntingly thick stacks of computer printouts on the corner of his desk, and I filled a plastic cup from his Braun coffee maker to fortify myself. It was early enough in the morning that the police station coffee hadn't yet attained its usual consistency of used motor oil.

"Got a dirty little chimney corner I can sit in and look at these?" I asked, tapping the printouts.

"Feel free to use my desk," Marko told me. "I'll be in a meeting most of the morning."

"Who's the meeting with? Sharon Stone?"

"What?"

"I figured from how dressed up you are that there must be a beautiful woman involved."

He got up from his desk. "Don't bust my chops today, all right, Milan? It's Monday, and I don't need your brand of crap." He straightened his tie in the mirror atop his file cabinet. "There's both Lake and Cuyahoga counties there. Up to you which one you tackle first," he said as he walked out.

I took off my coat and hung it on the hook behind the door. Marko's Brooks Brothers overcoat was on a molded plastic hanger. I'd bought mine on sale at the Burlington Coat Factory, so I felt okay about just hanging it up by the loop inside the collar. I sat down and pulled the files toward me; they must have weighed two pounds.

The Lake County Ford pickup owners seemed like a good place to start. Even though Princess True had died in downtown

Cleveland, it seemed more likely that if her death had not been an accident, someone from her own neighborhood would have engineered it.

I put my glasses on my nose and dug in. The pages had been turned out on an old-fashioned dot matrix printer, and the letters were faint and hard to read. The first name on the Lake County list was Abel. I groaned. My eyes were going to fall out of my head before I was finished.

But I got lucky on the third page, and the adrenaline rush almost made me dizzy. The hair on the back of my neck prickled as I read that a 1983 Ford pickup was listed in the name of one "Babb, Delores" in Perry.

Some people might think it was a coincidence; I personally don't believe in them. Babb isn't a very unusual name, but it's not exactly Smith or Johnson either. I was willing to bet the farm that Delores Babb was somehow connected to Dennis, his sister or his mother. Or even his wife, although I didn't think so. Dennis didn't seem the marrying kind.

I wrote down the address in my notebook. Then I whipped through the rest of the list. It took almost an hour. No other names jumped out at me. Delores Babb was to be all the morning's search yielded. I hoped it would be enough.

My eyes were burning from the strain by the time I finished, and I took off my glasses and massaged my eyeballs for a while. Then I picked up the phone and asked the operator if she could locate Lieutenant Meglich. She told me he was in with the assistant chief and couldn't be disturbed.

I swiveled the chair around so I was facing Marko's vintage Smith Corona typewriter, slipped in a piece of his own memo paper, and laboriously typed out a note telling him what I'd found, and that I was going to check it out. It was probably a good thing he wasn't there, because he would only have told me to stay out of it and let the police handle things.

Then again, no one had tried to run him down in the street.

I called Cassie to tell her I'd be late, and went down to my car.

It took the better part of an hour to get from downtown Cleveland out to Perry, where Delores Babb lived. The smokestacks of the inactive Perry Nuclear Power Plant loomed ominously over the whole area, more threatening somehow now that no smoke billowed from them, stark against a sky that was growing increasingly wintry.

There were no sidewalks out here; all that separated the road from the private property was a drainage ditch about seven feet wide, and the hardier weeds and grasses clung to its sides with a tenacity that was brave and touching. Crushed beer cans and other flotsam choked the bottom of the ditch. Scrub oaks, their branches naked awaiting the winter, and an occasional pine stood silhouetted black and bleak against the relentless cloud cover. Two large blue-black crows were having a shrill screaming match in adjoining trees.

The house was little larger than a cabin, I imagined it contained no more than two rooms. There was a concrete front step, cracked in the middle, in lieu of any kind of porch, and green moss showed through the crack. The gray paint on the aluminum siding was peeling, what little grass there was in the front was six inches high and a uniform light brown, and one of the side windows had been broken and then indifferently patched with electrical tape in the form of a drunken Y. Some kind of makeshift shed sat on a strange angle at the rear of the property, even more in need of paint than the house, and over the door a handsome pair of deer antlers had been crudely mounted. All over the grass and the gravel driveway there was evidence of a very large dog. Parked beside the house was Dennis Babb's old wreck of a Dodge.

I cut my engine and got out, my large feet crunching on the stones as I carefully tried to avoid the dog waste, and walked toward the front door. From somewhere behind the house I heard muffled, deep throaty barking. I mounted the step and knocked, waited but no one answered. I went around to the rear.

A woman backed out of the shed carrying a sack of dog meal. Locking the door, she stopped when she saw me and stood watchfully, leaning her broad blue-jeaned rump against it. She wore a man's army fatigue jacket over a flannel undershirt, and suede work boots shiny from long, hard wear. Her badly chapped lips made her look as if she'd put on too wide a swath of lipstick, and her hands were red and work-roughened with blunt-cut nails rimmed with half moons of dirt.

"Delores Babb?" I said. About forty, the resemblance to her

brother was unmistakable, right down to the funny glasses. Her eyes were small and squinty and a little too close together. The gene pool the Babb siblings had drawn from obviously had a few deficiencies.

She stuck out her lower lip the way Dennis often did. "Who wants her?" she demanded. There was a crackle in her voice, as if this was the first time she'd used it in a long while.

I tried my most disarming smile, for all the good it did me. "I'm with the Barbara Corns political campaign. Are you Delores Babb?"

She grudged me a small nod. Her lank brown hair, shot through with gray strands, looked as though it hadn't been washed for quite some time.

"Your brother Dennis has been volunteering for us."

She didn't say anything. It was obvious I'd have to work for every word.

"We haven't seen him for a few days, and we're worried about him, want to make sure he's all right."

It took her almost a minute to process the data. "Well, he don't live here. He use'ta, but he don't no more."

I jerked my head at the Dodge. "That's his car, isn't it?"

She stared at it as if it had suddenly appeared in her drive-way by magic. "Sometimes he leaves it here an' takes my truck. I ain't seen him since Friday. Don't know where he went off to."

"He has your truck now?"

"I s'pose." She set the sack of dog meal down with a thump, flexing her fingers. "So what you want with him anyhow?"

"Friday was the last time we saw him too. We're worried," I said again.

From inside the shed I heard a large dog snuffling and whin-ing—or maybe, from the sound of it, a grizzly bear. Claws scrab-bled at the bottom of the shed's flimsy aluminum door, and I could see it shake from where I stood.

"You try his house?" she said.

"No," I said. "Where is it?"

Her little eyes got even smaller. "Seems like if you was a friend of his you'd know where he lives."

"I'm more of a coworker than a friend," I said.

"Well, he ain't here." Her eyes were frightened, haunted, and I

was sure that it had very little to do with me. I didn't imagine Delores Babb had many visitors. Solitude often makes people unfit
for human contact, and she showed no inclination to be hospitable.

I put my hands in my pockets, trying not to intimidate her
further. "You could save me a lot of time if you told me where he
lived."

"Yeah, well, tough patooties, 'cause I ain't gonna."

"Look, Ms. Babb, Dennis could be in a lot of trouble. I'm just
trying to help him."

Her chin quivered a little, like Katharine Hepburn's, but the
resemblance stopped right there. "What kinda trouble?"

"Pretty serious, I'm afraid. And if he's driving your truck, you
could be in trouble too."

She curled her fingers into loose fists as if to hide the dirty
nails, and she blinked furiously. "You tryin' to skeer me."

"No, but it's important that Dennis contacts us."

"Ain't important t'me," she observed.

"It might be important for him."

She remained a skeptic. "You go find him, then."

"Won't you help me?"

"Why should I?"

"You'd be helping Dennis."

"Dennis done sump'n bad?"

"I don't know," I said. "Maybe."

Her eyes glazed over a little while she thought about it. Then
she gestured vaguely toward the roadway. "Git you on outta here,
mister," she warned, " 'fore I set the dog on you."

She put her hand on the doorknob and rattled it. The whining
turned into a throaty cough, then a thunderous bark that made
me jump in spite of myself. I didn't think she was kidding, nor the
dog either. I'm not usually afraid of dogs, but the depth and vol-
ume of the bark from behind the door was as impressive as hell.

"If you see him," I said, beating a retreat down the driveway,
"please have him call Barbara. Okay?"

She stuck her nose in the air and closed her eyes, I guess figuring that if she couldn't see me I wasn't there. Her hand didn't
leave the doorknob, though, and the barking grew louder and
more intense.

I was very happy to reach the safety of my car. I backed out of the driveway, noticing that Delores Babb never again opened her eyes to watch me go.

Dennis Babb had run down Princess True in the street, and since it had happened in downtown Cleveland he had obviously followed her there with killing on his mind. And he'd followed me to Kellen's house Friday night, probably waited down the block through an entire Chinese dinner, and tried to kill me too.

# CHAPTER TWENTY-THREE

**D**amn it, I stick my neck out a mile for you getting those printouts, and you go off by yourself to play hero!"

Marko was coatless, shirt sleeves rolled up to his elbows, and he was pacing angrily around his office, which effectively limited him to five steps in any direction. He was as agitated as I'd seen him since an unjust offensive interference call against him cost Kent State a touchdown in a game against Southern Illinois twenty years earlier.

I was getting used to Marko being bent out of shape with me, but I tried to defuse the situation anyway. I was tired of being yelled at. The last person to speak nicely to me had been Kellen, and that had been eighteen hours earlier.

"You're carrying on like I faced down a lynch mob with nothing but a slingshot," I said. "I went out and talked to a not too swift woman on a beat-up farm."

"What if you'd gotten killed?" he raged. "It would have been my ass."

"Correction," I said mildly, "it would have been mine."

"I swear to God, Milan, sometimes I think you need a keeper!" He fumed and fussed and pulled angrily at his mustache, then smoothed it down again. He lit a Winston, took two puffs, and squashed it out in the ashtray. Marko was having trouble making decisions this afternoon.

"If you want to play cop, why didn't you stick it out on the force where you belong and do it legally?"

"I didn't do anything illegal."

"You might have had the courtesy to let me know."

"I'd like to point out that if you hadn't gone off to a meeting I would have told you about Delores Babb and let you take care of it. I did try to call you. Ask the operator."

Lighting another cigarette and looking as if he were really going to smoke this one, he plopped down in his chair. "I suppose you ran to tell your goombah, Gaimari, about this right away, didn't you?"

I put both hands flat on his desk and leaned toward him. "No, as a matter of fact, I didn't—and I don't like your implication."

"Who gives a damn what you like?" he snarled. "You push me, Milan, you push me so damn hard. And all the time I feel like it's Gaimari doing the pushing. I don't like his fingerprints on me. Or on you, either."

I stood up. "I cracked your damn case for you!"

"Am I supposed to thank you?"

"No, you're supposed to go get Dennis Babb before he kills someone else."

He sucked air in through his teeth, and then he deflated. "Why did he do it?" he said quietly.

"Find him and ask him."

Marko took a deep drag on the Winston and blew the smoke out through loose lips. I preferred to think he hadn't deliberately blown it in my direction. "Jesus, I wish you'd stayed on the force."

"Why?"

"Because I'm a lieutenant now, and if you were still carrying a badge I could kick your ass good!"

"Marko," I reminded him gently, "on the best day you ever had in your life you couldn't kick my ass."

Things deteriorated between us from there. The upshot of my visit was that, while not exactly gracious about it, he did put out an APB on Dennis and notified the Lake County law enforcement people as well. But it wasn't going to be as easy as it sounded, I knew. I figured Dennis knew his attempt at me on Friday night had been one toke over the line, and he had gone to ground; that's why we hadn't seen him for three days. And any hunter knows it's a lot harder to bag your quarry when the quarry knows he's being hunted.

Victor Gaimari, for instance, knew I'd be loaded for bear when

I arrived at his office at six o'clock. That explained the presence of John Terranova reading *Playboy* in the outer office where the secretary sat. Terranova was clearly meant to be a deterrent to my getting out of hand with Victor. I thought about congratulating him on his civic-mindedness for contributing to Gayton True's campaign, but I reconsidered. Wisely, I have no doubt.

He waved at the door to Victor's private office. "Mr. Gaimari said you should go right in," he mumbled without getting up. He didn't seem as friendly as he had in my apartment, and the bulge beneath his jacket told me he was definitely on duty.

Victor was on the sofa against one wall, a drink in his hand. He looked artfully posed, like an ad in *GQ* for a particularly expensive brand of Scotch. Terminal Tower boasts spectacular views from just about anywhere; Victor's windows looked out on the twisting waters of the Cuyahoga and beyond to the steel mills, their furnaces glowing red-hot in the dusk. There is a terrible beauty about the mills, a raw, powerful spell they cast. My father, who had worked in the pits for most of his adult life, would probably have given me an argument about that, but viewed from a distance there was no denying their fascination.

"Milan! Right on time," Victor said. "Can I get you something? Oh, sorry, I forgot, this is strictly business. No socializing over drinks like gentlemen. Well, can you take off your coat and sit down, or are you going to hover over me and tell me what a shit I am?"

"I'm going to take off my coat," I said, doing so, "and then I'm going to tell you what a shit you are."

"It isn't exactly news," he said, eyes twinkling. "I rather pride myself on it."

I threw my coat over the back of a chair and sat. "Victor, you've played me for a sucker."

"How so?"

"You've been giving financial support to Gayton True right along with Barbara Corns. You gave John Terranova out there a thousand bucks to contribute to True's war chest and God knows how many other people."

"So?"

"Gamblers call that hedging your bets."

"I prefer calling it insurance."

"You lied to me. You said you wanted Barbara to win."

He wagged a finger at me. "I think if you'll recall our initial conversation, you'll find I told you no such thing. Evan Corns is a client of mine, of this brokerage. And a friend. His wife was running for mayor and I wanted her looked after because I felt things might get a little heated out there. I take good care of my friends—something you'd do well to remember."

"Can we do this without the commercials?"

He tasted his drink. "We've both kept our end of the bargain. I never lied to you in any way."

My stomach was doing acrobatics as I thought of poor Barbara and how hard she'd worked. "But you don't want her to make it, do you? You sabotaged her from the beginning."

"Is that why I hired her one of the best campaign managers in the state?"

"A black woman running an election in a white-bread-and-mayonnaise town like Lake Erie Shores? You knew the voters wouldn't like that. I should have figured it out earlier."

"All right," he said, and I could tell he was growing annoyed with me. "Let's say that my interests, and that of my uncle, would be better served if Gayton True remained the mayor of Lake Erie Shores and let it go at that. Grow up, Milan! Do you think for one moment Evan Corns believed that woman could challenge an entrenched, canny old warhorse like Gayton True?"

The hair on the back of my neck stood at attention. Pieces were beginning to fall together; I didn't much like the complete picture. Evan knew all along Barbara was tilting at windmills, but he'd put her through hell anyway. Somehow Victor convinced Evan to run her as a sure loser, insurance that True would be re-elected. I didn't know which man I loathed more.

But I knew which one was sitting in front of me. "You smug son of a bitch," I said.

His expression didn't change, nor did the tone of his voice. But he said, "Be careful how you talk to me, Milan. I'm getting older and I'm not as patient as I used to be."

"You're backing True, aren't you? You have right from the beginning. Because of the casino. You've had True's balls in your pocket all along."

He arched his brows and nodded.

"You only hired me to report back to you in case Barbara's people started poking around in things you didn't want to come out in the open."

He opened his eyes wide, Mickey Rooney at Boys Town, and nodded again.

"You never for one minute believed Barbara Corns had a snowball's chance in hell of winning this election, did you?"

He frowned and shook his head.

I chewed on my bottom lip. "You're a load, Victor, you know that? You're a real load."

He shrugged. "Is it on moral grounds that you object to a casino? The evils of gambling? Never put a couple of bucks on the Browns, have you? Never bet the spread?"

"The casino isn't the point."

He smiled. "I thought not."

"The point is that you set Barbara up to lose, all the while looking like a concerned friend and supporter. Why didn't you tell me? Why weren't you straight?"

He uncrossed his long legs and then crossed them again the other way. He was wearing what looked like ostrich-skin shoes that must have cost five hundred dollars, and smooth black socks. "Milan, I think we have to get something clear between us or else we're never going to get along: you are an employee. No less so than John out there, or my secretary, or Cassandra Pride. You were told all you needed to know in order to function properly and effectively do your job. You functioned well, and I appreciate it."

He looked at his watch, a Movado that gleamed on his wrist. "By this time tomorrow, maybe a few minutes later, the polls will be closed and your job will be over. You can forget all about Lake Erie Shores and Barbara Corns and go on about your life a few dollars richer."

"That stinks, Victor. On ice."

"You have a colorful way of expressing yourself, Milan. I like that. But I assure you that it doesn't stink on ice. It's business. Perfectly legitimate business. That's all politics is, you know— just a different kind of business. The flag gets waved and a lot of bullshit promises are made, but in the end it's all business. Dollars. We have certain interests out in Lake County, a certain agenda, and we did what we had to do to protect our interests. That's why we hired you."

He put his drink down, his affability instantly discarded. "You're a very righteous man, you know? I think you perceive yourself as some kind of Old Testament deity, dispensing justice and hurling thunderbolts at the Sodomites. You were very definite about not doing anything illegal, or anything that violated your quaint little code of honor. Well, rest easy, you haven't. You've done a perfectly legitimate job for which you're being paid a fair wage. What's your problem?"

"You used me."

He shrugged. "We all use each other, my friend. Think about it. No one ever does anything without a possible payoff. That's how the world operates. I did you a favor a while ago, now you've done me one. I don't see the harm."

"You wouldn't," I said.

Our eyes locked. A handsome man, Victor, well-turned-out in his expensive suit, sitting in his expensive office on his expensive sofa, and firmly convinced he was one of the untouchables under glass, that the dirt and corruption he slogged around in every day wouldn't rub off on his ostrich-skin shoes.

"Are we even now? In the favor department, I mean."

He sipped his drink, making the ice cubes tinkle musically. "I'd say we are, yes."

I stood up and put on my coat. "Then lose my phone number. I'm through doing business with you. Permanently."

"Until you need me again."

I took one more quick look out the window at the mills, a fiery vision of hell in the darkness—I figured I'd never see that view from this office again—and started for the door. Then a thought hit me.

"One more thing," I said.

He gestured broadly, generously, for me to go ahead.

"Al Drago. He's on your payroll, isn't he?"

His look never wavered. "Just like you, Milan."

I shivered as I walked through the outer office, even though the room was well heated. John Terranova looked up from his magazine. "See you around, Milan," he said.

I didn't even slow down. "Probably not."

# CHAPTER TWENTY-FOUR

I'm not sure what the conventional political wisdom is about the weather. I think I heard somewhere that storm clouds bring out the more liberal voters, and keep the conservatives home. Or maybe it's the other way around.

In any event, the first Tuesday of November brought with it northern Ohio's first lake-effect snow of the season, and when I awoke and looked out my window, all I could see was snow blowing horizontally, and a bunch of cars fishtailing crazily on the slippery street. I knew that if it was this bad in Cleveland Heights, it was going to be a blizzard out in Lake Erie Shores, and I wondered how it would affect voter turnout.

The lake effect is that weather condition peculiar to only a few places in the world, including Cleveland, occurring when a mass of cold air moves across a large body of water, sucks up the moisture, and then deposits it over the first available land mass in the form of rain or snow. Lake County, in the southeast corner of Lake Erie, is particularly vulnerable, part of what is commonly referred to as the Snow Belt.

I'd lived in the area long enough to recognize that this one was going to be a pisser.

I had mixed feelings to begin with about going out to participate in what I now knew to he a useless charade, but Barbara needed all the moral support she could get. It was the least I could do—I hadn't been much help to her otherwise.

Besides, I'd awakened in the middle of the night with one more piece of the puzzle.

I'd only had a TV dinner the night before, so I'd awakened hungry, but all I could find was a half-empty box of Lucky Charms from Stephen's last visit. I hope I'm never desperate enough to consider little colored bits of marshmallow an acceptable breakfast for an adult.

I got dressed, dug my rubber Totes out from the back of the closet where they'd remained ignored since last March, and tottered down the slippery sidewalk to Coffees of the World, a cavernous, high-ceilinged room where they offer fancy coffees and pastries by day and quiet jazz on weekend evenings, and had a couple of bran muffins and some hazelnut coffee. The healthful muffins didn't make me feel particularly self-righteous, and I'm one of those purists who think that the only proper flavor for coffee is coffee, but this was a morning for experimentation and meditation on the verities and vagaries of life. I'd taken my newspaper with me and read it at a table by the window, watching the traffic struggle past, the drivers bracing themselves for the rollercoaster trip down snow-slick Cedar Hill.

By the time I was ready to leave, the city's salt trucks had been by to ease the morning rush, and what had been white snow at dawn's first light was now brown and gray slush. Getting the car washed in weather like that is an exercise in frustration because it will only snow again a few days later, but the salt and chemicals used to melt the streets really play havoc with your paint job.

Then I did my civic duty and voted for the mayor of Cleveland Heights.

The freeway heading away from Cleveland was relatively traffic free, but that meant that the snow hadn't been pounded down and rendered decently drivable yet, and it was slippery going. Automatic transmissions have made the act of driving a car a fairly passive one, but not in Ohio in the snow, and I wrestled the wheel all the way out to Lake County.

The blue and white BARBARA FOR MAYOR signs I drove past on the front lawns of Lake Erie Shores seemed cruelly ironic, and it angered me that Victor and Evan had so callously toyed with the dreams and emotions of a decent, naive woman.

No wonder Evan wouldn't press the issue of True's son helping to count primary ballots, or capitalize on Earl Barnstable's indictment. No wonder he'd thought the Browns game more important than the campaign. Evan knew from the start that he was the head coach of a team that wasn't even seeded.

Was this what the electoral process is all about? Do the rest of us go dumbly through the motions when all along we're being manipulated and lied to? Have we become so damn docile that we let the kingmakers and power brokers, the Victor Gaimaris of the world, jerk our strings and watch us dance and jump like a bunch of wooden Howdy Doodys without minds of our own?

I got madder and madder as I drove, and like the man who went in search of a jack to change a tire in the hoary old joke, by the time I arrived at the campaign headquarters on the square I was ready to tear down the walls.

Cassie had assembled a large volunteer contingent this morning, and almost all of them were busy working the phones: "Hi, we want to remind you to vote today if you haven't already, and we hope you'll vote for Barbara Corns for mayor. She'll be good for Lake Erie Shores."

I wanted to stand up on a table and loudly announce to all of them that they were wasting their time, that they'd been wasting it for the last six weeks, but I didn't. They were all so earnest that telling them they'd been deceived would have been cruelty rather than kindness. Fighting in a just but hopeless cause can sometimes be ennobling for some people, a kind of purification, and at the end of the long evening ahead when the ballots had been counted and it was back to business as usual, they would wear the defeat like a badge of honor, having fought against the odds and borne their wounds bravely.

Laurie Pirkle had a phone to her ear, but of course there was no sign of Dennis. Cassie was busy briefing a band of volunteers who were dressed for the weather, instructing them to stand as near as the law allowed to the polling places and hand out campaign literature. I felt sorriest for them. They'd all catch colds and chilblains for nothing.

I stamped the wet snow off my rubbers. "Can we go somewhere and talk?" I said to Cassie when I finally cornered her back by the copying machine.

She looked ceilingward. "Milan, I don't have time for a heart-to-heart, today of all days. Why don't you grab a phone? Maybe we can get some lunch together later."

Before I could say anything, someone else demanded her attention and she was gone. I took off my coat, draped it over the back of a folding chair, and sat down at one of the tables, doing as she advised and picking up a telephone. I didn't contact any of the registered voters on the list in front of me, though. I called Marko.

"No sign of your Dennis Babb," he told me. "The Lake County sheriff checked his place in Painesville, and the landlady says she hasn't seen him for several days. I sent a couple of guys out to Perry, and they bounced the sister awhile, but I think she's telling the truth when she says she doesn't know where he is. They said she had a monster dog, a Hound of the Baskervilles she nearly sicced on them. Anyway, we have a BOLO on the truck, but Dennis seems to have turned invisible. He's either holed up in a cave somewhere or he's left town."

"He didn't leave town," I said, thinking of Dennis Babb trying to function in a strange city where no one knew him. "Guys like that have no place to go. What about Henry Ludlow?"

"Your chicken hawk? I turned it over to the locals, but they weren't too glad to hear about it. Even if they can get a warrant, which is doubtful, the man has a few bucks and he's going to have a lawyer screaming no probable cause."

"Kiddie porn is a federal beef if he used the mails."

He sighed. "Prove it, Milan. You know the drill. My guess is that it's going to be a tough bust."

I scowled as I heard him take puff on his a cigarette, and it made me realize I hadn't had one myself yet, but no one else in campaign headquarters was smoking, so I gritted my teeth. He wasn't telling me what I wanted to hear about Henry Ludlow.

"How's the election look up there? You gonna win?"

"Hope springs eternal," I said.

I hung up and brooded. After a while I put my coat on, went outside, and lit a cigarette, filling my lungs with poisonous smoke. I know it's not good for me, but I'm an addict, okay?

I bent my head low against the falling snow and walked down the block to a pay phone from which, using almost all the change I had in my pocket, I called the Federal Bureau of Investigation's Cleveland field office and dropped the dime on Henry Ludlow.

Although the fibbies didn't share Alice James's local mind-set

that nothing terrible ever happens in Lake County, they still said
they were going to need something more concrete than a tip in
order to move on Ludlow. But I gave them just enough—the connection between Ludlow and Earl Barnstable—to get them interested. And I cut a deal with them that I wasn't sure I'd be able to
follow through on.

It was a crazy move, especially since it was none of my business.
But a little girl I didn't even know was in jeopardy, and somewhere along the line Henry Ludlow was going to get derailed if
it took me the rest of my days to do it. I'd rather Dennis Babb got
away with Princess True's murder than let Henry Ludlow skate.

Big fat snowflakes had collected on my shoulders and my hair,
and I tried ineffectually to brush them off. It was a losing cause, it
was snowing harder now. I field-stripped the cigarette, scattering
the loose tobacco in the wind that swirled the snow and putting
the filter in my pocket to dispose of later.

Then I went back to the storefront and caught Cassie Pride in
a rare quiet moment.

"I'm going to be out for a while," I said.

She frowned. "It's Election Day—we need you here."

I wanted to tell her she didn't need any of us, but I didn't. I'd
only have to pretend for another few hours. Instead I said, "I'm
not good about calling strangers on the phone. I can do more
good where I'm going."

"Where *are* you going?"

"To fight city hall," I said.


The Lake Erie Shores Municipal Center was not as impressive
as city halls usually are in bigger cities. It was in an old colonial-
looking building off the square, which also housed the police department. The mayor's digs weren't hard to find, especially with
all the signs and arrows in the hallways. I proceeded around to the
side of the building until I found the right door. It had a window
of the kind of pebbled glass no one had used for forty years, and
gold leaf lettering on it proclaimed GAYTON M. TRUE, MAYOR.

The office was unexpectedly lavish for such a small town, with
rich wood panels and heavy damask drapes that matched the

lush maroon carpeting. The anteroom chairs were upholstered in good leather, which made the presence of Al Drago in one of them almost obscene, like a gobbet of spit on a linen tablecloth.

He was wearing his greenish suit again, and he heaved his bulk out of the chair when he saw me and stood blocking any further encroachment into the room. "What are you doing here, you fucking fink?"

"There's a good chance I didn't come to see you, Al."

"Nobody wants you around here."

"I have to talk to the mayor."

A deep breath expanded his chest to proportions that impressed even me. He seemed to get bigger every time I saw him, like some poor guy from a fifties horror movie who'd been zapped by atomic radiation and kept growing and growing. "Not today."

"Let's let the mayor decide."

"He pays me to decide."

"Victor Gaimari pays you."

His eyebrows climbed toward his hairline, making deep horizontal creases in his Neanderthal forehead. "You want it, don't you? You're begging for it."

"You want to tell him I'm here?" I said.

"What if I don't?"

I sighed, tired of the game. "I'm either going to go around you or through you, Al. But it'd be a shame to bust up all this nice furniture, wouldn't it?"

A smile played at the corners of his granite mouth, and he hitched up his shoulders. "I could live with that."

The door to the inner office opened, postponing the inevitable, and Gayton True came out wearing the vest to his brown suit over a white shirt and gold tie. His sleeves were rolled up neatly to just below the elbow. A working mayor.

"Well," he said when he saw me. "This is a surprise." He scrunched up his nose. "I'm sorry but I don't quite recall your name."

"Milan Jacovich."

"Yes," he said, and nodded twice, filing it away for future reference. I'm sure that if I met him in twenty years, he'd remember. "Forgive me. It's been quite a week."

"Yes. Please accept my condolences."

"That's very kind of you, under the circumstances. You know Mr. Drago here?"

I nodded. "We've met."

"Did you want to see me?" He smiled, fairly oozing charm and confidence. "I can't believe you came over to concede this early in the day."

"No, this has nothing to do with the election."

That slowed him down a little. "Then, what . . . ?"

"You want me to throw him out, Mayor?" Drago rumbled.

"Come on, Mr. Drago. I don't know what you're used to in *Cleveland*"—True drew out the word, his lips pulling back to show his teeth as if he'd uttered an obscenity—"but here in Lake County we're more hospitable than that." He shifted his eyes to mine. "You must realize what a busy day this is . . ."

"It won't take long," I said.

He put his hands in his pockets and jingled his change, thinking it over. "All right," he said. "Come on in."

His private office was even grander than the anteroom. Floor stanchions holding the U.S. and Ohio flags flanked an ornate antique maple desk the size of Connecticut on which was nothing but a Cross pen-and-pencil set. On a sideboard that must have cost five thousand dollars was a silver coffee service. The lawbooks and municipal codes one might expect to find in a city official's office were neatly arranged in a bookcase with a glass front, and the walls were covered with certificates and citations and photographs of state and local political bigwigs in gold frames, including one of the mayor with Al and Tipper Gore.

"Once again, Mr. Jacovich, I'll have to ask you to be brief," he said, sitting behind his desk like the absolute monarch he was. "This is Election Day, after all."

"All right, Your Honor," I said. "Direct and to the point. I want to talk to Earl Barnstable."

He pursed his lips as if he were about to kiss a baby.

"I figured you'd know where he is," I said.

"My connection with Earl Barnstable is an accident of marriage and nothing more," he said. "The little son of a bitch didn't even show up for his sister's funeral."

He hadn't invited me to sit down, so I stood there feeling

vaguely awkward. "No one is trying to connect you with him. As I said, this has nothing to do with politics."

"When you're a public official, everything has to do with politics," he said. "If I were to go into a store in this town and buy a six-pack of beer or a package of condoms, it's big news within fifteen minutes."

"I'll keep your name out of it, if that's any help."

He made a church steeple of his fingers. "Forgive me, but is there a quid pro quo in this?" He smiled. "Latin. It means if I do something for you, you do something for me."

"I have a master's degree, Mayor. I know what it means. What I don't understand is what you want."

"Well, now that's the thing, Mr. Jacovich. As far as I can see, you don't have a damn thing I want. And to paraphrase the Good Book, what doth it profit me to help you?"

I finally sat down unbidden, bulky in my heavy coat. "Better question is, what doth it cost you not to?"

His eyes almost disappeared. "I think you'd better explain that," he said, very slowly and deliberately.

"Let's begin with a one-thousand-dollar contribution from a recently released ex-con named John Terranova."

He took a long time before saying, "All right. Let's. I'm not familiar with this Mr. Terranova, but if he's an *ex*-convict, that means he's paid his debt to society and has the right of any other citizen to support whatever cause he chooses."

"Fine words, Mayor. But Terranova is a known associate and employee of some rather unsavory folks in Cleveland. He doesn't live anywhere near Lake Erie Shores, and due to his situation, it's doubtful he could afford to contribute a thousand dollars to a political campaign, especially one in a town where he is not a resident, one in which he has no stake."

True opened the top drawer of his desk, took out a little plastic box of Tic Tacs, shook two out into his palm, and popped them into his mouth. "So?"

"So I wonder how many more of your campaign contributions can be traced back to the same source, to say nothing of your . . . head of security out there." I pointed to the door. "If that were to come out, especially in view of your plans for legalizing gambling and building a casino here"—

That opened his eyes, all right.

—"how do you suppose the people who voted for you are going to feel about it? It could get ugly. Even a recall election. Best-case scenario is that it would cause you a hell of a lot of embarrassment."

"Your candidate has accepted campaign contributions from those selfsame sources," he said, slurping the Tic Tacs around in his mouth. "The sources that are paying your salary, if my information is correct."

"Oh, it's correct, all right. But you and I both know that you're going to win this election."

He allowed himself the ghost of a smile. "I wish I shared your confidence," he said. "All right—what's your suggestion?"

"You tell me where Earl Barnstable is holed up and I'll keep my mouth shut."

"If you don't, I doubt if our Murray Hill friends would be very happy about it."

"I'll take that chance."

He ran a finger over his lips, exploring them. "That's blackmail, isn't it, Mr. Jacovich?"

"It's for a worthy cause."

"Which is?"

"I'm trying to save an eleven-year-old girl from sexual abuse. How's that?"

He stood up as though it was an effort and walked around the room for a while. "I could have Drago throw you the hell out of here, couldn't I?"

"You could have him try."

He stroked his chin. "Feel pretty strongly about this, do you?"

"I wouldn't be here otherwise. You have nothing to lose by helping me—and everything to lose by not."

He frowned out the window, deciding whether to give Barnstable to me or to give me to Drago. Finally, chewing up what remained of the mints in his mouth, as if by making them disappear he could make me go away as well, he went to his desk, opened a drawer with a silver key, and pulled out a file folder.

"I'm assuming you're a man who keeps his word," he said, copying something on a memo pad with the Cross pencil.

"I wouldn't last ten minutes in my job if I didn't."

He ripped off the sheet and handed it over to me. On it was embossed, THE OFFICE OF THE MAYOR, LAKE ERIE SHORES, OHIO.

Below that he'd written an address and phone number. "You're a pretty tough guy, Mr. Jacovich. I hope I don't run afoul of you again."

"Is this your standard get-out-of-town speech?"

He laughed, although I don't think he found anything very funny. "Far from it. As a matter of fact, I was going to inquire whether you wanted a job."

Then it was my turn to laugh.

I crossed the outer office with Al Drago's eyes making two smoking holes in the middle of my chest.

"It's not over, Jacovich," he growled as I got to the door with the pebbled-glass window.

"I never imagined it was, Al," I said.

## CHAPTER TWENTY-FIVE

Earl Barnstable was living in Mentor under an alias in one of those postmodern apartment complexes that often serve as halfway houses for the recently divorced. This one boasted all the amenities—tennis courts and workout areas and saunas and a party room that could be reserved for weekends. It was called Lake Erie Pines, although there were no trees within several blocks; I have a great mistrust of apartment buildings that have names. The tennis courts lay under a blanket of snow, looking doleful and barren without their nets. There were lights, though, in case anyone wanted to come out of an evening and sock the ball around in the slush.

According to the paper Gayton True had given me, Barnstable had rented the apartment under the pseudonym Edward Barnes. Well, who ever said that porno peddlers were creative?

I eased the Sable into a designated visitor's spot and went inside. In the lobby, done in a pink and gray southwestern motif that clashed mightily with the snow swirling outside the picture window, I ran into a pretty thirty-five-ish woman who obviously worked there because over her right breast she sported a polished silver badge that said TESS. She was carrying an official-looking clipboard and an industrial-size ring of keys, and she treated me to a dazzling smile along with an eyebrow arch that plainly said she wondered what I was doing there.

"I'm Tess," she said unnecessarily. "Can I help you?"

"Just point me to the stairs."

She looked disappointed that I wasn't there to rent an apartment. "There's an elevator at the end of the corridor."

I thanked her and walked down the hallway. A muted instrumental version of "Sitting on the Dock of the Bay" with strings seemed to be coming out of the ceiling. On the wall next to the elevator was a large corkboard with circulars announcing the annual Thanksgiving feast in the party room, a bridge tournament, a nearly new Hoover vacuum cleaner for sale, a showing of *Lethal Weapon III* on Saturday night in the TV room, and a Sunday luau brunch. It all made me realize how comfortable I was in my own apartment at the top of Cedar Hill.

Apartment 237 was two down from the elevator. I knocked on the metallic door, and it was too loud for the hushed atmosphere in the hall. I waited and then knocked again.

The door opened a crack and a blue eye peered out.

"Yeah?" a male voice said.

"Mr. Barnes?"

No audible answer, but the eye blinked.

"Mayor True told me I could find you here."

Another blink, but the door didn't move. "Who're you?"

"Milan Jacovich. I'm a private investigator."

The eye widened, then squinted nearly shut. "Fuck off!" he said, and the crack began getting narrower. Fast.

I'd expected that. I got the toe of my shoe into the crack, and then shoved hard with my shoulder, a tactic that had served me well on the Kent State gridiron. The door flew open and the little man behind it went stumbling backward into the room. I went in after him and shut the door behind me. It sounded like the clanging of a cellblock gate.

Earl Barnstable looked like a dissolute cherub, with chubby cheeks, watery blue eyes, and an almost rosebud mouth; a pink scalp showed through his cloud of wispy blond hair. He wore khaki pants and a velour pullover with white deck shoes and no socks, and he'd hit the back of the sofa and almost fallen over it. By the time I had the door shut he was flailing around to keep himself upright.

"You better get out of here before I call the cops," Barnstable said when he found his breath.

"We both know you're not going to do that, Earl."

He pulled the velour shirt down over his round little belly and tried to recapture his dignity. "Whaddaya want?"

"Henry Ludlow."

"Never heard of him."

"Don't bullshit me, I don't have a lot of time. We both know you know Ludlow, that he was going to finance a porno distribution ring. The government would like to know that too."

He snorted. "Talk to my lawyer."

"I'm talking to you, Earl. Why don't we sit down?"

"Because you're not staying that long."

I unbuttoned my coat, figuring I'd be there longer than he thought. "I've made a few phone calls in your behalf, Earl. I'm here to offer you a deal."

He looked sullen and suspicious. I didn't blame him.

"You give the FBI Henry Ludlow and they're prepared to go easy on you."

"Put it in writing," he said, and started out of the room. I followed him into the kitchen, where a bottle of Jack Daniel's stood on the counter. He poured a few fingers into a wet-looking glass and took a gulp, neat. A real he-man, Earl, when he wasn't looking at pictures of naked children.

I took a scrap of paper from my pocket and held it out to him. "Nobody's putting anything on paper. But Agent Feder in the Cleveland office will be glad to tell you all about it."

He stared at the paper, afraid to touch it. His blond hair was damp at the temples.

"Take his number, Earl. He can probably talk the prosecutors into easy time in some minimum-security lockup if you play ball. You're a damn fool if you don't."

He licked his lips, uncertainty further softening the already weak lines of his mouth. "Why should I give them Ludlow? He never did anything to me."

"What's he doing to you isn't the problem." I waved the paper with Feder's number under his nose. "Think about Feder's deal, Earl. You go into a state prison, you might as well have 'Short Eyes' tattooed on your forehead. You know what happens to chicken hawks like you in the joint?"

He stared at me a second, and then he went back out to the living room, where he sat down on the sofa, hard. As I came in after him, he gulped down the rest of his drink, both hands wrapped around the glass like a Viking at a feast. Maybe it was the straight whiskey going down, but something made his eyes tear, and he blinked several times.

"You don't scare me," he said, but his face made him a liar.

I went over to stand directly in front of him, cracking my knuckles in his face. I must have looked like a mountain to him. "Let's try this, then. I'm going to break your fingers at the second joint, one at a time, until you make that call."

His breath caught, and the whites of his eyes showed. He put the glass down on the floor and stared at it, head down. "Don't hurt me, okay?"

I was ashamed of how disappointed I was that he was going to cooperate without physical coercion. I held out the paper to him, and he took it and stared at it for a long time. Maybe he was memorizing it.

There was a cordless phone on top of the TV and I went over and got it and brought it to him, extending the antenna.

His hands were shaking too hard to punch the numbers, so I did it for him. He held the phone a half inch from his ear; I could hear the ringing, the metallic voice that answered.

"Is this Agent Feder?" he squeaked.

I leaned against the counter and waited until he had done what I wanted him to. Then he put the phone down on the floor next to his empty glass. "I'm supposed to go in and see him tomorrow," he said without looking at me.

"Make sure you keep that appointment, Earl. If you don't, I'll come back. And I won't be smiling." Buttoning my coat, I started for the door.

"What's it your business anyway?" he said, his voice cracking like a thirteen-year-old boy's. He started to stand up but his knees were shaking too badly and he fell back down against the cushions. "What do you get out of it?"

"I'm a father," I said.

• • •

It wasn't quite what we call a whiteout, when the snowfall is so thick that you can't see twenty feet in front of you, but the short trip from Mentor to Painesville through the blizzard on a snow-slick freeway was difficult enough. I even turned off the car radio to better concentrate on my driving, and by the time I got to the squat red brick building that housed the editorial offices of the *Bulletin*, my neck was stiff and my eyes were burning.

I parked at a Denny's down the block a way, thankful that I had a car big enough to plow through the drifting slush but missing my little Firebird anyway. I went inside and ordered a bacon cheeseburger and fries—it was too late in the day for the Grand Slam Breakfast—and then headed for the bank of pay phones between the two rest rooms. There was no directory on the shelf, so I had to dial 411 to get the *Bulletin*'s number.

"Donald Straum, please," I said when I finally reached someone.

"I'm sorry but he's out to lunch," she said pleasantly. There was more truth in that than she realized, but I didn't say so. "Do you know when he'll be back?"

There was a brief pause during which I heard her breathing, and then she said, "About two thirty. May I take a message?"

I looked at my watch. That gave me thirty-five minutes. "That's all right," I said. "I'll call back."

At two twenty-five, burger-sated, I pulled out of the lot and parked directly across the street from the newspaper office, getting out only long enough to put a quarter in the meter. Then I got back in and sat behind the wheel chain-smoking Winstons and waiting.

At twenty minutes to three Donald Straum pulled up in an old Mustang that looked as though it had been through the bombing of the World Trade Center. I was out of my car to intercept him before he could get through the door. I'm pleased to say that I think I scared the hell out of him.

"Don't you touch me!" he warned, looking around to see if assistance might be in sight. He wore an extra-long red scarf wrapped around the collar of his tweed coat with one end trailing in the wind.

"I'm not going to hurt you," I said. "Except maybe to bust your dialing finger."

He gave me an owl's blink behind his glasses; the lenses were beginning to catch the snowflakes. "What?"

"I'm surprised at you, Straum. A journalist ought to know that 'adulterous' is spelled O-U-S."

His chest heaved with surprise, and he fluttered his fingers at the knot of his tie like Rodney Dangerfield; I guess he wasn't getting no respect either. "I don't know what you're—"

"Let's not waste time. I know you're the one that's been calling Barbara, and sending those stupid notes, too. But you stepped in it when you called me."

The wind gusted suddenly, and he backed up a little, as if it had blown him off balance.

"You dumb bastard. In the mall Saturday, you said, 'You're dead, fucker'—the same thing you whispered to me on the phone. Not smart, Donald."

He backed up another two steps; now his back was against the brick wall of the building.

"I should have picked up on it then, but I'm more the slow and steady type. What was the point, anyway? Just trying to be a pain in the ass? Or did you think that if you shook Barbara up badly enough to make her blow the election it'd cause trouble in her marriage, and she'd leave Evan and come back to you?"

A red flush suffused his face; I'd hit home.

"Alice James wouldn't like that very much, would she? That's why she made me ask you to leave at the dinner the other night— she didn't want to do or say anything indiscreet in front of her husband."

His mouth opened at that one. "It's none of your—"

"I'm tired of people telling me it's none of my business, Straum. Until tonight when the last returns are in, Barbara Corns *is* my business. And so are threatening phone calls to my home in the middle of the night."

"You can't prove it!" he said.

"Sure I can. From your house to my house is a toll call. A simple check of your telephone records . . ."

He slithered along the wall toward the door, but I grabbed his elbow.

"You're touching me again!" he shrilled.

I was at that, and I squeezed that nerve we all have in the elbow, just to make sure he remembered it. He jumped at least six inches off the ground. "I'll do more than that if you don't knock it off—starting with a formal complaint to your publisher. And I'll tell Evan Corns what I know. He's a lawyer and I'm sure he'd just love to haul your ass into court." Snow was blowing down my collar, and I hunched my shoulders against it. He thought I was going to hit him, and this time he jumped nearly a foot. "If he doesn't, making harassing phone calls is a criminal offense, and sending harassing letters through the mails is a federal one. So you behave yourself, or I'll see to it that you swing."

I let go of his arm, and he rubbed it.

"If your paper is planning on having someone cover Barbara's headquarters tonight," I said, "I suggest they send somebody else."

His look of outrage would have made me laugh if I hadn't been so cold and wet. "Freedom of the press!" he crowed.

"Never heard of it. If I see your face tonight I'll throw it right through the front door—and I just might forget to open it first."

I could see he believed me, and it shook him. He took off his glasses and wiped away the snow with gloved fingers. "You're a real fascist, Jacovich. You know that?"

"And you're a pathetic and scared little sneak, hiding behind a press card and an erection that won't go away. I wonder how in hell you can stand to see yourself in the mirror—although with that silly beard from 1968, I guess you don't see much."

He bowed his head; his blond curls were soaked with melting snow.

"Remember what I said about tonight," I said, and started for my car.

"You son of a bitch!" he screamed after me, but it was almost lost in the howling wind.

I stopped, half expecting him to come after me. But he was neither that brave or that dumb. He stood there quivering with humiliation, tears on his cheeks; whether they were from the wind or something else, I couldn't say.

"You're so goddamn smart!" he raged, mucus coming out of his nose. "Haven't you ever been in love?"

My anger went from a rolling boil to a simmer, and for just a moment—a brief one—I almost felt sorry for him. "Yeah," I said. "I've been in love."

And I went back across the street to my car almost feeling sorry for me.

# CHAPTER TWENTY-SIX

So it was all but over, my Lake County adventure. Henry Ludlow was probably going to jail, the mystery of the phantom phone calls was solved, I'd severed my uneasy ties with Victor Gaimari, and with any luck at all Marko Meglich would find Dennis Babb and charge him with Princess True's murder and the attempted murder of Milan Jacovich. And I'd accomplished all of that with only a little bullying and blackmail and intimidation.

I'm such a fine fellow.

Now all that was left was the painful process of sitting with Barbara Corns, an optimistic smile painted on my kisser, and listening while the election returns trickled in and buried her dreams.

There is of course an ancient if not very honorable tradition in politics of picking a patsy to run in a can't-win race in exchange for present perks and future considerations from the party. The difference here was that the patsy had not been told this was a lose-lose situation and was campaigning her head off, even though she hated it, trying to be the best candidate she could. It's a lousy trick to pull on anyone—especially if it's your wife. But we all have our priorities. Evan Corns didn't much care about breaking Barbara's heart as long as Victor Gaimari was happy.

I couldn't even think about it for a while, much less face it. So I called Cassie and told her I'd show up around six o'clock unless she needed me before that.

It's tough killing time when you aren't in your own home, and

I rejected several ideas like going to a movie or sitting in a bar somewhere. I wound up spending the next few hours at a reading table in the Painesville Library along with about three dozen junior high kids who were working on their school assignments and occasionally forgetting you were supposed to be quiet in a library. I don't remember what I read, though, so it couldn't have been very good.

When it got to be a quarter of six I got up and put on my coat. It felt heavy, like chain mail, and I realized how tired I was of politics. I had only to somehow make it through the evening, as the sad and pointless enthusiasm gave way to bitter disappointment and regret, and then it would be finished.

The snowfall had diminished from a full-fledged blizzard to big fluffy half dollar–size flakes falling straight down from the sky. The sidewalks in front of the stores had been dutifully shoveled and the salt trucks and snow-movers had been around, and although the yards and trees were still pristine white, the streets were messy gray slush. The traffic on I-90 was sluggish, almost sullen, as the suburbanites made their slow way home to sit by the fire and watch *Wings*, the light from their windows beckoning to those still outside.

Most of the shops on the square had closed early because of the weather, and the municipal parking lot was deserted save for several cars belonging to Barbara's volunteers, who were gathered together for warmth to get the election returns firsthand. The 'dozers had pushed the snow into big ridges, some of them several feet high, and the number of parking spaces had diminished by nearly a third. But the first big storm of winter tends to make people cocoon in their homes, surprised by the bad weather even though it's as inevitable as the sunrise.

I wondered what things were like in Cleveland Heights, but I was comforted knowing that the areas on the northeast shore of the lake were usually hit harder by snowstorms than those closer to the city. Cleveland's West Side hardly gets any heavy snow at all.

Inside headquarters someone had bought every helium balloon in Lake County, and they floated about the room like disembodied heads in a grotesque waltz, bumping against the ceiling and each other, their strings hanging down into everyone's face like flexible and mobile stalactites. The volunteers were running around trying to look excited, proudly displaying their BARBARA FOR MAYOR buttons, and many of them wore straw boaters with red-white-and-blue hands, which looked like surplus from the Bush-Quayle campaign. Evelyn Culbertson was there, going around touching everyone on the arm and leaning too close to people when she talked to them, and Norma Bish was present as well, sporting a big red sunburst BARBARA button with a flowing red ribbon and looking as though her macaroni-and-broccoli casserole had just taken second prize at the fair.

I stood in the doorway surveying the scene and allowing the sudden heat to penetrate my cold hones. I pondered whether perhaps the lake effect isn't only a climatic condition. Maybe it's what happens to people when they know they're going to get snowed on for months at a time without even a peek at the sun, when every morning getting out of your driveway is an adventure, getting to work is like cross-country skiing, and opening your heating bill every month is courting a coronary. These good folk of Lake Erie Shores dancing around in their little hats and buttons amidst the balloon strings looked positively loony.

Laurie Pirkle wasn't there, I noticed, and I wondered if Barbara, on this the most important night of her life, was going to have to stop and get her to bring her to the party.

In the middle of one long wall of the room a blackboard had been erected on an easel, the old-fashioned kind that is actually black, the way they'd been when I went to school. A line had been drawn down the center, and BARBARA was written in red chalk on the left; on the other side, in blue chalk, the same hand had inscribed TRUE. Not as sophisticated as the electronic tote boards on *ABC News*, but it would do.

Cassie came over to me, her eyes puffy from the cold she'd been fighting, a weary slump to her shoulders. "The polls close in forty-five minutes," she said. "All we can do now is wait and hope."

"Any feel for things yet?"

She shook her head. "None of the precincts have reported. What have you been up to all day?"

"Mischief," I said. Henry Ludlow and Earl Barnstable had nothing to do with the election, and I didn't think Cassie would be very interested in them, tonight of all nights.

I grabbed a slice of pizza from one of several boxes that were spread out on the front table. An unimaginative pepperoni and cheese. I took a bite; it was as cold as a personal injury lawyer's heart.

I munched the pizza as if I were enjoying it and washed it down with a can of Dr Pepper from a nearby ice chest. I would have figured out some way to serve hot chocolate, or at least coffee, but it was not my party.

Just before seven o'clock Kellen walked in, the snowflakes clinging delightfully to her bangs and to the beret she was wearing. The way her eyes lit up when they caught mine made several parts of me light up too.

I met her at the coatrack, trying to appear as if it were a casual encounter. "I was hoping you'd be here," I almost whispered.

"Me too you," she said as she hung up her coat.

"I would have called, but it's been a crazy two days."

"You have cheese on your mouth."

I wiped at my face with a napkin.

"The other side."

I wiped again, and she nodded her satisfaction. "Are you staying to the bitter end?"

"Why bitter? You know something I don't?"

She shook her head. "Just a guess. Look, I'm going to head home about eight thirty. Why don't you come over after you finish here? I'll whip up a salad or something. Pizza's no meal for a growing boy." Her eyes danced. "I even stocked up on Stroh's, just in case."

"You've got a date," I said.

She looked over her shoulder at the milling well-wishers. "I suppose we have to go mingle."

"It's a dirty job but someone has to do it," I said, and she squeezed my arm before moving off into the crowd.

"Seven o'clock," Cassie announced loudly. "The polls are closed."

Several people applauded; they were so wired they would have clapped for a balloon busting. Later that evening they did.

Their biggest ovation was reserved for the candidate herself, who arrived at half past seven on her husband's arm, all bundled up in a mink coat I'd never seen before. I guess when you're run-

ning for office you don't want to appear too grand to your constituents, nor you do want to risk offending the animal rights people
or anyone else who votes. But now that it was all over but the
shouting, Barbara had opted for warmth and comfort.

And glamour. She'd taken great care with her makeup and
was beaming confidently. For the first time I saw what Donald
Straum and Evan Corns must see in her.

Evan was dressed in his usual corporate drab overcoat over a
dark suit, only tonight he'd added a little English racing cap to
keep the snow off his head. It wasn't sporty enough to make him
look the least bit relaxed; he was pinch-mouthed and sour-faced,
and the smiles he bestowed on the welcoming and cheering volunteers were forced.

No one noticed it but me. Then again, they were all ignorant of
Evan's perfidy, so I was the only one looking.

Once the Cornses got their coats off and properly stowed, Barbara went around to all the volunteers, shook their hands and
thanked them individually for all the hard work, and on every
one bestowed a big hug. She was wearing a clinging, calf-length
white wool dress with a red and blue scarf and looked very elegant, even though she hadn't taken off her fur-lined galoshes.
Her obvious sincerity as she talked to each person there made me
feel lousy about what was coming.

At last it was my turn. "You've been very special to me, Milan,"
she said, taking my hand in both of hers. "You're a strong man,
and you've loaned me some of that strength, and I'll never forget
you. Thanks for being my friend when I needed you."

She stood on tiptoe and pressed her cheek to mine for a second. Hers felt warm and flushed. Then she gave my hand an extra
squeeze and moved on to Norma Bish.

At seven forty-five the phone rang for the first time, and the
noise level in the room dropped to almost zero. Cassie glanced at
Barbara, then snatched it up on the third ring.

"Barbara Corns headquarters," she said. She listened for a moment, jotted some figures down on a yellow pad, thanked whoever was on the other end of the line, and hung up. She looked
at the figures, then walked over to the blackboard and picked up
the red chalk.

"Fourteenth Precinct," she said so everyone could hear, and under Barbara's name she wrote *134*. Then with the blue chalk, she wrote *159* under True's.

A disappointed murmur ran through the room, and Barbara's smile dimmed a little.

I had moved over next to Kellen. "Close," I said, trying to put the best face on it.

She shrugged. "Close the wrong way."

"Hey, that's one precinct," Cassie said brightly and too loud. "It ain't over till it's over."

A few people clapped. Most of them headed for the ice chest. A young woman in a flowery print dress and low heels took off her straw hat and fanned herself with it; the air in the room was getting close from too many people breathing it.

When the phone rang again I glanced at my watch. It was two minutes after eight.

Cassie listened, wrote, and then added the figures to the black-board. "Ninth Precinct," she said in a voice that suddenly sounded tired.

We stared at the totals. Barbara 126, True 166.

Evan ran his hand over his face like Wallace Beery in *Min and Bill*. He was sweating, and he tugged the knot of his tie away from his neck and loosened the top button of his shirt.

Kellen shook her head, and when she spoke it was in a tense, low whisper. "That's the hill precinct, where the church is. A lot of senior citizens up there, and middle-income people. We should have won it." She looked at me. "It's not going to get any better, Milan. It's going to get worse." The phone rang every few minutes after that for the next hour, and each time it did the bell tolled for Barbara. Cassie dutifully put up the numbers, and they weren't good. True in the Second Precinct, 176–141; 183–155 in the Fourth. With each posting of the precincts, True's lead increased a little bit more and the mood in the Barbara for Mayor headquarters grew a little less partylike, a little more sombre.

Barbara had ensconced herself on a folding chair in the middle of the room and was sitting with her hands clasped between her knees, looking as if a building had fallen on her. As each new set of figures was written on the blackboard, her head sank a little lower. Even Evelyn Culbertson's natural ebullience had evaporated. She stood near the door, wringing her hands and showing a lot of teeth. Kellen hugged Barbara good night, gave me an unobtrusive little wave, and left. I felt deserted, impotent, useless.

So far Barbara had only carried a single precinct, and that by seventeen votes.

By just before ten o'clock, True had run up nearly a three-hundred-vote lead with only three precincts unreported, and we all knew the miracle wasn't going to happen. County Chairman Guilfoyle's endorsement had come too late. The people who had flocked around her for weeks, trying to get her attention, were now almost pretending Barbara wasn't there; no one looked at her, and only Cassie came over to put a sympathetic hand on her shoulder. Barbara didn't acknowledge it, or even move. Gayton True had been reelected to another four-year term as the mayor of Lake Erie Shores.

Evan got on the phone with Tyler Rees over at True's campaign headquarters in the basement of the Presbyterian church and formally conceded, and then he made a stiff-necked little speech of appreciation to all the volunteers who had believed in Barbara and her cause, to everyone who had worked so hard and given of themselves, di-dah di-dah didah.

I wanted to punch his lights out.

And then it was over. Evan and Barbara went home in stony silence, the volunteers dumped their straw hats in the trash bins and did likewise. The room was deserted except for some empty pizza boxes with the grease congealing on the cardboard, three cases worth of empty soft drink cans, and about three dozen balloons doing their ghostly dance, bumping against the buzzing fluorescent light fixtures overhead.

And Cassandra Pride and me.

She was sitting at one of the long tables, her chin cupped in one red-nailed hand. "It's pretty hard to unseat a longtime incumbent like True, unless he happened to rob a bank in broad daylight without a mask. And to send a green, untested candidate against him . . ." Her mouth twisted and a dimple appeared in her pretty brown cheek.

I looked at the final figures on the blackboard. "Barbara lost by three hundred and four votes."

She nodded. "Not exactly a landslide, but moral victories don't feed the dog."

"I'm surprised it was this close. Barbara's a nice woman, but she's pretty pitiful as a campaigner."

"Just shows you how sick of True the voters here were."

"May I ask you something?" I said.

"I don't have many answers. If I did, we'd be doing a victory conga out into the parking lot."

"If we'd released the information about Darryl True stuffing the ballot box in the primary, it sure as hell would have made him look bad."

She nodded. "So?"

"If we'd used it, if we'd fought back by bringing up Earl Barnstable and his kiddie porn . . ."

"Would the totals have come out differently?" she finished for me.

"Would they?"

She sighed. "I'm not Carnac the Magnificent," she said. "'If' is the biggest word in the English language."

"Educated guess, then."

"I have an advanced college degree, but I'm not sure I'm educated. I'm smarter than I was six weeks ago, that's for certain." She put her hands flat on the table and hauled herself up out of her chair like she weighed four hundred pounds, rotating her head on her neck. I could hear it pop from across the room. "Yes, sure, it might have made a difference."

"But Evan wouldn't let you do it."

She shook her head. "He wouldn't even talk about it. You saw that."

"Yeah," I said. "I did."

Looking around the deserted room, I went and picked up two of the empty pizza boxes. "Let me help you clean up this crap."

"Screw it," she said, waving her hand. "We'll get some cleaning people in here tomorrow to do it." She batted aimlessly at a balloon, sending it bouncing into its neighbor and creating a weird domino effect as almost all the balloons in the room suddenly jerked into motion. It was eerie.

"My first loss," she said. "My first losing campaign."

"It wasn't your fault."

"I know it. If they'd let me run things the way I wanted to, we might have had a chance. An outside chance, granted, but a chance. As it was . . ." She raised her arms and then let her hands flap against her thighs. "It's just such a damn shame about Barbara. In the end she really wanted it to happen." She smiled ruefully. "That's politics."

"Come on, Cassie, let me walk you out to your car."

"No, I just want to stay here for a while and think about things," she said. "Thanks for everything, Milan. And especially for that night at Cap'n Andy's. You're a good guy."

"You too," I said, and went to take her hand. I hugged her. Her perfume was citrus and spice, like Constant Comment tea.

"Sometime in the next few weeks," she said, "let's get together. I'd like you to meet my husband. Maybe the four of us can have dinner or something."

"The four of us?"

"Kellen," she smiled.

I felt myself blushing. It's an involuntary thing, blushing, like sneezing, but it's still pretty embarrassing for a guy forty years old. "Right," I said. "The four of us."

I put on my coat, slipped my rubber Totes over my shoes, and went outside into the deserted square. It was a picturesque little place, Lake Erie Shores, and up until now they'd taken a lot of trouble keeping it the kind of small town that Norman Rockwell immortalized and is now all but gone from our landscape. I wondered what this square would be like at ten o'clock on a Tuesday night after they built the casino and another idyllic little corner of America bit the dust.

It had stopped snowing, but it was mushy underfoot, and I was glad I had the Totes to protect my shoes. I walked around the building to the back parking lot where I'd left my car. Most of the arc lamps had been turned off; only one remained glowing at the far end of the lot. When there's snow on the ground in Cleveland, it never gets completely dark. The snow seems to glow pink, almost as if it has swallowed up what precious light there is during the daytime and hoarded it for the middle of the night when it's needed.

For me it was good news/bad news time. The bad news was that a nice woman had been devastated by forces beyond her control, forces that were aided and abetted by her own husband, and the bad guys had won. The good news was that I was on my way over to Kellen's for salad and snuggling.

I was glad about that. Until I saw Al Drago smoking a cigarette, leaning against the fender of my rented Sable.

"It's time, fink," he said.

# CHAPTER TWENTY-SEVEN

He took one more drag on the cigarette and flipped it away. Scattering sparks, it made a glowing arc in the darkness and hit a pile of snow, where it hissed and went out.

"You knew it was coming," he observed. He was wearing corduroy slacks and a wool turtleneck. He must have left his overcoat in his car.

I nodded, unbuttoning my own coat. If there was anything in the world that was inevitable, it was that Al Drago and I were eventually going to tangle. I'd known it since I blew the whistle on him and got him bounced from the police department several months before. I'd been expecting it nearly every day since then, and when I'd discovered he was working for the other side in this election, I'd known it would be sooner rather than later.

"What took you so long, Al?"

He pushed himself away from the car. "Mr. Gaimari made me wait till the election was over."

Just two guys passing the time of evening in a parking lot. "Is this on Gaimari's orders?"

He made a guttural sound in the back of his throat that might have been a laugh and shook his head. His breath was foul, whether from the cigarettes or what he'd eaten or just as a normal condition I didn't know. "This is between you and me. You know why."

I knew why. It had to do with macho. It had to do with revenge. It had to do with Drago's compulsion to hurt people. It really had little to do with me.

I let my coat fall off my shoulders so it wouldn't hamper my movements and tossed it over the hood of the Sable.

His mean little eyes were like two lumps of coal in his pasty white face. "You packing heat?"

"No. You?"

He held his arms out away from his sides so I could see he wasn't wearing a weapon.

I gestured to his feet. "No ankle gun?"

"You got it wrong, fink. I'm not gonna shoot you. I'm gonna beat you half to death, that's all."

I yanked my tie off and stuffed it into my pocket; I wasn't going to give him the chance to grab hold of it and strangle me with it. The cold wind bit at my bare neck.

Drago smiled a little at my caution and nodded approvingly. This wasn't his first street fight.

But it wasn't mine, either. I'd had my share, and I was ready.

"Your call, Al."

"Yeah," he said. He began circling me very slowly, his enormous hands doubled into fists and held waist-high in front of him. He was like a huge bulldozer moving across the parking lot, a seemingly irresistible force.

"I'm gonna knock out some of your teeth, fink," he said, breathing through his mouth. "Maybe I'll take out an eye. Break some bones. The kind that don't heal so good, like an elbow, maybe. Or a knee."

I wasn't afraid of Al Drago—I didn't let myself even think about being afraid of him. But he was a big, brutal man and I knew that no matter how tonight turned out, I was going to get hurt. The extent of that pain was going to depend on me. Anticipation made the adrenaline race through me.

I raised my hands, higher than he had his, curling them into loose fists, and shifted my weight to the balls of my feet. My feet felt heavy from the rubber Totes, but I didn't have the time to slip them off. I moved to my right, his left. He was no boxer—a man that large and strong doesn't have to be. I wasn't much of one, either, but I figured it was my best chance with him. If I let him get close, he'd use his superior weight and strength to crush me.

I snapped out a left but it didn't quite reach him. It gave him something to think about, though, and he backed up a step. I followed quickly with another left, and this one caught him on the cheekbone. It probably stung—it stung my knuckles, anyway—but it didn't seem to do much damage. A guy like Drago has to get hit pretty hard to even feel it.

"You fight like a faggot," he said. He feinted with a left and clubbed a sidearm right toward my head. I moved away from it so that when it landed on my shoulder a lot of the steam was taken out of it. But even a near miss from someone as powerful as Drago was enough to jar me.

I gave him a short, hard punch in the ribs and backed up. That one made him grunt.

He dropped his elbows and moved in, and I landed a couple of good ones around his face before he uppercutted me in the gut, knocking the wind out of me. It was like getting hit with a tree trunk. I tasted cold pizza at the back of my throat.

And then he was all over me, hands reaching for my throat, legs pumping, trying to knee me between the legs. I stuck my butt out as far as I could, and then his knee came pile-driving into my abdomen but at least not where it was aiming. I hammered at his body, his sides, but he didn't seem to notice. His thumb went for my eye, but I ducked my head and it dug into my cheek so hard it forced my teeth apart.

He wrapped his arms around me, pinning my own arms against my sides, and squeezed hard. If I had been any slighter around the middle he would have broken me like a number 2 pencil.

Knowing what was coming, I turned aside so that his butting forehead smashed into the side of my face instead of the bridge of my nose. Pain racketed around inside my head.

I ground my heel down onto his instep, and he loosened his grip enough so I could get my arms free. Then I hit him as hard as I could, right on the breastbone, and when he stepped back I threw a roundhouse right that bounced off his ear and made him yell. I followed it up with a one-two combination; one shot caught him on the nose, and blood spilled out of his nostrils and down over his mouth.

He backed up, spitting to get rid of some of the blood, and then he lowered his head and rushed. It was like being back on the line for Kent State, and I knew what to do. I slapped him hard on the side of the head, knocking him a few feet off course.

He straightened up, and my left jab popped into his eye socket, stopping him in his tracks. My right missed, and that's when he hit me on the side of the face so hard that it knocked me down. My brain seemed to rattle around inside my skull. Then he kicked me, hard, in the thigh. And again, this time near the hip.

I rolled around in the slush, dizzy, trying to keep away from his heavy-shod feet, but one of his kicks took me in the side, and I felt a rib crack.

Trying not to breathe, I got myself to my knees, and when I saw the toe of his shoe rushing toward my face I grabbed his foot and twisted.

On dry level ground it wouldn't have done much, but the footing there in the snowy parking lot was slippery, and he went down with a crash. I think the earth shook.

I clambered to my feet, a poison arrow of pain stuck in my ribs, and when he tried to rise I hit him in the eye again. He snarled, rolling over and away from me, and scrambled up.

Blood was bubbling out of his nose, and his right eye was nearly closed. His mouth was contorted with rage and he was making a growling noise deep in his throat. He came at me again.

I moved quickly to my left, hoping he couldn't see me too well out of his bad eye, and threw another punch, which hit him on the side of the neck and didn't seem to have any effect. I went for the bad eye again, and this time I made him yell.

His fist thudded into my shoulder and my left arm went numb. I landed two more rights to his face, this time drawing blood from his mouth. One of his teeth dug into my knuckles, and the thought that he might have AIDS or some other disease transmittable through the bloodstream—or be rabid—flickered in and then out of my consciousness.

No matter how much I hit him, it didn't seem to faze him. It was as though he was impervious to pain and injury. He just kept coming and coming, and I realized that the only way I could stop this fight before he killed me was to disable him.

I stepped back, giving him a clear shot. He was a brutal fighter but artless, and when the overhand blow came I grabbed his wrist and, using his own momentum, twisted it up behind his back, putting my leg in front of his and shoving hard. He tripped and fell down on his face, with me still holding on to his arm. I landed on him with both knees, forcing the air out of him, and jerked his arm higher up against his back, and then I very deliberately bent his thumb back toward his wrist until I heard it snap.

He yelled again and with his enormous strength lifted the upper part of his body off the ground, throwing me off. And then there we were in the slush, facing one another on our hands and knees like two feral dogs fighting over a scrap of rotted meat. Blood dripped from his nose and mouth, and his right eye was a narrow slit. He shook his giant head violently as if to clear it, and a string of saliva flew through the hard, cold air.

I knew how he felt. Every part of me hurt, and every breath was like a knife thrust.

I dragged myself to my feet as he struggled up himself. He was holding his right hand, the one with the broken thumb, away from his body, and his breathing was as ragged as my own.

We began to circle each other again, and except that his thumb and my rib were broken and we were both hurting a lot, we seemed to be right back to square one. It struck me how pointless the whole thing was, two grown men hammering at one another's bodies, trying to inflict pain over something that wasn't going to change no matter what the outcome. I suddenly felt kind of silly.

"Al," I gasped, "how about we call it even?"

"Fuck you," he said, and spit out another mouthful of blood, and maybe a tooth with it.

"This is a kid thing. We're too old to do this."

"Maybe you are." He bent his knees.

"What's it going to prove?"

He straightened up for a second, his gorilla brows furrowing. It was a concept I don't think he'd considered before. Then he said simply, "What does it ever prove?"

"Nothing." I pressed my elbow against my ribs, against the stabbing pain. The side of my face throbbed and pulsed; it felt three feet wide. "It doesn't prove a damn thing."

He remained motionless for about ten seconds. Then he said, "Come on," moving around again cautiously, left fist up and right hand dangling at his side.

A gust of wind blew the drifted snow around like desert sand, and with the cold I realized that my pant leg was torn at the knee from when I'd fallen. I had a bloody scrape there, but compared to my other hurts it was negligible. I got into my boxer's crouch again, my rib grinding. I was sick of the whole business. I'd tried to stop it, but Drago wasn't going to let me.

We were both too weary to get fancy, and when we finally engaged it was graceless and clumsy as we flailed away at each other, Drago slicing karate chops with the edge of his hand to avoid more damage to his thumb, although they must have been more excruciating for him than for me. In a boxing match neither of us would have scored many points with our flurries, but no one was judging, and the heavy blows took their toll on both of us.

I went in slow, banging my sore fists into his stomach, but he was a solid slab of muscle covered by a layer of flab; he felt like the heavy bag in a gym. I tried going for his ribs, almost heedless of the jackhammer blows raining on my neck and shoulders, except that with each one that landed, my own punches lost a little more steam.

And then I got too close, a bad mistake, and he looped his right arm around my neck in a punishing headlock, bending me at the waist, and with his left hand he repeatedly drove his fist at the top of my skull.

Jesus, it hurt! My ears were ringing, and I came close to blacking out, but then he stopped, and with his third knuckle extended he went for my eye.

I scrunched my eyes shut and tried to pull my head into my neck like a turtle. Dizzy and hurt as I was, I still had the presence of mind to slug away at his kidney. On the fifth punch he groaned, letting me loose, and staggered away. He turned back to me, and when my vision cleared I could see that his face was distorted with pain and that he'd wet the front of his pants.

From the corner of my vision, which was a bit blurry, I saw movement at the entrance to the parking lot, but I couldn't allow myself the luxury of taking my eyes away from him for a second. He lurched toward me, favoring his right side where I'd punished his lower back. His smashed and battered face was almost bestial, his mouth slack, his bloody nostrils distended like those of a tired racehorse. The eye that remained open glittered with a hatred as senseless as it was disturbing.

I could barely lift my arms, but I did, for protection, and as we came together I knew that for this to be finished, one of us was going to have to kill the other.

He hit me openhanded on the side of the face again, high up near my eyes. My ears rang anew, and I socked him in the mouth, falling away, so there wasn't much to it but nuisance value, but it rocked him a little bit anyway. My fist came away bloody.

And then the movement I'd seen with my peripheral vision intruded onto my consciousness and I looked up to see an old white Ford pickup truck moving purposefully toward us, picking up speed as its tires hissed through the slush.

"Look out!" I hollered, and launched myself over the hood of the Sable, sliding on top of my coat and tumbling off on the other side onto my head.

"Fuck!" he screamed.

From flat on my face I looked under the car; all I could see were Drago's feet in his big heavy brogans frozen in place, and then the wheels of the pickup, spinning impossibly fast, and I felt the sickening impact, felt it all through my body. The shoes left the pavement, going almost straight up. The Ford's engine was roaring, but not so loud that I didn't hear Drago when he hit the ground. It was a sound like a watermelon being dropped from a third-story window.

I pulled myself up and looked across the car in time to watch the truck careen crazily for a moment on the slick tarmac. Then it powered around a snowbank on two wheels, heading out onto the square.

Al Drago was crumpled up about thirty feet away like a ruined and discarded doll, his neck bent at an impossible angle and blood spreading out in a widening pool beneath his head and his midsection, staining the snow dark red. He didn't move; from the awful position of his head I didn't expect him to.

It was sad but fitting, somehow, that the last word of such an obscenity of a man would be obscene.

I fumbled in my pants pocket for my keys, my sore knuckles scraping against the fabric, and unlocked the car and slid in, jab-bing blindly for the ignition. The engine caught, coughed, and then began purring. I floored the accelerator and the car leapt forward churning up the slush and leaving quite a bit of rubber on the parking lot pavement and a stench in the air that wouldn't quite overpower the coppery smell of blood.

# CHAPTER TWENTY-EIGHT

The Sable shot out of the parking lot like a Patriot missile, and I hit the street just in time to see the pickup bounce crazily over the curb as it tore counterclockwise around the other side of the deserted square on its way out of town. I smiled grimly at the irony of it—run people down with your truck and kill them, but don't go the wrong way on a one-way street.

I had no such scruples and turned left instead against the nonexistent traffic to cut several hundred feet of the distance between us. I wasn't much worried about being stopped by the police for the flagrant violation; on a snowy, slippery night like this they probably had their hands full with motorists who'd slid off the road into trees or whose cars just wouldn't start.

The truck's taillights disappeared down a side street, and I followed them, cursing to myself. On clear pavement the Sable could easily overtake the ancient, wheezing pickup, but the side streets of Lake Erie Shores had not yet benefited from the ministrations of the salt trucks and snow-movers, and the white Ford's high undercarriage made its passage through the snow a lot easier than mine. I gripped the wheel tightly, hoping I wouldn't go into a skid.

He knew the town better than I did, and our trip through the white, silent streets was like navigating a fun-house maze. He made so many quick turns trying to shake me that I became disoriented, not sure anymore in which direction we were heading. The drumming pain in my head and body from the beating I'd just taken didn't help my equilibrium any.

Finally I realized he was heading in the direction of the free-way. I took a deep, satisfied breath, hardly noticing the sharp pain in my ribs. On the uncluttered interstate I could easily overtake the truck; what I'd do then I hadn't figured out.

He roared through a red light and I followed, trusting there would be little traffic out on a night like this—I was wrong, and I narrowly missed being creamed in the intersection by a Dodge minivan. It braked hard and skidded around almost a hundred eighty degrees so that it was facing the wrong way, and the driver gave me a futile, angry blast of the horn as I cut in front of it. I couldn't hear what the driver was saying, but your imagination is as good as mine.

I was more interested in keeping my quarry in sight. The pickup was racketing down a side street again, white smoke spuming out of its tailpipe into the icy air. The street curved at the end where it turned into another street. At the bend, the truck's tires slipped on a patch of ice, and it sideswiped a parked Lumina, sending sparks flying, but it only slowed for a second before picking up speed again. I followed it with only a sidelong commiserating glance at the newly dented Lumina.

Another turn or two and we were on a dark rural road, run-ning straight as an arrow over hills and through valleys. My stom-ach lurched as I hit the bottom of a depression and sailed up the other side. This was almost as much fun as the Mean Streak roller coaster at Cedar Point—or would have been if I wasn't aching in every bone and muscle.

The reflecting green and white sign at the side of the road ad-vised me that we were approaching the interstate. I had no way of knowing which direction the truck would ultimately go, so I just kept my eye on it, maintaining a distance of about sixty yards between us.

Up the westbound on-ramp it went, heading toward Cleve-land, with me after it. I'd at least guessed right about the pau-city of traffic on the freeway; nobody in their right mind goes out driving on a night like that, and except for the occasional dark bulk of an eighteen-wheeler on the road only because it had to be, both lanes were empty.

My fuel gauge showed a quarter tank of gas, and since I didn't know the Sable very well, I wasn't sure how far that would take me. But I figured the pickup, at its ripe old age and generally in a state of disrepair, wasn't too well suited for long distances.

I thought about Dennis Babb up ahead of me, and wondered what dark forces at work in his childish brain had led him to snuff out a human life, not once but twice, and then to undertake this foolish flight into the winter night. Panic, I supposed, was making him run. But what had made him kill?

The speed limit on that stretch of highway is fifty-five, and I figured it was pushing it hard to maintain that in the beat-up Ford. I closed the gap between us without much trouble, but I wasn't in any particular hurry. He knew I was there behind him, knew he had nowhere to go. He was running on fear, and almost empty.

The pickup was booking pretty good in the left lane, and I kept pace, the scenery flashing by all clad in virginal white, but when we got to the Grand River exit he suddenly cut across the freeway and went bouncing down the exit ramp, tires screaming, and I had to brake hard and wrestle the wheel to avoid overshooting it. As it was, my right wheels went up onto the berm beside the ramp, and only the speed at which I was driving kept me from becoming mired in a snowbank.

The stoplight at the bottom of the ramp might as well not have been there. The white truck went rushing through it, making a turn on two wheels and almost tipping over. I couldn't imagine what refuge he thought he'd find in Grand River, a town of ship repair yards, boat landings, dry docks, and concrete factories and stoneworks. But he turned away from the town, toward the facility Morton Salt calls the Fairport Mine. A Cyclone fence stretched along its perimeter, and its towers were gray against the dark sky.

And then he turned in at the darkened entrance to Headlands Park.

The park is a recreation area, with picnic groves and a sand beach with dunes that slope down to the shore of Lake Erie. It's a popular weekend destination for families during the summer months but desolate and deserted in winter. There's probably no colder spot in the state of Ohio.

A chain was stretched across the main roadway about a hundred yards into the park, with a red stop sign hanging from it, but the truck plowed through, snapping it as if it had been a piece of string, and went bucketing off into the darkness. At that point the truck cut off its lights, which made it more difficult to follow.

I drove across the chain, mindful of the roadside signs reading ICE–UNSAFE, suddenly thankful my rented Sable was so much heavier than my own Sunbird. On the pavement broken chips of ice glistened like dirty diamonds.

Once in the park, the roads meander in a series of lazy figure eights past the rest room facilities and the picnic tables toward a parking area down near the lake. The only light here was that reflected from beyond the fence of the Morton factory. I might have lost the truck, but since this road was off limits to the driving public during winter, the city crews hadn't plowed or salted it, and the pickup had left deep ruts anyone could follow in the fresh snow.

Even so, it was slow going for me, my rear wheels spinning and churning, kicking up twin plumes of slush behind the car. Here in the deep stuff, the pickup and I were even.

The white truck was camouflaged in the snowy landscape, and there were quite a few trees here, but every so often I caught sight of it lumbering along, sometimes going in the opposite direction from me across the open space where in the summer there was grass. But I didn't dare leave the pavement in this weather, at least not knowingly. So I followed the tracks, the car jouncing along over the drifts and skidding on sudden ice. I noticed at one point that he'd doubled back on his own trail, so apparently he didn't have a plan. He was just running.

The wind was pretty stiff out on the headlands, and so much snow was blown against the windshield that it might as well have been falling from the sky. I turned off my own headlights—the snow glare was sending frissons of pain through my battered head. Besides, it was easier to see with the lights off.

An eerie feeling, driving along in complete blackness with only the faint luminous glow reflecting up from the snow, knowing that somewhere out there was a maniac who had already killed twice behind the wheel of a truck big enough to turn the Sable into scrap metal.

I wanted to stop and get my bearings, but I was afraid that if I didn't keep moving the car would become mired. So on I drove, squinting through the glass, trying to catch sight of the white pickup.

I found it when I practically rear-ended it; I jammed on the brakes, causing the Sable to fishtail wildly. The Ford had been abandoned in the middle of the roadway, as close to the lake as it was possible to get without going out onto the sand. The driver's side door was open, and a set of footprints led out toward the water through the snow-covered saw grass.

What the hell was he going to do? Swim to Canada?

I got out of the car, my bruised body protesting and my cracked rib grating painfully, and began following the tracks. Immediately my shoes were full of snow, and I couldn't much feel my toes anymore. Rubber Totes are fine for walking around city streets in winter, but out where the snow was two and three feet deep they were next to useless.

I had to lift my knees high with every step, and it was an effort just pulling one foot after the other out of the drifts. After just a few moments I was out of breath. I'd taken even more of a pounding from Drago than I'd thought.

Drago. Dead Drago. As I trudged, I started examining how I felt about that. The world was not going to miss Aloysius Drago, and I sure as hell wasn't. He was a mean, stupid man who had hurt a lot of people, abusing the powers of the badge he'd worn until they had to take it away from him.

But he was a human being, flaws and all, and didn't deserve to die that way. Nor had Princess True. Nobody deserves to die that way. That's why I kept going, to get to Dennis Babb and stop him before he killed somebody else.

Somebody like me, for instance. It wasn't as if he hadn't already tried.

I came up over a frozen rise, feeling as if I'd just climbed the Matterhorn, and for the first time I could see Lake Erie beyond the beach, its surface frozen and stark from the day's storms. Clumps of shrubbery and beach grass clung gamely to the side of the dune atop which I stood, looking like white chrysanthemums under their covering of snow. There was no sign of Dennis Babb, or of anything else alive on that beach.

I was still wearing only a sports jacket and slacks with an

open-necked dress shirt, all of it thoroughly soaked, and the wind off the lake was punishing me almost as badly as Drago had. I hunched my shoulders against it, although I'd heard on television once that hunching made you feel colder, not warmer.

"Dennis?" I yelled, and the wind threw my own voice back at me. "Dennis? It's Milan."

I waited. In vain.

"Dennis? Come on out. It's easier this way. I'll take care of you." Still no reply, no movement that I could discern. I moved along the crest of the dune to my right, the snow getting into my pant leg through the rent at the knee. I was as uncomfortable as I could remember, broken and bruised and wet and chilled to the bone.

I banged my shin on a rotted old driftwood log that was nearly buried in the snow—one more painful area to deal with. "Dennis!" I yelled.

And all at once the log exploded, and a big chunk of it flew up past my face. It was only afterward that I heard the sharp crack of the rifle, and I stumbled backward and fell down the other side of the dune, landing flat on my back with my feet higher than my head on the incline. This was a hell of a time to be making snow angels.

Where had he gotten the rifle? Then I remembered the deer antlers over the door to the shed at his sister's house. Unlike legitimate hunters, Delores Babb probably lived on the venison she shot and didn't much bother observing the legal deer season, and so it made sense that her deer rifle had been in a gun rack on the back wall of the truck's cab all along.

I hadn't even seen where the muzzle flash came from. But it didn't matter—he wouldn't be there anymore, anyway.

How many shots did he have left, I wondered. Most deer rifles I knew about could carry four rounds in the clip and one in the chamber. But not even the wildest good ol' boys went yahooing around in their trucks with a round chambered. So I figured he had three shots left—assuming he didn't have a pocket full of ammo.

Struggling in the deep snow to extricate myself from my upside-down position, I laboriously got to my feet, which must have looked pretty comical, and considered my options. The smartest thing to do was to go home. But Dennis Babb was not right in the head, and he was armed. God knew who he'd decide to waste next. I had to stop him right there on the frozen beach before he hurt someone else—and without any firepower of my own.

The first thing I did was to make my way back to the truck, looking over my shoulder every few seconds to make sure he wasn't coming after me with his deer gun. I leaned into the cab and pulled the hood latch. Then I quickly removed the distributor cap, tossing it as far as I could into the drifted snow. It hit with a barely audible plop and disappeared in white quicksand; if Dennis got by me, he was going to have to walk home.

I climbed the ridge again, further north than I had the first time, to about the place where I thought the shot had come from. About halfway up I dropped to all fours and crawled the rest of the way, the fluffy snow getting into my mouth and nose. When I was a kid I used to like to eat snow; at this particular moment the charm of it was lost on me.

I inched my head up very slowly over the top of the dune, keeping as low as I could. In a way it reminded me of nights in Vietnam, except that it didn't snow there. There was just the heat of the day and the chill of the night and snipers behind every tree and the squalor of Saigon and little brown children who'd been booby-trapped to explode when touched.

It isn't often that I think about Nam; even less frequently do I talk about it. It was just something I did a long time back when I was very young, and mostly I've been able to let go of the bad memories. But there are times . . .

I shuddered, and it wasn't from the cold.

Nothing was visible except a vast expanse of white all the way to the horizon. Far behind me I was aware of the thrum of heavy machinery from the salt mine and the LTV Steel lime Plant, and the wind moaned off the water. Otherwise the loudest sound was my own breathing. I pressed my elbow against my side to ease the pain a little. It didn't help.

There wasn't much to be done. Dennis was armed and I wasn't. I could sit there all night and freeze to death—a bad idea, and one that made me realize I'd had a date with Kellen for right about now. I hoped she'd understand.

Or I could stand up and let him take another shot—a *really* bad idea.

The only other course was to make something happen.

With fingers aching from the cold, I fashioned three snow-balls the size of baseballs, packing them tightly so they wouldn't fly apart in the air. By the time I finished they were rock hard and icy.

I crawled back up over the top of the dune and looked around again. Off to my right there were several clumps of ragged bushes, and I thought perhaps that might be where he was hiding. Either that or he'd dug himself a foxhole in the snow.

I raised up on my knees and fired the first snowball at one of the bushes, unable to stop my yelp of pain as the broken bones in my side ground together. The snowball hit, and from the furthest bush the rifle barked twice, the muzzle flashes like firecrackers in the dark. I dived face first into the ground, hugging it. The first bullet hit about twenty feet in front of me, kicking up the snow; I don't know where the second one went. But I learned two things from the experience: first, where Dennis was, and second, that he was a lousy shot.

I lifted my face up, my hair and mouth and eyebrows full of snow. I could hear movement out there; he was moving away from his cover, his feet crunching on the crusted snow. I slid backward down the berm and moved to my right again, doubled over more from pain than to keep out of sight. It was becoming excruciating to breathe now because of the broken rib, but the cold was rendering my other bruises numb.

It had started to snow again, not as fiercely as earlier in the day, but the kind of Christmas-card snow they sing about in *The Sound of Music*, so pretty until you have to shovel it off your driveway. It lessened the visibility even more, but since he had the rifle I viewed it as a plus.

There was a stand of naked black trees at the top of the rise, about sixty feet from where I was, and I headed for them. They wouldn't provide much cover, but they were better than nothing.

I almost made it.

As I began my upward climb, I looked up to see a dark, wide silhouette at the crest of the dune, sighting through the scope of a rifle. The barrel swung toward me, looking like a cannon, and I dived and rolled as it spurted fire, and the bullet thunked into the frozen ground behind me.

If I was right about the rifle, if he hadn't chambered a round, there was no more ammunition.

If I was wrong, I had about three seconds to live.

The shooter disappeared over the rise, and I went charging up the dune in pursuit, scrambling and clawing through the thigh-deep drifts. I got to the crest and started for the trees, and when I reached them the stock of the rifle smashed against my chest, dropping me to my knees.

There wasn't much steam behind the swing, but in my condition it was good enough to fell me. The bulky figure moved through the trees, and I staggered up to follow. We were heading into the wind, snowflakes blowing straight at us, and I could hear a high-pitched moaning—the sound of terror. My legs were longer, and in about thirty seconds I had caught up at the top of the ridge.

Don't ever let anyone convince you that football skills are never used after one's playing days are over. I used my best tackling technique, the one I'd had to use when the ball carrier got by me, and wrapping my arms around the broad waist, I brought my quarry down at the top of the dune. Locked in a grotesque embrace, we rolled over and over each other, every revolution sending an agony telegram from my rib cage to my brain, until finally we came to rest in the deep snow at the bottom of the hill that was the beginning of the sandy beach.

It didn't feel right, somehow—I registered that upon impact—and halfway down the incline I came to realize that it wasn't Dennis Babb I had tackled. We rolled through the deep snow and when we stopped my face was pillowed between two large breasts.

"It's all right, Laurie," I said, my breath coming in great painful gasps. "I'm not going to hurt you."

# CHAPTER TWENTY-NINE

There was a jurisdictional dispute between the police departments of Lake Erie Shores and Cleveland as to who got her. Cleveland, having lots more muscle, won, and it was a good thing for me, because my old friend Marko Meglich was a lot more free with information than the suburban police might have been.

The story that came out under psychiatric examination was a sad one.

Laurie Pirkle, like Dennis Babb, was fixated on Barbara Corns. Idolized her. Practically worshipped her. Obese, homely, and introverted, Laurie didn't find acceptance in many quarters, and Barbara's welcoming arms, even though open only because she was campaigning and would take help from anyone, were the only warmth the young woman had known in her short lifetime.

So when on that ill-fated night of the chamber of commerce mixer Laurie had seen the devastating effect Princess True had on Barbara, she'd decided to do something about it.

Dennis Babb borrowed the Ford pickup from his sister, Laurie borrowed it from him, and she followed Princess into Cleveland that Sunday with no particular plan in mind other than to somehow get her out of the way. She'd waited patiently while the mayor's wife brunched with friends, and then, as Princess was crossing Prospect Avenue for a spot of shopping at The Avenue, Laurie seized the moment and ran her down in the street.

She had enticed Dennis Babb into giving her the truck by going to bed with him.

Laurie's only previous sexual encounter was with a boy from

her small-town high school who had deflowered her on a dare and then blurted the story all over the neighborhood, thus precipitating her exodus to Lake County. Dennis had been a virgin—not too many women wanted to get naked and sweaty with someone like him—so Laurie's body was the most welcome and generous gift he'd ever received.

The thing about killing is that once you've gotten away with it, it becomes easier. And when Laurie felt that her position at Barbara's side was being threatened by my entry into the campaign, she'd tried to dispatch me, too, the following weekend in front of Kellen's house. This time she'd gotten the pickup not by using her womanly charms but by frightening the crap out of Dennis, telling him that his sister's truck had been the instrument of destruction in Princess True's murder and that if Dennis didn't cooperate with her, she'd see to it that he would he blamed. So he loaned her the truck for the Friday night attempt on my life, and like a frightened animal, went into hiding. We found out later he'd been living for four days in an abandoned industrial building in Painesville, subsisting on Big Macs.

As to her killing of Al Drago, I'm not sure which one of us she was actually aiming for, but I'd like to think that Drago's unspeakably cruel treatment of her at Laird's Steak and Chop House had moved him ahead of me on the most-wanted list.

Evan Corns arranged for an associate of his to represent Laurie in court. She hadn't planned things very carefully—it's never a good idea to involve anyone else who knows the story when you're planning a major crime—and they pretty much had her dead to rights. She entered a plea of not guilty by reason of insanity to a charge of vehicular homicide, and was remanded to a state mental hospital for psychiatric evaluation and treatment.

There was talk of indicting Dennis for aiding and abetting, but no one in the prosecutor's office thought they could get a conviction, and the matter was allowed to fade away quietly. Dennis was allowed to fade away quietly too.

I spent three weeks taped up like a mummy until my cracked rib knitted together, the first two with a bad cold I'd gotten playing in the snow on the beach at Headlands Park without a jacket. The swelling on my face abated eventually, and my black and blue bruises faded to green, then yellow, then away.

Marko and I never mentioned the conversation we'd had about Victor Gaimari. He bugged off work and that spring we went to the Indians' home opener together like old times and drank beer and ate brats. Later that summer he fell in love, hard, with a twenty-three-year-old caterer's sales rep named Ashleigh. Ashleigh had major hair; I guess nobody had the nerve to tell her that just because Dolly Parton does it doesn't mean it's still in style. Ashleigh dallied with Marko until right before the holidays and then dropped him to return to her old boyfriend, although not before Marko had bought her an expensive diamond tennis bracelet as a Christmas present he could ill afford. Custom jewelry does not come with a money-back guarantee, and Marko wound up selling the bracelet back to the jeweler and taking more than a forty percent loss.

On the journalistic front, some time in February Donald Straum got caught making calf eyes where he shouldn't. Mr. Arlen James, in defense of the sanctity of his marriage, made a single phone call to the publisher of the *Bulletin*, who happened to be an old fraternity brother of his, and Straum was advised to seek employment elsewhere. And there was no golden handshake, either. When last heard from, Straum was writing a television criticism column for a small suburban weekly in Indiana and probably cutting a wide swath through the lonely matrons of Muncie. He was undoubtedly penning his first novel in his spare time.

Mrs. Arlen James—Alice—went to Cancun to forget.

Aloysius Drago was buried out of the same church where I had made my first communion, Saint Vitus parish in the old neighborhood. I had known his last name was Slavic, but until his death I hadn't realized he was of Slovenian descent. For years there has been a wide schism between two segments of the Slovenian community in Cleveland. Descendants of immigrants from the early part of the century, like Al Drago's parents, didn't much associate with those who had appeared after the Second World War, like my family. There were a multitude of reasons, political and otherwise, and from a modern-day perspective it seems rather silly, but that's the way it is. Slavs hold on to old grudges, even almost fifty-year-old ones.

I went to his funeral—don't ask me why. Maybe because if not for me he'd still be alive, although I know that doesn't make any sense. I've been known to send myself on guilt trips before. It was a damn good thing I showed up; there were only two other people present. One was Drago's uncle, an embittered old man in his seventies, who when I offered my condolences observed with a shrug that shit happens. The other was a rather pretty dark-haired woman dressed in black who sat with head bowed during the funeral mass and the eulogy and left the church immediately after it was over. I never found out who she was.

Earl Barnstable was tried and convicted and is doing seven to fifteen for several counts of using the United States mails to distribute and purchase pornography featuring underage children. True to FBI Special Agent Feder's word, he's doing his time in a federal country club–style lockup in Maryland, which was once the temporary residence of several people whose names you would know, men who in a bygone era could drive through the gates of the White House with a simple wave to the Secret Serviceman on guard.

Henry Ludlow, on whom Barnstable gladly rolled over, was convicted of possession of obscene material and is doing shorter but harder time in the state correctional facility at Mansfield. They tried to prove federal violation for receiving obscene materials through the mail, and the Lake County prosecutor tried even harder to make a case against him for sexual molestation of his eleven-year-old daughter but couldn't seem to make it stick and finally plea-bargained a deal.

When Gayton True attempted to build a casino in Lake Erie Shores and turn it into the gambling capital of the North Coast, a group of irate citizens led by Barbara Corns formed an action committee, yelled bloody murder to the papers, and even got up a recall petition to unseat him. But a good politician knows when to fold 'em, and True was finally intimidated enough into shelving his casino plans—temporarily at least.

Which meant Victor Gaimari had spent a lot of money for nothing. He paid me what he owed me, including the bill for the repairs to my Sunbird, but he didn't call me down to his office or to some Italian restaurant on Murray Hill to present the check, nor did he have it personally delivered. It came in the mail in about a week without a note, a thank you, or a kiss-my-ass, and Victor and I didn't speak until we greeted each other coolly at an accidental meeting at the Cleveland Play House. I guess I am no longer the mob's private detective of choice.

Victor and his uncle, the don, who had been counting heavily on the casino being built in Lake County, weren't pleased by Barbara's activism and made their displeasure known to Evan Corns, who in turn tried to call his wife off. But Barbara, who had cried for a week after losing the election, was suddenly emboldened and told Evan to put his head where the sun doesn't shine. Their marriage, shaky at best, couldn't survive their political differences and about a year after the election they separated, too late for Donald Straum, already gone to Indiana.

The casino incident, however, cost True a great deal of credence; the Japanese might say that he lost face. So when it came time to elect a new county party chairman, he didn't even stand for the office, issuing a statement that his duties as mayor were far too burdensome to even contemplate taking on such a responsibility. Evan Corns, having been bought off in the past election by Gaimari and D'Allessandro, had no such reservations and jumped into the running. He was soundly thrashed in the voting by Judge Guilfoyle, who would snooze through important committee meetings for another four-year term. No harm was done, though, because the judge appointed Barbara as his deputy, and in her quiet, almost mousy little way she ran the entire county in deed if not in name, although every party bigwig in the state recognized her contribution.

Tyler Rees went to Columbus as special legislative assistant to the Speaker of the Ohio House of Representatives. Talk is, he'll run for secretary of state two years from now.

Cassandra Pride very quickly landed a job as head of public relations for Marbury-Stendahl Advertising on Chagrin Boulevard in Beachwood, with whom I'd had less than pleasant dealings in the past. Two evenings a week she taught a class in government at Cuyahoga Community College's metropolitan campus.

After my rib healed, she and her husband Jim and Kellen and I did indeed go out to dinner together at Piperade, downtown on Prospect Avenue not two blocks from where Princess True had been killed. Jim was a delightful guy who looked like Wesley Snipes, had a voice like Barry White, and a sense of humor like Bill Cosby. It was a fun evening, with lots of laughs and no talk of politics. In my business you sometimes get out of the habit of laughing, but that dinner reminded me how again.

Oh, and about the broken date on Election Night—Kellen forgave me.

A NOTE FROM LES ROBERTS . . .

Thanks for "electing" to read The Lake Effect.

Next up in the Milan Jacovich series is The Duke of Cleveland.

The question I'm most often asked is "Where do you get your ideas?". Even though I'm tempted to say there's a little guy in New Jersey who sells ideas for twenty bucks each, the fact is that ideas come from everywhere. The Duke of Cleveland was inspired by two visits I made--one to the pottery studio of the brother of a friend, which I describe in detail in the book, and the second to an old public school in the St. Clair–Superior Corridor that has been transformed into residence/studio spaces for a variety of artists, sculptors, and craftspeople.

I wanted to say something about art collecting, and Milan's ongoing love-hate relationship with smooth-talking mob guy Victor Gaimari seemed to offer the perfect background.

When I got halfway through the book, I discovered to my chagrin that I had inadvertently recreated the Dashiell Hammett classic, The Maltese Falcon, setting it in Cleveland instead of San Francisco. I had to go back to the beginning and retool the entire novel. I hope you'll read The Duke of Cleveland and agree the effort was worth it.

-- Les Roberts

## ACKNOWLEDGMENTS

The author has several thank-yous to extend:

First, to the Ohio Arts Council for helping to make this book possible.

To Gail Medland Roberts, one of the beautiful people of Denver, for a terrific idea that wouldn't go away.

To Pete McDonald, for sharing his expertise about tire forensics.

To Bruce M. Hennes and Carolyn Hasslett, for a peek into the real world of local politics.

To Lieutenant Lucie J. Duvall of the Sex Crimes Unit of the Cleveland Police Department, and to Officer Terry Colton and Officer Rick Smrekar of the Sixth District, Fourth Platoon.

To William F. Miller, who reports on ethnic affairs for the *Plain Dealer*.

Sometimes an author encounters an irresistible name, so my thanks to the real Evan and Barbara Corns and the real Cassandra Pride for graciously allowing me to use their names even though they don't resemble their namesakes in this book.

All the other characters are fictional, and any resemblance to persons living or dead is purely coincidental. And Lake Erie Shores is a fictional community.

Finally, and very belatedly—four books belatedly, as a matter of fact—my love and warmest appreciation to Diana Yakovich Montagino and to Milan Yakovich, D.D.S.

# Now available in quality paperback:
# the Milan Jacovich mystery series . . .

**PEPPER PIKE**
Introducing Milan Jacovich, the private investigator with a master's degree,
a taste for klobasa sandwiches, and a knack for finding trouble. A cryptic
late-night phone call from a high-powered advertising executive leads Milan
through the haunts of one of Cleveland's richest suburbs and into the den of
Cleveland mob kingpin Don Giancarlo D'Allessandro.   1-59851-001-0

**FULL CLEVELAND**
Someone's scamming Cleveland businessmen by selling ads in a magazine
that doesn't exist. But the dollar amount hardly seems worth the number of
bodies that Milan soon turns up. And why is Milan being shadowed at every
turn by a leisure-suited mob flunky? One thing's certain: Buddy Bustamente's
fashion sense isn't the only thing about him that's lethal.   1-59851-002-9

**DEEP SHAKER**
Ever loyal, Milan Jacovich has no choice but to help when a grade-school
chum worries his son might be selling drugs. The investigation uncovers a
brutal murder and a particularly savage drug gang—and leads Milan to a relic
from every Clevelander's childhood that proves to be deadly.   1-59851-003-7

**THE CLEVELAND CONNECTION**
The Serbs and the Slovenians traditionally don't get along too well, but Milan
Jacovich makes inroads into Cleveland's Serbian community when an appeal-
ing young woman convinces him to help search for her missing grandfather.
Hatreds that have simmered for fifty years eventually explode as Milan takes
on one of his most challenging cases.   1-59851-004-5

**THE LAKE EFFECT**

Milan owes a favor and agrees to serve as bodyguard for a suburban mayoral candidate—but these politics lead to murder. And the other candidate has hired Milan's old nemesis, disgraced ex-cop Al Drago, who carries a grudge a mile wide.   1-59851-005-3

**THE DUKE OF CLEVELAND**

Milan dives into the cutthroat world of fine art when a slumming young heiress hires him to find her most recent boyfriend, a potter, who has absconded with $18,000 of her trust-fund money. Turns out truth and beauty don't always mix well—at least in the art business.   1-59851-006-1

**COLLISION BEND**

Milan goes behind the scenes to uncover scandal, ambition, and intrigue at one of Cleveland's top TV stations as he hunts down the stalker and murderer of a beautiful local television anchor.   1-59851-007-X

**THE CLEVELAND LOCAL**

Milan Jacovich is hired to find out who murdered a hotshot young Cleveland lawyer vacationing in the Caribbean. Back in Cleveland, he runs afoul of both a Cleveland mob boss and a world-famous labor attorney—and is dealt a tragic personal loss that will alter his life forever.   1-59851-008-8

**A SHOOT IN CLEVELAND**

Milan accepts an "easy" job baby-sitting a notorious Hollywood bad-boy who's in Cleveland for a movie shoot. But keeping Darren Anderson out of trouble is like keeping your hat dry during a downpour. And when trouble leads to murder, Milan finds himself in the middle of it all.   1-59851-009-6

# Get them at your favorite bookstore!

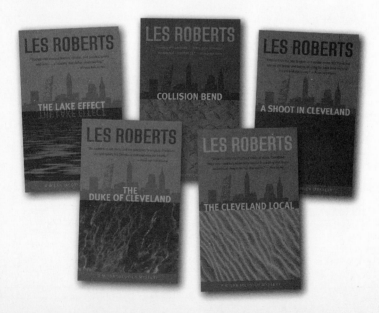